TRAPPED PRINCESS

N. MALONE

MORE FROM THE AUTHOR

Etani

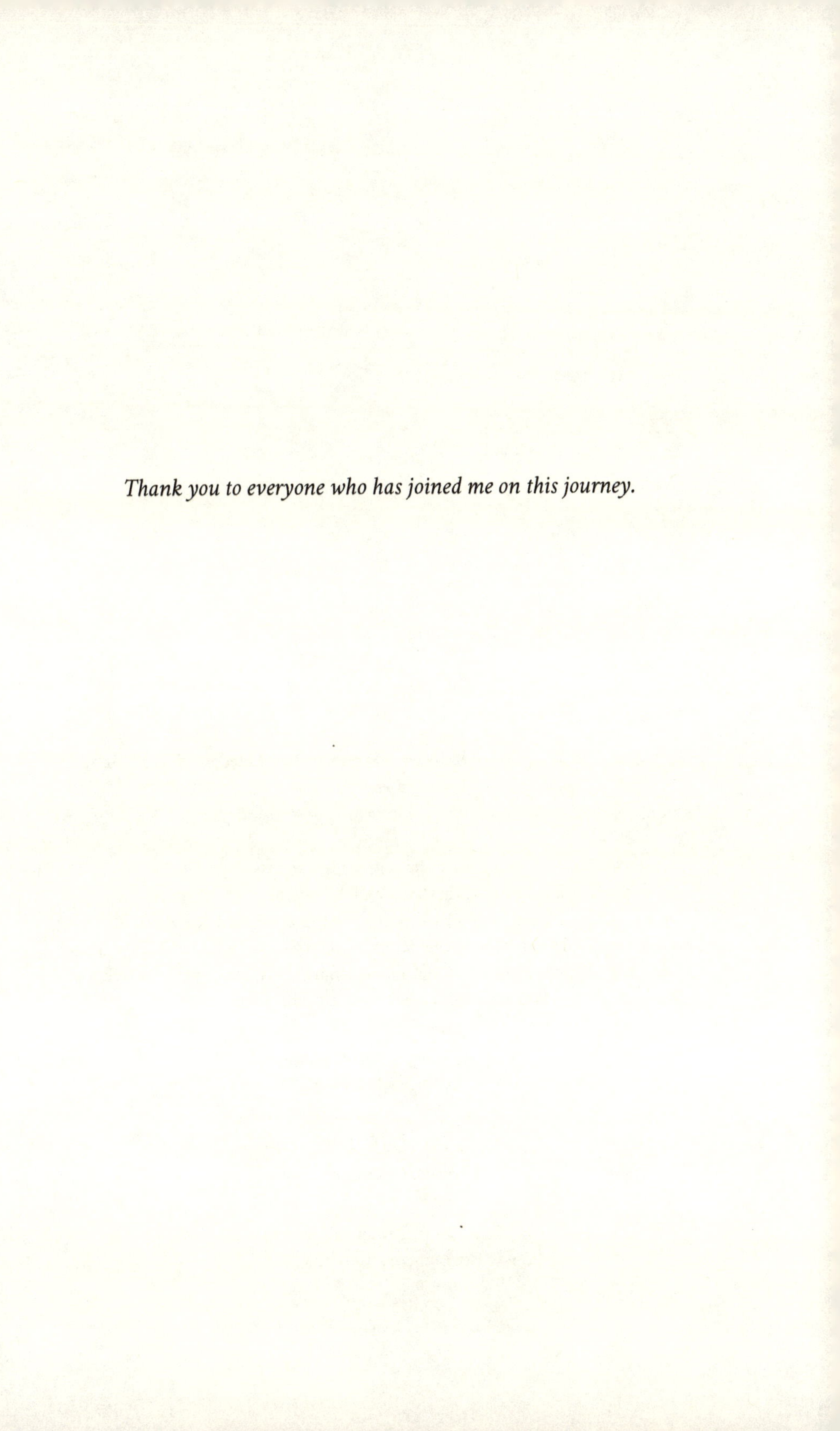

Thank you to everyone who has joined me on this journey.

Front Cover Design by DAZED designs
www.dazed-designs.com

Rear Cover Design by Cascuda
www.twitter.com/Cascuda_?s=09

TRAPPED PRINCESS

HOW CAN IT POSSIBLY GET ANY WORSE?

Returning to Ayathian from the human town was uneventful. The Wild Hunt had failed and needed some time to recover. That, coupled with the Dryads being still offended, allowed them to pass freely. Etani knew Epharis wanted to linger in Faerie, but it was not safe for him and she was not about to let him loose to explore, no matter how badly he seemed to want to.

Being there was precarious for both of them. She was still struggling to come to terms with the idea of her being captured and her new situation. Almost always she seemed to overlook her station. Yet another thing she did not have the time to tell her sisters and as her failings piled up, they began to gnaw on her until her stomach hurt.

Keeping a firm grip on the Lich's arm, she all but dragged him along, refusing to let him linger, regardless of how hard he tried to make her stop so he could look around.

The only time she relented was when they stopped for a last glance of the spiral city, but she barely gave him two minutes to stare around in wonder. His expression was hard and searching as if he tried –in those minutes before she was yanking on his arm again— to absorb everything he could.

Etani was glad he did not object because the last thing she needed was to force him along or get him angry. It would be impossible to get him to move if he dug in his heels. Even the little things mattered and if they were not careful, they would be captured.

Finally, they reached the location they had arrived at only hours before. The grass was still scuffed from their frantic pace. Letting out a slow breath, she bit the tip of her finger and drew a shaky line in the air, carefully pushing the doorway open. When he hesitated, she grabbed his hand and yanked him through, trying to ignore the longing in his features, reminding him that he had no choice.

They stepped through into her room in the palace and the place was strikingly clean. What was equally perplexing was that Alaric was sitting in one of her chairs. As the King's eyes latched onto their joined hands, Epharis quickly dropped hers.

Not caring that Alaric had seen them stepping through realities or that Epharis might be struggling with his disconnection from Faerie, she wordlessly walked out to the balcony.

Even the Lich had to tap into Faerie's magic to exist. Their concept of arcane magic was only a delusion, simply because all magic came from Faerie and he had been dosed heavily with it when he had been in that world. The Lich was now denied that huge strength and share of power, as well as the premise of what he could become if they were permitted to live in Faerie. Their power would be boundless, their strength and energy unequalled, and the most important part for him, they were more alive than dead in Faerie.

Settling in one of the lounges on the balcony, she ignored the two men as they spoke—or rather bickered—but when Alaric stomped onto the balcony and glared at her, it was evident he was not having any of his brother's nonsense.

"You cannot avoid me," he barked, but she ignored him.

"Alaric, this is not the time."

"Shut up, Epharis."

Turning her empty eyes from the sunset to the two men, she simply looked at them, her fingers still clasping the cat necklace and the hairpin.

"You never answered my proposal," the King insisted, his eyes fixed on hers.

"What proposal?" Epharis asked, his face going wary.

"We're getting married," Alaric announced.

All of a sudden, Epharis lunged at his brother, punching him straight in the face.

SHE WATCHED THE FIGHT DISPASSIONATELY, not caring that they tore apart the newly-repaired furniture, not caring that blood was shed and the walls of her room were destroyed. Not even when Epharis threw a chair out of the glass balcony doors, aiming for his brother who managed to duck at the last minute, spreading glass shards around her on the stone balcony and –no doubt—into the garden below.

Had she been in the right state of mind, she might even have cheered the fight on, but she could not find anything humorous in it; she could not feel anger, regret, or anything of the short.

Within a week she had lost three people who were important to her. Her sisters had been her reason for living, and Nayishma was her first and only friend.

When she realised—through her muddled thoughts—that she did not even have the chance to tell her sisters Letari and Avadari about Nayishma, she could not take it anymore. Hiding her head inside her arms and leaning on the balcony railing she cried quietly, ignoring the men and blissfully ignored by them.

At some point, the sounds of their fighting and yelling became distant and she assumed that they must have wandered somewhere else in the castle. Something touched her shoulder, but she ignored it, her body still trembled, and her breath was caught in her throat as she tried to think over everything that had happened. She could not possibly process things with her mind feeling as though it had been stuffed with cotton.

"Etani?" A low, soft voice spoke in her ear and she registered that it belonged to one of the vampire twins.

Unable to answer, she only shook her head. After a moment, her lounger dipped on both sides as they sat down with her, without saying a word. The person on her right put his hand on her back gently patting and drawing soothing circles. The person on the left touched her shoulder tightening his hold for just a moment.

When she was all cried out and was finally able to lift her head, it was dark and both men gazed at the city while she did her best to compose herself.

"Are you okay?" Jaia asked gently, brushing her hair back from where it stuck to her face.

She shook her head again, unable to speak right away.

Kai on her other side wrapped his arms tightly around her, hugging her while a fresh wave of pain ripped through her.

Fresh tears began to roll down her cheeks as she stared into the black eyes of the vampire, his twin holding her almost hard enough to hurt. It stung to remember that they were twins.

"My twin and little sister are dead," she whimpered, barely able to get the words out.

Jaia's face went pale and Kai's arms slightly faltered.

"Oh Etani, I'm so sorry," Kai whispered against her shoulder, resting his forehead there.

Unable to look away from Jaia, he grabbed her hands and held them tightly in his own.

He knew how it felt to lose a sibling, having witnessed what happened to Kai before he was turned.

Leaning against Jaia's side, Etani rested her head on his shoulder while Kai moved to sit behind her, holding her tight as the night passed.

When dawn was upon them, the two vampires were forced to retreat. She watched them go and saw Kai trying to conceal the fact that he had been crying for her. Once alone, she turned her eyes to the city and watched as the sun rose, lighting up the world.

She stayed there until well past midday when someone

approached her from behind; she ignored them and continued to stare blankly into the distance, her mind repeating the events of that night over and over. Something was itching at the back of her mind and she was doing her absolute best to ignore it even as it nagged her.

Someone was sitting on a lounger on the other side of the balcony, silently leaving her to wallow in her misery, but close by in case she needed them. She did not know who it was nor did she care.

That nagging thought was scratching painfully inside her psyche trying to be noticed.

Finally, determined to ignore the thought, she turned to her company and saw the elf assassin Aelen sitting across from her. He had been watching her, calm and relaxed.

Meeting his blue eyes, she chewed the inside of her cheek while that thought finally burst unwelcome into her mind.

Letari was not coming back. It had been too long. It should only have taken a few hours to a day at most.

Letari was not blessed with immortality and as that realisation dawned on her, she began to think once more. If her twin was not coming back, then she did not want to be there either.

"If I asked you to kill me, would you?"

He did not so much as stir, his eyes boring into hers. "Why would I?"

"Because I would have asked you to."

His brows drew close in a slight frown as he contemplated her words. "Are you asking?"

"Yes," she whispered.

Aelen watched her for a long moment, taking in her request. "How?"

"Heart or brain."

He nodded once and stood. He did not ask anything else. She was in pain and had asked him a simple favour. She had suffered at his hands, at the hands of the King and the hands of the Prince, now all she wanted was peace. He would give her at least that.

Moving behind her, his hand was light on her shoulder as she stared at the city.

She did not feel the blade piercing her back and sliding smoothly through muscles and tendons. She did not feel as it pierced her heart and her blood spilled. She did not feel it when he lowered her onto the lounger and slowly pressed down on the knife, driving it up to rip and tear at the organ, or when the blade left her heart. Nor did she really feel it when he brushed the hair back from her face, wiping away the tears from her cheeks.

She only felt an incredible relief as the world began to fade into nothingness, the sky above her the last thing she saw before her life was snuffed out.

Dying was not as terrible as everyone made it out to be, or at least that was how she found it. By her estimations, throughout her rather long life, she had died about one hundred times, The Ghost's mercy making it one hundred and one. She was grateful that he had given her what she wanted without question or argument.

She could only imagine Epharis' reaction when he found her body and watched it disintegrate into the wind.

Etani opened her eyes and saw that she was sitting on the ground that was no ground, her legs crossed and pulled up against her chest, her arms resting atop of her knees that were not knees. She was not a ghost, but she did not have a body; she simply was.

Pushing herself to her feet, she looked down and found two ribbons that protruded from her chest, a black one led along the path that was no path, the other was a deep crimson that went off behind her somewhere.

She knew that the first ribbon would take her back to life.

But the other…

Turning around, she looked at the distance, and the longer she looked, the more the heavy mist began to take shape, forming into figures.

They were shifting and incomplete, nothing but a face set into an amorphous, vaguely human shape with a tattered grey ribbon protruding from their chests.

That was the land of the dead, every one of those figures was a dead mythical who had yet to pass on to their next lives.

Some chose to stay, to welcome their friends and family when it was their time, some were too scared to move on and others too stubborn. And then, there were those who wanted to watch over their loved ones.

There was no colour to that world, only a white path, grey smoke, and a pale grey sky. She was grey too, even though she could see herself as she was in life, rather than as the shapeless forms she saw around her.

As she stepped off the path, the crowd began to shift restlessly, her mere presence an affront to the dead unless she stayed on the path.

They moved away from her, none paying any real attention, only trying to keep away, much like the shark swimming through the school of fish. They kept a good three feet from her, leaving her encircled but untouched.

The ribbon she followed led her deeper into the crowd of creatures, her pace slow and careful.

Each step left her feeling more strained and exhausted. She was pulling her tether to life tighter and it was straining to hold her. She did not care, she wanted to find the end of the second ribbon before it snapped.

She knew her little sister Avadari would not be there. The destruction of the sword that had ended her life had freed all those who had been trapped and she would have moved on immediately. Ava had never been afraid of death and even welcomed her next life. Ava *was* the strong one, not her. The bravest woman she had ever known.

There were instances that it had bothered Etani, but she had finally embraced the fact that her sister was weird. There was no point in trying to find her in that place.

She felt an odd tugging sensation at her mind and chest and as she glanced back, she saw one of the spirits caught on her life ribbon, trying to move past it but unable to do so. It tugged the ribbon, straining it and she felt it as it began to fray. An odd fluttering at the back of her mind.

Turning back to her path, she hurried to reach the end of the crimson ribbon that she suspected—or maybe hoped—would link her to her twin and burst into a small clearing.

Letari sat there, her form curled into a ball and she looked so small, like a child.

It was not entirely wrong, Letari's mind had snapped when they were only young after the loss of their mother, and then her twin's first death. Letari had never truly grown up.

Without thinking, she extended her hand to her sister, the head lifting to look up at her.

At first, Letari seemed confused before recognition dawned on her, extending her hand to grasp Etani's.

As their hands touched, she faintly recalled a warning to never touch the remnants of the dead. Not ever. But it was too late, and with their fingers coming into contact, pain surged through her as the ribbon that linked them turned black and exploded, throwing them both backwards.

They had both been forcefully slammed into life.

PANIC FILLED their mind as they struggled to understand what was going on while trying to reach the surface before they drowned. How ironic would that be? Drowning in the pool of their rebirth?

Bursting through the surface, her arms refused to work properly as their minds struggled to fit together in the space designed for one, both fighting to gain control. Eventually, they managed to get to the shore and drag themselves out of the water, naked and disorientated.

"Have to get back…" she gasped

'No, not going back!' Letari's frantic scream in her head left her reeling.

"Calm… think…"

'No, run now! Danger! They see!'

She turned around to see a figure in a white robe was staring and then bolted from the cavern.

Both minds swore in unison and both hands were lifted, both were bitten and two lines in the air were drawn.

Both tried to pass through each opening, but they only had one body.

Swearing again, Etani crushed her sister down and threw their body through the opening, staggering to run as she knew their people would be after her.

Her new body was clumsy, as it was not used to functioning, but she managed to overcome her confusion and run as fast as she could.

Letari was not happy, snapping and fighting to get control to the point where she caused them to stagger, threatening to overturn them. With one hand on her head, in their mind, Etani managed to squash Letari and gain control and so, they were able to run faster and faster as the muscles began to work.

It was always hard in the beginning, a new body meant new muscles and they did not like being forced to work so soon. But Etani knew exactly where she was. It was not the first time she had to run from the cavern, and she knew how to avoid the town, except it was now a very large town. She had never bothered to learn what country she was in, nor why the people there were all so uniformly pale with dark wooden houses.

Cursing the plague that was humanity, she changed course, heading North, and sprinted as fast as her long legs could carry her almost as if she had wings.

Thanks to her mixed breed, it was impossible to try and chase her down, as she was simply too fast. There had been a cruel joke that she had to be part cheetah thanks to her speed, but she did not find it offensive. The shape of her irises, her reflexes, her ability to see well at night, and her speed all made her think there might have been a werecat somewhere in her family tree.

She ran at full tilt for a good hour until it was safe to stop, panting hard and leaning against a tree.

She needed to find clothing and figure out what was going on.

'We have to go back,' she thought to Letari.

'*No, don't want to go back. Lich is bad.*'

'I don't care, we have to.'

She had to wonder if the Lich felt her return to life as well as her death and how long she could get away with hiding out in the countryside. She did not think it would work, but it was fun entertaining the thought.

Heading first West and then doubling back, she knew that whoever tracked her would think she had continued North. But her way was in the South towards Ayathian. It would take about a month to get there and she was tempted to cut through Faerie, but she needed clothes first.

By the time they found a village, it was close to sunrise and she quickly stole some clothes, fashioning a few stones to appear like coins and leaving them as payment.

The money would change hands at least six times before turning back into stones and by then it would be hard to trace it back to the owner of the pants and shirt she had stolen.

Keeping off the main roads, she headed South for another hour before she decided to slip between realities.

It was odd to think that Faerie was smaller than the human world, so stepping three paces could open onto a different realm to the one you opened those three paces back. That was why they were so focused on intent. If one intended for an opening to appear in a particular spot, it usually opened onto that spot. But one still had to try and line it up properly or they could open a door from their own home and end up falling into an active volcano. It also depended on the time of day, weather, and the mood of the Courts at the time.

No one ever claimed Faerie made sense.

Enjoying the feel of the wind against her face, she bit into her finger and entered Faerie. The moment her feet touched the grass, her mind felt warped as it struggled to feed two minds in one body with the magic of Faerie.

Bending forward, she heaved—nearly vomiting—as she tried to focus enough to see what she was doing. Stumbling blindly, she leant against a tree and tried to remain still, despite the world around her waving and swaying.

It settled painfully slowly and, finally, she was able to see again.

'*Don't like*,' the voice in her head muttered resentfully.

"Me neither," she replied aloud, finally able to straighten up.

Setting off through the trees, she paused to see in the distance. Ahead of her, there was a forest made entirely of enormous red-capped mushrooms. Staring, she tried to figure out what it was she was looking at when the warmth of the place registered.

Oh no, she had slipped through into Summer.

GLANCING AROUND HER, she immediately knew she was a trespasser. One did not cross into another Court without invitation, even if you were not formally aligned.

She started running again, even though she had no idea where she was. She had never been in Summer before and did not know where she should go in order to get to a specific part of the world. In the distance, she could discern the roiling clouds of Winter and headed for the corner that would be Ceress. She quickly realised that she was not alone as the sound of hooves approached and a Centaur with a large spear came onto her.

Cursing, she spun, prepared to fight but he simply looked at her with his big, soft brown eyes.

"Hail, stranger," he called out.

He had chestnut-brown skin and a large, tall body to match his incredibly broad chest. His mane and hair all a similar shade of rich, warm brown. He was shaggy, his shoulder-length hair done in braids and a skirt was covering his back, laden with a waterskin, horn and a large belt with coins that jangled merrily. Across his back was a quiver with a bow.

"Good day, Centaur," she greeted, eyeing him warily. "I meant no disrespect. I came here by accident and am leaving as quickly as I can."

The Centaur nodded and smiled at her, his posture relaxing. "Good. For a moment I took you for a Winter spy."

"Celestrial," she replied quickly, taking the moment to rest while she had the chance.

He looked surprised as he studied her, but she shrugged. "Half-bred."

"Didn't know they had those," he admitted cautiously.

"No, and they don't like it very much. I've been on the run for a long, long time."

"Why not join one of the other Courts?"

"I prefer the human world, actually. If there's one thing to say for humans, their politics are less… deadly."

The Centaur let out a laugh, knowing full well what she meant. "Well Celestrial half-breed, you are about two hours' sprint from the border to Celestria."

She frowned. "Celestria?"

"That is the name of the Court."

"No, it's Ceress," she insisted, confused.

"Before it was Celestria, now it is Ceress. Thus, the name of your kind. Do they not teach history to your young?"

"No, not at all. What is your name? When I have some time, I might have to call upon you to learn more about this Celestria." She was still frowning as she tried to take in all the new information, unable to think why they would change the name.

"Barron Browncoat."

"Barron Browncoat, it is a pleasure. I'm Etania Daewen," she introduced herself, accepting his proffered hand.

Smiling, the Centaur shook her hand, but something shifted in his eyes.

"It is an honour, young one. You should hurry now. Before long, the Hunt will start."

Etani nodded and without wasting any more time she sprinted off, feeling his eyes boring onto her back.

2

NEVER TRUST A LICH

*S*he crossed the border between Summer and Ceress just as the horns of the Hunt sounded. They were not after her, but it was their everyday routine to hunt in search of spies or trespassers. Discovering a spy was a pretty common occurrence and it made things more interesting for the Courts.

Once back on familiar ground, she was able to move freely as she headed for the spot she had used for their travels a few days earlier. Once again, she slipped through the door and into her magically once again clean room.

How it managed to get repaired so quickly she would never know, but she found everything to be in perfect order.

The blood from the lounge had vanished, the furniture had been repaired, and the wall was back up. That made her wonder if an enchantment had been cast so that the castle could repair itself.

She did not have to ponder for long, for as soon as she was done perusing the room, the dividing door between her and Epharis' rooms burst open with such a force that the handle put a large hole in the wall.

Etani turned towards the noise just in time to see him lunging at her.

13

Dancing back, she dodged his advances, only to have him come at her again.

She had forgotten the events of the days past, forgotten that she had asked the assassin to kill her and that she had dragged Epharis on a merry chase through Faerie where he had gotten a taste for what he could be in that world. Her mind had banished the thoughts of how she had strived to avoid him for months before that.

Etani evaded him time and again, trying to put some distance between them, but he finally cornered her.

Planting his arms against the wall on either side, he bared his teeth and leant closer, only to stop when she looked up at him.

"What happened to your eyes?" he snapped, his rage temporarily subdued.

"What do you mean?" she asked, baffled by the change in mood.

Grabbing her upper arm in a painful grip that was just shy of breaking her bones, he dragged her into the bathroom and thrust her at the washing basin to face the mirror.

Startled by the sight of herself, she jerked back, noticing that her left eye had changed from vivid blue to a mixture of green and blue.

Epharis loomed over her, glowering.

'Pretty,' the voice remarked, but Etani ignored it.

Her eyes moved from her reflection to his as his fingers curled around her upper arms, clenching so tight it burned.

"Epharis," she said cautiously, only to have him yank her back from the basin and slam her face-first against the wall, pinning her with one forearm pressed on her nape.

"You have been keeping secrets," he whispered to her ear.

His free arm traced her skin, searching for weapons. Finding her unarmed, he spun her around and pinned both of her wrists above her head, reaching up to clench her jaw and forcing her to look at him.

He studied her face, turning her jaw so her eyes reflected the light.

"That is the colour of your sister's eyes, is it not?" he asked coldly, and bruises formed under his fingers as he moved her face the other way.

"Yes," she replied, her mind racing to find the way to get out of the situation.

If she tried to defend herself, it would only enrage him, so she remained still as he looked her over.

Something seemed to catch his attention, his eyes flicking down to her shoulder. "You are injured," he said almost accusingly before his gaze returned to her face.

Jaw clenching, his brows furrowed as a thought crossed his mind, and he seemed to be considering something she couldn't fathom.

"You were dead," he said finally, releasing her jaw and reaching behind her to run his hand through her hair, searching for the vials he knew she hid in her long strands.

"That doesn't usually last for long," she retorted, wincing as his fingers gripped her black strands.

Jerking her head back, he forced her to look up.

"You were gone for three months, Princess," he snarled, his face barely an inch from hers.

That was unexpected. To her, it seemed as if only a day had passed. "Three months?"

When had she lost the time? Had finding Letari taken that long?

"Three..." he dragged out the word in a deadly whisper.

His eyes were glowing now, a warning sign that his anger was about to reach boiling point.

"Epharis, I—"

She never finished her sentence. Epharis moved his hand from her hair and covered her mouth as his fingers ground her wrists together. Wincing, she could do nothing but stare up at him.

"So many secrets… So many things hidden away in that brain of yours," he mused, that deadly whisper sounding worse than any amount of yelling or screaming. "How about I pick it apart to find out what's in there?"

She shook her head as much as his hand on her mouth would allow.

"Perhaps I was too gentle with you in the dungeon. Would you like to revisit?"

His eyes grew wider at the prospect, while her pupils dilated in fear. On the inside, she was crushing down her raging twin, trying to keep her from barging in. They were in grave danger and she had to remain calm.

Again, she gave a little shake of her head, as much as she was able to.

"Are you going to be a good little monster and tell me everything or do I have to hurt you?"

She shook her head for a third time, staring into his eyes in an effort to appear harmless and obedient.

Taking his hand from her mouth, he clenched it into a fist and, drawing it back, sank it into her stomach. Only then did he let her go, looming above her as she dropped to her knees, wheezing.

"That was for lying to me."

Grabbing a fistful of her hair, he half-dragged her from the bathroom back into the living room and threw her onto the couch. Etani struggled to sit up, her arms moved protectively around her stomach and she gasped for the air that had been slugged out of her.

He sat down across from her. "Who are you? The truth," he demanded, crossing his right leg over the left at the ankle and resting his arms over the backrest of the chair. He did not blink, he simply watched her and waited.

She straightened up. "Before I came here, I was just Etania, the Celestrial half-breed on the run. Here, I was told I was also the Princess of the Winter Court. I found out after *you* had."

"And you are from this fourth Court?" He asked with eyes narrowed, aware that she had been about to lie.

"Yes, there are four Courts."

"Who else knows?"

"The vampire twins."

Given the deal she had struck with the brothers to try and set her free, she had to tread carefully now. Epharis nodded, but she could tell the news angered him even more, as he was not the first to know.

"What is the other Court?"

"It has been named the Heathen Court. It's where the ones who do not fit into the normal Courts go. It was once Spring."

"And this Ceress was Autumn," he concluded.

Etani nodded in confirmation even though he had not expected her to. "You cannot die."

"I can die just as any other creature. I simply do not remain dead unless I wish to."

His brows rose and she let out a drawn sigh.

"When a mythical dies, we go to another realm to await our next lives. We linger there for as long as we need to come to terms. Once there, I see a ribbon that leads me back to life and my twin. I simply follow it and am reborn."

Her words were met with silence that stretched until she was finally forced to continue.

"There is a cavern under Ceress City and beneath it, there is a blue pool that no one knows where the water comes from. When some Celestrials die, we are in that water and swim out. No one knows why this happens, and with every generation, less of us are born with the ability to be reborn. When you are reborn, you return to the state you were in when you died for the first time. I was about twenty-three the first time, so every time I return to the body of a twenty-three-year-old and begin to age from there. Die and you start over."

"Why are less born with that ability?" He asked, absorbing the information.

"Some say it is punishment while others claim it is because there has been no new blood. Our ability to procreate is dwindling, but the older generations will never allow another species to enter the gene pool. My mother fell in love with a man from the Winter Court who had come to Ceress as a spy. They soon married and produced my sister and me in secret. When an admirer of my mother found out, he reported it and we were sentenced to death. My father pleaded to die in our place so that our lives could be spared. Cain was the one who killed my father. After that, my sister, mother, and I were taken to the city and, by the orders of Queen Illia, mother remarried and died birthing Avadari. It was said that my mother's death was her punishment for producing half-breeds, but it only came after she gave birth to a pureblood. I think that she was murdered once she had given birth to the one who could replace her, but only after her place had been taken by my sister. That way the Council would preserve its precious population ratio. I never told my sisters that…" she trailed off, forcing back her tears.

Letari had gone silent in her mind, listening hard to the thoughts that flashed through her head.

"After mother's death, Letari and I were left on the streets and when our usefulness ran its course, we were banished from the city. A while later Avadari joined us in the forest, but it took us so long to convince her we were her blood. The council found out, and decided we were a bad influence. So, we fled into this world to hide and we've been running ever since."

Etani was not looking at him anymore, her eyes affixed on the table that had been destroyed so many times and, yet, looked perfect. She did not know why she was telling him all of it, but she could not bring herself to stop talking.

"Why were you gone for three months?"

"I don't know. I can't place the missing time. I can only assume it was because I remained in the spirit world. Maybe that's why my tether to life started to fray, I stayed there too long."

"What of your eye?"

Immediately she knew she needed to keep that detail from him. The need to protect her damaged sister was too strong, he could never know. "I don't know. I have no explanation for why it happened, but it should reverse with my next death," she lied.

He grunted and stood, beginning to pace. "What other talents do you have that you are keeping from me?"

She flushed and bit her lower lip. "Would you like a list?"

He growled, and as he turned on her with his glowing eyes, Etani shrunk back.

Eventually, she let out a huff and decided to have an out. "Well, as you know I can create a host to put myself in. I can kill with a kiss, I can resurrect, I can travel between worlds, I can glamour myself and certain objects though not permanently."

Etani paused, tapping her mouth with her finger, trying to think. "What else… my healing ability is good, and, with some effort, I can see through most magic and glamours as well as charm with music. I'm skilled with a knife, bow and arrows, throwing knives and the like. I am a capable acrobat and possess basic knowledge of street fighting."

She racked her brains, trying to think anything else, but she had covered –pretty much—everything.

"What about Alaric?" He pressed, and she frowned in confusion. "You are to marry him."

Her expression went blank as she tried to process the information when she finally recalled the event. Blood and rage, so many corpses and that man demanding she marry him.

"I will never marry him."

"You may not have a choice, Etani. He has sent an emissary to gain access to the Winter Court. He is going to demand your hand provided they are given information and access to you."

Her face went cold, and she swallowed hard, trying to get past the lump in her throat. Jumping to her feet, she started for the door determined to hunt the man down and wring his neck, but Epharis was on her in an instant, preventing her from leaving.

"But he can't marry you if *we* are already married," he whispered, and his lips brushed her ear.

She could almost feel his lips pulling back into a nasty grin and his arm sliding around her middle. She did not have time to respond before he was yanking her into that crushing blackness that was his ability to move great distances at a speed she could not comprehend.

Ripping their way back into being, she flung herself away from him and dropped to the ground, retching even though that time she was at least able to breathe.

Epharis stood over her, making sure she would not try to escape.

WHEN SHE FINALLY LOOKED UP, taking in her surrounding, she discovered that he had brought her to a place odd, dark, and broken. She was sure it had once been a church of some sort but, for some reason, it had fallen apart. Vines grew over nearly every surface and all around her there were stained stone pillars, rotting remains of benches, and shattered glass windows. There was even a hole on the roof that allowed leaves and debris from the trees to fall inside. She could see through the opening.

Reaching down, Epharis grabbed her upper arm and hoisted her to her feet, bringing her before a man who made her recoil. It was another Lich and he was staring her with cold amusement.

"Glad you could join me," the man said. His black robes along with his rotting beard matched their gloomy surroundings.

Etani struggled to yank her arm free, but since his grip proved unbreakable, she tried to land a kick at his leg. He growled as he looked down on her, baring his teeth.

"Be still or I will restrain you," he snarled, tugging her roughly to stand closer to him.

She tried to pry his fingers off to escape his grip. He did not budge, but she never stopped trying. Not even when the bearded Lich spoke in a tongue she did not know and concluded that she never wanted to hear again.

Around them the vines began to move, creeping away from the walls and along the floor to reveal that the walls had alcoves, and inside each one there was a person.

Straining to see them all, she counted six bound and gagged figures.

"Got to have sacrifices to bless an unholy union," Epharis informed her with malicious cheerfulness.

The people consisted of a mixture of both human men and women and they all seemed terrified. Judging by their clothes, they were all peasants, furiously striving for their freedom.

Something touched her foot and she jerked back and looked down to find that one of the vines had just reached her while multiple others were creeping towards her feet. Epharis repositioned his grip to her upper arms, rendering her powerless to escape the vines as they crept their way up her legs.

The bearded man spoke a word and she cried out as hundreds of thorns stabbed into her legs, holding her in place more effectively than Epharis' grip on her arms.

The Lich let her go, his smile was pure malice. How many times had she forgotten what he was under the delusion that he cared about her?

Too many.

The bearded man began to intone in a deep voice that made her heart jump and her blood turning cold in her veins. She chanced a look at Epharis, and his eyes rested alight and hungry on her.

He must have been experiencing the same thing. They both could smell each other's blood.

A single vine crept on each of their sides and curled around both of their left hands, the thorns digging into their skin.

However hard she tried, she could not shake it off, any attempt to free herself resulted in ripping her skin even further. She now knew why her position had her facing Epharis.

Turning to her, he took her hand in his, the vines interlocking their hands and withdrawing from their palms before tightening to trap their hands together.

"Epharis, please don't do this," she whimpered, straining to pull away as blood oozed from their palms, mingling between their fingers.

"It will all be over soon. Once you are fully mine, Alaric won't be able to touch you," he crooned, using his right hand to stroke her hair.

It was impossible to know whether his driving force derived from possessiveness or jealousy over his brother, but neither was good for her. He had concluded that a forced marriage to her was the best solution, and that would be the end of it.

"I'll do anything," she pleaded in a vain attempt to stop that madness, her body straining to pull free, but the more she struggled, the higher the vines crept up onto her arm to keep her in place.

"This is all you need to do. When the time comes, consent to be my bride. Simple."

At that stage, she somehow doubted her consent was a requirement. A keening wail made her jump, whipping her head at the sound. The voices of the people inside the alcoves changed into screams. She whipped her head at the sound the voices of the people inside the alcoves as they changed into screams. The vines had reached their chests, filling the decrepit building with the tantalising scent of human blood.

The Lich priest handed Epharis something on a little silver platter and taking advantage of her distraction, he pried her jaw open and dropped whatever it was into her mouth. His hand immediately clamped down over her lips to keep her from spitting it out.

"Swallow," he snarled while she tried to dislodge it.

But it had begun to dissolve on her tongue, and she swallowed, having no idea what it was or why she had to eat it. It left an unpleasant tingling taste but, a moment later, warmth spread out from her stomach.

The vines began to darken starting at the tips protruding from the humans and creeping towards them in an ominous journey.

"Epharis please!" She cried and she struggled once more, resulting in spilling more of her blood.

Using her free hand, she tried to rip the veins free, but it did little to release her.

The vines at her feet turned black first and she gasped as first a trickle, and then a flood of cold energy filled her, her pupils immediately expanded and he watched as swirls of ink pooled out to fill in the colours of her eyes, turning them black and empty. Her lips itched as they darkened and the blackness began to spread from her eyes into the delicate veins around them, spreading out as the deaths of the humans fed her. The energy had flooded into him as well, and his chest expanded as he sucked in a deep breath and his eyes flared into a silvery green glow.

Blackness wormed up the vines that kept their hands interlocked, spilling into their joined fingers, just as the blood they cupped in their palms began to heat.

The bearded Lich smiled as he watched them and posed a question Etani did not hear.

Epharis spoke gently and the question was asked again. A gentle squeeze of her hand brought to her mind his earlier words. All he needed was her consent. It did not matter why he needed it or what for, he only needed one little thing from her.

"I do," she promised softly, not entirely sure what she was agreeing to.

Energy flooded her system, heightening her senses.

The vines retracted from their bodies and she felt arms going around her, one at her hip and one at her upper back.

Holding her in his arms, he dipped her body backwards and planted his cool lips on hers.

She only hesitated for a moment before she was looping her arms up around his neck to return his kiss with unparalleled passion.

Absently, she noted that she had no urge to analyse her desire for him. None at all. Not even when he lowered her to the floor, hovering over her and kissing her harder.

She did not care when his trembling fingers tugged at her clothes and exposed her naked body to the priest. The only thing she cared about was how good it felt to be in his arms.

Her fingers worked on his clothes even as his hands explored her form, stroking and touching her naked flesh as his robes fell away.

Gasping at the feeling of him, she shifted to straddle his lap, her front pressed hard against his chest. Arms tight around his neck, she kissed him hard and hungrily.

Slowly, he pressed her down onto him and soon she felt something tear in her body, followed by a burning sensation. But she did not care. All she wanted to be near him.

Their bodies moved together, his arms exploring her back, gripping her rear as he helped her move atop him. Finally, he lowered her onto her back, remaining buried inside her.

With her legs wrapped tight around his middle, he thrust hard into her, eyes wide and hungry as he gasped her name and admitted how deeply he had loved her for so long.

She silenced him with another kiss, her tongue exploring his mouth.

Epharis had worked himself into a dark, demanding pace, not caring if he hurt her and she returned the favour by sinking her sharp little canines into the nape of his neck.

He grunted at the pain and his fingers curling in her hair to pull her back from the bite.

The sight of his blood on her mouth aroused him even more and he licked the blood from her lips, growling his pleasure.

Their kiss was long and rough, his hips bruising hers with the force of his desire.

It was when she moaned his name that he found his release, clutching her to him and driving himself as deep into her as he could, spilling himself inside her with a primal roar.

His back bled from her nails, but, at that moment, the only thing they cared about was not to sever their union, to remain locked with each other and get as close as possible.

Lifting her from the floor, he knelt with her in his arms, her legs still tight around his middle and he growled his contentment as his forehead pressed against hers.

"Epharis," she murmured gently, her fingers passing through his hair.

"Etani," he almost purred in response, his lips tracing a line across her jaw to her lips.

Impatient, she turned into the kiss, matching his greedy fervour with her own.

She could feel him hardening inside her once more, his need growing stronger.

A delicate cough interrupted them and they both looked up at the bearded Lich, who had been there to witness their consummation.

Epharis looked angry at the interruption, but the Lich only handed him a small bag of something she did not care for, motioning to something she did not see. Her attention was focused on the bite marks, they were still bleeding, and she studied the beauty of his blood as it trickled down his neck.

His arms tightened around her, clutching her to him as the priest left and Epharis grinned, looking down at her. Picking her up, he slammed her back into the pillar, gripping her wrists with his hands and took her again, hard, and rough with little mercy for her body.

And she relished every second of it.

3

MARRIED LIFE

They returned to the castle the same way they had left it, yet that time the journey did not bother her. She was rather curious about what he had in the large bag he had collected after they had dressed, some hours later and only after he had spent himself several more times. The man was insatiable.

Returning to their room, she looked around but found nothing out of place, the buzz of the consumed souls soothed her, and she was able to think again.

When he noticed her buzz was fading, he picked out a small chunk of something and offered it to her.

Taking it, she sniffed and frowned as it had almost no smell at all. Seeing her hesitation, he directed her hand towards her mouth and she obediently ate it.

Not having a clue what it was for or why she needed to eat it, she shrugged it off and headed for the bathroom to bathe, followed closely by her new husband.

When she stripped, she noticed her body was covered in lingering bruises where he had gripped her, but nothing serious. They would fade soon enough.

Epharis' shoulder however still bled.

"Perhaps we should clean and dress it," he said, slightly concerned for the bite.

Murmuring her agreement, she crossed to the basin and crouched down to reach the small cupboard under it. Picking out a small glass bottle, she returned to him and poured a dribble of alcohol on the wound.

It began to bubble, and the Lich winced, but then the holes healed.

"Odd," she murmured, unsure of what could be causing it. "Maybe my saliva doesn't agree with you."

He grunted his agreement and watched as she moved around, preparing for her bath, and bundling her long hair up with the aid of two sticks to keep it out of her face.

Standing before the mirror, she looked up when he approached from behind, his arms going around her possessively. Leaning down, he smelt her hair and she smiled, not caring that her eyes were still a deep, bottomless black.

She turned to him and helped him undress for the second time, taking his hand and guiding him into the bath with her. She waited for him to settle before inching closer, his eyes widening when she straddled him.

"Now husband," she purred, reaching behind him to grab a washcloth, and intentionally pressing her breasts against his chest. His cheeks flushed slightly, and she felt him growing aroused again as she settled back against his thighs. "It is *you* who must submit to me."

Her tone was teasing, but the words sent a zing of electricity between them. She knew it would be a challenge, albeit a playful one, he would nonetheless rise.

Dipping the cloth in the water between them, her lips parted as she pressed it against his chest, dragging it slowly down. His breath stopped when her hand moved past his navel and he growled, grabbing her wrist.

Soon he was clasping both of her wrists, moving her hands behind her back, and securing them with one of his large fists. Glaring at her, he leant down and traced his lips across her jaw and up to her ear, the gentleness of it making her shiver.

Using his free hand, he arranged himself and then gripped her rear hard, lifting her off his lap just enough to enter her.

She gasped in delight, her back arching at the joy of being his and the hunger he had instilled in her.

Her body moved on its own accord, unable to keep still as pleasure flooded her system. Still, he held her wrists, keeping her controlled as he groaned, watching her body with greedy eyes.

Only after he had been spent did he release her, but he was quick to wrap his arms around her when she settled against his chest, her eyes shut and content to simply lie in his arms.

It was only a few days later when they were discovered.

They were in bed with Epharis atop her and their lips locked in a fierce, passionate kiss as his body moved against hers. Her long legs were wrapped around his waist and her arms around his neck. He was not being particularly gentle with her, taking out several centuries of loneliness on her soft body and leaving bruises everywhere he touched. But the pain only heightened their pleasure.

The sight and sounds of their intimacy had sent the maid scurrying in horror and it was not long before Alaric had found out. His fury was legendary, but it was nothing compared to the fury they faced when he walked in, right as Epharis reached his peak and his lips had found hers.

The heat that radiated off the King was all the warning they needed, both turning in time to see Alaric reaching for his sword.

Epharis flew off her and she immediately grabbed the blankets to cover herself.

Alaric kept staring at her, watching what *he* could have had if it were not for his brother.

"I'll deal with you later," he snarled at her and turned on Epharis. "This is the last time you ruin my plans, Epharis. First, you snatch her from my fingers, and now you snatch her from my bed."

"We are married, Alaric. She is in the right place."

Etani frowned, irritated by the implication that her only place was in one of their beds—preferably under one of them—and pushed herself out of bed.

"Fight it out like children if you want, but I was never going to marry you, Alaric," she threw over her shoulder.

For that matter, she was never going to marry Epharis either.

The thought flittered through her mind and was gone, like so many other negative thoughts against her husband since their marriage. She dismissed it like the rest and picked one of the little chewy balls of reddish stuff that Epharis had brought back. She had grown a taste for them that was bordering on addiction. She popped it into her mouth and chewed it, looking back at the two.

"You can't have me," she said after swallowing, and revelled in the flood of energy that filled her body.

Alaric looked like he would have very much liked to kill her then, licking her fingers free of the last oily residue the little ball left behind.

Her attention turned back to Epharis and she smiled, happy to see him unharmed.

Alaric stalked towards her and she backed up quickly, but he only bowed before her. Tucking something into his pocket as he straightened, he turned and stalked from the room.

"That was weird," she said slowly, not understanding what had happened.

What had gone into his pocket?

Epharis joined her and he traced his fingers along her jaw, making her shiver.

Looking down into her eyes, he smiled and leant down to kiss her forehead.

"Don't worry, my love, he won't bother us again," he murmured, not seeing the way her cheeks flushed and eyes welled at the endearment.

Sliding her arms around his waist, she snuggled into his chest, feeling safe in his embrace.

THEY SPENT the following days alone in their rooms, reading and making love at regular intervals, only stopping for bites of the chewy balls she had grown to crave.

He did not seem to mind how many of them she ate, paying little attention to how many she consumed or how often the little crystal bowl had to be refilled. But the large sack was beginning to dwindle and that made her nervous.

"We're almost out of these things," she observed, chewing her second treat for that hour.

He looked up and grunted gently.

"I'll get more," he promised, motioning for her to join him.

It had been about a month since their marriage and Alaric had not returned. Not a single person bothered them, leaving them to enjoy their honeymoon in peace.

Settling into his arms, she looked down at the book he was holding in a way that allowed them to read at the same time.

His fingers were tracing up and down her side and it was not long before she had dozed off in his arms under his gentle ministrations.

But when she opened her eyes again, he was gone. The blanket someone had placed on her slid off as she pushed herself up.

"Princess," a soft, sad voice spoke up and she jumped, jerking the blanket back up over her chest.

Looking around, she found Kai and Jaia sitting on the couch. Kai's face was bright red, no doubt from the sight of her naked form.

"What are you doing here? Where's Epharis?"

Her head felt fuzzy and she turned to pick one of the balls only to find the bowl empty. Immediately her eyes searched for the sack, but it too was gone.

"We're here as your friends," Jaia said slowly, seeing her panic when she could not find the treats she had come to crave more than air itself.

"Where?" She whimpered, turning on the twins.

Kai lifted one of the treats before him.

Jumping to her feet, she clutched at the blanket, barely mindful of her modesty as her body screamed for the little thing he was holding. Jaia moved as she did, approaching her slowly, his hands outstretched as though he was striving to placate a wild animal.

"Give me that, Kai," she said, doing her best to remain calm, but her attention was now on Jaia, his defensive posture was triggering her need to attack.

"Etani, these aren't what they seem," Kai offered. "They're drugged. Epharis has been dosing you with something."

She refused to listen, her attention flicking between the treat and Jaia who was very carefully keeping himself between her and his brother.

"Don't come any closer, Jaia," she warned, taking a slow, calculated step back from him.

"You have to listen to him, Etani. Epharis has been drugging you so you won't fight him. It's to make you desire him and want to please him."

"Epharis loves me," she snapped, shaking her head angrily that he would dare to insult the man she loved.

"No, Etani, he's a Lich, he can't love you. But he is so incredibly possessive of you. I've never seen control so complete before. He will do anything to ensure you stay with him, but we don't know why yet," Kai sounded sad as he told her, and she narrowed her eyes in anger at him.

"Shut up, Kai. You don't know what you're talking about."

"Then why are your eyes still black?" Jaia asked. "We saw you at the ball, your eyes go black when you feed, but you haven't fed, have you? Answer me, Etani, have you fed today?"

She glared at him, refusing to answer.

"This drug is tricking your instincts into thinking you are feeding with every one of these. At the same time, it is filling your system with hormones and a mind-altering drug."

"If he cannot love me, then how are we able to be together?" She hissed, inching closer to Kai.

"We don't know. It might be the drugs allowing him to… copulate," Kai offered, flushing. "But he cannot love, Etani. It's not possible."

Inching her way further under the guise of countering Jaia, she made her move when she was within range, but Jaia was prepared.

Her lunge for Kai's hand was met with Jaia's body slamming into hers, knocking her to the floor. She rolled with him, taking him off guard and pinning him to the ground with her knees, her hands going to his throat.

He snarled at her, fangs bared, and she growled back.

Kai had moved as well, tucking the ball into his pocket, and coming up beside her, his foot swinging back and connecting hard with her ribcage. Something broke and she fell off the vampire

Rolling, he moved to straddle her stomach, Kai grabbing her ankles before she could knee Jaia in the back.

"What now?" Jaia demanded, grabbing her wrists, and holding them away from him although she had already left four deep gashes in his cheek as she struggled to get him off her.

"Drain her!" Kai cried, striving to pin her down until, eventually, he sat on her legs.

"No!" She yelled, panicked, as she wriggled and squirmed under them.

"Sorry Etani," Jaia murmured.

Gripping her wrists with one hand he cupped her jaw with his other, forcing her head to the right and exposing the slender length of her throat to him.

"No, Jaia don't!"

But it was too late for her threats. His fangs sank deep into her throat and she screamed as his body jerked as the taste of her blood hit his tongue.

His saliva that would slow the clotting process in a human burned like acid and her heart pounded, only making it easier for him as he released her wrists and wrapped his arms tightly around her, lifting her to meet his lips.

After only a few seconds, Kai got off her legs and crawled around to monitor how much his brother blood intake.

The blackness in her eyes faded with each pull of his mouth and her head began to spin.

"Jaia, I think you've taken enough," Kai said and tugged on his brother's shoulder, earning him a solid punch to the face.

Creeping back in a crouch, he kept his arms tight on her, dragging her with him as he drank faster, unable to get enough.

Kai's voice had risen into a panicky yell, but she was not in a state to comprehend what he said. Her numb body was unable to feel anything except a warmth that spread through her from a point at her throat and a grip on her that was too tight.

Something crashed and those arms released her, taking their warmth with them. She was left cold, floating in a hazy greyness that felt unbelievably good.

'Hey E? We're not alone.' A little voice said from somewhere and they both looked down to see something small and glowing, curled into a ball in the general region of her navel.

Her eyes opened and she blinked at the bright light coming through a tiny crack in the curtains and the balcony doors, flooding the room and temporarily blinding her. She looked around and found a huddled figure sitting in the darkest corner with his knees tight against his chest and his head down.

"What?" she croaked.

The figure moved, head tilting and pushing himself up. It was Kai and he quickly moved to close the gap in the curtains. Only once it was dim again did he lift his head and smiled at her brightly.

"You're okay!" he cried and approached her, sitting down beside her.

"What happened? Where's Jaia?" she asked, her head feeling uncomfortably fuzzy.

"He is down in the basement. I...I missed the part where Fae blood is addictive," he sounded sad, his eyes lingering on her throat in a way that made her immediately wary.

"We all make mistakes."

She was trying to placate him as she sat up, finding she was dressed in a black satin gown.

"I need some water," she said, feeling she was not going to be able to walk across the room to fetch it herself.

Kai jumped up and rushed to the pitcher, filling a mug. She drank it gratefully, her eyes sliding shut in delight.

"I can barely remember anything that happened," she started, trying to wade through the fog of confusion and wild emotions.

"Well, you got married to Epharis and he had been drugging you so you could love him. King Alaric brought us one of the treats to study and when we figured out what it was, we came straight here. Epharis is on trial for…" he trailed off, trying to decide how to word it and deciding that simply going very quickly would work best. "Drugging, kidnapping, forcing marriage upon and raping a Princess under the King's care. Plus, treason for disobeying a direct order," he finished, taking air into his lungs.

She gawked at him, trying to process everything he had said along with that last thought she had before she had fallen unconscious.

Touching the area below her navel, she felt it there. A tiny beat of a soul, pulling on her energy and leaving her feeling even more drained.

Kai watched her, not understand until he went over what he had said and connected the dots.

"Oh no… that's not possible… that's not possible! Lich can't procreate," he said, jumping up and wringing his hands as he paced.

"They can't, or they have never been known to?"

Kai stopped dead on his tracks, staring at her in horror.

"You can't be pregnant, not with that creature's spawn!"

His words cut through her and she drew back from him, hurt by the cruelty while the voice in her mind growled, teeth bared at the tone.

"He tried to make me into a Lich and failed, but I still changed, I'm at least part Lich."

He realised what he had said and looked more afraid than ever, coming back to her, and holding her hands in his.

"We'll figure something out, I promise," he said gently.

She did not know what there was to figure out. Exchanging a glance with Letari, the other mind only shrugged. After a moment, she nodded and when he embraced her, she leant into him.

A WHILE LATER, she made her way into the bathroom and glanced at herself in the mirror. The sight before her made her freeze. The bite was only small, two little holes that had sealed shut, but the skin around it had darkened, and little tendrils had spread out from the dark patch.

"Kai?" she called out, bending in to examine the spot.

Kai padded into the room, letting out a sigh of relief when he saw her fully dressed.

"Oh," he breathed as his eyes lowered. "Jaia… he couldn't stop. I had to hit him with a chair to let go. He almost initiated the process of turning you. That's what happens when enough of our saliva enters the bloodstream. It will go away in a few days."

Etani nodded, wondering at how many things she could be turned into before she finally exploded.

"I'll wait in the sitting room," he said and retreated.

After a quick bath, she got dressed and braided her hair. She opted for a shirt with a high collar to hide her neck, but the tendrils were still visible, seeming to move with every beat of her heart.

Kai was waiting patiently when she joined him, her slow movements a sign of her exhaustion.

"What will happen if Epharis is found guilty?" she asked as she casually headed for the jug to get some more water.

"He will be executed."

The mug dropped onto the tray as she turned to him. "What? Where is the trial?" she demanded.

Damn, she could not let the monster die or she would join him.

"In the throne room I thin—" He was cut off as she gripped his arm and yanked him towards the door and out into the hallway.

"He's cursed me so I couldn't kill him. If he dies, I die, and there's no coming back from a soul-linked death," she said, and he immediately upped his speed.

Bursting into the throne room, the scene threw her off.

The King was seated on his throne, looking furious. All around, there were about one hundred chairs, each one occupied with a grim-faced man or woman, all of them of some variety of mythical creature.

Epharis was on his knees, his arms bound behind his back by the same chain he had once used to bind her. The loop was tied to a hook dug into the marble floor, keeping him from standing up.

Looking around, his eyes lit up at the sight of her, but then they darkened as he took in her face.

"Your Majesty," she said urgently as she swept into the room until she was standing beside Epharis.

King Alaric looked at her, a moment of pity showing on his face before he schooled his features.

"You can't kill him," she said, causing a murmur to form somewhere behind them.

Kai had lingered back, looking anxious.

"Why not? You cannot be defending him after what he has done."

"I'm not. I'm only saying you can't kill him. If you do, I'll die right along with him. We are linked."

The King's face darkened as his eyes fell on his brother who just shrugged and grinned at him.

"I see," he said darkly, considering the options. "Very well, then. In exchange for his life, you will agree to work for me. Since Epharis will be imprisoned, you will need to stay busy," he spoke deliberately, slowly.

She was suspicious and so was Epharis. He growled and his eyes skimmed over her form with the same possessiveness he had all those days.

"Agreed," she said, not taking her eyes off Epharis.

Her hand lifted and she touched her stomach, the movement seemingly random and yet the intent in her eyes had Epharis following her movement. The moment that realisation sank in he was intent on reaching her, struggling against the chain.

"For all the crimes stated, Epharis, you are to be confined to your rooms for the foreseeable future. You will have no contact with the Princess ever again."

The King stood and held out his arm to Etani. The crowd clapped, and she dropped her hand from her stomach and moved away from the Lich.

The last she saw of Epharis was his expression turning to one of pure, unadulterated murder as he saw Alaric's arm wrapping around her and turn her away from him.

The King had taken everything from him, his freedom, his wife, and now, his unborn child.

4

THE KING'S REQUEST

ollowing the King through the halls, they moved out of the back of the castle and into a room that was almost entirely made of glass. She came to a stop, looking around her in wonder.

The room was so warm that she felt as if she had stepped from one reality into a tropical one.

Sweeping past him, she found the room filled with strange and beautiful plants.

"What is this?" she asked as she moved deeper into the room.

"It is called a greenhouse. A room that is kept warm and allows plants to grow all year long," he said quietly as he followed closely behind. "Your eyes seemed different," he observed after a while.

"It's a long story," she replied, crouching down to lift one flower and inhale its wonderful scent.

The entire room was remarkably beautiful.

"I will listen if you talk," he promised, and she realised he was standing right behind her.

Standing, she turned to look into his eyes. "I don't feel ready to discuss the events just yet."

Alaric nodded once and let her explore. She was not foolish

enough to believe he was any different from Epharis. But while Epharis had a cold and dark evil in him, Alaric was more likely to hit her if she displeased him. When it came to those men, she supposed it was a choice between physical and mental abuse.

The King offered her a dark violet rose and she took it, smiling warmly at the pretty and perfect flower.

They spent an hour exploring the garden room, talking only when necessary.

"I have a task for you," he finally said as they were leaving the garden.

All the while he had been watching her closely, his eyes lingering on her throat and the vivid dark marks on her pale skin.

"We are having trouble with the Weoreneian King after the incident. Since you were close to the Princess, I was hoping you would… consent to a visit to Weorene to meet with Nayishma's father."

The words hung in the air, only the mention of her best friend's name stinging her. But she had agreed to work for him and refusing would put her and Epharis' lives at risk.

"Alright, I will go," she agreed, knowing she had little real choice in the matter.

Leading her back, he guided her to where her new rooms would be. He had placed her in the royal quarters, near him. She thanked him, but inwardly she much preferred her smaller rooms away from the King. The rooms were enormous, and she did not care for the empty space, nor did she like the hideous pastel colouring of the rooms.

SHE WAS GIVEN two days to prepare for the trip and she used them wisely, packing everything she would need and handing everything to the guard who loaded it all outside her room for collection.

Since she would be spending a week there, she had prepared for a lot of reading.

When the time came, she put on a black fluffy dress and a veil, as was befitting to a royal emissary into Weorene. She understood why Nayishma had hated the veil so much. It was impossible to see through it.

Once she was helped into the carriage, she turned and was stunned to see Izziah climbing in after her and looking flustered.

Before the door had shut, and in full view of everyone, she punched the Drow right on the nose, and she heard Alaric's booming laughter from the stairs.

His nose bled profusely, and she spent the entire two-day trip glaring at him and refusing to answer when he tried to strike up a conversation. She still refused to talk to the Drow male when she finally got out of the carriage and into the swampy city.

"Welcome to Weorene, Princess," a voice greeted her, and she squinted her eyes through the fabric at a man whose body ended at the waist and formed a long, snake-like tail.

"Naga," Izziah remarked and Etani had to agree with his fascination.

They were not the most common species, and they were extremely dangerous if you went against them. Most could kill with a single bite, and they were incredibly strong.

"Thank you," she replied politely, accepting the Naga's proffered arm.

"Dinner is in a few hours. Until then, we will show you to your suite. I'm afraid you and your companion will have to share a double suite, as we are full up with representatives paying their respects. They feel the need to stick around to help."

The poor man sounded put upon and she could not help but smile as she started walking, leaving the Drow to follow them.

The city was a series of long strips of buildings and houses inter-sected with swampy water that moved sluggishly. Oddly enough, it did not smell as bad as she thought it would. She quickly found out that her veil was also effective at keeping bugs off her face, though the sight of them still made her skin crawl.

Izziah was having issues with them, something she took great pleasure in, as a series of small boats guided them to a large island that held the castle.

It was huge and a rich, muddy brown colour. Squat and square, looking as though it was built to endure and not to look pretty.

Accepting their guide's hand once more, he led her up the stone steps to the door. But rather than a wooden door, they found layer upon layer of that frothy fabric that had made up their gowns at the ball.

As they passed, each layer parted and fell back down behind them, keeping the vast majority of the bugs away from the castle. It was as if they were stepping into a magical portal.

The inside of the castle was large and square, the front door reaching directly onto the throne room with a series of doors around the room leading off to the rest of the building, with a second storey above them having a wide balcony and even more doors.

The man sitting on the throne was short and sturdy with red hair and a big red beard with plenty of grey streaks. Approaching, the Naga bowed deeply.

"Emperor Varsas, please allow me to introduce you Princess Etania, emissary to King Alaric of Ayathian. Accompanying her is Lord Izziah of Ayathian."

The Emperor's face turned red, looking like he might blow up, but Etani curtsied low and, going against custom, she spoke up.

"Emperor Varsas, I am here on behalf of King Alaric, however, I am also here to beg for your forgiveness."

Immediately, the man's anger fizzled out, staring at her, confused.

"Nayishma and I were close friends, it was my responsibility to keep her safe that night and we were separated. I was unable to reach her in time. Please forgive me for not being able to protect her."

At some point, the tears had sprung up and her voice wobbled at the end, adding a tragic note to her plea. The man looked devastated as he pieced together who she was.

"You're Etani?" he asked, sliding off the throne and coming to stand before her. He took her hand and she shivered at the warm humanness in him.

"Yes, your Majesty," she replied, confused by how well informed he was.

"Nayishma told me a lot about you, she wrote daily. I am sorry you have suffered as much as I."

"I wish I had been able to reach her. She was my best friend and I loved her deeply," she whispered, not wanting anyone to be able to listen in on their conversation.

"She loved you, too," he replied with a sigh. "There is nothing to forgive, you are not to blame for an assassin getting through that lazy man's defences."

He moved away from her and sat back down on his throne.

"Please, you have travelled a long way, get some rest and we will talk at dinner."

Glad for the easy escape, she and Izziah were led to their quarters.

SHE WAS SHOCKED at the size of the room and the windows, and even more so since they were all covered in a fine mesh that seemed to be exceptionally effective in keeping all the bugs out. Immediately she removed her veil and as she turned, she noted that the Naga seemed shocked at her boldness.

"Princess, Lord," he bowed his way out of the room and closed the large wooden doors behind him.

The moment they were alone, she turned and glared at Izziah. "You are to stay away from me during this entire trip. If you so much as touch me, I will break your arm."

With that, she left the startled man alone in the sitting room and retreated to her room.

Having time to change and remove a few layers of the veil so she could see, she tried to figure out how the bath worked, only to quickly learn that the water came out of a metal spout above her and she squealed as boiling water came down.

Flattening herself against the side of the stall, she used the very tips of her fingers to turn the second knob and the water began to cool.

Finally stepping under the spout, she basked in the novelty of having a hot bath while still standing up, the water washing away the grime down a little hole in the bottom of the stall.

Fascinated, she tried to figure out how that thing worked, but she was drawn back by the heat and spicy smelling oils.

She stayed in there longer than she intended, enjoying it far too much and when she stepped out and got dressed, she only had a few minutes to apply her veil and head out before the knock for dinner came.

Wearing a long silvery-white dress that had been picked out for her, she dropped the thinner veil over her face and stepped out into the hall with Izziah close behind, looking as though his bathing experience had not been as delightful as hers.

That time, their guide was a reptilian that did not speak at all, only wordlessly directed them through one of the doors from the empty throne room into a corridor leading to a series of large rooms. Even the smallest of those rooms was still massive, but it housed a large wooden table and a few dozen chairs.

The Emperor jumped to his feet at the sight of them and hurried around to pull out Etani's chair, blinking slightly as he noticed the change in her veil that gave only the slightest hint of her face beneath.

"Oh Princess, please do not stand on custom for our sakes, you do not have to wear the veil inside the castle."

Immediately, she took it off and placed it on the seat beside her, relieved by the freedom. "Wonderful, I was not sure how I was going to eat while wearing it."

The King blinked several times, but when he understood what she was saying, he laughed at the jest.

"So, what does Alaric plan to do about this incident?" he asked after they had settled, and they had both their wine and water glasses filled.

"The perpetrators were executed. All of them," Izziah offered, taking a sip of the wine, and letting out a soft noise of appreciation. "It was discovered that a High Priestess had gone rogue and ordered the hit, following her belief that a prophecy called for the Princess to marry King Alaric."

Etani kicked him under the table and he jumped.

Emperor Varsas looked devastated by the news. "A prophecy? Did the oracle die?"

The question threw them both off and they exchanged a look.

"Not that we have heard," Etani said gently, unsure of the question.

"So, they killed the wrong woman."

Etani's eyes immediately dropped to the table and she heard Izziah suck in a breath as realisation dawned on him.

"I'm afraid so, at the time Etania's presence was still unknown to most," Izziah said.

"Where are you from, Princess? Ayathian doesn't have a Princess of their own."

"I am from Faerie," she said evasively, and the man looked surprised, his eyes going to her ears and then back to her eyes.

"I assumed you were an odd elf," he said and Izziah snorted.

"No, I am one of the Fae."

The Emperor nodded and looked at Izziah.

"From the Under Dark originally, but I was accepted into the ranks of Alaric's trusted allies along with my brother," he flicked a glance at Etani, not speaking the name aloud.

"Interesting companions I have," the Emperor mused with forced cheerfulness.

Dinner was served and the meal was similar to what Nayishma had always eaten.

It turned out that the meats were large rodents and even larger insects, all of which tasted wonderful and Etani ate heartily, even if it did nothing for her. She did her best not to think about what she was eating, instead, she tried to focus on the taste.

After dinner, they stood to leave but the Emperor asked her to stay. She watched as a wary Izziah left, his eyes narrowed.

"Princess, I would ask that you join us tomorrow evening for a small party. It is the six-month anniversary of Nayishma's death and as is custom, we celebrate her life."

"Do you not do that immediately after death?"

"No, that is a time for mourning, we wait six months and then celebrate. It isn't for a week really, but we wish to celebrate with your presence."

"I would be honoured," she replied sadly, and the Emperor nodded with a sad smile of his own.

Once she was dismissed, she followed the Naga to her room, and he opened the door for her, closing it firmly behind her once she was inside.

"You're alright," Izziah breathed and she swept past him, throwing the veil onto the couch.

"I'm fine, excuse me," she tried to leave but he caught her arm and she swung on him, but he jerked her forward against him to throw her off balance.

"Stop being angry at me, Etani," he snapped. "You know why I did it, you know why *we* did it. I did not know Drizdan had that plan."

"Well you're stupid, the man is insane," she hissed, trying to free her wrist but his arm went around her, keeping her trapped. "Besides, he can give up on that plan because I'm already married."

"What? To whom?"

Grabbing her left wrist, he pulled her hand up in search of a ring. Instead, a dark line had formed that she had not noticed before.

"The Lich," he snarled and threw her arm away.

Wriggling herself free, she turned and, using the momentum, she slapped him as hard as she could.

"You and your brother can never keep your hands to yourself. Do not touch me Izziah, I'm not your doll to be manipulated. You tried to sell me, and you would have gone ahead with it if you hadn't been discovered. You had gone to negotiate my price when your brother was threatening to rape me. *Promising* to rape me."

"How could you marry that monster?" he yelled, clearly not listening to her as he clutched his face where she had struck him.

"That's none of your business," she snapped, and he grabbed her arm once again, keeping her from escaping.

"You're a Princess of the Winter Court and you're married to a Lich?" he yelled once again and his hold on her wrist became painful.

"Let go of me," she cried, twisting her arm to try and free it.

Finally, he let her go and she took some steps back, clutching her bruised wrist.

"Has he touched you?" he demanded, his eyes raking down her form.

She lifted her chin and turned away from him. "I'm carrying his child," she threw behind her back and slammed the door to his livid face.

Locking the door was not enough, so she shoved a chair under the handle just to be sure. Then she headed for the bed and dropped onto it, fuming. The cackling in her head only added to her sour mood.

A LONG BLACK gown and a matching black veil were sent to her in preparation for the next evening. The veil, while it hid her face almost entirely, the fabric allowed her to see out. Stepping out of her room, she ran her fingers down the silken fabric and glanced around to find the Drow.

Izziah had also dressed well. His suit matched her dress and with a cautious smile, he lifted a silver circlet to her.

Careful not to touch her more than necessary, he settled it onto her head. By the time they left the room to an oddly quiet palace, her instincts were already frayed. She did not want to think that Nayishma was dead, she wanted to focus on the beauty of the woman in life but that was not how things ran in that place.

The Naga led them down the hall and into the quiet and eerie throne room filled with people wearing black.

"Creepy," Izziah breathed, looking out over the mass of figures.

She could not help but agree, glancing around when their guide bowed and left them just to the side of the mass of figures.

"Thank you all for coming to mourn the death of our most precious daughter," Varsas called out from the throne. "Not only will we remember the perfection that was the Princess Nayishma, but we will celebrate the beauty of her, and the happiness of her life."

That was odd, she had been so sure the man had loved her, but she did not think he found his daughter overly beautiful or precious. Especially since he was throwing his lesbian daughter at an abusive man in the hopes of marrying her off.

The crowd broke into smaller groups and she noticed that much of the conversation revolved around Nayishma's life and what she had done. She was an incredibly kind and generous woman, striving to help others in need and sharing what she could with the city.

She loved birds, was gentle and sweet, represented the future of the throne and they all missed her almost as much as Etani did.

It was painful to hear it all, recollecting those precious last moments with the dying Princess and the tender kiss that pulled her free of her failing body. She could not help but recall it, even as it burned her soul.

Dancing had started and she accepted an offer as soon as it came, barely seeing the face of the tall man, only his black-jacketed chest as he pulled her seamlessly through the steps of the dance as though they were his second nature.

The dancing lasted for hours, growing slowly more upbeat until finally she was passed on to Varsas. He was looking rather flustered as his hands slipped into hers.

"I am glad you were here to see this," he said, squeezing her fingers.

"Thank you for asking us to stay. It feels good to be able to celebrate her, even in death. I am glad that we can move past this and look to the future."

Their difference in height made it somewhat difficult for her to follow his lead.

He smirked at her. "Yes, I am sure it will be interesting. Why don't you stay for a while? I'm sure someone of your rank could use the break from that overbearing arse."

"I'm afraid we must decline, we are needed back in Ayathian," she said, half-tempted by the offer.

"Ayathian won't be the safest place for much longer, Princess."

"Why not?"

"Because there *will* be war."

She froze, staring down at him as she took that information in.

"You will go to war with Ayathian?" she hissed, removing her hands from his.

"He allowed an emissary and my only daughter to be murdered under his watch," he snapped, glaring at her.

5

ESCAPING WEORENE

"That was not Alaric's fault," she retorted as fear crept up inside her.

Had he planned the entire thing?

If so, why had he even agreed to her presence there?

"He allowed a faction of his people enough momentum for an assassination attempt. What if it had been you, Princess? What if they had realised they were looking at the wrong woman?" he spat, sounding bitter as his eyes scanned her up and down.

"I don't know," she whispered, hating herself.

She was to blame for Yish's death, not Alaric.

"You and the Drow will stay here as my honoured guests until after the war," he stated and made a gesture she did not recognise.

Two guards moved towards her and she gasped. Her eyes searched the Drow who was oblivious as he danced with a young woman who looked utterly enamoured by him.

Hurrying through the dancing crowd as quickly as she dared so as not to cause a panic, she caught onto Izziah's hand before he could be taken by another woman. He seemed shocked to find her before him and pulling him into a dance.

"Varsas is trying to have us captured. We need to get out, the war won't be prevented. We have to warn Alaric."

Her eyes scanned the crowd, but the guards did not seem ready to intervene and risk a scene.

"Right, we need to escape. I'll have the carriage arranged. Grab whatever you can," he growled, squeezing her fingers, and they parted.

He headed for the nearest maid while she ran towards the doors to the throne room.

As soon as she was free of the throne room, she picked up the hem of her skirt and almost running. Guards and servants stared at her curiously, but they did not seem to be aware of the situation yet.

Making it into her room, she gasped as she found six guards already in there and she backed up quickly, right into the arms of someone else.

The Naga wrapped his arms around her middle, holding her against him while she began to squirm, furious that they would dare contain her like that.

Turning, she drove her elbow into his ribs and he immediately let her go. Ducking under his arm she sprinted for the hall to find Izziah was heading her way. His eyes slid past her to the guards after her.

His face paled at the sight and he reached out his hand. Clasping onto it as he pulled her along with him, the pair ran full pelt to the main palace entrance without being stopped. It would seem that not everyone was aware of the importance of their arrest just yet.

Feet pounded after them as they skidded around the corner and burst out of the gauzy fabric and into the humidity of the swamp.

"This way."

Izziah pulled her along with him, running for the nearest boat and all but throwing her into it as he grabbed onto the pole that allowed him to push the boat away from the land and steered them towards the next landmass where they could swap the boat for another one.

"What did he say?" the Drow demanded, looking around as the guards were piling into the other boats, some even jumping straight into the water.

"That we were to stay as honoured guests. That it wouldn't be safe in Ayathian."

The moment the next island was within reach, she pulled them closer while he jumped out to help her. Once they were both standing on solid ground, he kicked the boat away from the island, leaving it to float lazily down the stream.

"Damn dress," she hissed, and she bundled it up. The massive thing was not only making it hard to keep up with him but also she was frequently being snagged on shrubs. "Why do they demand we wear these stupid things?"

"It's harder for a woman to escape dressed in one of those," Izziah reasoned, glancing around as the guards were crawling out of the swampy water like monsters.

They ran as fast as they could across the island, ducking between houses and alleys before coming to the next river and looking around wildly, spotting a boat further down.

Heading that way, she jumped into it and he poled them along quickly, anxious and sweating in the humid air.

"Not far now," Izziah gasped after a few minutes.

His body was straining to keep them moving, and she acknowledged that, but had she reached for the pole, he would have hissed at her. Instead, she grasped the shore again and pulled them closer, shoving herself up and out of the boat before pulling him out with her.

He looked exhausted, stressed, and sweaty, but he ran along with her as she tugged at him, knowing how difficult it was to get the boats to move. When they reached the final crossing, she shoved him into the boat before he could touch the pole.

Pushing them off the bank, she looked back at the guards who were starting to wilt under the heat and strain of running after them.

'Behind,' flashed in her mind and when she looked down at their boat, she shrieked to find a grey-skinned lizard-looking reptilian crawling up over the gunnel.

Spinning the pole, she slammed it down on top of its head and it buckled. Quickly, Izziah shoved it off the edge of the boat and back into the water.

Poling them along as quickly as she was able, she was left panting, her muscles aching as she worked to push them along, while it was hard to tell whether the boat was moving at all.

Finally, he reached for a post to tie the boat to and they scrambled out. Once again, she turned and shoved the pole into the face of another guard who was surfacing, sending him crashing back into the water. They ran to the dock where a carriage seemed to be waiting for them.

"Oh, thank you mother," Izziah cried.

They both gathered their strength, running as quickly as they could for the carriage and almost falling against it.

Izziah turned to the driver and handed him several coins. "We need to get back to Ayathian ten minutes ago."

The driver nodded in understanding and opened the door for them. Etani was shoved inside and scrambled into the sweet-smelling space. Glancing around, she concluded it was not the same one that had brought them in. This carriage had seats of plush crimson velvet and walls stained so dark they were nearly black.

Deciding it did not matter what carriage they had so long as they had one, she reached for Izziah and pulled him in with her, the man still gasping slightly as he clambered in and collapsed onto the seat opposite hers.

The door slammed shut and she looked out the window as arrows were nocked.

Reaching for Izziah, she shoved his head down and ducked as well as the arrows thudded into the side of the carriage, two ending up inside with them.

Lifting her head, she pulled the circlet and veil off and stared out as the archers prepared once more, but the carriage was already moving, and the horses seemed to fly with their speed.

Izziah straightened his back and a hint of a smile appeared on his solemn face, before he slumped back against the seat and closed his eyes, trying to get his breathing under control.

Heading back out of the city at top speed, she cursed the man who had become so obsessed, cursing men in general, for that matter.

They had fled, leaving behind their belongings, but she was glad she had worn the hairpin and necklace, or she would not have consented to their leaving until she had retrieved them.

Izziah had fallen into a sullen silence, his eyes often lingering on her middle more than was warranted, but there was nothing she could do to stop his foul mood. What was done was done and there was no saving any of them.

War was coming to Ayathian and their attempt to stop it by visiting Weorene had been pointless.

It was hard to tell how long they travelled but, at some point, Izziah stopped the carriage long enough to retrieve a falcon from the storage compartment.

"To warn King Alaric," he offered with a sheepish look. "We planned this before we left. He knew that even with the peace agreement, war was still a possibility."

She did not argue, simply watched the bird flying fast in the direction she knew Ayathian to be.

They had been lucky to get out at all rather than ending up the political prisoners the Emperor had intended them to be the whole time. They had been even luckier to get the carriage, as it moved faster than Izziah could run.

THEY TOOK some time to stretch their legs and move about. Izziah offered the driver one of the horses and excused him, stating they could get back the rest of the way without him and it would be easier for him to get home himself. That was fine by her and, soon enough, their driver was galloping away, leaving them behind with a carriage of three.

Etani paced slowly along the road, her eyes were cast downwards as she chewed on her nail, thinking hard about what they were going to do.

"Do you know much of what Alaric's army is like?" she finally asked him.

"No, I imagine he will try and recruit from the outlying districts. He rules over at least half of this continent to hear him tell it."

Izziah pulled off his jacket and shirt to hang them over the door to dry, groaning as the cool breeze calmed his skin.

"What is the difference between an Emperor and a King?" she asked, her eyes lingering on the road they had just come down, wary in case someone had followed them.

Izziah perked up. "None at all, actually. In essence, they are the same thing, but it's believed that depends on how the title was gained, the location and the like, but really, they are the same. It's an ego thing, wanting themselves to sound like they are more important and powerful than they are."

"Alaric having an ego? Never," she scoffed, making him laugh. "Ten minutes and we head off again?" She turned to him, finding him still watching her. "What?" she snapped.

"I still can't believe you are carrying that monster's child," he growled, glaring at her.

"Mind your own business, Izziah."

Pushing past him she climbed back into the carriage, frustrated that he was still bringing up the subject.

It was not his business and he had no right mentioning it. It was *her* life, *her* body and now, *her* child.

After the short break was finished, the Drow pulled his clothes back on, slammed the carriage door shut, and climbed up to the seat as they headed off again.

The first day slipped by uneventfully. Alone in the carriage, she did nothing but stare at the world as it passed by. They were forced to stop at sunset, and he climbed into the carriage with her, bringing along a blanket for her as the carriage had no glass in the windows.

They were forced to huddle closer together, with their backs pressed against each other's and using the blanket along with her dress to keep warm.

Neither of them slept well, but it was still preferable than no sleep at all.

Early the following morning, they continued on and at the first town they came across, they swapped their horses for fresh ones, purchasing a fourth one as well. Etani went hunting and found herself a human she barely paid any attention to. Returning to the carriage, Izziah had removed the arrows.

Their supply of money was dwindling and they could not afford to buy them both new clothes, even with Etani glamouring coins for them—something Izziah was not happy with. He bought himself enough food to last him the remainder of the trip even though she thought it was almost twice what a person would normally eat, something Letari seemed to agree with.

Minding her own business, she climbed back into the carriage and they left the village.

The second day was nearly as uneventful as the first, with the exception that he had provided her with a handful of books, keeping some for himself up on the seat.

At least that gave her something to do and she sighed, finishing the first book before they were even forced to stop to swap horses.

They were going too fast and she knew it, but they were in a hurry to get back.

IT WAS NEARING mid-afternoon when she heard Izziah yelling, someone swearing as the horses reared with the carriage coming to a crashing halt. Etani slid off her seat, landing in a heap on the floor and looking around her, confused.

"Stay in the carriage," Izziah called out to her and something about his voice made her freeze, affixing her eyes on the window.

It was not like she could not defend herself, but she was no longer the only one that needed defending. The child inside her had to be protected, and she cared more for it than herself.

"Get out of here, we've got nothing of interest to you," Izziah yelled, but she could not make out the answering growl.

There had to be more than one. Something near the back of the carriage shifted and she froze, unable to see what was happening through the curtains and unwilling to reveal herself.

When someone walked around the side of the carriage, she did her best not to make any noise as she turned to observe the shadow as it passed.

She carried no weapons, nothing but a small book to defend herself, but she hoped at least Izziah had something.

"We aren't rich, we carry nothing of profit to you," Izziah said.

"Who's in the carriage?" a deep voice growled, causing her shoulders to tense.

"No one but my sister," Izziah lied and then she heard him grunting followed by the sound of flesh hitting flesh.

"Why don't we go say hello to your sister then?" That voice was lecherous, and she quickly picked up the book, ready to whack anyone on the head.

"Leave her alone!" Izziah cried and she looked up as the shadow moved around, pausing beside one of the doors.

The moment the door was yanked open, she froze. Before her there was no stranger, but none other than Drizdan. Her heart skipped a beat as terror washed through her at the sight of him.

"Afternoon," he growled, and when his eyes shifted from her, she gasped as something pricked her side.

Whipping around, she found Izziah holding a syringe, the barrel empty and whatever it contained already coursing through her veins.

"Izziah?" she whimpered, her head beginning to spin as she moved to slap him, missing by over a foot.

Catching her wrist, he pulled her closer and grinned.

"Don't worry, Princess, we won't fail this time," he promised as everything faded to black.

6

RETURN TO THE UNDER DARK

When she came to, she found herself tied elaborately in the carriage. Glancing at her hands, they were bound before her with a chain similar to the one Epharis had used. One end of the chain was tied to one door of the carriage, around her wrists and then across the other end, attached to the other door. A shorter chain secured her wrists to the ceiling with a second chain around her ankles.

At least she was able to lie down, but as she straightened up, she found Drizdan sitting across from her and grinning, his white teeth bright in the candlelight.

"Evening Princess," he greeted, and she jerked back from him, her back hitting the wall of the carriage with a thud.

"Everything okay?" Izziah spoke out.

"Just the Princess saying hello," Drizdan replied, his black eyes never leaving hers.

Since she saw him last, he had gotten a tongue piercing and now Etani observed how the little silver stud appeared against his dark red tongue, but somehow it worked for him.

Reaching out, he tilted her jaw to inspect her neck and the lingering bite and its scar that refused to budge.

"Got yourself a vampire problem?"

She glared at him, her eyes sweeping the carriage for anything that could help her.

"Don't worry, I already searched you… thoroughly," he leered, and her cheeks flushed at the thought of his hands running over her body. No doubt he must have taken great pleasure in searching her too.

Pressing her head back against the carriage wall, she stared at him as if she were trying to silently will him not to move against her.

Etani gestured at her bonds. "Taking a page out of the Lich's book?"

"Very much so, quite the genius, that man," Drizdan said as he shifted his weight.

Lounging, she found the position oddly attractive, his legs spread wide, leaning back and to the side as though he did not have a care in the world. One arm was placed at the backrest of the seat, giving him a lazy and sultry air.

His eyes dropped to her cleavage that was all the more enticing since her arms had been pulled forward and close together.

"Nice dress," he said, reluctantly lifting his eyes back to her face. "What happened to your eye?"

She was surprised by the sheer number of people noticing the green specks in her eyes. They must have been observing her closely.

"Long story…" she started, but with no intention of getting into it.

"We have plenty of time. We're at least a day from our destination." Reaching out, he grabbed her legs and, pulling her slightly forward, he nestled his knees between hers. "Or we could find other things to entertain ourselves. I heard your Lich has already gotten a piece, why not me too?"

She recoiled, pushing herself back against the wall of the carriage and as far away from him as possible.

"Keep your hands to yourself, Drow scum," she snapped and his face darkened.

Etani had not even seen him move, the sound of the blow resonating loud in the carriage followed by a sting to her face.

He reached out and gripped a fistful of her hair, pulling her closer while his free hand pushed up the hem of her skirt, his rough fingers scraping her inner thigh.

"Don't think for a second I would hesitate to take you by force, Princess. There's no one around for miles to hear you scream and we both know Izziah won't do a damn thing to help you."

His fingers scraped her undergarments, his nails scratched her thighs while she gritted her teeth.

"Get your hands off me, you bastard," she hissed, refusing to be intimidated by him.

"Stop the carriage," Drizdan yelled to his brother who immediately obliged.

Her heart began to race as she stared into his eyes that were alight with malice.

Reaching down, he pulled the chains around her wrists and ankles free of their loops and jerked her off the chair and onto her knees before him, while her arms were still restrained above her head.

Izziah stepped off the carriage and came around to see what was going on. The moment he took in the sight before him, he stopped. Etani was on her knees with Drizdan's hand still under her skirt, his face exhibiting his feral intent.

Turning away from the carriage, he left her to her fate, and she immediately hated him for it.

Spinning her around, Drizdan forced her forward onto the bench, her arms bent back painfully as he slid down behind her.

"All you had to do was be nice to me, Etani," he hissed as he gathered her dress and threw it up over her back.

Leaning over her, he dragged his tongue slowly up the side of her face, the feeling of that little metal stud stinging her skin, but she refused to make a sound or give him the satisfaction of knowing it hurt.

Then he grasped her inner thigh, forcing her legs to part, growling his irritation at her refusal to cooperate.

"Damn woman, obey!" he snarled and lifted his hand, intending to slap her when a horn sounded in the distance.

His hand froze mid-air and his head jerked in the direction of the sound.

Soon after, running footsteps reached them and Izziah was at the window. His face was carefully schooled, but she saw the pity in his eyes and hated him all the more for it. He had walked away and facilitated his brother into doing whatever he pleased.

"We have to go," Izziah snapped as the horn sounded again.

It was getting closer.

Cursing, Drizdan pulled up his trousers and threw open the door, stepping out. She immediately dropped to her side, allowing her skirt to fall back down and cover her legs.

"Get in, I'll drive," Drizdan snarled, thwarted by whatever it was that was heading their way.

Izziah climbed in, but when he moved to help her to the seat, she recoiled from his touch, unable to even look at him. She remained on the floor of the carriage, focusing on Izziah's retreating back as he walked away from her, leaving her to his brother.

BY THE TIME they had arrived, she had huddled herself as far into the corner as she could, her arms stretched out to where they were trapped. The door opened and Drizdan stood there, smirking at her.

He reached up to undo the chain, motioning for Izziah to do the same with the other side. She was all but dragged out of the carriage, the short link between her ankles making it hard for her to walk.

Kneeling, Drizdan fixed his eyes on her. "Harm me in any way and what I was going to do to you in that carriage will be the least of your concerns," he said and yanked the hem of her skirt and removed the chains from around her ankles to facilitate her walking.

Once again he stood and as his eyes landed on hers, she saw that same malicious need that had her stepping back from him, only to have him pull her closer.

"As soon as I'm alone with you..." he whispered, but never finished what he had to say as Izziah approached.

The white-haired Drow looked between the two of them and then moved on, approaching a group of six Drow men and one Drow female.

Drizdan lingered behind to watch the group. Leaning over her, he licked her jaw, laughing softly when she shuddered. "I'm glad you did not scream, it's more fun when they stay quiet. I can enjoy myself more when not interrupted."

She tried to tune him out, but it was difficult with his hot breath on her cheek and his eyes hungry on her chest. At least she had Letari's profanities to focus on, as the woman started screaming at him.

Waving them over, Drizdan pulled her towards the group and she noted that all the men looked similar, all in various shades of black, dark purple and dark blue, with white, red or black eyes and silver or black hair.

The woman was tall and slender, with her skin so inconceivably black. Her hair was pure silver and she looked haughtily at Etani.

"Is this your Princess?"

Izziah nodded. "Princess Etania of the Winter Court, yes."

The woman reached for her, touching her jaw, and turning her head, focusing on the bite on her neck.

"Vampires are such pesky creatures. Don't suppose this one is doing too well," she said and released her. "Very well, put her in the carriage. You two can go in there with her and a guard."

She turned away at Drizdan's pout, trying once more to dig in her heels even as she was pulled into the new carriage. Drizdan settled beside her, toying with the chain and occasionally whipping her with it just to see her jump.

Izziah and the nameless guard sat across from them, pointedly ignoring his cruelty.

She did not know what to expect from the Drow city, but passing through a small opening in the side of a sheer mountain face was not one of them.

The pathway they followed was precarious and narrow, the carriage passing through at a speed that made her nervous. Her companions seemed unconcerned by it, staring out the windows as they descended deeper under ground until the passage opened into an enormous cavern. The city was huge while every building, spire and tower had a sharp, knifelike angle at the top.

It was dark, but the place was kept well-lit due to large green balls. They entered the gates of the palace and the moment Izziah and the guard got out, Drizdan took advantage of the situation to move his hand higher on her thigh through the dress.

"You know, if you want a baby, we can get rid of the Lich's and I can put one in you. Might take me a few hundred tries though."

She knew he was just trying to scare her, knew he just wanted to torment her, but she still shivered. Grinning, he pulled her from the carriage and onto the rough stone of the cavern floor.

She could not help but wonder whether everything there had not been carved out of the mountain itself. It appeared to be perfect, without any hint of joins in the stone.

Approaching the palace, she looked around herself in wonder, not having a clue what she was going to do. No one knew where she was, except maybe Epharis and he would be locked up for an exceedingly long time, unable to get to her. She might be angry at him for drugging and forcing her to marry him, but he would be able to save her.

At the top of the stairs sat an enormous statue. From the waist up there was a woman, but her bottom half was that of a huge spider. She looked both beautiful and terrible, a spear in one hand and a ball of something in the other.

Drizdan pulled her past the statue and she resisted going anywhere near the thing, but they eventually went inside.

THE INTERIOR of the palace was exotic, all dark lines softened only by green and red strips of fabric fluttering gently.

Women were everywhere, most of them naked or wearing only metallic skirts.

Undeniably, the Drow women were uncommonly beautiful, their dark skin almost shining in the green light.

The woman on the throne had deep violet skin and long black hair that trailed past her midriff. She wore nothing but a silver coloured belt that hung a single strip of black fabric at her front and back, her chest uncovered and her eyes were an odd silver that stood out from all the rest for its strange—almost flat—colour.

Glancing at Izziah, she realised he was the only one who also had silver eyes. She had thought they were only lords, but she had a feeling they were the Queen's sons.

"Bring her closer," the Queen ordered and Drizdan obliged.

All eyes were on her as she moved forward. They all remarked the rumpled, dirty, strange-looking creature in their midst. The Queen picked up a device from her throne and slid it over her fingers, turning them into sharp metal talons.

Stepping down from the top tier of the dais, she moved sensually forward while a younger woman appeared, holding a little glass bottle with a green liquid on a small silver tray.

Using the device she had slipped over her fingers, the Queen cut the crook of Etani's inner arm.

A single drop of blood hung from the point of the talon. Lifting the bottle, the drop of blood fell in and the crowd gasped as the green liquid turned to a blinding white light that filled the room.

Etani was sure she had seen that light before. Aelen had a light just like that.

"Welcome to the Under Dark, Princess," the Queen smiled coldly, even as the crowd began to cheer.

To her abject terror, when she realised that the apartment she was given had three rooms, she knew that the two Drow that had captured her would be in those rooms as well. Guards were stationed outside every room, as well as the main door to the apartment and albeit their presence made her feel slightly safer, it was odd all things considered.

The chain was not removed, but rather her hands were allowed more freedom to be able to do the normal things a person needed to do, like eat and bathe.

The days turned quickly into weeks and then eventually a month, all with no news of Epharis, Alaric, or anything to get her hopes up, and she was rapidly losing weight.

The tiny ball of light inside her was siphoning off all her energy faster than any wound and she looked gaunt before the first month was up.

Finally, she was forced to venture out of her rooms. Izziah looked up from his book and his eyes widened at the sight of her. She looked fine, clean, and neat but incredibly thin.

"I'll send for some food," he said quickly and hurried from the room.

Turning, she saw Drizdan leaning in the hallway to his room with a vicious smirk on his face. "A bit thin for my tastes, but weak means easy."

A guard coughed to remind him of their presence and Drizdan, frowning, turned to follow his brother out of the room.

Etani glanced at the guard and even though his returning stare was blank, his eyes *did* trail down her stomach. She had begun to show, mostly due to her lack of body fat. Flushing, she turned away from him and set herself down on the couch.

Looking down at Izziah's discarded book, she wondered where the books spread over the table had come from given their mad flight from Weorene. But then, she realised that the two men had been born in the Under Dark and the books had probably still been there for them if they returned.

Picking one of them up, she sighed when she realised they were in another language.

"Botany, Princess," the guard offered, making her jump. Her senses were dulled, and she had not heard him creeping up on her. He took a quick step back, frowning. "Apologies, I did not mean to startle you."

"It's fine," she replied weakly, lowering her eyes to the book, and opening it to examine some of the names.

She recognised a small number of the flowers that had grown in the compound in Ayathian, but the names were gibberish to her.

"One of the few things I did not inherit from my father," she sighed, placing the book down.

"What's that, Princess?" he asked curiously, and she looked up at him.

"The inherent ability to understand all languages known to any species in this world or any other."

He blinked in surprise.

"I did not know Fae had that ability."

"Yes, most of them do. My sister did, but not me. I get brute strength and speed, she gets languages and shape-shifting," she had never gotten over her twin's luck and the giggling voice in her head was not of any help.

"Sister?"

In all probability, he did not seek to press her for more information rather than give her someone to talk to.

"Mm, my twin. She died a few months ago," she broke off, the last sentence coming out strangled.

Tears welled in her eyes and she was surprised to see him offering her a little square of white fabric. Thankful, she accepted it and used it to dab her eyes before her tears could escape.

"Sorry, I might have stained it," she apologised, handing it back.

His eyes were wide with amazement as he tucked safely away in his pocket the little fabric with the little spots of watery black.

A smell hit her like a slug to the stomach and she whipped around to see Izziah returning with no less than three bearded men wearing nothing but ankle cuffs and loincloths.

She did not so much as think about what she was doing. Instead, she leapt over the back of the couch and her hands were soft on the face of the first man, cupping his cheeks as her lips found his.

The man was dead before he knew what happened and she shivered as his life filled her, vibrating through her like a song. The second man was gone only a breath later, the third looking too dead to care. He looked at her as she approached, her black eyes reflecting in his. He reached for her just as she reached for him, welcoming death to free him from his suffering.

The thump of the third body hitting the floor was incredibly loud.

No one was breathing as they seemed frozen at the sight of death standing amongst them.

Izziah was not all that phased by the events, but he watched with fascination as her form filled out before their eyes, the dullness of her skin and hair brightening, and a soft pinkness filling her cheeks.

"I've never tasted a Drow before," she purred, reaching for him.

He danced back and metal-clad arms wrapped hard around her body.

The metal burned her, and she screamed, jerking violently away from him. The shock of the metal had knocked her right out of her feeding frenzy, and she turned on the guard with eyes wide and feral.

"What… What happened?" the guard asked.

Looking down at a small strip of skin that smoked itself away into nothing. But when the patch that had peeled away on her shoulder healed before his eyes, realisation dawned on him.

"Our armour has iron in it. Princess, I'm sorry, I did not know! Please forgive me!"

He sounded genuinely terrified and she looked at Izziah, not understanding.

"You have the right to his death for hurting a woman," Izziah said, panting slightly

"You weren't to know. Go back to your post and we won't speak of this again," she finally said, filling in the story in her head and knowing she did not want him to die for it.

He had been kind to her and was only protecting one of his own.

Realising the threat the men around her posed, she sat down in the couch and faced them all. It was clear by some of their expressions that they realised the threat they posed to her as well.

The three bodies were quickly removed, and the room was spotless once more.

Drizdan returned several hours later, his eyes sweeping the room and finding her immediately.

"Looking better, I see," he stated calmly, only slightly disappointed.

"Come and find out," she challenged.

For a second, she was sure he was going to, but then he shook his head and turned away from her.

"Ensure she is given a steady supply of food. We can't have our guest dying on us before negotiations are completed," he called out, and with that, he disappeared into his room.

"What negotiations?" she asked, looking at Izziah who looked annoyed by her question.

"My mother is negotiating your return to the Winter Court with your grandmother."

For some reason, the realisation that the Winter Queen was her paternal grandmother struck her as ludicrously funny and her voice rang out in a laugh.

"What is it?"

"I just now realised that my grandmother is Tatiana, the Queen of Winter. From a half-breed on the run for about nine hundred years, I go to being the Princess of Winter. Do you not perceive how insane all of this is?"

For some moments, he looked taken aback by her words, but then he understood what she was saying and grinned widely.

"How do *you* even know I am a Princess?"

"Because of that test mother performed on you. It would only be triggered by a royal of Winter. There is one for Summer as well, but it glows yellow."

Well damn, that put a hole in her thoughts.

"Aelen had a light just like that," she recalled, frowning.

"Yes, it is a fairly uncommon thing, but some keep them for lights due to the purity of the colour. I don't know where he gets the blood, or even if it is the same test," he said, and she nodded slowly. She would like to find out for herself, but given her circumstances, it seemed impossible. "But from what I understand, the light will last for centuries if you don't introduce anything else to it, like water."

"When do you suppose I will be leaving?" she asked and, for an odd second, her mind went to Epharis.

"A few days most likely," he said, and something in his tone made her look up. "We resent the fact that we had to do this. I regret my actions, but I cannot take them back now."

"No, you'll have to live with them for the rest of your existence," she said coldly, unforgiving of his role in her situation.

At least he had the good grace to look ashamed.

It did not take a couple of days after all.

The next day, she was informed that she needed to prepare for her trip, and she was terrified. She did not know what to anticipate from those people who were supposed to be her family. At least with Izziah and Drizdan she knew what to expect, but not with that new group. Not with people whose sole interest in her was that she was heir to the throne and able to produce more Fae. Those people would not allow her an ounce of freedom.

Nevertheless, she packed a bag with the few things she possessed, consisting mostly of clothes and a few pieces of jewellery, and the guard who had been so kind to her carried it out.

As the day wore on, Drizdan had gotten moodier and Izziah had started pouting.

"I'd say I'll miss you but given our circumstances..." she said to Izziah, letting her words trail off.

Then, she turned and glared at Drizdan. "One day I'm going to kill you for daring to lay a finger on me."

He smirked. "And when that day comes, Princess, I'll finish what I started."

Hatred burned inside her, and she turned her back on the two men who had so completely ruined her life. As she walked from the rooms, the guard led her along.

"I hope I never see them again," she said quietly to the guard who smiled sadly.

"Princess, Drizdan is obsessed. He will follow you to the underworld and back just so he can watch you from a distance."

Taking out a clean handkerchief, he tucked it into her pocket. "Don't forget, some of us Drow aren't terrible people," he said gently and opened the door.

"What is she wearing?"

That was the first thing she heard from a Winter Court member and she turned to see them all.

They were not what she was expecting. A small woman with long silver hair and pale skin, an ogre who looked more tired than intimidating, a snowy white Centaur and an elf with black hair and bright yellow eyes.

She did not know what she had expected, but three entirely normal-looking people were *not* it. Maybe she thought they would be covered in ice or look exotic.

The one who had spoken was the small silver-haired woman as she moved forward, looking Etani up and down.

Etani wore Drow attire, consisting of black horse leather pants and a vest with soft boots, while her hair was loose down her back. She thought she looked perfectly respectable.

But they all wore heavy cloaks with fur lining.

"She can't wear that. She'll freeze to death before we get there."

"Leave me here then, I have no interest in going to Faerie."

The Centaur snorted his amusement at her comment and moved forward, reaching down to gently grasp the chain that bound her.

"You have an attitude, girly. Want to keep it or want to keep this?" he asked, lifting the chain that kept her arms bound.

"Call me girly again and my next pair of pants will be out of your hide," she hissed as he boomed a laugh.

"She's Winter alright. Come on Princess," he tugged her chain and she stumbled forward after him.

"What about our deal?" the Drow Queen demanded, standing from her throne.

"The team will be here later to install the gate to Faerie," the Centaur announced, dragging her behind him while she stubbornly dug in her heels.

"Good," the Queen said and sat back down, her eyes on Etani.

Etani stared at her, making a silent promise that one day she was going to return for that woman.

Leaving the palace with her ragtag band of Faerie, she saw a carriage awaited them. Staring at it in dread, the ogre stomped forward, looking like he wanted nothing more than to take a nap.

"It's half a day to the nearest passage," he offered softly, and she nodded in understanding.

Climbing into the carriage with the elf and the silver-haired girl, she settled into the seat and crossed her arms over her chest.

"Now don't be mad, you know we can't leave you in the Under Dark with those savages," the elf said as the carriage set off. That was strange. She had not seen any horses nor was she hearing any.

"Yes, because my comfort is the reason why I am being taken to Winter," she retorted, and her two companions exchanged a look.

"Well, no, but you're safer in Faerie," the elf finally said.

"I'll be safer once I'm left alone. I've survived fine this long," she lied.

The silver-haired woman laughed at that. "Is that what you call being kidnapped?"

She glowered at the woman and turned her attention to the window.

The city slowly shrank as they climbed back up the mountain, with the Centaur running ahead and the ogre following behind while the carriage was moving smoothly all on its own.

Bursting back out of the mountain, several things happened very quickly.

She was blinded by sunlight and the carriage swayed. Something tingled on her arm and when she glanced down, she saw an arrow sticking out of her arm, and the ogre bellowed.

Looking at her companions, they were very much dead, and she could not really say she felt sorry for them. Most of their kind were difficult to kill anyway, she would not be surprised if they woke up before long. The carriage shuddered to a stop and she pushed herself off the seat and moved to the window to peer out.

Opening the door, she stepped down to see a large brown and tan wolf going after the Centaur who had bolted. To the other side, the ogre was facing Aelen and a man she had not seen before. He was a vampire, but the sun did not bother him. White skin, crimson eyes and hair that was thick and long enough to reach his lower back.

Looking down at her arm, she gave the arrow an experimental tug, but it was not budging. Cursing whoever had shot her, she saw an elf striding towards her, readying its bow. She arched a challenging brow.

"Stop, Winter scum," the elf yelled, and she realised that despite its physique she was a female.

"It's not every day the rescue party shoots the one they're trying to rescue," Etani said in a casual voice, the woman's face going white. Turning, she saw the Lich looming over her and, in the next second, his arms encased her.

The world snuffed out by the robe, his face inches from hers as he searched her face and then her body for injuries, stopping only at the arrow sticking out of her arm.

"Epharis... what took you so long?" she asked, nearly overcome by the odd urge to fall into his arms, before she was able to squash it.

"How is it?"

"It's fine," she replied, irritated that he had ignored her question.

He lowered the darkness from around them and breathed a slow sigh of relief, though his arms were still possessively around her.

The Centaur was long gone when the ogre followed on his footsteps. His arms and torso were bleeding heavily but he would survive.

The group turned to her, seeing the arrow, and then turning on the elf who shrugged. "No one told me what she looked like."

Etani offered her arm to Aelen, knowing he would make quick business of the stupid thing. Indeed, he moved forward and with one hand holding her arm out in front of her, he shoved the arrow the rest of the way through and snapped it off, pulling it free.

The hole healed quickly, and she flexed her fingers. "Much appreciated."

Loud stomping sounded and Alaric appeared, looking irritated.

"You missed the party," Epharis said, his hands finding her shoulders and he drew her back against his side. She did not resist, wondering why the King had come to help.

"Drow," he grunted, his eyes finding her and aside from the blood, she was perfectly fine.

The vampire lingered back from the group, watching with interest and she perused him from afar. She was fascinated by him and his ability to be out in the sun. For an instant, he met her eyes but could not hold his gaze and looked elsewhere, shuffling his feet slightly.

Deciding to leave questioning for another time, she looked up at Alaric who was now very intent on Epharis' arms on her. The Lich made no attempt to hide how possessive he was.

"Why did you wait so long?" she demanded, irritated.

Alaric shook his head, confused. "It's by chance that we learnt of the deal. We thought you were still in Weorene."

She opened her mouth and then shut it again, trying to process.

"Izziah sent a hawk…" she trailed off, but his frown made things clearer. The hawk had been sent to Drizdan, not the King.

"You don't know? The emperor has declared war. He is going to attack."

Alaric nodded as though he had expected it. "Very well. We shall be prepared then. We should get going. Those two might return with help."

She knew they likely would, given the Drow would be expecting their gate and the Fae were not good at holding up deals that go wonky, especially when it went wrong on their end.

"Where were they taking you?" Alaric asked.

Etani glanced at the people who had worked to keep her safe. "They were taking me to the Winter Court,"

The wolf padded into view and plopped down on the ground, rolling onto its back and wriggling to clean the blood off its fur.

"Catherine," Alaric addressed the creature.

Etani was stunned by the small woman's ability to fit into the form of the enormous wolf. At the sound of her name, the wolf looked up but when she decided that no one expected an answer from her, she returned to her cleaning.

Offering her arms to Epharis, he removed the chains that bound her and she stretched, relieved to have regained full range of motion. But then, the chain went into his pocket and that gave her another reason to worry.

After a few minutes, the group set off down the track towards a large copse of trees. Among the trees, there were horses tethered and judging by their stomping, they looked annoyed.

Immediately, she went still at the sight of those creatures and when one rolled an eye in her direction, the whites began to show. She took a quick step back and Epharis stopped, looking at her curiously.

"Horses don't like me," she explained, telling the truth. The horses were getting anxious the longer she stood nearby.

"What? Why not?"

"Same reason I expect Catherine isn't here. They can smell predator."

The further back she moved, the calmer the horses became but they were all watching her now.

"Go ahead, I'll run."

Epharis looked doubtful and a little annoyed at the speed loss, but that only amused her. Removing her boots, she threw them at him and grinned, then set off at a sprint in the direction of Ayathian.

Only Catherine was able to keep pace with her. The rest of the group had to try and keep up. The two bounded ahead, leaping from boulders and fallen trees as they raced.

Every muscle in her body was singing in joy at the freedom and she laughed when Catherine began to howl her own pleasure at the run.

When the group decided to stop for the night, they were forced to backtrack and find a place to set up camp. Both she and Catherine had to stay as far away from the horses as possible so as not to spook them.

Skidding to a stop, she turned on Catherine with a wild grin. "Beat you, fur face."

Catherine sniggered at her as she sulked by the fire, but there was no actual malice.

Epharis made room for Etani, and she automatically moved to sit beside him, his arm protectively around her.

"What happened at Weorene?" Alaric asked.

"Everything seemed fine at first. They were celebrating Yish, but then he said that it would be safer for me to stay since war would be coming to Ayathian. He said we would be his honoured guests, but they tried to capture us. We were only there for two days when we fled. We did not get the chance to have any major discussions, nothing."

Alaric hung on her every word; Epharis' hand had crept down and was resting against her stomach, stroking her swelling belly through her vest.

Aelen was listening, but his focus was on the fire. The second elf had decided to leave them halfway along the day and the vampire was sitting alone, staring into the distance at nothing.

When everyone had eaten except Etani and Epharis, they settled down to sleep.

At his request, she lowered herself down onto Epharis' cloak and fell asleep.

Soon, they all followed suit with the vampire offering to stay awake and watch over the group.

THEY WERE AWAKENED by the sun early the next morning and they quickly packed and headed off again; this time she and Catherine stuck near to the group, circling around and around as lookouts for the King and Prince.

It had been stupid for them both to come looking for her, a risk she was not worth, but she was glad they had saved her. Not even for a second did she think that it was over between her and Winter, but for now she was safe.

Late that night they reached Ayathian, after deciding to slow down to a walk and continue by moonlight rather than camp again when they were so close. By her estimation it was past midnight, but not yet near dawn.

Coming to a stop at the outcropping she had stood on that very first day, she studied the city and then the group, realising how different things had changed. She had been so empty, lonely and hungry.

Now she was all those things, but she also had those people who were approaching, and a tiny life growing inside her.

Shaking off her thoughts, she dropped down the outcropping and started for the path, Catherine joining her after only a minute.

"I enjoyed our run. Perhaps we could do it more often," she proposed to the giant canine.

Catherine growl-barked, nodding at Etani and giving her a hard shoulder bump that sent her crashing into a bush.

If that was how the wolf wanted to play it, then it was fine by her. She was up and after the creature in a second.

Catching up, she slapped the wolf on the shoulder and bolted in the other direction, changing course when the group got near.

At some point, she thought she had seen something or rather

someone standing on the outcropping above them, but when she stopped, there was nothing.

Heading back up the hill, she paused and looked around but there seemed to be no hint of anyone or anything around. Not even a footprint in the dirt.

'You see?' she thought.

'*Stranger, not threatening,*' Letari thought back, evidently more interested in something else.

Shrugging it off, she headed back down and joined the group as they were dismounting.

As soon as he was off his horse, Epharis rushed to her.

"Did you get hurt? I'll skin her alive," he snarled.

She assumed he was referring to Catherine and she shook her head in frustration.

"I'm fine, Epharis. I'm quite capable and certainly, I don't need to be treated like a delicate doll."

Huffing, she faced the hill, and that was when she saw it. The man standing there with faintly glowing blue eyes was watching them, but when he discerned that her attention was on him, he quickly turned away and vanished.

She did not feel malice coming from him, but she could not be entirely sure.

Allowing Epharis to pull her along, she had her gaze affixed on the spot even though the man did not appear again.

Approaching the castle, she allowed the men to lead the way inside, Epharis only lingering long enough to kiss her hard on the mouth, causing her to jerk back. His fingers were tangled in her hair, keeping her from escaping but he released her quickly, leaving for his room.

When she quit staring after him, she turned back to see both Alaric and the vampire watching her.

Ignoring them both, she headed in the direction of her rooms, just glad to be back where she belonged.

She was on the way to her rooms when the vampire caught up

with her. Sensing him, she spun on him and he jerked back with reflexes on par with her own.

At first, he looked irritated, but that was soon replaced by amusement. "My apologies, I only wished to speak with you."

It was the first time she had heard him speak above a mere whisper. His voice was a low purr that fitted him, sounding sexual and dangerous in equal parts. That had to be one of the perks of being a vampire.

"I heard from the twins about you."

"What did you hear?" she asked warily.

"You are an assassin by trade, skilled in fighting, potions and arcane magic?"

She nodded once, not sure what he was getting at.

"I wish you to train me," he stated simply, and her eyebrows rose. "I need to know how to defend myself. You see, I *am* the vampire King."

7

THE VAMPIRE KING

he man had shocked her to no end, for she did not know it was possible to be a vampire King, only a Queen. Unless the Queen was dead, and then her title would go to…

"You killed a Queen?" she whispered, appalled by the thought.

The vampires would have been in turmoil, the loss of their Queen a devastating blow, leaving them powerless until another could be found. Unless she was killed by her own kind. In that case, the power moved to the nearest eligible vampire. But it was supposed to be women only, never a man.

"I did… accidentally," he said and when she looked doubtful, he took a deep, fortifying breath. "She was going to kill me. I never thought I possessed the strength to kill her. Then… she was dead."

It was not much of an explanation, but she would accept it for the time being.

Looking him over, he did not look much like a King, but he was exceptionally attractive in a dark way, his face chiselled and sharp with a lithe body dressed in black.

"Why do vampires always wear black?" she asked, deciding to focus on one thing instead of the million other questions littering her mind.

"It absorbs and holds light and heat, keeping our bodies warm."

That was a simple explanation, but she appreciated how easily he replied. "Very well, I'll teach you."

THE NEXT DAY she found him waiting outside her room. In all honesty, she had not expected him to be so eager, but she shrugged and led him to the courtyard.

It was still so weird to see him in sunlight, but she tried not to dwell on that.

"Self-defence first," she announced, believing it to be the most important part. "If you wouldn't mind, please aim at any part except my middle," she said, and his eyes instantly dropped to the barely noticeable bump there.

"Are you sure you should be doing this in your condition?" he asked, dropping his guard. She took advantage of it and landed her fist on his jaw, sending him sprawling.

"Never drop your guard, no matter what your attacker says," she said, waiting for him to get back up.

His eyes were alight like a red candle, but he contained himself and started towards her, his face set.

She grinned and the fight began. He was not skilled, but he was obscenely fast, able to counter her blows like they were nothing. Yet he was reluctant to strike back, at least before she kneed him in the stomach. That was when he lost his cool. He slammed his palm on her chest, throwing her back and to the ground. She might have been winded but used the roll to flick herself up to her feet. Then her hands touched her knees as she bent forward, wheezing. He hurried after her, catching her arms and lifting her upright.

"Oh, I'm sorry... I did not hurt you, did I?" he sounded panicky.

Focusing on herself, she felt down but that light was still happily glowing away.

"We're... both fine..." she said between gasps for air. Straightening up fully, she knew she would have a spectacular bruise.

"Good shot, that was fantastic," she commented, leading him back into the arena.

"Thank you, I did not mean to, though. I lost my temper."

"You need to control and use that strength even when you are calm," she said and turned to face him.

"Sit down," she instructed, and he obeyed.

Folding herself down before him, she took his hand in hers and placed it against her chest, right over her heart.

"Feel how steady it is? We can fight all day and I will remain calm. I can tap into my rage and hatred without losing my composure."

The man was staring at his hand, feeling the steady, abnormally slow thumping of her heart and she frowned as he licked his lips.

Releasing his hand before he had the chance to get worked up, she pushed herself to her feet and helped him up.

"How about we work on some fun elixirs for the rest of the day?" she suggested with a smile as she reached up into her hair, carefully unknotting and unwinding the strands.

He looked dumbstruck as she handed him a vial and she grinned.

"Your hair is a remarkably effective and often overlooked place to hide defensive objects. You can keep that one. If you throw it on the ground, it will shatter and let off a large amount of smoke. Extremely efficient for escapes. I'll show you how to tie these into your hair, yours is thick enough to work."

He was looking down at the vial, then up at her in bewilderment but she only smiled.

Leading him back up to her rooms, he followed her into the spare room a servant usually used, but she had turned into her private laboratory.

"I make all sorts of things, experiment a bit, try and invent new things, but it's not easy work," she explained and she bent down to study a small tube that she had left the day she had gone to Weorene. It would have been perfect had she been gone a week, but the mixture had dried to nothing.

"So, what are you hoping to learn?" she asked as she straightened, catching him turning his attention quickly away from the region of her backside.

"Anything that can be effective against vampires."

She bit gently on her lower lip and his eyes focused on that tiny, razor-sharp fang. His own were almost twice the length of hers.

Etani leant back against the table deep in thought. At some point, her eyes lit up and she rushed to a cupboard and picked an assortment of things, lining them up neatly on the bench. She started from the easiest and ended at the ones she still could not make without Epharis monitoring her.

Once she had set them all out she picked up the first vial and offered it to him.

Taking it into his hands, he gave it a gentle shake.

"This is a corrosive agent, fairly common item. It burns the skin and is highly effective if thrown onto the eyes. All of my bottles can be opened with the thumb, so snap it off and dash it."

Nodding he took the bottle.

"You can get it in most general stores," she informed him as she wrote down the ingredients on a piece of parchment, adding its name and where to buy it.

"Next is this one," she lifted the bottle, quill in hand and giving the red powder a little shake. Her eyes still on her work. "Works on just about every species in this world and a lot in Faerie. Inhaled, swallowed or in the eyes and they will drop like a brick. Be careful though, as it's easy to inhale it yourself. Taking a nap with your attacker might be nice, but he might wake up first."

He moved up beside her, taking the vial. As he watched her writing some strands of hair fell on her face and she brushed it away.

"There is a spare pouch under the sink, you're welcome to it. It holds ten vials." Collecting a handful of spare bottles, she placed them out on the bench, preparing for his attempt at making it.

"These are for you, it's not that hard but you will need gloves and a mask to make it."

He nodded, seemingly only half paying attention as the sun began to warm the room. He had been standing still for too long and she looked at him curiously, seeing his eyes had begun to glow.

"Are you alright?" she asked, unsure of what was wrong with him.

He was staring at her, battling something inside him. A low growl reverberated from deep within his chest and that was when she knew she had to leave the room quickly, but not trigger his instinct to hunt her.

Slowly, she took a step back and his eyes snapped down, then back up. His movements mirrored hers, already on the prowl.

Deciding it was not worth trying to keep him calm if he was already hunting her, she bolted for the door.

He was faster and she almost ran into him, sidestepping him, she tried to move around but his hands closed on her arms. Turning her, he slammed her back against the wall.

The empty jar she had been holding shattered and she felt dread as pain crept up her hand. He was at her throat, inhaling deeply but the smell of blood did not reach him until he had already withdrawn.

"Think, try and work through the haze," she said in a calm and soothing voice, trying to bring him down.

But she knew better than anyone that suppressing bloodlust was nearly impossible.

The smell of her blood hit him and, suddenly, he was no longer breathing as if he were savouring the smell and taste of it in the air. Sliding his fingers down her arm, he lifted her hand as though to show her evidence, a small cut in the fleshy part of her palm below her index finger.

His movements were so slow she thought he was going to stop, but his tongue was long as he slowly licked the blood from her skin.

She saw the tiny pins of black that were his pupils suddenly swell up to cover the red almost entirely and the growling stopped.

He let go of her hand and placed two fingers against her jaw, tilting her head and exposing her throat, her heartbeat pounding there, visible to him. Leaning forward, he licked the side of her neck while her shudder seemed to excite him even more. Grazing a sharp fang over the delicate skin, he found the existing scar and let out a low —almost sensual—laugh.

"Not your first time, is it?" he purred in her ear, nuzzling her jaw.

Her eyes went to the row of bottles and she knew she had to get to them. His throaty laugh did things to her body she did not comprehend, nor did she wish to.

Yet he responded to her body's response to him in a vicious cycle. His breath washed over her skin as his arm slid around her and she realised too late that she had been trying to make friends with a vampire King, not just a normal vampire. He was dangerous, able to seduce any creature, just like a siren could seduce men, and it was working exceptionally well on her.

Her body was nearly vibrating while his responded in time until she was sure she would have ripped her clothes off to offer herself to him, had she not still been able to think rationally.

A tiny prick at her throat had her breath catching and he hissed his pleasure at that tiny sound.

Again, he licked her skin and she wondered absently if that was what was causing the reaction.

She knew immediately that it was the case, his saliva was like a shot of hormones into her system, riling her up in readiness for him to mate with, and feed on, her.

Stretching out her arm for the cabinet, she quivered as his hand traced just under her breast, hating it but unable to make it stop.

Shifting, his arms went around her, and he turned, lowering her form to the floor, his own body settling atop her, making her entire being scream for more. Unconscious of the action, she had parted her legs for him, and he had eagerly settled between them, regardless that they were both still wearing pants.

The first grind of his groin on hers had her mind suddenly going blank, ripped back from logic and into need.

She looked up at him, his sharp fangs glistening with his saliva and all she could ever want was for them to sink into her throat.

Her hands moved to him, tracing slowly up his back, her finger catching the fabric and drawing it up. Turning her head, his lips met hers, hard and heavy. His saliva tasted sweet and her free hand found his face, clutching him to her.

Her nails dragged along his skin and he gasped in shock and then growled in pleasure as he realised she could give as much as she got. It excited him more than anything she had previously done.

One hand lowered on her body, catching her pants, and sliding them down her hips, his nails grazing the soft flesh, making her shiver.

The smell of blood and pheromones was thick in the air, driving him into a frenzy of need and when her nails bit into his back to draw blood, his reservations snapped. His fangs sank deep into her throat, a mere half inch above the site of the first bite and her blood filled his mouth.

He went rigid, the taste more than he could ever realise from a single drop and he swallowed greedily.

His hands went to her vest, ripping the buttons off and peeling the tight fabric away. His hand found her breast and she gasped in pleasure, his nails biting and then gentle. He did not want to waste her blood, so he did not break the skin.

Her own hands had gone to his trousers, trying to push them down but she could not reach far enough and even as he drank, saliva filled her system and she found herself floating high on a sense of him.

His attention moved from trying to mate with her to striving to get more blood from her, his grip going from sensually painful to simply painful as he gripped her wrist, pinning it to the floor.

She gasped, attempting to tug her hand away, but his hold was unbreakable.

Her vision began to darken, even as she squirmed under him, arousing him further as she went from arousal to fear and then desperation. He could taste it when fear filled her, making her blood all the sweeter.

Distantly, she noted that the effects of blood loss were happening at a considerably faster rate with him than it had with Jaia and she wondered why that might be.

A sudden pang of fear went through her as she thought of that tiny life inside her. It did little to break the spell of him, but it gave her the strength to move.

Barely clinging to consciousness, she lifted her arm and placed her hand against the back edge of the small cabinet that she stored empty bottles and tubing, pulling it. The last thing she heard was it coming crashing down.

When she began to come back to reality, she vaguely wondered if she was ever going to wake up from something that was not being knocked out or drained into unconsciousness. So far, it did not seem all that promising.

Her eyes opened and met the ceiling of her room in the new suite, mentally criticising the pastel green colour that had been chosen, as she did every time she saw it. She got it, they were a lady's rooms, but really, the colour was revolting.

Looking first to her left and then her right, she blinked at the wanton destruction that had taken place, including a *very* ruffed looking Alaric sitting in the corner.

At first, the fact that the King was in her room did not register. Her eyes drifted off to a large set of claw marks on the wall and she began to examine them when everything clicked in her mind, and her eyes snapped back to him.

"Glad to see you're back to normal," he said sardonically.

"What happened?" she croaked and winced, her hand going up to her throat, finding it heavily bandaged.

Frowning, she sat up and tugged at the bandage but stopped when Alaric's hand came down lightly on her wrist, offering her a mug of water.

He sat on the edge of her bed while she greedily gulped down the water. "Might want to leave that alone, you haven't healed yet."

Looking up at him, she arched a brow at his casual white tunic and grey pants. His feet were bare and the sight of the blond hair on his feet made her feel oddly uncomfortable. Why was he barefoot in her room?

"Not healing?" she asked a few seconds later when the realisation finally registered in her struggling brain.

"No, not healing. It seems that Versalis' saliva has a powerful anti-magic ability. It is even preventing your own body from repairing in any form."

She swallowed the water she had taken in, and the feeling of her bandage moving against her neck ached in the most delightful way, immediately bringing the vampire's face to her mind and she found herself suddenly, illogically craving his touch.

"I see," she breathed, unable to help a little shiver of anticipation that ran down her spine. "So, what happened to my room?"

His brow furrowed. "You don't recall?" he asked, looking around the room to inspect the destruction.

"I was unconscious for the hundredth time since coming to this wretched city," she said, unreasonably irritated with the man.

Trying to get her mood under control, she found herself thinking again of the vampire, his bright red eyes, and the feel of his tongue on her throat. Shaking her head to clear her thoughts, she squinted at the King but a high-pitched giggle had started in the back of her mind.

"You destroyed it, plus three other rooms and threw a guard through a very expensive stained-glass window," he said, and he frowned when she gave him a blank stare. "You can't recall any of these?"

Shaking her head, she looked around once more, trying to figure out what had happened. "I need to speak to Epharis," she said, knowing he was not going to be happy about it.

"Out of the question, he is imprisoned."

"In his room," she retorted, bringing her attention on the claw marks.

Pushing herself out of bed, her head swam dangerously, and she grabbed the bed frame to keep from falling face-first onto the floor.

Frowning, she stared at the bed frame. She distinctly remembered she did not have one at the foot of her bed. Reaching out, she clutched the arm of the King, who had rounded the bed to help her.

"This is wrong," she breathed, unable to let go of his arm, but the feel of his warm skin made her want to jump away from him in repulsion. He was responsible for so much of her suffering, but her mind seemed unable to focus on that. It kept drifting back to the vampire.

Extending her left arm, she tried to reach for the wall, but it was not possible to do so unless she took at least three steps. But she was not sure that was going to happen because she would have to let go of Alaric and he was the only thing keeping her upright.

Cursing in her mind, she curled her fingers around his shirt and tugged him forward, taking a single step that made her legs shake.

"What is wrong with me?" she pleaded, hating that his hands went to her waist, but having no other choice to get to the marks.

"Significant blood loss that would have killed anyone else," he replied as he helped her take the last two steps so she could use the wall for support.

Leaning her forehead against it, she breathed slowly as the exertion of taking only three steps had exhausted her. She had never felt so incredibly weak and confused. Forcing through it, she lifted her hand and traced a finger through the mark, her eyes narrowing as she used her handspan to measure out the damage.

The depth and width of them were a perfect match for her nails.

"When the guard heard a crash, he went in and found you both on the floor. He said he couldn't get Versalis off you and finally he had to stab the vampire to get his attention. The poor man had never been so scared in his life, but he held him off long enough for help to arrive. They carted him off to the dungeons to calm down. He was fine by the time they got down there and was asking after you, but we locked him away to be safe. When I arrived, you were sitting in the corner, cursing like a sailor at the guard who was trying to help you. Your eyes were green and you… you bit a chunk out of his cheek. After that it was a game of catch the Fae, with the Fae being a ravenous killing machine who liked to taunt people," Alaric said softly from behind her, his hands ready to catch her should she fall.

"Versalis is his name?" she breathed and stroked the gouges, imagining they were his abs.

"Yes, he was let go early this morning. He's been sulking in the throne room ever since."

Turning to him in surprise at the passage of time, the world around her spun in one direction and her brain spun the other. Alaric caught her before she could hit the floor and she clung to his shirt, the smell of him filling her nostrils at the closeness of his warm flesh.

"Alaric," she sighed, and her mouth began to water. Without a warning, she licked from his collarbone up to his chin in one long, slow drag.

He had frozen at the inflection of her voice, the soft sigh of his name that had him quivering, but then that tongue. She looked up to see him looking down at her and black wisps crept into the whites of her eyes.

He jerked away from her and while she kept a firm grasp on his shirt, he was no longer holding her.

Swaying, she stared up into his face, her right hand releasing his shirt and her fingers trembled as they touched his lips, dragging them down gently in abject fascination at their softness, the warm colour.

She made a soft humming sound, her smile almost drunk. He looked down at a trickle of red that had crept down her throat to pool at her collarbone, her bandage having soaked through.

"Hungry," she mewled, dropping to her knees and then, face forward onto the floor.

8

A NEW KIND OF ADDICTION

Swimming into consciousness once more, she basked in the feeling of someone gently stroking her hair. It felt nice, someone just petting her like that, and she felt dreamy as she hung in the blackness of her closed eyes.

A warm and spicy smell lingered in the air and she was hypnotised. She wanted to roll into it and curl up in the warmth; she wanted to feel it all around her. When her eyes began to drift open, she was first irritated to see that obnoxious pastel green above her, but then she was distracted by a low rumbling voice murmuring to her.

Humming, she turned her face and nuzzled her cheek into a hard chest clad in black. It felt so wonderful to be in strong arms like that, fingers combing through her hair and a soft voice murmuring sweet nothings to her in a language she could not understand.

It felt so… black?

Her eyes sprang open as she tilted her head to look up at who she was currently snuggling. The red eyes that were peering down at her were soft and warm.

Jerking back from him, she tried to process what was going on. The room had been repaired, a guard was on the floor near the door with blood pooling under him, Versalis was in her bed, stroking her bare shoulder. The strap of her nightgown had been pushed down to expose more of her pale skin.

Wriggling herself back, her body felt like lead and he watched her as a smile crept onto his pale lips.

"Where are you going?" he purred, the sound of his voice making her stomach clench in a way she did not understand.

"Versalis? What are you doing?" she whispered, and his eyes lit up at the mention of his name.

Rolling onto his hands and knees, he crawled closer to her and she found herself watching the way his body moved, particularly down his shirt when it hung loose, subject to gravity. He was incredibly muscular, and she wondered what it would taste like to bite his chest.

Shaking her head, she inched backwards, close to the edge of the bed, but he followed.

"I've come to be with you, of course," he crooned, looking a little put out by her not knowing.

He grabbed her calf and tugged her closer, her entire body jerked towards him as her back hit the bed.

Gasping at the sudden movement and the way the world swayed, she could only watch as he crawled over her, smiling. "You're happy to see me as well?"

She nodded before she had even registered the words and he breathed a sigh of relief. The feeling of his breath on her skin made her tingle in the most delightful of ways.

"I don't like this," he said, lifting one hand to touch the bandage around her throat.

"I'm sorry," she replied, not knowing why she had apologised, nor caring.

"I'll take it off for you."

Settling his weight against her thighs, he leant over her and tugged quickly at the knot keeping the bandage in place, his warm hand was light at the back of her head while he unwound the bandage to expose the still oozing marks.

"Much better, you shouldn't hide them," he said, leaning down to nuzzle her jaw to the side and inhale the scent of her blood.

"I won't," she breathed, her entire body singing for him. "Do you want to taste it?"

Why had she suggested that? Why was she so desperate for him?

He did not reply, instead, the long length of his tongue dragged over the bite marks, her gasp audible in the quiet room. He shivered and growled his pleasure, even as she quivered under him.

Curling his arms under her, he lifted her from the bed and into his arms, allowing her to sit up with him seated in her lap.

Her hands shook as she traced her fingertips in delicate dances along the small of his back, tucked up under his shirt to find bare skin. The touch seemed to have an electric effect on him.

Nuzzling her head out of the way, he locked his mouth over the bite and sucked greedily, the minor amount of healing her body had been capable of no match for his hunger.

Her entire being felt as though it were vibrating with the first traces of his saliva that entered her system and she buzzed with it, feeling as though she were both drunk and high.

Clinging to him even as he clutched her harder, she felt her world rotating on its axis as he fed on her again, unable to stop until he was full.

She faded once more with the feeling of him wrapped around her, encasing her in warmth and pleasure.

THE NEXT TIME she was able to open her eyes, she found that she had been bound to the bed using the gold chain Epharis had found to be effective at containing her, the man himself sitting in the corner of the room with a book in his lap, a curtain pulled open just enough to let in light for him to read, but not to disturb her sleep.

"What?" she croaked, pulling weakly at the chains.

Epharis looked up and snapped the book closed, the sound making her jump and she squinted, the brightness of the sun from his direction making her eyes sting.

"Welcome back to the world of the living, my love," he said grimly as he stood and placed the book down on the chair.

Making his way to the table he filled a mug of water and moved to her side. Gently lifting her head with one hand, he tipped the cup to her lips and she drank slowly, her throat feeling raw and angry.

"Your sister is quite the troublemaker," he said, and she choked on the water.

She spluttered, but he did not do anything to help her, merely watching as she coughed up whatever she had inhaled, her eyes watering.

"Yes, I did not think it would be a surprise. I told you not to keep secrets from me," he sounded livid and she looked up at him through swimming eyes.

"What are you talking about?"

The blow came out of nowhere. One second, she was looking up and the next she had strained her shoulder under the force of the slap, her cheek on fire.

"Lie to me again and I'll do worse," he promised in a low, lethal voice.

Tasting blood, she nodded and lowered her eyes to the bedspread.

"Good. Now how is it that your sister is still alive?" he asked, sitting at the edge of her bed.

"When she died, I asked Aelen to kill me, I wanted to be with her. I forgot you're not supposed to touch the dead, not ever. But I wanted to comfort her, she was so sad and small... when I did, we rebounded and when we came back, we were both in my head."

He lifted the cup to her lips again and she drank, washing away the taste of blood.

"And she comes out when you fall unconscious. Why did you take off your bandage? You bled everywhere."

His words took a good ten seconds to register. "I don't understand. She comes out? How?" That was the real question and the giggling in the back of her mind was not helping.

"I hoped you would know, but if I could hazard a guess, only one consciousness can be active and in control. Your weakness was her weakness, but with her manic energy and total disregard for self-preservation, she is strong, dangerous and doesn't care much for the damage she causes," he said dryly, watching her as she sipped more of the water.

"Well, that's inconvenient."

"Why did you take off the bandage? You were almost dead."

"I don't remember taking it off," she said with a frown as she tried to remember what had happened. She had a vivid dream of waking up to the vampire in her room and then feeding on her, but she could not recall taking off the bandage.

He was studying her carefully, undoubtedly hunting for lies or half-truths. "For the time being, we are going to keep you restrained, for the sake of the guards and everyone within a ten-mile radius. I brought more of the elixir I made for you, the one you tried at dinner. It will help you gain energy faster since you're too weak to feed."

Standing, he left her side and collected a small silver bowl from the end table beside the door. It had a little silver lid on it, keeping in the smell but when it hit her nose, she wanted to recoil.

"That isn't the same thing," she said warily, eyeing it and him. She had not forgotten his drugging her to make her obedient and submissive.

"Yes, it is," he snapped, growling when she turned her head away from his offering.

"Guard!" he bellowed, and a nervous-looking guard burst into the room. "Come and hold her mouth open."

The guard hesitated but eventually approached, willing to face her rather than the Lich.

She clenched her teeth, but the pain of his fingers as they dug into the join of her jawbone forced her mouth open and Epharis spooned the mixture into her mouth. Clamping her mouth shut, she glared at the guard with as much malice as a kitten in her current state, but the paling of his face made her think she got her message across.

"Swallow," Epharis ordered and she turned her glare on him.

Even now, she could recall their wedding night and his order for her to swallow the drug that had resulted in their passionate love-making on the church floor. She shook her head, grunting when he slapped the guard's hand away and gripped her jaw with his long, sharp fingers. Forcing her head back, the mixture slid to the back of her throat and she choked, finally swallowing to keep from drowning in it.

The taste of it repulsed her and her stomach heaved, but she managed to keep it down.

"I will not allow your stubbornness to harm my child, Etani."

The guard jerked at the words and his eyes went to the swelling he had not noticed before. It was not common knowledge that the Princess was pregnant by the Lich.

Slowly, and with the help of the guard's strong grip, they force-fed her and while the zing of energy filled her and sped up the blood production, it also caused the holes in her neck to bleed faster.

AFTER A FEW DAYS, she had almost started to feel back to normal. That was, up until Epharis left and Versalis slipped into the room, locking the door behind him.

He smiled at her, taking in the fullness of her figure as she lay atop the blankets.

She stared at him as a flood of desire and happiness overwhelmed her, followed by a sudden wariness of her situation. Her arms were bound and she was unable to escape.

Crossing the room, he crawled up to the bed, not pausing until he lay on top of her.

"Versalis you can't—"

He cut her off with a hard, hungry kiss and she shuddered as pheromones flooded her system at the first taste of him.

"I've missed you... but the Lich wouldn't leave," he said, sounding angry at the inconvenience.

Her eyes were heavy as he kissed her again and again, his fingers light over her jaw and down her throat to untie the bandage that was only an hour old. He kissed her feverishly, his lips overly hot and needy on hers.

As soon as the bandage was out of his way, his mouth found her throat and he began to drink greedily, his hands heavy on her sides and back as he clutched her to him.

Gasping in pain, she realised he had bitten her again, not getting his fill fast enough and opening the healed holes first once, then twice to add a third bite.

The door rattled followed by a low growl. But Versalis did not hear that. He was too engrossed in his pleasure to care about what was happening to the rest of the world. He drank deeply, unconcerned about the pain or damage he caused her and in turn, he pumped her system with saliva and pheromones to leave her craving for more.

When the door burst open, Versalis had already lifted his head, meeting her hooded eyes, and smiling as he bit his lip. Kissing her hard, she tasted his blood and her entire body sang with the taste.

Sucking on his lip, he drew back and turned to see Epharis looking as though ripping the vampire to shreds was entirely possible. The Lich was too enraged to even move, his eyes alight with a green fire but Versalis turned and flung open the window, leaping out and vanishing into the night.

"No," she whimpered, reaching for the window but she could not move her arm more than a few inches.

Groaning, she strained against the chains, her head spinning and her teeth beginning to ache.

"Versalis..." she called out, feeling his loss more keenly than anything she had felt before, including the loss of her sisters.

Epharis rushed to her side and grabbed her face, urging her to look at him. "How many times, Etani?" he snarled, and she looked at him, unable to understand what he was saying.

Licking the smear of blood from her lip, she turned her head back to the window, hoping Versalis would be there, but it was empty, and the sight brought tears to her eyes, devastated by his absence.

Epharis swore and unhooked the chains that kept her bound to the bed, bundling her up in his arms and carrying her from the room.

"No... he will come back," she gasped, squirming weakly in his arms.

"Don't worry, he'll find you," Epharis said through clenched teeth.

The news calmed her, and she panted gently, exhausted at the feeble attempt to free herself from his grip.

Resting her head against his chest, she felt her eyes growing heavy.

"His blood tastes like the sun," she breathed.

Epharis went stiff under her as she fell into a deep sleep.

9

WITHDRAWALS AND RETURN

When she stirred from her sleep, she found she was cradled in strong, hard arms but the smell was wrong. The colour was right, a deep black but it was not the satiny softness of Versalis' shirt, it was a somewhat rough fabric that she did not like at all.

Irritated at the difference, she squirmed and tried to escape, making about as much movement as a snail.

"Shh, Etani it's okay," Kai's voice was soft and warm as he held her tightly against him.

She was sitting crosswise in his lap, her left arm pressed against his chest and her head on his collarbone. Grumbling, she nuzzled her face into his neck, content at the smell of him. It was not Versalis, but it was close.

"What has he done?" a voice demanded.

"He is trying to bind her. A blood doll," another voice said, sounding disgusted.

"What is that?" the first voice asked.

She wanted them to shut up and she screwed up her face, trying to block out the sound by burying her face deeper into the warmth of Kai's neck.

"It's a way of keeping someone alive for as long as the vampire wants. It's usually a human, fed on almost daily and fed vampire blood to help them recover faster. It floods them with endorphins and pheromones to keep them pliable, almost sexually aroused and the vampire can feed as much as he needs. It's a common practice amongst the higher-ups," Kai said, his voice reverberating through her left ear bone, making her growl.

Lifting her head off him, her neck wobbled, and she would have fallen off his lap, had he not been holding her so tightly. Finally, she opened her eyes and grunted at the blinding stabs into her eyeballs.

"Why is it so bright?" she complained feebly.

The voices went quiet as something plopped on her head. Squinting her eyes open, she found one of the twins' hats on her head. Humming happily, she tugged on the rim to settle it firmly.

"I like your hat," she slurred slightly.

"Thank you. You can borrow it for now," Kai said, and she followed his voice, still only barely able to see.

"How long will she be like this?" the first voice asked

"For a human, about a month. For Etani, I can only assume that if you can get food into her, it will fade quite fast. But I don't know if she will be able to keep food down. He did not intend to, but with what I did, and now him, she has started to change. She may not be able to eat normal food. If we can get her off the saliva for long enough, it will reverse, but it will be rough, and the withdrawals will be terrible."

The voice finally registered, and she turned, flinging out her hand for the owner of the voice.

"Jaia," she cried, delighted to know he was there with her.

His hand was gentle as he held hers. His skin felt delightfully warm and she gave him a little tug to bring him closer, but he resisted.

"Jaia, come and join us," she whined.

"He can't, Etani. Not yet," Kai offered gently.

She turned to him and he ducked his head to see her face under the brim of the hat. She opened her eyes a little more, her lower lip stuck out in a petulant pout.

"He still craves your blood. Now be good and stay where you are."

Glowering at him like an impudent kitten, she locked her fingers with Jaia's and clung to his hand, refusing to let him go.

"What are the odds of her surviving all this, along with the baby?" the first voice asked, sounding almost defeated. She still could not figure out who it belonged to.

"At this point, I'd say fifty-fifty. I'm sorry Epharis, I wish I had better news, but he has worked fast and hard. It should have taken months, not days," Kai said and bounced his knee to shift her weight, causing her to sway dangerously, his arm around her back flexing to keep her upright.

"What can be done to better those odds?" Epharis asked.

She frowned at the name, a face began to swim into her head about the owner of that name, but it was still eluding her.

"Who's that?" she hissed, the sound of groaning wood loud in the sudden silence.

"You know who that is, Etani. He's Epharis," Kai said with an odd tone in his voice.

"It's to break familial ties. She won't remember most people she has any emotional connection to. The stronger the emotion, the longer it takes to return," Jaia said in a strained voice.

"What about you two?" Epharis growled.

"We are vampires and our closeness is usually enough to bring the memories back, at least in fractions."

There was a grunt and she tilted her head back, squealing when the movement had her entire body swaying. Falling back, her back arched and she flung her hand up to catch the hat. She grinned drunkenly at the startled sight of the person who was assumed to be Epharis, peering at him upside down.

"Nice tattoo," she said, zeroing in on the elaborate tattooed band on his ring finger.

"Thank you," he said coldly, and she looked up to his face.

For an instant, their eyes locked, and her smile faded, remembering something but unable to latch onto it. His brows drew together at her loss of smile and confusion. Jaia tugged her arm to help her back up and she slumped against Kai's chest, bewildered, and somewhat scared.

"What about Versalis?" Kai asked as he shifted his arm to keep her from toppling back again.

"Alaric refuses to stop him from going anywhere he pleases," Epharis said. "Why is it that vampires are so easily enchanted by her?"

Kai lowered his head to Etani's hair and breathed in slowly before he spoke, the rush of her scent leaving his voice breathy.

"You recall the feeling you had the first time you set foot in Faerie?" there was a pause. "Etani smells to us like that felt for you. She is born from magic, it runs through her veins, it practically glows off her. The smell of it is so tempting any vampire will struggle around any of the Fae. For some reason, they smell so strongly of Faerie that it drives us mad."

She looked up at Kai with a dreamy smile. "Does my blood hurt you, Kai? I don't want you to hurt," she whispered, and slid her arms around his neck, hugging him tightly. His arms tensed around her in return.

"Hush, Etani, everything is going to be okay," he murmured.

When she looked up, she could see his strain through the tight cords in his neck. She did not like it when he was stressed, especially when it was her fault. Lifting her fingers, she slid the delicate digits under the bandage and then pressed them tenderly against his lower lip.

Several things happened very quickly: his eyes rolled down to meet hers and she smiled even as his lips parted and his tongue touched the smear of red. The colour change in his eyes was so instantaneous she did not know it was possible.

Something grabbed her from behind, there was a feral growling and she was all but ripped off the lap of her friend. She felt something cold against her back, iron-strong arms around her waist and the sound of a blow with a growl of pain.

Looking up, Jaia was being held back by his brother and his face was red where Epharis had hit him while snatching her away.

She noticed that Kai's eyes were a vivid red. "Kai," she pleaded, reaching for him with crimson still staining her fingers. "Don't be sad Kai, I'm here."

Kai seemed to quiver at her words, and she saw the struggle as her blood glistened on his lip. Unable to resist, he licked it away and shuddered, yet he refused to let go of his struggling brother.

Eyes finding Jaia, she smiled when his hand reached for hers.

"Please, let me go," she pleaded, wanting to go to them.

Her blood was singing to them and she wanted to offer it to them so they could be happy.

Kai's shoes slid on the carpet as Jaia strained to get to her. Epharis heaved but she was having none of it. Jaia's fingers grasped hers and he yanked both couples closer, his tongue wet and slick on her fingers.

Grasping her arm, he sank his teeth into her wrist, and she gasped, allowing him only a mouthful before Kai punched his gut so hard, his feet left the floor.

Epharis spun her and she was pulled from the room and a raging Jaia. She resented being pulled away, needing to get back to him. He needed her and Epharis was denying him.

"Epharis, stop! He needs me," she cried, squirming in his arms but she could not match his strength to so much as pry a single finger off her. "Please, you have to let me help him."

"I'm not risking my child to feed a vampire," he growled. "I knew I needed to keep you locked in a box." Something in his tone made her pause and she looked up, realising she still had Kai's hat on her head.

"In a box?" she asked, sobering fast in the face of his fury.

"In a very secure box, away from everyone. No vampires, no Alaric, no Winter Court."

She did not like the sound of that at all. How was Versalis going to find her if she was crammed into a box?

"You can't put me in a box," she said slowly, but then she wondered if it was possible for him to do exactly that.

"Watch me," he snarled.

And so, she did.

His box was the bedroom in his suite, making it already difficult for anyone to reach her. On top of the protections already placed on the room to keep others from getting in, he placed more to prevent her from getting out. Sadistically, he had removed the bedroom door, but much like the wall around the castle that Alaric had set up to keep Cain out, she could press against an invisible barrier in the doorway and window.

At that point, she knew better than to think he was not capable of anything.

After he had thrown her unceremoniously on the bed and ordered her to sit and be good, he had started his rage-induced work on her protections.

"You can't keep me in here forever," she said, knowing full well that he could do that for as long as he liked.

"Just until you have given birth," he muttered, focusing on the window and the yellowish ripples that spread out from his fingertips in the air.

Well, she could not fault his paternal need to protect, except that it was a tad on the extreme side.

She crossed her arms over her chest and watched him work, realising that any attempt to escape would either result in her face-first on the ground, or him hitting her again. Neither was desirable and so she sat and watched, her mind slowly processing the fact that she was pregnant.

BY THE NEXT DAY, she had gotten bored, prowling around her new home for several hours. A tantrum had done nothing. She smashed his things and the only thing she succeeded at was him glaring at her from the doorway. Throwing the water jug through the window had only resulted in her having no water while the window repaired itself before her eyes, even as the jug did not return. Apparently, it repaired itself because Epharis had accepted it from a guard and now it too taunted her from the sitting room.

By the second day, she had started to feel the effects of withdrawal, her skin burning but she felt frozen. Her head ached and she sat against the door frame, pleading for him to let her out.

He did not.

The elixir he had left for her to drink was ignored and the smell of it repulsed her, but she did not dare smash it for fear that he would force her to drink it with the help of the guard. Instead, she abandoned it on the table and watched him, begging him to release her any time he looked her way.

By day three she had flown into a rage, screaming at him, and snapping off the decorative ball on the footboard of his bed, lobbing it at him through the door.

He ducked but it was a narrow miss.

"Let me out," she screamed at him, kicking the door barrier but that only hurt her foot, making her even angrier.

In the next moment, the second ball was through the door, lodged in the wall in the precise location his head had been a moment before.

She stood and screamed at the top of her lungs and to both of their surprise, the window exploded outward. She stared at it and then back at him before her eyes settled on the window again, as a huge and nasty grin formed in her lips before directing her gaze at him for a second time.

Before she could suck in enough air to scream again, he tackled her to the ground and, as a result, she found herself on the bed, bound and gagged.

After the first week, he was forced to feed her, and she was not going down easy. The guard's finger was spat at his face after she had bitten it off. That was entirely his fault for removing the gag and trying to silence her with his hand.

He howled, as his blood flowed before he was excused from his duties.

Instead, Epharis used the chain to bind her entire body down, including her head.

She glared up at him, sweating and shivering as he dug his fingers into her jaw to pry her mouth open and spoon the elixir into her.

After she had thrown up the first lot, he went slower, giving her only a spoonful or two at a time and letting it settle before giving her more. He only released her after she had promised not to throw things or scream again.

Versalis found her on day nine, the sight of his form at the window making her quiver and she hurried to him, her hands pressed against the barrier.

Opening the window from the outside, his eyes were greedy as he took her in.

"Versalis, he won't let me out," she whispered, aching for him when his hand pressed to the barrier on the other side, a hair's breadth away and yet unable to touch her.

"I'll get you out," he promised.

She leant closer and he pressed his forehead against the barrier over hers. She could almost taste him, yet he could be on the moon for all the good it did them. The bites on her neck and wrist had finally healed and the sight of the scars on her skin angered him. It meant she was returning to her natural state and his work was being undone.

They both hated it, but she did not have the strength to get out.

Almost night after night, he returned to her window ever since he found her, simply hanging there from the side of the castle and either talking to her or watching her while she suffered.

Epharis did not seem to know about the visits and she was not about to tell him, but he was suspicious of her obedience when he fed her, and she silently ate to hurry his leaving her room.

She hated it when he lingered to check on her, making sure both she and the baby were progressing okay. Both were well enough, but as soon as he was gone, she was at the window with Versalis.

He glowed in the moonlight and the sight of him seemed almost magical to her.

"I want to be with you," she whispered, leaning against the barrier and he looked sadly back at her.

"I know, my darling, but it won't be long now," he soothed.

She sighed and smiled at the news, her fingers stroking the barrier over his cheek.

He stayed with her all night, standing on the windowsill with his fingers dug into grooves his repeated visits had earned him in the stone.

It was the next night when whatever it was that he had been working on came into effect.

From the grounds below her window, she could hear someone chanting and she pushed herself up from the bed and made her way to the window, trying to see what was down there. Pressing her hand against the barrier, she was leaning against it when suddenly it was no longer there and the strong, hard arms of Versalis caught her before she could topple over.

Hanging forward out of the window, she saw the man below who was looking up at them with a markedly fanatic gleam in his eyes.

Something crashed behind her, and she saw Epharis bursting into her room, the sparkling of the barrier dissipating in bright golden ripples.

She met his eyes and she was torn between glee that Versalis had finally reached her, and concern for the look of terror on his face even as Versalis picked her up and flung her over his shoulder, climbing up the outside of the castle to the roof.

She saw the moment when Epharis realised exactly how it had happened and did something she had never seen him do before. Toxic green fire seemed to bloom in his hand from nothing, but she was not sure that was possible. He threw the ball down at the fanatic man who made no effort to get out of the way. Her ears popped as the man was engulfed in green light and was left a mangled, blackened skeleton.

As he looked up, she stared at him with horrified fascination, but he did not share the sentiments as his eyes were alight with fury.

"Etani!" he bellowed, and her stomach clenched at the sound, watching as he flung himself back from the window and away, she did not know where.

Reaching the roof, she huffed as Versalis adjusted her on his shoulder and she lifted herself to look backwards at him.

"Versalis, I can walk," she said, rather glad she had been dressed when he arrived.

He ignored her, crossing the roof and peering down the side at the distance.

A noise had her looking up, but Versalis did not seem to notice.

Kai and Jaia had seemingly appeared out of thin air and she gave them a little sarcastic wave.

Kai gave a tiny wave back, then lifted his finger to his lips in a gesture that she should keep quiet.

She nodded but yelped when, suddenly, they were airborne.

He had leapt across to one of the towers and climbed up into the room at the top. Realising it had been her room, she was somewhat happy to find it well and intact. She would not have put it past the King or Prince to destroy it to ensure she could not hide there again. But it was possible they did not know about it.

Putting her down, his hands cupped her face and he kissed her deeply and passionately. She felt the exact moment the endorphins flooded her system, but there was no resisting it and she returned the fervour of his kiss. Drawing back with a smile, his fingers found her hair and that sent shivers down her spine.

"Alone at last," he murmured, drawing her towards the new bedding he had obtained.

She followed eagerly, allowing him to draw her down but something was itching at the back of her mind.

"*No, this is wrong,*" a tiny voice kept saying.

He was nuzzling her neck, stroking her arms and down her sides, exploring her as she gave that little voice a shred of attention and it was immediately screaming at her.

Drawing back from him, she shook her head in an attempt to clear it.

"Versalis, we have to stop," she sounded unsure and when he paused, she wriggled away from him.

He followed, looking hurt at her words.

"No, Etani, just give in and everything will be better," he caught her hand and lifted her wrist to his lips, kissing it gently, but stopped when he saw the bite.

His eyes narrowed and he followed the line of her arm up to her throat, no doubt connecting the dots in his mind.

"Those boys are getting to be a problem," he said slowly, the threat ominous.

Shaking her head, she drew him in for a tender kiss, her mind working sluggishly to keep him distracted from her friends. They would find her soon enough. She was sure of that.

"I will not let them taste you again," he growled against her lips and gripped her thighs.

Dragging her towards him. Her back hit the floor and he leant over her, bunching her nightdress around her hips. Leaning down, he gripped her hair and forced her head to the side, rough in his anger.

She gasped as his fingers trailed over the bite marks on her throat "Versalis, stop!"

"Hush, you're mine," he growled and sank his teeth into her flesh.

Her voice rang out in a cry of pain as he began to feed, the bite stinging and the pressure of his hunger making her veins burn, unable to keep up.

She shuddered as the familiar coolness started at her extremities, his weight atop her being all the warmth she could find. Reaching between them, he lifted the hem of her dress, pushing the bundle of fabric further up to her waist to leave her exposed.

He did not have time to start on his clothing when first one, then two sets of boots sounded heavy on the floorboards. Versalis looked up, his sudden movement tearing her skin and blood began to flow heavily.

Looking up at the two, he smiled and deliberately moved. Lifting his wrist to his mouth, he bit down and turned, smashing it down over her mouth.

Kai cried out and Jaia rushed forward, but she could not focus on that. As soon as she tasted him, she was sucking at the wound, the flood of energy that lit her system better than any soul she had ever tasted.

She only got two mouthfuls when Jaia hit Versalis and he left her, only to be replaced by Kai a second later. He yanked her from the floor, trying to figure out what to do before, finally, he grabbed her jaw and tried to shove his fingers past her tongue. He was trying to force the blood back up.

He howled when she bit him, tasting his blood then and she flung herself back from him.

He came for her again, his eyes frantic. "Etani, I don't want to hit you, but you have to bring it back up," he said urgently, stalking after her even as she backed away, her arms going protectively around her stomach.

Her head was spinning and she blinked hard to try and steady it. An odd redness was coming around the edges, turning everything slightly pink.

"Stay away," she said, backing herself against a wall.

Kai was on her in an instant, his left forearm going against her throat. Ignoring the nails that cut cleanly into his arm, he met her eyes and she saw the decision he made, seeing both her pain and the muddy redness in her eyes

"Forgive me," he pleaded and drew back his arm.

'Protect,' flashed through her mind as his fist drove forward and slammed into her stomach, she felt her legs go numb and she dropped, vomiting up all the blood she had managed to consume.

Heaving, she expelled everything that had lingered in her stomach and she slumped to the floor, watching as the redness in her vision returned to normal.

Whimpering, she could hear fighting and Kai pleading for her to be okay, almost begging her to be alright

Her eyes closed and she willingly surrendered to unconsciousness, eager for the relief.

10

NOT QUITE FAST ENOUGH

When she came to sometime later, she found herself once more bound to her bed and feeling awful. Epharis was pacing, his anger emanating from him in almost visible waves but as soon as he saw she was awake, he grabbed her shoulders and shook her.

"Is it okay?" he yelled in her face and she tried to twist and turn her body in an effort to get him off her. He calmed down enough to take a step back and she was able to think once again.

"It's fine, and so am I, thanks for asking," she snapped, tugging at her arms to try and loosen the hold of the chain that she loathed.

"We couldn't hear it when we tested you. The doctor was sure you had lost it."

"It's still there," she assured him and turned inwards to be sure.

Yes, it was still there, and the weird little thing was making strange sounds. Almost humming to itself. She shook her head at the oddity that was children and considered it, noting that while it was quite a lot bigger, something had curled around it, making an effort to protect it from the blow.

"Do you know anything about Fae gestation lengths?" she asked idly, still watching the thing and whatever it was that was curled around it, curious.

"No, your kind are very secretive," he snarled, and her brows rose in response to his attitude.

"I take it Letari was an issue?" she said as she gave the chains a little jingle

"She was silent. Those were just a precaution," he said, and she was left wondering at the thing wrapped around the light inside of her.

"What happened to Versalis?"

Her breath caught as she uttered his name, and she found her body craved him. She half resented having to go through withdrawals again, but she longed for him all the same.

"I wonder why you forgot me so completely," he said, side-tracking her and she blinked, trying to change course. How long had that been nagging at him? "The twins said those with stronger emotional ties go the longest before returning," squinting up at him, she found he was smirking at her. "Do you care about me, my darling?"

He was goading her, she knew it but still, she made an effort to kick her blankets at him.

"I don't love you, Lich," she hissed and when their eyes met, she looked away, uncomfortable.

Maybe she surely was sick. The Lich had managed to worm into her affections while drugging her out of her mind, but there was something there, and she hated that he brought it up.

"We can always consider more than one child, you know, wouldn't it be fun to try for a second?"

He was grinning at her, knowing he was getting to her but also, was enjoying the blush and her attempts to kick him.

Short after that, he left the room leaving her chained and alone.

It was not until sometime later when Kai knocked timidly on her door.

"Etani?" he asked, his voice small, but he looked somewhat relieved.

"Kai? How is Jaia?" she shifted to sit up better, her shoulders aching from being in the same spot for so long.

Kai inched into the room, peering around for something and then relaxing when he did not find it. He hurried to her bed and sat down beside her, removing the chains from where they were linked over the headboard.

"Come with me, we need your help," Kai said and tugged at the chains to get her moving.

She allowed him to pull her from the bed, clutching his arm to keep herself upright but it was not that bad. She must have been out for a few days.

Following him, they made their way deeper into the castle and down several corridors she had never seen before. They turned off at a seemingly random door and she expected to see a room, but instead, she saw a set of stairs leading down a tight spiral.

Kai tugged her down and she trod carefully so as not to fall. They must have gone down only a single level when they came to another door. Pushing it opened, they entered a room very similar to the suite she had been living in next to Epharis, decorated in dark greens and violets.

Kai did not give her time to look around when he started walking again, pulling her down a second flight of stairs into a room she did not expect.

It was a spacious room split into four sections with one being empty aside from a bench and the passage to the stairs. The other three sections of the room were broken up by massively thick stone walls. The wall facing them, however, was made of layer upon layer of glass so thick it warped the air. In the section to her right sat Versalis on a stone bed with furs for comfort.

THE URGE TO go to him stung her brain like acid and she forced herself to look away into the other two sections.

The middle section was empty, clean and sterile with nothing but a bed. In the room to her left she saw Jaia, his body pressed up against the glass and staring at her, saliva dripping down his chin.

She recoiled immediately, but she was only able to retreat a foot before the chains stopped her and she looked from it to Kai and then to Jaia.

Fear washed through her and the scent of it caught Versalis' attention as well as riling Jaia up all the more. His fingernails left deep gouges in the glass.

Versalis approached the glass, drinking her in, even as he tried to figure out what was going on.

Kai's eyes bore into her. "Etani, he's mad with blood lust but I can't get him to drink anything. It might be your blood he needs."

She was standing as far back as she was able with her arms outstretched before her, the chain tight but she was unable to pull it free with it looped around his hand.

At his words, she gasped, planting her feet on the ground when he tugged at her forward. "Kai you can't be serious."

"It's okay. I won't let him do anything to you, trust me," he said, frowning when she shook her head.

"Etani please, it's the only thing I can think of. Don't make this hard."

Her eyes turned from Jaia to Versalis who had his cheek pressed to the glass, trying to see who was in the other cell, looking anxious.

"Kai, look at him," she cried.

She did not like this at all. No, she did not blame him for resorting to it, but she was less than keen on dying to feed a vampire, regardless of who the vampire was.

Kai gave the chain a jerk and she stumbled forward. He looked both annoyed and frustrated at the situation.

"You would force me?" she asked with a pleading tone.

"I will if you don't help. He's my brother, I can't let him suffer."

Her eyes met his and her fear clashed with his resolve. Dread filled her and Versalis punched the glass as Kai wrapped a second loop around his hand, dragging her forward.

"Kai please, we can figure it out!" she whimpered but he was no longer listening.

Pulling her forward, she found herself hypnotised by the horror that was Jaia as she was shoved against the glass.

Horrified, she saw Jaia licking the glass over her throat, his eyes wild and feral.

"I'm sorry Etani," Kai said gently and opened a small hatch she had not noticed.

He kicked the back of her knee and she dropped, almost smacking her head against the glass.

Kai gripped her left arm and opened the hatch, forcing her arm through.

The glass was thick enough to reach from her shoulder to just below her elbow, leaving her forearm exposed to the ravenous vampire.

Before she could pull away, Kai placed his hand on her nape, holding her down on her knees, the angle making her unable to pull herself free. She heard Versalis trying to break the glass, but she could not focus on it, only on the footsteps that rebounded through the open hatch.

Suddenly Jaia appeared calm as he approached her exposed arm and, taking deep breaths, basked in the scent of her fear.

He knelt down and tilted his head, staring deep into her eyes for a long moment. She did not think he had any recollection of who she was, but he soon turned to her arm.

His hand was cool and gentle as he curled his fingers around her wrist and forearm, tenderly holding her. Leaning down, he licked her from elbow to palm and she shuddered at the feeling, trying to resist the sudden rush of desire that flooded her system.

She felt him smile against her wrist and when the scent of her need reached him, his mouth opened, clamping down on her. He bit her once, then again and again, seeming to chew on her flesh, resisting the blood until he could hear her cries of pain.

She gritted her teeth at the first bite. The second seemed less but then it came again and again until finally, she could not hold in her pain and the room echoed with her distress. Smiling once more, he began to drink deeply, his fingers digging into her skin to keep her from escaping.

She did not know when the tears had started, but they dripped onto the floor below her. Versalis had gone silent, listening to the sounds of the vampire lapping at her bloody, ruined wrist, her panting breaths and Kai's slow breathing.

Finally, Jaia released her and she was allowed to pull her arm back.

Jaia was looking at them, confused as he wiped the blood from his face. Looking down at the sticky red on his normally white gloves, he looked up to Kai who had dropped her chain and stepped up to the glass

"What happened?" Jaia demanded, and his crimson eyes returned to black, as he looked around the room, confounded.

The instant she had been freed, she backed away from the glass, her back hitting the wall and she hugged her arm close to her chest. She was panting hard, and her head began to ache as she tried to figure out who it was that consumed her mind, occupying her every thought. All the while, she thought it was Versalis, but it was also Jaia.

Shaking her head to clear it, she looked to Versalis who has managed to splinter the first layer of glass. He was staring at her arm, his expression furious.

She needed to get away from them all and she spun, scrambling up and sprinting for the stairs and towards the exit.

Kai was after her in the next breath, but she had a head start. She did not know if his speed could match hers, but she was not eager to find out. Bursting into the sitting room, she grabbed a chair and jammed it under the door handle just as Kai tried to get through. He grunted and the door splintered, but she was already backing away.

"You have to let me explain," he yelled through the door, but she was done listening to excuses.

Instead, she turned and ran for the door.

The door and chair splintered as he kicked the door, but she was already passing through the second, running up the flight of stairs.

Screaming, she felt his hand on her ankle and she turned as she fell, ensuring she fell on her backside instead of her front. Taking advantage of her stance, she drove her heel into his nose, but he refused to let go.

Dragging her back down, he caught one of the chains and huffed in relief, wrapping it twice around his hand.

"Damn it all, Etani, listen to me."

He caught her free wrist and pulled her closer, even as she aimed a kick squarely between his legs.

He dropped, but it did her no good. Jaia appeared just in time to take hold of the second chain, wrapping it lightly around his fingers.

Turning on him, she had been about to punch him when Kai jerked the chain and she fell back, cracking her head on the step.

Her world was spinning, and she grasped her head with both her hands, feeling the wetness of blood.

Something grabbed her ankles and pulled her down the last few steps and back into the sitting room, as the door quickly shut and locked.

"There we go, now you two be good," Jaia said as she peered at him through a curtain of her hair.

She was sure she had a concussion, but it would fade soon enough.

"How do you feel?" Kai asked, pulling her to her feet and helping her onto the couch, the chain tied securely around the wooden arm of the couch.

"I don't know. I have no way of knowing how long it will take."

"What about that *thing* inside her?" Kai asked. "They couldn't hear it when they checked."

"Could it be dead?" Jaia asked, his voice hopeful.

"It's possible, but Epharis seemed fairly cheerful when he left her alone. I think he would have been in a rage if it were lost."

"It's problematic, this whole situation is trouble for us."

She lowered her arms and blinked, taking a moment to process that not all the blood on her arm was from her head. The chew marks on her arm were oozing, only adding to her confusion.

Suddenly a hand appeared and a set of six fingers snapped in front of her, making her jerk back.

"She hit her head," Jaia said, his fingers gentle as he tugged at her hair, unable to see through the blood and sticky hair.

"I think that was you," Kai said, moving away and collecting something.

She had spotted a twin pair of threads that had come loose on the rug, focusing on them to try and clear her head but the harder she focused, the more her brain hurt.

SOMETHING wet and cold touched her neck and she jumped back, sliding off the couch and onto the floor in a heap. A pair of hands pulled her back up and someone held her head gently against his stomach while another one worked on the back of her head.

"It's not bad, might have a concussion though. She's not acting right," Jaia said and Kai huffed in agreement.

Letting go of her head, she looked up to see two sets of twins, the four men swaying together and apart again. The sight made her stomach churn and she wanted to vomit all over their pretty rug, but nothing came up.

"What is it with men constantly trying to keep me chained up?" she asked, sounding groggy even to herself.

"Etani, are you alright?" Kai asked.

"Fuck off, Kai."

He looked taken aback but Jaia laughed. "Well you *did* kidnap her, force her to feed me and then refuse to let her leave," he said, moving to attach the second chain to the opposite couch arm.

"Says the man tying me to a chair," she said moodily.

She squinted at their feet, trying to force four into two but it was not happening.

"Yes, well that can't be helped," Jaia said, tugging at the chain and moving to sit across from her.

Lifting her head just enough, she glared at him through wet hair.

"I am looking forward to when Epharis finds out and rips your head off. He might even let me keep it."

Jaia exchanged a look with Kai and frowned.

"That is a cause for concern. The Lich will have figured out someone let her go," he said, and Kai sat in the armchair to her right.

"If you keep me here that makes you no better than *him* downstairs."

Jaia stiffened, looking angry at the insinuation. "We are considering our options, not turning you into a blood doll for our sick fantasy," he snarled.

"Tell yourself whatever you want, Jaia, but you are keeping me here for your own selfish reasons, too. You're *exactly* like him."

Springing up to his feet, he balled his hands into fists. "Shut up! If it weren't for your Lich, we wouldn't be here! If he hadn't drugged you, we would never have had to feed on you!"

She glowered up at him, not giving him the satisfaction of agreeing with him.

The silence that ensued felt thick between them.

Kai sighed. "It was my idea to drain her."

He sounded remorseful, but she held no sympathy for him. Using the chains to sit up, she swallowed again to keep from throwing up, the world spinning and slowly she eased herself back against the backrest of the couch.

Tilting her head back, she closed her eyes.

"No sleeping," Kai said.

She chose to ignore them both, feeling their eyes on her but she was going to pretend they did not exist until they went away.

At that point, she figured it was just a waiting game until Epharis had drawn his conclusions and came down there to look for her.

But as it turned out, they had the same thought. After only an hour of trying to get her scrambled brain back together, she was moved down into the recently vacated left cell. She did not have the energy to fight and so when she was sat down on the bed by both men, she immediately laid down on the hard stone, the furs doing little to cushion it.

At that point, it could be needles for all she cared. All she wanted was to sleep. A second later, a pair of hands gripped her shoulders, rolling her onto her back.

Looking up, she was shocked to find that one Kai and one Jaia were above her and Jaia was biting his wrist.

Recalling the events in the tower, she immediately clamped her mouth shut and Jaia gritted his teeth as he worked to get her mouth open.

Finally, Kai sat on her chest, freeing up his hands, not that all that fanfare was necessary since she was in no state to be defending herself. Squirming, she flicked up her right leg and caught Kai around the neck, bending him backwards.

But that distraction was all Jaia needed. Digging his fingers into the joints of her jaw, he forced his wrist against her mouth, blood dripping onto her tongue. Etani turned her head, trying to spit it back out, only to have Jaia gripping her hair, keeping her from moving.

Whimpering, she knew she would have to either choke or swallow, neither overly appealing to her. In the end, she swallowed and felt it burning its way down to her stomach.

Kai and Jaia moved with effortless synchronicity, Jaia sliding onto the bed and lifting her until she was leaning against his chest, his arm plastered against her mouth.

Kai moved to bind the chains together behind her back after he had released himself from her leg. Giving in, her tongue traced the bites and Jaia shivered behind her.

Clutching her tight to him, he rested his cheek against her hair and allowed her to drink freely.

Kai squeezed her fingers gently before moving away to watch, but she did not try and escape again.

With her eyes sliding shut, she considered the heat that was spreading through her body, making her feel as though she were glowing from the inside out. When she opened her eyes again, her vision had begun to turn pink and Jaia reluctantly drew his arm back from her.

Craving to prolong the connection to him a moment later, she leant forward, frowning at the loss, but, at the same time, something in her had begun to fray.

Someone was shouting from another room, loud and furious but she was no longer able to pay attention. Turning, she buried her face in the neck of the man behind her, the man who smelt amazing, delicious and erotic yet entirely normal all at the same time.

Strong arms encased her, and she sighed, her fingers curling in the fabric of his shirt, making her feel that a new connection was forming that would overtake the old.

Versalis no longer lingered in the back of her mind, it was now Jaia.

11

ESCAPING AYATHIAN

*E*pharis came only a few hours later after the castle and grounds had been properly searched, but she could only vaguely hear the conversation from their cell. Jaia had not left her, and all the while, he kept stroking her hair and murmuring sweet words while she drifted in and out of consciousness.

The shouting from the other cell had long stopped, but she could still recall the sound of crunching bone and chipping glass.

Versalis was just as trapped as she was by the twins.

Instead of trying to comprehend what was going on, she basked in the warmth and comfort that Jaia could bring her. Her body was curled in his arms, his right leg under hers and his left behind her back, giving her something to cushion her back rather than the wall.

The door slammed and Kai came back down, glancing to the cell that contained Versalis before coming into the cell they were staying in.

"He's gone for now, but I think he suspects us. We do not have much time before Alaric is forced to come down here.

As Jaia moved, she made a soft sound of distress, her face burying deeper into the crook of his neck. He was gentle as he pressed her back and she reluctantly opened her eyes, squinting at the brightness of the candles on the walls.

"Come on sweetheart, we need to go somewhere where you'll be safe," Jaia said gently and she nodded, willing to do whatever he asked so long as she got to remain at his side.

Helping her to her feet, she rolled her shoulders, but there was little she could do with her arms behind her back.

In a dream state, she was led out of the room. However hard she tried, she was unable to focus, having just enough sense to look over in the direction of the far cell. Versalis looked like a mess, blood smeared on the glass where he had broken himself trying to get through, his eyes wide as they locked on her.

He watched her until she was up the stairs and out of sight, but even then, she could still feel them.

Entering the sitting room, she was allowed a moment's rest on the couch, her head spinning and her sleepy eyes following Jaia everywhere he went. They appeared to be packing, but she did not know what for.

Finally returning to her, Jaia cupped her face and kissed her forehead. "Come now, darling, it's time to leave this place," he said gently, helping her to her feet, and she willingly obliged.

Something was gnawing at her as he said it and she frowned, trying to remember what was that inside her, telling her not to leave. Whatever it was, she let it go and followed Jaia, Kai coming up behind her. Stepping into the hallway, they did not head for the front door. She soon found out that the castle had a back door. They took the route through the quiet kitchen and into a small road that seemed to work as a loading dock for the castle's kitchens.

Jaia took her arm gently, hurrying her along and her nightdress swung around her bare feet, making it obvious they did not belong. The trip by foot only lasted ten minutes and they came to a small alley somewhere in the seedier part of the city.

Knocking on a door five times and then once, followed by three slow taps, it opened and a small, balding man squinted out at them.

"We need to leave," Kai said urgently, and the man sighed, motioning them inside.

Once the door shut behind them, they headed down the hall and into a large room filled with black carriages.

The old man seemed to be studying her, but she barely noticed, only caring that Jaia was helping her into the carriage and had settled close at her side. She did not know what Kai was doing, but the man mumbled his thanks and shuffled away, leaving them alone for a moment.

"How long do you think we have?" Jaia asked, slipping his arm tightly around her and she sighed happily.

"A few days at best; it will be rough, but we have to do it."

She felt eyes on her, and she peeked at Kai. She had been angry at him for something, but she could not recall what, so she smiled. His tense shoulders eased, returning the smile. Someone stomped up to the carriage with what sounded like two horses, taking the time to strap the horses in and then climb up onto the carriage.

Kai pulled the cords on the curtains and the carriage fell into darkness.

Leaning against Jaia, he lifted her chin with his finger and lightly kissed the tip of her nose, making her smile at the tender gesture.

"I'm going to look after you," Jaia promised softly against her hair, pulling her into his lap with his cheek resting atop her head. "Everything is going to be okay."

She dozed off easily to the soft sound of his voice and his arms wrapped tightly around her.

WHEN SHE AWOKE SOMETIME LATER, they were moving and she felt groggy and nauseous, her hand going to her head that was still somewhat aching.

"Where am I?" she asked, trying to figure out why the entire world was shaking.

She realised her hand was free and she could feel her wrists, no longer restrained by the chains. Glad for it, she reached out for a curtain, but someone stopped her, pulling her back from the window.

"No, Etani," A sleepy voice said, and she glanced at the vague outline of a man beside her.

It appeared that the carriage had been modified, the seats of the carriage pulling out and the backrests folding down to make a bed. They had been curled up together with her snuggled securely between Kai and Jaia.

The one who had spoken had been Kai and she jerked her hand back from him.

He swore, sitting up sharply and Jaia on her other side moved as well, alert and wary.

"What is going on?" she demanded, feeling confused and somewhat alarmed, but mostly just angry.

Kai reached for her, but she parried his grasping hand and drove her palm up into his nose, relishing the satisfying crunch. The force of the blow knocked him back against the carriage wall, the driver swore and kicked the horses into a faster speed.

She nearly fell on top of Jaia, but she caught herself just in time. She was so tired of vampires trying to control her. So sick of them abusing her like this. Jaia had been a little slow on the uptake, at least until she shoved Kai's nose into his brain, and he slumped to the bed, unconscious before she turned on him.

"Etani calm down," Jaia said, and she very nearly locked up under the words, but she was not going to give in that easily.

When he made a move for her, she threw herself back, planting her foot against his chest and pushing him back again. He swiped her foot away and she was reaching for the curtain, ready to kill them all if that was what it took. He did not try and contain her, instead, he sank his fangs into her shoulder, his arms going around her only as an afterthought.

She cried out in pain, shifting and kicking the door of the carriage, but it did nothing to get the doors open. Jaia moved back onto the makeshift bed, dragging her with him, his fangs breaking her skin as he bit her again and then a third time.

Screaming, she struggled violently. Absently she registered that the carriage had stopped, a moment before the door opened and both of them toppled out, landing hard on the stone floor of what appeared to be a cave. Falling apart, she rolled away and threw herself to her feet, her hand gripping her bleeding shoulder and backing away as quickly as she dared.

Jaia leapt to his feet just as quickly, prowling after her with murder on his face.

In the carriage, Kai had begun to stir.

Their driver was an enormous man with a mass of red hair and beard, looking confused by the scene and not sure how he could help.

Facing off against Jaia, he lunged and aimed to punch her head, but she was prepared, ducking to the side and landing a solid knee to his ribcage. She threw him back a good three feet, but he rebounded and swept her legs out from under her, catching her before she could hit the ground. His kindness earned him a punch to the throat, and he dropped her the last few inches, clutching at his throat and struggling to breathe.

Kai swore again, crawling out of the carriage to help his brother, but she was quick to turn on him, landing a brutal kick to his side as he came within reach. He crashed into the wall of the cavern and slid down, more angry than hurt.

Someone caught her from behind, but she stamped down on her attacker's foot and drove her head back to connect with his nose.

SPINNING AROUND, she brought her elbow down on the side of his throat, dropping Jaia like a rock. She knew that would mess up all the nerves in his neck and buy her a little more time.

Following a sliver of light, she spotted the exit of the cave and rocketed towards it, past the baffled human giant, but Kai had already planned for her escape attempt.

Coming at her from an angle, he caught her around the middle and knocked her into a wall, her shoulder jarring under the impact but she returned the favour, using the same elbow she had used on Jaia to drive into nearly the same spot. Kai was down but he was still clinging to her in agony, refusing to let her go. It gave Jaia enough time to reach them, the gold chain glistening in the air as it looped around her upturned arm.

Jerking her arm back to get away from the closing loop, she found herself caught, but she yanked hard before he could get a good grip on the other end. It did not matter though. In a flash, he crashed into her and pulled the loop tightly, binding her wrist.

Pulling hard, she stumbled over a snarling Kai and fell to her knees, panting softly as Jaia lifted the chain, forcing her arm up.

Looking up at him, her fury was met with his own, knowing just how close she had come to escaping and realising that their current attempts were not enough for someone of her species.

Kai pushed himself up, grabbing her arm and bending it , spiteful enough to enjoy her cry of pain before accepting the chain from Jaia and binding her arms tightly behind her back, one end snaking up to bind around her throat, keeping her arms up at an uncomfortable height. The other end was left loose to be held or to hogtie her if she decided to be difficult.

"Harder to keep contained than a wet cat," Jaia remarked when Kai had finished binding her.

Both men took a step back to look at her kneeling form, as it lay ruffled and angry before them, but otherwise she was unharmed.

"I don't think you took enough," Kai said, grabbing her arm and roughly pulling her to her feet, still smarting after she had tried to kill him.

"I'll fix that once we're back in the carriage," Jaia said, his voice a low growl.

She was forcefully stuffed into the carriage, the makeshift bed making it difficult to get in without hands and the brothers climbed in after her, both angry and wanting revenge.

"Maybe if you do too?" Jaia suggested, pulling the carriage door shut and the driver locked it from outside.

"Do you want to risk us both becoming addicted?" Kai asked, but his tone said he was seriously considering the option.

Pushing herself into a sitting position, she squinted in the gloom until her eyes adjusted and she was able to see them reasonably well. They were watching her, trying to decide what to do with her.

Taking an internal stock of herself, she found no lasting injuries. The thing that had protected the little light inside her had a bruise and she was eternally grateful for what she could only assume to be the soul of her twin encasing her womb and keeping the foetus safe from harm.

"Too much of a risk, she's dangerous," Kai was concluding when she came back to herself.

"Well, we'll just have to move faster, harder. It's possible Versalis helped her build up an immunity to a degree, she's fighting it," Jaia said thoughtfully.

Turning to look at her, he frowned at her glare. Rolling onto his hands and knees, he started towards her and she immediately used her legs to push herself back as far as she could.

"There's always the other option," Kai said slowly with his eyes averted.

"I am not a rapist," Jaia said, easily deflecting her attempt to drive her foot into his face when she had run out of space to back up into.

"I know, I was just saying."

Jaia grabbed her hips and jerked her forward, her upper body falling back, and he leant over her, easily able to use one arm against her shoulder to keep her down.

Kneeling between her knees, he had her nearly defenceless and they both knew it.

Using his free hand, he nudged her head to the side using two fingers and chuckling when she resisted. "Come on Etani, you know this is going to happen whether you want it to or not."

He leant and brushed his nose over the growing number of scars along her throat. But Etani refused to surrender just yet. Lifting her foot, she slammed her heel down on his calf muscle and he grunted in pain. He bit down harder than necessary, her teeth clenched to keep from making a sound and she struggled to contain the rush of desire that flooded her, knowing she was fighting a losing battle. There was no stopping the endorphins that rushed into her.

Giving a soft whimper under the strength of his first pull, he relaxed on top of her, the arm that had been on her shoulder sliding down to trace over her thigh. His nails felt smooth on her skin and he dug them in, in response to her shiver. He did not stop until she was barely clinging to consciousness, her eyes fluttering as she tried to focus on what was happening.

He was still lying on her, warm and safe, but the position felt wrong. When he bit down on his wrist and placed it against her lips, the wrongness vanished, and she drank greedily.

Leaving her to drink until Kai finally told him to stop or he would risk turning her, he pushed himself off her and settled against her side, smiling when she wriggled herself closer to him, content and safe.

When his arms closed around her, she immediately felt like nothing in the world could harm her.

He tucked her head in the crook of his throat and she fell into a happy doze, soothed by the feeling of his fingers tracing along her hip and the curve of her waist.

Jaia and Kai were still talking quietly, but she did not pick up anything they said.

GETTING BACK TO CONSCIOUSNESS, she found herself once again snuggled tightly between the two men. Kai's back was against hers while Jaia's body was curled around her, and she used her form to curl protectively around her swollen belly. She woke into a happy sleepiness, pushing herself up just enough to see what was going on, but the darkness outside only highlighted the darkness inside, and the warmth inside the carriage only made her sleepier.

With as much strength she could conjure, she wriggled free from the two men, making her way to the edge of the bed and tapping once using her shoulder. They did not appear to be moving, so she hoped she would be allowed out.

The door was not locked, and she slid out. Their driver did not stop her and as she breathed in the night air, her smile seemed to confuse the man even more.

"Where are we?" she asked, not sure why she wanted to be out of the carriage, only that she needed to get out and move.

"About thirty-five miles Northeast of Ayathian," he said, watching her warily.

"Do you know where we're going?" she asked, pacing a few steps away before coming back, trying to get some movement back into her sore legs.

"Not exactly. I only know that we have another day of travel, possibly two as we will need to stop for horses."

She looked at the pretty, brown-coated horses and found they did not seem even remotely bothered by her, even when she got close enough to smell their warm bodies.

"They grew up around werewolves and the like, they are used to the smell of unusual creatures," the man offered as he moved up behind her, taking up a few strands of her hair and waving it before the horse.

The horse just gave them a look like they were insane.

"Odd, do you provide this service often?" she asked, inching closer to the horse to see the fine little hairs on its soft nose.

She had never seen a horse up close before. It was entirely brown aside from little white bands around his hooves and a white stripe down his nose. She did not know much about horses, but she thought it was pretty.

"Fairly often, as the needs demand. Please don't eat the horse."

"I eat humans, not horses," she retorted. The man stepped back, but her amusement was cut off when the horse tried to eat her hair. Jerking back, she glared at the creature. "Bad horse, you don't eat hair."

The horse only looked at her with a flick of the ear as if to say, 'what are you going to do about it?'

She turned away from the obnoxious beast to see Kai stepping out of the carriage. Jaia was stirring inside their vehicle. He *did* look a little full and sluggish, cupping his repleted stomach.

Approaching her, Kai raised a small water skin and she closed the distance to him, glad for it.

"What is the story with you three?" the man asked, watching as she drank.

"It's private business," Kai said, using his sleeve to wipe a few drops of water off her chin.

Wrapping his arm around her, he hugged her close to his side and she leaned into him, his warmth calming her down even if he was not Jaia.

"Apologies, Sir, I meant no disrespect," the giant of a man said, bowing slightly.

"None was taken," Kai said, guiding her back towards the carriage and Jaia.

Jaia accepted her eagerly into his arms and she dropped down beside him, barely able to move without their help.

"Think we can undo the chains a bit, at least let her use her hands?"

Jaia hummed his response, inhaling the scent of her hair and too lazy to care.

Kai released her arms, her groan loud as she was finally able to stretch them. Settling on an alternative, he linked both arms to the chain and her throat, leaving her able to use her arms but not fully, nor was she able to fully extend them.

Being confined in the middle of the carriage, she would not be able to reach the windows.

12

PROMISES AND A HUSBAND RETURNED

*A*ll three of them slept for most of the trip, waking long enough to take a walk or move about. Jaia was not keen on feeding again, feeling sluggish from the amount he had already consumed and reluctantly going out to run to burn off some energy.

The day and night had passed, and they all needed a break, moving around stiffly.

Etani did her best to stretch. She found a tree and was contemplating how best to climb it when Kai joined her.

"How are you feeling?" he asked, watching as she extended her arms as high as they would go, but it was not enough to reach the branches.

Stymied, she turned to him. "Well enough."

Much of her buzz diminished but not enough to make her hostile yet. It was almost time for Jaia to dose her again, but he was being difficult when he already felt so full.

"Good, and the *thing*?" When she looked confused, he motioned to her stomach and her brows lifted.

"The thing is called a foetus, Kai. A baby, and it's fine," she said, turning away from his look of disgust and apprehension.

"What do you suppose will happen once you have given birth? Do you think Epharis will let you keep it?"

She went still, freezing in her perusal of the tree bark and the possibility of climbing it that way.

"You know he will take it and leave you behind, alone and childless."

His words cut through her, even though she tried to ignore him.

"He will leave you, take that child and teach it to be like him. A man who drugs his wife into loving him."

"Shut up, Kai," she hissed, her eyes filling with tears but with her back to him, he could not see.

"A man who will hit her if she doesn't obey, who enjoys torturing other creatures. A man who would probably beat and torture your child!"

He was full-on shouting now and she shook her head, moving away from him. He grabbed her arm, keeping her from escaping and turned her to him.

"You know it's true. That *thing* is all he wants. You are merely the vessel in which *it* is being carried."

His grip was painfully tight, and she pushed him back. He paused when the first tear fell down her cheek. She did not say anything as she ran away from him into the field. He did not follow her. Perhaps they both knew she was too weak to outrun them now.

Sinking into a cross-legged position, she stared down at the ground and watched a little red beetle with black spots crawling along a stem of grass. Her hands were on the top curve of her belly, the only part she could reach.

"Don't worry, I won't let him take you," she whispered to the little life inside her, hating herself for being so weak.

After an hour or so, Jaia found her still there. He looked much refreshed as he sat next to her.

"He told me what he said. I'm sorry, Etani," he offered gently, dropping his arms when his first attempt to embrace her was rejected. "You had to know this was a possibility."

Extending her hand, she leant forward to allow the little bug to crawl onto her, moving on little black legs along her finger.

"Knowing something and being informed of it while kidnapped are two different things."

Her soft words made him look at her. She was quite lucid but still weak. That meant she was relatively harmless.

The bug tickled as it crawled along her forearm and she leant sideways, training a blade of grass in the path of the beetle and lifting it away. At first, the bug seemed disorientated, but then went on its merry way down the grass blade before fluttering its wings to fly away. Watching it, she tucked her arms around herself, exhausted and cold.

"Let's go back, we'll be there in a few hours," he said, not touching her, but it was clear he wanted to.

"Where are we going?" she asked, doubting he would tell her.

"Our old home. It's long abandoned but it is a good place to hide while we get things in order."

"Are you going to turn me?"

"No, Etani, I need your blood. But…" he trailed off and she knew what he was going to say. He intended to make her into his blood doll, forever craving his attention and bite for eternity.

"What did Kai mean when you said you weren't a rapist?" she asked, watching as the grass moved in waves as a gentle breeze picked up.

"The process normally takes a few months, but it can be… sped up through… sex."

He looked uncomfortable while she nodded in understanding. "So, you're going for the slow method."

"Kai doesn't want to admit it, but the other way is a lot less dangerous, it's logical."

"Logical rape," she remarked, laughing softly.

His frown made her blink, not understanding.

"It wouldn't be rape if you had fed first," he said slowly, and she narrowed her eyes at him.

"It would make you like Epharis, drugging me into desiring you."

Much to her dismay, that did not seem to bother him all that much just then. Jaia pushed himself to his feet as the sky began to lighten. She reluctantly accepted his hand and followed them back to the carriage and climbing inside.

If nothing else, she was safe until nightfall.

THE DAY PASSED in a haze of boredom and her own feverish withdrawals, but they were making her wait. Getting angsty, she pouted in the corner, watching as they conversed quietly.

She was becoming warier of them by the hour, her hostility growing but she knew they would make their move when they were ready. They had been forced to stop after a horse threw a shoe and by the time the man had returned from the village, the sun had begun to set again, so they decided to get out and walk.

Stepping down, the man was hitching up the horse and when he noticed that the seats were back in place, he frowned.

"We will walk the remainder of the way, thank you for your service," Kai said, offering him a handful more coins.

The man beamed, jumping up onto his carriage and trundling away in the direction they had come.

It was a good hour before they reached the place. It was an enormous, square building with hundreds of windows and a large square front door that was flung wide.

Walking inside, the place was spotless, not the dusty and mouldy thing she expected.

The hallway was tiled in black and white, the walls a creamy peach colour. Straight ahead lay a sweeping staircase with an archway on either side. Along the hall were two doors stood open on each wall, leading to large dining and sitting rooms.

"The bedrooms are upstairs, kitchen is through the left arch, dining through the right. Five rooms and two bathrooms," Kai mentioned.

Her eyes lit up at the word 'bathrooms' and she immediately

headed that way, followed closely by Jaia, who was given very pointed instructions to stay out after he tried to follow her in. He did however remove her chains to give her a full range of movement.

She ran the bath as hot as she could bear it, and sank in, the heat only barely touching the coldness of her flesh and by the time she got out, the water had begun to cool.

Dressing in a robe that smelt of lavender, she looked at Jaia who was dozing on a little bench.

"Over there," he said, pointing at a door.

Her room was small and cosy with dark green and silver colours. She rather liked it. Some clothes had been set out for her that were not to her taste, but she had nothing else.

Jaia returned only after she had finished and had combed out her hair. "It's only for a short while," he said, coming up behind her.

She was surprised that at least one legend was not true. She could see him perfectly fine in the mirror.

"Yes, I know," she said gently and saw that his eyes were lingering on her throat.

Shivering at the heaviness of his gaze, she moved away from him only to stop as he caught her arm, drawing her close to him. His body felt hot and she melted into it, catching herself suddenly and moving back.

"Your resistance to my blood is growing stronger," he said gently, following her even as she moved away until, finally, he was lowering her onto the bed.

"Perhaps that means you should stop," she retorted, mimicking his tone and squirming to evade him.

He curled his fingers around her calf and pulled her back. He settled between her knees and that small smile on his lips made her stomach twist. The man was too attractive for his own good.

"Perhaps that means we aren't moving fast enough," he countered

"We could come to an agreement. You don't have to turn me into a slave," she said, and he paused, looking down at her in surprise.

"An agreement?" he asked intrigued.

"A deal. We could make a deal."

"What sort of deal?"

"I feed you whenever you need it and you don't turn me or make me into any sort of blood toy or puppet," she bargained, unsure if he would go for it.

Jaia twitched slightly and then shook his head, his hands sliding up her thigh.

"Just be good, relax and we can live happily forever," he said and sighed when she shook her head.

"Jaia, just listen! I can arrange it so you are both allowed back into Ayathian, there will be no blame. Please, just stop."

He was listening, she knew he was, but her panic was working like magic and she forced herself to calm down.

"I'll be yours, any time you need it. Any time, day, or night, I'll come to you without complaint. Kai will be pardoned and safe, *you* will be safe," she was pleading with him now, knowing that if it failed to work now, it never would.

He stilled and stared at her suspiciously. "Go on," he murmured, making it clear she was on borrowed time.

"Kai and you both safe, no blame and no repercussions. Me whenever you desire it, not a word from Epharis."

He frowned. "Any time I want? Any way I want?" She nodded, guessing what he meant. "I also want a favour from you. One owed favour."

Fear zinged through her, a primal need to rage against him, something feral and wild like a bird trapped but she nodded. "Deal?"

He grinned. "Etani, you can be so difficult."

Gripping a fistful of her hair, he yanked her head to the side, jarring her neck as he sank his teeth almost viciously into her throat. Her hands flung up to try and throw him off her, but then froze, sinking back to the bed as the deal between them dictated she would not resist.

With one hand occupied, he kept her head turned with his jaw, his free hand sliding to her inner thigh and scraping his nails across the delicate skin. She gasped, doing her best to stay calm, fearing what he might do to her and what their deal actually entailed. But then, he moved his fingers from her thigh and up to her hand, using her nails to slash across his wrist.

She could not move enough to turn away, pinned under him with her head trapped in place.

Unable to escape, his blood dribbled into her mouth and she reflexively swallowed to keep from choking. That familiar flood of desire coursed through her system and she shuddered under him, his weight making her insides quiver.

Releasing her face, he gripped the skirt of her dress and pulled it up, revealing the fact that she had not been provided with undergarments. His growl of pleasure made her heart pound and she surrendered to her fate.

WHEN SHE OPENED her eyes the next morning, she found herself unable to recall the night before, only that blood had soaked the bed and her dress was on the floor along with his clothes except for his trousers that were unbuttoned and hung dangerously low on his hips.

She did not feel afraid or even angry, only fascinated at the sight of him there, a hint of light shining through the window and yet the sun did not burn him.

Lifting her hand, she placed her hand in the light, curious, before she pulled her hand back and, no, nothing happened.

Cautiously, she reached out and touched the spot, pressing gently, but he did not burst into flames.

His eyes had opened at some point and he watched her playing with the light, a hint of a smile on his lips.

"The house is protected," he murmured sleepily.

She looked from him to the window and back again, putting two and two together.

"You can be in sunlight here?" she asked, waving her hand in the beam to make the light dance on his hip.

"Mm," he murmured, reaching for her to draw her back to him.

Settling down by his side, she snuggled into his arms and sighed.

"You're in a good mood," she observed.

"I have a full stomach, a beautiful woman and the sun. Why shouldn't I be happy?"

The reason for being unhappy burst into the door only a few minutes later. Kai went bright red at the sight of them and although she had her back to him, it was more than she ever wanted him to see.

Jaia jerked the blanket up to cover her hips.

"They must have found out. They're coming," Kai said, breathless and still shocked at the sight of them in bed.

Jaia groaned in frustration and pushed himself out of bed. He caught his pants just in time to keep them from falling down and quickly did up the buttons, both men locking on her as she sat up, her long hair covering her backside from Kai's view. It was odd, she did not think they had slept together regardless of how the situation might seem from the outside. She thought he might have touched her though, explored her body while they fed, but she did not feel any of the signs that they had been intimate.

Etani pointed to her dress from the night before and Jaia collected it for her. As she was pulling it on, her eyes focused on Jaia and the way his body moved as he hurried to dress.

Glancing at Kai, she found him staring back at her, a look of concern and sadness on his face that he wiped away quickly.

Crawling off the bed, she accepted Jaia's hand and he led them out to a balcony that ran across one wall. Kai lifted his finger to draw their attention and she squinted, just able to see the dust cloud.

"How did they know?" she asked even though she might have an inkling.

First Izziah's betrayal, then knowing exactly where to look on the compound, knowing where to go in the Under Dark.

All the lies and misdirection…

"He's still monitoring me!" she yelled, stalking forward and glaring at the cloud as though she could spear the Lich right through the chest with her glare.

"Monitoring how?" Jaia asked sharply.

"A crystal ball for all I know. He knew where to find me every time!"

Fuming, she turned to the twins. They seemed scared and she knew why. In the case of the house being damaged, it would expose them to sunlight. The sudden terror at the loss of Jaia bit at her stomach and it clenched, making her feel sick.

"Basement?" she asked, and they nodded. "Go. I'll wait here."

They did not argue, instead, Jaia touched her cheek and they left, hurrying to get down into the basement where they would be safe.

SEVERAL HOURS PASSED before the cloud was close enough for her to see them clearly, many horses heading their way.

Finally, when they were close enough, she simply walked from the building towards the group, feeling a little awkward but there he was, Epharis looking huge on a horse that… was blowing smoke out of its nostrils and had a green flame for eyes.

She did her best to ignore that creature even if it surprised her. Instead, she decided to focus on her approaching husband. She did not recognise any other faces in the crowd, no werewolf or anything.

"Etani, come."

She was immediately angered by his choice of words, addressing her like she was his dog.

"No," she retorted, and the horse pawed at the ground.

Dismounting from the horse, he approached her slowly. He wore armour over his robe to cover his chest and sword arm, the armour steely grey and tarnished gold but it worked surprisingly well for him with his glowing green eyes, dark violet robes and long silver hair.

"What did you say?" he asked as he approached her, coming to stop a mere foot from her.

"I said no," she replied, her chin lifting in defiance.

He looked very much like he wanted to strike her, but he resisted the urge with her belly between them.

He studied her and a slight frown came over his face. "You have gotten bigger."

For a second, she felt offended, but then she realised he meant her belly.

"That happens when you're pregnant," she quipped but they both knew what he meant.

She was growing at a rate in which was uncommon for most species and at her current speed, it was likely she would be giving birth in about three months.

"Don't get smart. Where are the vampires?" he demanded, and she noted his fists clenching and unclenching.

"Gone. They left in the night," she lied easily.

"Gone where?" he barked.

His anger did not scare her, the tiny creature in her stomach was her protective shield.

"I did not ask."

His eyes rolled from the house down to her and then narrowed, his teeth bared in response to her raising her eyebrows. "What happened?"

She was enjoying that, far too much. "Jaia and I made a deal."

"What deal?"

He stilled and his burning eyes bore into her, before flicking down to her swollen belly. She knew perfectly well that he wanted to hurt her. Badly and in new and unique ways, but he could not. Not right then and not for months longer.

"That you, along with Alaric and that King in the basement will not harm, accuse, or prosecute them for taking me. That my blood will be at Jaia's beck and call when he needs it, and... a favour." Her lips curled, hating the mere thought of it.

He reached out for her, but she immediately danced back, her arms going around her belly in an instinctive defence that was entirely new to her.

Snarling in fury, he suffered impotent rage. "And what if I refuse?"

"Then I go back to being his blood doll... and become his bed mate." She tacked that last on, only because she knew it would enrage him, considering how possessive he was of her.

Green sparked in his eyes and the fire began to burn, but she forced herself to remain calm and think rationally.

"You promised this, did you not?" he asked through gritted teeth and she nodded. "Very well, we'll wait. Call back your pet vampires and we will return tonight."

She smiled, glad to have finally gotten something, but as she turned, he grabbed her arm and his lips found her ear. "If you set foot in a bed that isn't mine, I'll make you wish you had never existed."

The cold threat made her shudder and she looked back at him unable to hide the fear in her eyes.

She nodded once and turned away from him, heading back in the direction of the house.

Calling them out, she trembled and ignored everything they said to her as they waited for the sun to set.

13

HOW TO ANGER A HUSBAND IN THREE EASY STEPS

They headed back at full speed.

Etani almost ripped out of her skin and onto the neck of his horse as he had one arm tight around her.

They headed back to Ayathian at a speed she did not think was possible for horses. But they galloped at full speed all night, reaching the city a few hours before dawn, and she was stunned. She knew Epharis' horse was not alive, but the others seemed to also be dead and running entirely off his magic.

Getting down, he dragged her after him and set her on the ground, his eyes searching her face and then her belly before the two vampires approached.

"You two are pardoned," he snarled, and their expressions of relief made it entirely worth the trouble she was going to be in later.

She had not forgiven them, at least not yet, but she could understand their reasons. As Epharis' grip pinched her arm like a vice, she gave the pair a small wave, her eyes staying on Jaia, crushing down her burning need to be at his side.

She could manage to tame that need. At least she hoped so. His blood sang in her, the saliva leaving her craving his bite in ways she did not try to comprehend. But she would see him again soon.

Epharis was exceptionally fast in throwing her back in her box and she sat down calmly, looking up into his fury that could not touch her at that moment. Her calmness was entirely false and precarious, but she could not help but revel in it just a little bit, especially when it angered him so much.

"Is the baby safe?" he demanded, and his anger faded just slightly when she nodded.

"Safe, well, and I think Letari may actually be protecting it."

Pausing mid-pace, he wheeled to look at her incredulously. "Protecting it?"

She frowned, trying to draw on the drug-addled memories to mix and match the story, finding one that would not implicate the brothers.

"I fell out of the carriage and when I checked, I found something wrapped around it. It seemed bruised, but the baby was fine, and she hasn't come out at all. I believe she has wrapped herself around it to form some sort of barrier that draws on my energy to... I'm not sure, form an actual physical barrier? A magical one? Something that is keeping it safe."

Epharis studied her face, searching for a lie but it was mostly the truth and the realisation made his brows draw in a frown. "Why would she care?" he asked, baffled.

"Letari might be crazy, but she is still a woman and my twin. She wanted to be a mother, and that is her family in there. You're surprised she would do whatever it took to keep it from being lost to an accident?"

She did not like what he had implied about her sister. At that moment, she registered that she was missing the occasional laugh that came from the back of her mind. Her sister was otherwise occupied watching the baby and keeping everything else out.

"Do you believe it would be unable to be harmed with her there?" he finally asked.

"I don't believe she can stop everything, but a great deal."

He nodded and then narrowed his eyes at her. "How long have you known?"

"I noticed something was there in the tower. But I only started to suspect a few days ago. I am not certain. I can't get a read on her. But when you had me chained, you said she was not an issue. I thought that was strange. So, I am connecting links that may not be there, but what else would be curled up around it and crooning?"

He could not fault her reasoning, still, she could tell he did not like it and his eyes lingered on her belly thoughtfully.

"Do anything to harm my child and I'll rip your soul out and shove it down your throat," she threatened and her fiercely protective tone surprised them both.

He lifted his hands in a sign of surrender, but she knew better. When those arms moved around her belly, she glared at him.

"I won't hurt it," he promised, dropping his arms, and coming to sit at her side.

She noted dryly that he only specified he would not hurt the child, but she let it pass for the time being.

"What was the army you brought with you?" she asked and stood.

Making her way to the closet, she picked a pair of pants she felt might still fit her. Wriggling into some much-needed undergarments and then her pants, she threw the dress into the corner and sighed when the stupid pants would not do up.

Epharis had not responded and she looked at him, finding him staring at her with his mouth slightly open. Flushing, she lifted her arms to cover her chest, but his warning growl had her dropping them again. Her cheeks flamed as he took her in. Her belly and breasts were swollen, and she was almost naked, standing in a patch of sunlight.

That surprised her because she had not even realised the sun had risen. He neared her carefully as if any sudden movement would either shatter the illusion or have her running. She remained still and met his eyes when his hungry stare finally rose to her face.

He reached for her and his pale skin lit up in the sunlight, making his silver hair glitter.

In the sun he looked less angled and harsh, softer and warmer in a way she could not place.

Reaching to touch her burning cheeks, he cupped her face in his hand and her eyes closed, pressing her cheek into his palm.

He leant down and she met his lips gently, the kiss so tender it was barely enough to feel. He held her face in one hand while his other went around her bare back to draw her closer to him. Etani went willingly, though she was no longer able to press that much of herself against him.

His kiss deepened but never became aggressive. If possible, it became passionate and she felt herself melting into it as her fingers clutched his robe, drawing him closer even as he drew her into him.

He removed her tangled hair off her face and ears in a way that made her shiver.

A delicate cough had them both freezing and Epharis looked to the side. "Brother," he greeted calmly as though he had known Alaric would be coming to see her.

Her cheeks flamed again, and she turned her back to the King, realising he could see them both from the side. Her rush of pleasure was draining fast and a nasty voice had pointed out that he may have planned the whole thing so Alaric would see them together, glowing in the light of the morning sun.

"Good morning," Alaric growled, and she knew he had been standing there for some time, watching them.

Epharis tightened his arm around her, holding her to his chest to guard her modesty and she found herself glad for at least that aspect of his possessive nature.

"Your Majesty is there something you needed?" she asked, too embarrassed to look at him.

Instead, she rested her head against Epharis' chest, trying to hide inside his robes.

"I came to check on you as I was informed you had returned. It appears my brother has done the job well."

She was not entirely sure what he meant by that, so she only nodded her agreement.

"She is quite well," Epharis offered and reached behind him.

Pulling a long tunic down from the closet, he handed it to her, and she quickly pulled it on, glad it fit.

Finally stepping back from the Lich, she glanced at the King and then at Epharis, his eyes hot on her. She tried to figure them out, but it was impossible.

"Good, would you like to go for a walk, Princess?"

Her first instinct would be to refuse, but the thing was that Epharis did not want her to go, so she decided to go if only to spite him.

"Certainly, might I have a moment to prepare?"

Alaric nodded and left the room, leaving her alone with a glaring Epharis.

"Not a word," she cut in before his mouth had even opened. "I am fully within my rights to go anywhere I like so long as it does not violate our deal. You cannot force me to stay h—"

"I'm your husband, I can force you to do anything I like," he snapped, cutting her off.

"You could, but you won't. If you want me to play nice with you, you need to give me my freedom or I'll make your existence a living nightmare you can't wake up from."

She was not sure where her confidence came from, but she wanted to make it clear to him that she was not about to bow down before him.

Wriggling out of her pants and tunic, she threw them at him and pulled on a dress instead; it was tight, but it still fit around her.

"Order me some new clothes, would you, dear husband?"

She knew she had pushed her luck and she danced out of his reach, laughing softly as she fled.

THE WALK in the garden was pleasant, their pace slow and easy and she was beginning to wonder when he was going to start on her. They made their way around the corner of the castle when he turned on her and she noted dryly that he had waited until the guards could no longer see or hear them.

"Why did you marry him?" he snarled, furious.

"I don't recall having much of a choice. I *do*, however, recall drugs being involved," she said sarcastically, turning to face him when he stopped.

"Get it annulled, then."

She blinked, her lips pulling down into a frown. "Is that possible? He's the Prince. You're the only one with the authority to do that."

She was wary of his intentions.

"I can, but it would require agreement on both sides. Your other option is to seek out the priest," he said thoughtfully.

"Why are you so interested in who I am married to? Or is this brotherly concern?"

His face twisted and she had to smile inwardly at the sight. "I don't care who he marries, as long as it's not *my* Princess."

Anger flared up in her, burning like acid. "I am not *your* Princess. Nor have I ever been."

Her voice came out harsher than she intended, and she flushed at his indignation. It did not make her words any less true.

"You were my Princess since the day you set foot in this city. No, since the day you were *born*," he said with righteous anger.

It took a moment for what he was saying to sink in, and she closed her eyes, taking a deep breath to keep from shouting at him.

"I am not the Princess of your prophecy, Alaric. Prophecies don't exist."

Her eyes opened and she found him glaring at her with fanatic zeal.

"My destiny was foretold. I am destined to be the King of legend with a great Queen at my side who will bear the greatest dynasty in history."

Tilting her head slightly to the side, she studied him in his pride and insistence that he was that King.

"You may be that King, but I'm not the Queen. I am married to your brother, I am carrying his child," she tried to say it gently, but it was difficult to face such blind devotion calmly when her life was on the line.

Her words seemed to hit him like a blow, and he stared at her hard.

"No, perhaps you are right," he said with a calmness she found even more disturbing.

Men like him did *not* change their minds like that. It took weeks to just chip their resolve and then longer to get them to stop clinging out of sheer stubbornness.

"Thank you for the walk Princess, I hope to do it again sometime in the future."

And with that, he turned away, leaving her there alone and confused.

Deciding not to go back to Epharis just yet, she went in search of the twins, hoping that they could shed some light on the situation. Making her way into the rooms she had been detained in, she knocked gently on the door at the bottom of the stairs.

Kai opened the door a moment later and his face split into a wide smile. "Etani, we weren't expecting you for a few days, please come in."

He pulled the door open and she stepped inside. Jaia and Versalis were sitting on opposite sides of a board with black-and-white squares. Atop the board, there were small figures in odd shapes. Both men were intent on the board, however, Jaia's hand was immediately on hers when she was within reach as though they were magnetised.

Settling close at his side, she watched as Jaia moved a piece that she did not know, both looking up but Versalis was looking at their joined hands, witnessing their closeness.

"Your turn," Jaia said, refusing to let go of her even under the scrutiny.

"You told me you did not bind her," he said with a calmness none of them expected.

"He didn't, a deal was struck," Kai offered carefully.

Kai had come to stand behind her, his hands gentle on her shoulders but she knew he would be ready to rip her from the seat if the need arose.

"We were able to come to an agreement, Versalis," she said gently, not fully grasping the situation, but she felt coming there so soon might have been a bad idea. "I did not mean to intrude. I can come back another time."

She meant to move, but Kai's hands on her tightened and she knew better than to try and resist. He was not detaining her, only keeping her in place while Versalis struggled with whatever was going on in his head. Jaia was tense at her side, everyone was waiting for someone to make a move, everyone waiting for everyone else.

Finally, Versalis managed to get himself in order and focused back on the game.

ETANI FORCED A SMILE AT KAI; he bent down and pressed a gentle kiss against her forehead.

Everything would be fine, and she knew it. She had Jaia and Kai and, so long as Versalis did not pitch a fit, they would be able to live together comfortably.

The game went on for almost an hour, the two men murmuring to each other, but she did not understand what it was they were playing, nor what one had to do to win.

If she could hazard a guess, she would say that one had to get their tallest piece to beat the matching piece of the other colour, but she was not entirely sure.

"It's called chess," Kai informed her as he sat at her side, intent on the game.

Nodding, she had heard of the game but had never seen it played before, watching as Versalis grew angrier by the second and finally threw his pieces down and slumped back against the couch, defeated.

Jaia grinned and scooped up the pieces, packing them carefully away into little velvet bags and collecting the board to put it away.

"So, what did you do to her?" Versalis asked, watching her.

"We struck a deal," Etani said slowly, unsure of his mood.

"Did you sleep with him?" he snapped, still angry at the defeat.

"No," Jaia said while Kai shifted slightly at her side. He looked confused, especially given what he had seen in the room. "We did not have sex," Jaia repeated for the sake of his brother who relaxed slightly.

"But you thought they did?" Versalis asked sharply.

"They were… naked in bed," Kai blushed, squeezing her hand.

She felt the heat coming up her cheeks as well, looking into his tender black eyes before she rested her head against his shoulder.

"I know how it looked, but we never got that far. I couldn't bring myself to do it, even after—" Jaia paused, taking in a deep breath. "Even when she was begging for it, I couldn't take advantage like that. Not after what Epharis did to her."

She studied his demeanour and she knew that, at that point, she had wanted him. The flood of desire had left her aching for him and she was not the least bit surprised she had begged him for more. The need was incredible.

Dropping her eyes, she reached for him as he did for her, she pressing her lips against his fingers and he running his free hand over her hair.

Before Versalis could speak again, there was a knock and everyone went still, looking towards the door. Kai stood and went to answer it, wary of who it might be.

Opening it, he was shoved back by Epharis, who was fuming as he searched around for her.

When he saw her, he seemed to relax. "Did he hurt you?"

"No, he only wanted to talk," she said, studying the man as he glared back at her, angry and frustrated, but he seemed to calm down with her words.

"Come for a walk. we need to talk."

Arching a brow at the demand, she glanced at the others before she sighed and pushed herself to her feet, kissing Kai's cheek as she passed him, allowing Epharis to draw her back up the stairs.

Only after they had reached the garden, did he speak, his glare never leaving his face. "You are being reckless, Etani. You are not putting only your life at risk."

"I was perfectly safe," she lied, turning away from him in frustration, and continued down the path.

She heard him suck in a breath, but a sickening thud claimed her attention and there he was, crumpled on the ground.

She didn't get to see what had happened as something crunched, and everything went black.

14

NIGHTMARE OF A MONSTER

When she regained consciousness, her wrists were on fire. She gasped at the sudden loss of peace into a world of pain and blinked to clear her vision. Her hands were beside her face and her wrists encased in thick and dark-grey metal.

Trying her best to concentrate, she found that the more she tried, the more focus seemed to evade her.

Her wrists were not the only place that hurt. The back of her head was smarting, and the smell of blood led her to believe someone had attacked her with some sort of blunt weapon.

She was leaning up against a rough stone wall, her wrists clamped in shackles that appeared to be nailed into the wall.

That meant she was in a dungeon of some sort.

Turning her head slowly, she surveyed the empty and surprisingly clean cell. It was as if it had been cleaned to await their arrival.

Sweeping her eyes across the rest of the room, they fell onto Epharis as his head rested against his chest. Blood covered the back of his silvery head, too.

At least she was not alone in her suffering. He had not been bound in iron as she had, but rather a thin gold chain ran from one ring to a wrist, across to his neck, then to the other wrist before snaking up to a second ring. She had to marvel at the irony there, seeing him bound using the chain he so regularly loved to use on her.

His position made it impossible to lower his hands below his ears and he could only lean around a foot from the stone. He had not stirred yet while his short breathing made her wonder if he had been close to death and was now recovering. The thought of him being killed scared her and she squirmed, wiggling herself out as far as she could, her arms and leg extended to the fullest.

She only succeeded in poking his calf with her toes, but he did not react.

"Epharis, wake up," she hissed, not wanting to alert whoever held them.

He did not wake up and she let out a low sigh, she pushed into a more comfortable position. Sitting with her back against the wall, her legs bent out in front of her, and her arms up to her right shoulder, she rested her head against the stone. So, she waited, without knowing for who or for how long.

If her guess was right, almost an hour later Epharis began to stir, rolling his head to the side. He grimaced when his head thunked against the stone and he grunted in pain.

Finally, he looked up, his eyes zeroing on hers and then drifting to her arms, down to her belly and then her feet. She could almost see the list being ticked off in his head.

Etani alive? Check.

Arms bound in iron? Check.

Baby well? Check.

Was she able to kick someone's testicles into their throat? Check.

Only after he had assessed her, his eyes stopped focusing, and she knew he was taking stock of his injuries.

"At least I have a cell buddy this time," she quipped when he seemed to be alert again, his eyes sweeping the cell. "The chains make for ironic karma, don't they?"

He grunted and focused on her again, studying the iron and the red welts around her wrists.

"A few hours," she said, knowing he was trying to use the damage as an indication of how long they had been locked up.

He nodded and tugged at his chain, but it had been looped around the ring at least three times on each end.

"Can you reach?" he asked with a motion towards the ring.

She sighed. "I could barely reach you but might as well try again."

Pulling herself up, she stepped forward as far as she was able to. With her arms outstretched, she lifted her foot off the ground and extended. Her wrists burned and she gritted her teeth to keep silent as the iron chafed her skin, tearing it and finding new skin at the base of her hands.

It sizzled but they both ignored it, solely focused on her movements.

Given her current position, she could not reach and so she sighed, straightening. Once again, she turned to face him and stepped forward again, her back arching as she lifted her foot and found she could just touch the ring with it.

The sudden burn on her toes nearly had her on the floor in shock, but she ignored it, trying to focus.

Giving up on that, she motioned to the chain and he pulled it forward. Catching it between her toes, she gave it a little tug, but it had been knotted.

"Damn it all," he hissed, and she dropped her foot. "When did you learn to do that?" he asked. He watched as she twisted on the ball of her foot and straightened. It was not all that impressive; she'd learnt it to be called a backbend and was commonly used in gymnastics.

"It is part of a religious belief somewhere I can't remember the name of, but they perform this as a form of meditation and battle," she said, avoiding the question as she returned to her side of the room.

Planting her foot on the wall, she tried her best to simply rip the iron out of the wall, using her legs and back but it would not budge.

"What is this place designed for?" she asked when she finally sat down, frustrated.

"If we're in the castle dungeons, it's for creatures like us."

"Well that's inconvenient," she replied, the two exchanging a look before settling into a sullen silence.

Her arms had begun to sting from the prolonged contact with the iron and she studied the lines that streaked down her forearms; the iron poisoning was destroying her veins.

"How long is this going to take?" he finally spat when—by her estimation—eight hours had gone by since they woke up.

"The waiting is over," a voice said, and a key was jammed into the door.

The sound of that voice made her stomach clench in terror. Her blood went cold at the sight of Drizdan, as he stood there with two other Drow men.

"What are you doing here?" Etani and Epharis said in unison, both ignoring the other in their death glare at the man.

"Now, now. There's no need to be like that." He seemed cheerful, his gaze flicking to Epharis before settling and remaining on her. "Hello again, beautiful," he purred, stepping into the room.

The two Drow moved in behind him, pulling a trolley along with them. It rattled loudly in the quiet room. Whatever was on top of it was covered with a white cloth.

He approached her with a smile, but she waited, letting him get closer before she shifted and kicked up, the top of her foot, scoring him in the stomach.

All his breath left him, and she only had enough time to pull her leg back before one of the men jumped on her, almost flattening her to the floor.

"I told you to bind her legs," Drizdan wheezed.

The man did not have a particularly good grip on her and while Drizdan was still bent over, she kicked out with all her strength. Her foot collided with his face, flipping him back onto the ground.

Epharis took over, swinging one leg around Drizdan's neck, the other coming to meet the first and locking at the ankle. His calves flexed and Drizdan began to choke, his air cut off.

She drove her knee between the legs of one Drow and he rolled off her.

Turning, she watched as the second Drow tried to release Drizdan, the man already turning black rather than purple. Pulling herself to her feet, she stepped forward and used her foot to shove the Drow headfirst into the wall.

Epharis was grinning at her, but then his eyes flicked, and she turned in time to see a fist coming to her face. She had just enough time to think, *'well damn'* before her head snapped back and she dropped, caught by the Drow before she could hit the floor.

THAT WAS the second time someone had hit her in the head that day, and her head spun violently. Someone lowered her to the ground, binding her ankles as her companion left to help with Epharis, who had Drizdan on the verge of losing consciousness.

The Drow punched Epharis as hard as he had hit her—if not harder—and pried his ankles apart, allowing Drizdan to roll free and gulp down as much air as he was able.

When he stood again, he kicked Epharis hard, the sound of ribs breaking echoed loudly. Drizdan kicked him again and again, only stopping when he was dragged back by his companions.

"You need him alive," a Drow reminded Drizdan and he turned to her.

Immediately, she pulled her legs up to her chest, protecting her stomach.

Drizdan smirked at her. "Don't worry, you and I have a future date," he snarled, motioning for the two that he was fine.

Binding Epharis' legs just as hers had been, they were effectively trapped with the three Drow looking down at them, breathless but satisfied with their handiwork.

"Now that we have all calmed down, we can chat," Drizdan

announced, his malicious smile turning from her to Epharis and back again. "I have a little game I like to play in situations like this"

He approached her and crouched beside her even as she shrank back from him, but his eyes were on Epharis

"It's called *Choice*, and it's quite simple, really. I give you two options and you get to choose."

Epharis looked like he wanted to say something very unpleasant but chose to keep his mouth shut. Finally, he nodded his understanding.

"Perfect! Now your first choice is..." he trailed off, pretending to be thinking, but they both knew it was just a game and he had it all planned out. "If the beautiful Etani here were to lose a finger," he mused, touching the ring finger on her left hand. "Or that sharp tongue." He touched just below her lower lip and jerked back when she snapped at him. "*Which* would it be?" he asked as his hand flung out and backhanded her on the cheek.

She gasped in pain, rolling her jaw but it was not broken. Looking up at him, his eyes bore into her soul and she was left dreading what exactly it was he had planned for them.

"Finger," Epharis said, without breaking eye contact.

They both knew what was coming. It was obvious and yet Drizdan whipped the cloth off the tray with a flourish like it was some great surprise.

"It was the name, was it not? I'll have to change it for next time."

When neither of them gasped in horror, he pouted, looking a little put out, but he still picked up a large pair of clippers used to cut tree branches and shrubs. She was glad they were at least clean.

Her eyes slid shut as she felt the blades against her finger, and she gritted her teeth to try and stay quiet. She did fairly well, remaining silent until the final click when the blades came together, but then her scream rang through the room.

Drizdan laughed, seeming to get drunk on her pain.

"Good girl, scream for me," he growled, making no effort to hide his arousal.

Forcing herself to go silent, she panted heavily and stared at her bleeding hand. The iron meant it would take longer to heal and blood was flowing down her arm to pool beside her, soaking her skirt where she sat.

Reaching for her, he gripped her jaw and forced her to look at him. "Now, where should move on to next? Ah, I know. Those beautiful eyes… or a foot?"

He forced her to look at Epharis even as he looked to the Lich. He met her eyes and swallowed, trying to figure it out. There was a risk of killing her if they removed her eye, but her foot was slightly less dangerous, meaning she would no longer be able to run or defend herself.

"Eye," he finally decided, and she whimpered.

HE GRITTED HIS TEETH, refusing to take his eyes off her as one of the Drow moved behind her, his arm curling under her jaw, the second going over in a headlock.

Picking out a small knife, Drizdan studied her eyes, unable to decide which one to pick.

"I think the green flecked one, I don't like that change," he said and leant down, the knife pressing against the corner of her eye. "I always found those eyes hypnotic, electric, and sexy."

Slowly he pushed the blade into the underside of her eyelid, and she did her best to stay still even as she screamed. When he leant back, her mangled eye was resting on his hand. Cackling, he threw it onto the trolley. He looked down at her, one half of her face coated in blood and the other black with her tears.

"Don't look at me like that, Etani. It's all games," he said, wiping a tear from under her remaining eye.

The Drow released her, and she dropped against the wall, waiting for the grand finale, she did not know why it would be three, she just knew it.

"Now, Epharis, here's the big one… your child or your wife."

The room went so silent they could hear her blood dripping from her elbow into the pool on the floor. No one had taken a breath, and everyone was frozen as though captured in a painting.

"W-What?"

Her entire body had gone cold as she realised what was happening. All the games led to her death and—by extension—the death of her child.

Drizdan was watching her, waiting for her to realise.

"Ah, she's got it," he whispered with a sadistic grin. "Your child or your wife, Epharis," he repeated, his scorching gaze never leaving her face, no doubt relishing on the fear that flooded through her, the way her body tensed and she drew her legs closer to herself, protecting the swelling at her middle.

"Are you insane?" Epharis asked, too horrified to be shocked.

"Not at all," Drizdan said jovially, finally tearing his eyes off her and turning to Epharis. "Not at all. Those are your choices."

Turning to Epharis, she saw the horror on his face. It was simple really. It would either be the baby or her *and* the baby. He really had no choice.

Either way, he was going to lose his child.

"Why are you doing this?" he snarled, his entire body straining against the chain but there was no freeing herself from his greatest and most dangerous invention.

"Because it's fun, because I wanted revenge, and because I have my orders."

"Orders from whom?" Epharis snapped.

Drizdan leaned to Etani's ear, but he spoke loud enough for everyone to hear.

"King Alaric."

15

GAMES, LOSS, AND TRAITORS

King Alaric.

Those two words burned into her like a blade, sinking into her very soul and slicing her. Each syllable a deep cut that left her bleeding at the betrayal.

Epharis had gone feral, raging and trying his best to free himself. But Etani had gone entirely still, that name playing in her mind over and over.

King Alaric.

King Alaric.

King Alaric.

The moment she would be out of that cell or just as soon as she got back from her rebirth, she was going to kill the King.

While both Etani and Epharis tried to take everything in, Drizdan picked up a knife with an abnormally long and coal-black blade that seemed to hum the closer it got to her. It touched her throat and she could feel the whispers rather than hear them.

"Where did you get that?" she whispered, too horrified by their situation to even be scared any more.

"A gift from the King. Your little immortality trick is a problem, so we have a special knife that will keep you nice and dead," Drizdan explained as he drew the blade leisurely and tenderly against her flesh.

Blood oozed and she felt a horrible, terrible sucking sensation inside her that pulled her towards the knife. She recoiled against the wall with eough force to bruise her shoulder. Her head swam while her consciousness was pulling her towards the knife as her body went the other way.

It felt weird, as though she had left herself for an instant, only to snap back in like a blow to her entire being. Her mouth watered, but she managed to keep from throwing up.

Epharis was still raging, swearing and speaking in tongues, but nothing worked. His chain was too good, even for its maker. When he finally wore himself out, his eyes were on her in desperation.

"You have to choose, my dear man," Drizdan said brightly, his eyes still lingering on her with interest.

She could not look at either of them, staring instead at the blood between her feet and wait for the words that would end her life, one way or another.

"I can't," Epharis yelled.

Drizdan grinned. "You know Etani... I think he does actually love you," he said in a stage whisper, delighting in their suffering.

Her head lifted and her eyes landed on Epharis. His face was a terrible mask of agony, tears glistening on his cheeks. They both knew she was not getting out of there alive and she swallowed, nodding her acceptance to him. She would go out like the soldier she was. Her chin lifted, ready for the word that would result in the knife coming down on her.

"The baby."

The words were like a physical blow and her heart stopped for a second.

No, no, no! He could not do that! He was not allowed to let her live!

"No!" she screamed, refusing to accept that he would choose to let her live even after killing her child.

But the Drow were already moving, one wrapping his arms

around her torso and the other grabbing her legs, forcing her to lie flat on the ground. She thrashed, screaming and straining to get herself free, even as she heard Epharis sobbing across the room. Drizdan's grin was sadistic as he knelt beside her, having replaced the black knife with a long, silvery blade.

Struggling to hold her down, the Drow at her legs sat on her knees, placing his hands on her hips to keep her still as Drizdan cut her dress open.

Desperate, she sucked in as much air as she was able and the scream that left her was terrible.

Drizdan spun away from her, his hands covering his ears that had begun to bleed.

The Drow above her that got the full blast of the sound was bleeding through his nose and ears, as she ruptured his eardrums. Falling back, he collapsed onto the floor, pressing his forearms against his ears in an attempt to block out the sound better.

Running out of air, she sat up, her hands reaching for the Drow on her knees and she reached for his throat, sinking her nails in the tender flesh.

HER FINGERS CUT through tendons and muscle like they were butter, meeting in the middle and she pulled towards herself, the front of his throat exploding towards her. He fell to the ground, choking as blood filled his lungs and she spun, slamming her back against the wall for protection.

The two men were still incapacitated, but Epharis was fine; his hands already covered his ears before everything began.

"Were you a banshee in another life?" Epharis snarled, his hands coming away red.

"I'll kill you," she screamed, hating him for daring to choose her over their child.

She yanked at the wall, wanting nothing more than to rip his heart from his chest, but she could do nothing, she could barely even stand up.

Buying herself only a few minutes, she was surprised to see the door opening and two more Drow entering the room, their ears red with blood.

"What in the abyss' name was that?" Drizdan shouted even though the room was fairly quiet now.

"Banshee?" one of the men asked, but they found no such creature in the room.

They only found the dead Drow, another one who seemed to be entirely deaf or dying, Drizdan, and the chained pair.

"We need more men to contain the bitch," Drizdan yelled.

One of the newcomers dragged both the dead Drow and the other one from the room. She did not know how many men Drizdan had brought with him, but she was in trouble.

Now that it was just Drizdan and her, she strained harder against the stone. Drizdan looked up, alarmed, following an ominous creaking sound. ·

Her entire body strained against the stone and a puff of dust appeared.

Swearing, Drizdan moved to the tray and brought a large hammer down on her knee. Her scream was loud, but not the same pitch as before. Her knees gave out and she slumped against the ground, panting and gasping for air.

As soon as Drizdan had dropped the hammer back onto the trolley, he was on her. Ripping two strips of fabric from her dress, he forced the first into her mouth, cursing her when she tried to bite him, and then used the second to bind around her head to keep the wad in place. Finally, he stood, wobbly on his feet.

"What are you, woman?" he growled, and for good measure, he drove his foot into her ribcage.

The gag muffled her scream well and he smiled when she curled up around her belly again, unable to defend herself, knowing he was going to win.

When the men returned, their numbers had doubled, and they

took in the scene. Three had bleeding ears, the fourth did not, though he looked a little disorientated.

Drizdan motioned to her and they moved forward. She fought them as best as she could, but with her arms and legs bound she was helpless lying on her back and her arms extended straight and strained above her head.

With two men sitting on her legs, her knee was on fire, one hand in her hair, another on her throat and the fourth man deciding at the last minute to sit on her chest. She was effectively restricted and entirely unable to see what was happening.

Not that she needed or wanted to see what was happening anyway, her fear bottoming out into a calmness that made Epharis look away from her.

Drizdan collected his knife and dropped back to his knees beside her, his hands rough as he pushed the shredded fabric that covered her torso away. His hand pressed against her abdomen firmly, feeling around for what he was aiming for and then he looked up.

"Got her?" he asked, and all four men nodded, muscles straining, and fingers clenched harder.

Epharis could not take his eyes off her now, seeing her tears as the knife slid across her skin, opening her abdomen.

She did not scream, she could not even see the room around her, instead, she had turned inward, throwing herself down, striving to join Letari in the protection of her womb.

The knife cut deeper, just grazing the protective muscle that Letari had manifested in order to protect the delicate creature inside her.

Fingers prodded at the muscle, testing it and pressing to see if it could be moved, but finally the knife dragged along it, cutting deep, even though the knife did not stay sharp for long.

It was quickly replaced, and the second knife changed route, cutting soft flesh to find the edges of the unusual muscle, attacking them instead.

Both she and Letari tried to hold it in place but, in the end, it snapped free and their little ball of light was exposed. It made a happy little hum at the feeling of their being near, not understanding.

The knife was gone, and then it drove through the thin skin of her womb and that little light snuffed out.

THAT SNAPPED her back to consciousness, letting out a terrible, wailing sound that had men going rigid atop her, the sound one of absolute loss even as her body jerked, rough hands digging and then a weird sucking sound as Drizdan removed the entirety of her womb along with the parts that went with it.

She was bleeding profusely, the puddle under her growing larger and larger by the second.

Working fast now, Drizdan threw the lump of flesh and fluid onto the trolley and pulled her abdomen back together. Something was grabbed from the trolley and warmth spread from little spots that dripped onto her.

Drizdan moved away, grim and determined as he did whatever he needed to ensure that thing was gone. When he finally turned, the men were getting off her, bloodied and pale.

She did not move, her eyes locked on the ceiling, breathing slow and fading. She was willingly giving in to death. She welcomed it. The instant she would be in that world of ghosts she would snap the ribbon and stay there, just another dead thing refusing to ever welcome a new life.

She could feel death reaching out for her, arms outstretched and welcoming her as an old friend, but something spoke, while another voice growled a word. Her head was being lifted and the gag was removed from her mouth, but she no longer paid attention to what was happening to her body. Soft drips of something fell onto her tongue that tasted exquisitely painful. The drips turned to a pour and she swallowed reflexively, her realisation of what it was coming too late.

Death faded from her vision, and she knew she would need another way to reach him.

She blinked, her eye turning to see Drizdan who had a bottle of red liquid in his hand, she could no longer see death but rather the room and the Drow beside her. He had fed her vampire blood to keep her from dying.

"Why?" she whimpered, her voice breaking on the simple word.

"We can't have you ruining the game," he explained with a cruel grin on his face.

She turned her head away from him, feeling her body sewing itself back together, the vision in her missing eye beginning to reform, blurry and indistinct.

Standing, he moved away from her and the trolley was pushed from the room by his foot, crashing into the wall across the hall and then he turned on the two of them.

"Wasn't that fun? Good choice, Epharis, I'd hate to be left wanting."

"What?" Epharis asked, confused as he finally tore his attention from her.

"Well, as payment for my work tonight, I get to have a bit of fun with the pretty Princess for a few days," he said, reaching under her to lift her body from the bloody stone.

DREAD FILLED her and she turned her head to see Epharis. He looked horrified, but there was nothing either of them could do.

"Don't worry, my man, I'm not going to defile my future wife," the Drow crooned, nuzzling his cheek against her hair and laughing when she cringed away from him. "I want her to be good and pure for when I get to have her."

Epharis fought against his bonds. "She'll never submit to you."

"You of all people know what the laws are. A wife cannot refuse her husband's advances. You can't tell me you haven't used that against her," Drizdan leered, his hand sliding up to grip her breast.

Flinching away from him, she did her best to remain silent and still, wishing it would all simply stop.

Epharis did not reply, his face white and rage burning in every pore of his being.

"I still get to keep her, and so long as I don't kill her, Alaric doesn't care what I do."

With that, Drizdan carried her limp form into the cell next door.

Dropping her onto the bed, she looked up at him blankly as he crawled next to her.

"You have no idea how long I've been waiting for this moment," he breathed as he tugged at the remains of her dress and leant closer. His tongue was hot on her breast, tasting her skin and shuddering in delight. "But I will have you soon enough, my beautiful Etani. And when that happens, you will belong to me."

She did not respond, her entire body burning with the knowledge of what had happened to her, what had been taken from her. She could not cry anymore, she only felt horribly empty.

Her lack of response only angered him, and he drove his fist to her cheek, earning a cry of pain that only urged the sadistic man on. He revelled in hitting her, in using the scraps of her dress to choke her until she was close to passing out. When she refused to respond, he dragged her from the bed and kicked her until the sound of her spine snapping alerted him to her state.

Finally, frustrated, she watched in horror as he stood over her. She had never seen a man pleasure himself before, the sight was repulsive to her and yet she was afraid that if she looked away, he would force her to help him.

Rather than risking that, she remained silent and stared him in the face, hating *him* and everything he had ever done. Never before had she felt so strongly about another being, not even Cain. At least with Cain, she knew what she was getting herself into. Drizdan was insane, sadistic, and vicious. He revelled in hurting her and making her suffer. Cain was only doing what he thought was right, but Drizdan did whatever made him happy.

His moans in the quiet cell grew louder and she clenched her eyes shut as he found release, shuddering as his semen landed over her exposed breasts and stomach.

She wanted to vomit, her stomach roiling but nothing came up.

When he was finally done, he scooped up his semen from her skin and smeared the cooling substance against her cheek, making her gag.

"You can run for an eternity, but I will always find you," he whispered. "In this world or Faerie, there is nowhere you can go that I won't hunt you down. You will be mine, there is no point in denying it. It's already arranged and is only a matter of time before you, and your body, belong to me."

His eyes skimmed over her body and he sighed. She recoiled as he reached for her, but he was faster and his fingers curled in her hair, using it as a handle to drag her from the room. She had to bite her tongue to keep from making a sound, her bare feet scraping on the stones as she struggled to keep up with him.

Returning to the other cell, Drizdan threw her from him and she landed hard on the stone floor. He approached her but she tried to scramble back. She tried to twist away but he caught the chain and pulled her closer to the wall, locking her in place.

Both the floor and the wall were covered in blood and bits of gore, making her shudder as the blood stuck to her skin.

"I need to give my report, but I'll be back soon," Drizdan cooed, smirking at Epharis before he swept from the cell.

Leaving them broken and alone.

16

YOU CAN NEVER TRULY ESCAPE A NIGHTMARE

Etani could not bring herself to speak, mortified and humiliated by Drizdan's show, but also incensed at Epharis and his choice to spare her over their child.

"I can't lose you, too," he said after long minutes of silence.

She peered at him as she lay huddled against the wall to make herself as small as possible.

"I can't lose you," he whispered again and dropped his gaze from her furious and hate-filled eyes.

Silence stretched between them until Drizdan returned.

He smiled broadly. "Oh no, trouble in green pastures?"

When no one responded, he shrugged and yanked her away from the wall by her hair. He then positioned her on her knees, her fingers clenched and smoking around the chain to keep from bending her arms back. Kneeling at her side, she bit her lip as she heard something whistling and she screamed at a loud whacking sound, before something long and thin connecting against the backs of her thighs.

Again and again, the switch struck her while she struggled to remain silent. Tears had begun to trickle down her cheeks after the second blow, blood filling her mouth where she had bitten her tongue in an attempt to remain silent.

The sound of the switch was loud in the small room, followed by a sharp smack and her gasps and whimpers of agony. He only stopped when he was covered in sweat and she found him staring down at her with a burning intensity, the front of his trousers bulging with his arousal.

"You're so beautiful when you're crying," he whispered seductively as if unable to take his eyes off her.

Drizdan stood and she recoiled at the sound of his dark laughter.

"See, Epharis? You only have to beat her enough to make her obey. Just like any good pet," he crooned as he cupped her chin.

He forced her head up, but she was unable to meet his eyes. The room was silent for a long moment as Drizdan studied her, his breathing heavy with exertion.

"As much as I'd love to hold you down and fuck you, I'm willing to wait," he said, and she had a feeling that he spoke more to convince himself than anything else.

Without a word, the Drow left the room, but he did not stay gone for long. Seconds later, he returned with a short and narrow knife in his hands.

"Lie down on your back."

She hesitated, glancing towards Epharis. She might be angry at him, but she was terrified of Drizdan.

Her hesitation cost her, though, and the back of the Drow's hand connected with the side of her face, sending her sprawling on the hard, stone floor.

Rolling her jaw to see if it were broken, she heard a faint click in the joint, but she could not focus on that when Drizdan grabbed her legs and dragged her closer to him. He was on his knees, the sight of him looming over her like that, sent a thrill of terror through her, certain he had changed his mind on not defiling her.

He did not, however. Instead, he rolled onto his backside and lifted her right leg onto his thighs. The position was intensely uncomfortable, her hip burning within a few seconds as he forced the joint to twist in a way it was never designed to go.

Clenching her jaw, she refused to make a sound, knowing he was going to do something terrible to her.

The knife slid cleanly over her skin and she jerked back, but with his arm around her thigh, she could barely move. Again, the knife danced over her skin, cutting deep lines into the soft, sensitive flesh.

It only took a minute, but when Drizdan drew back, both his hand and the knife were bloody.

Shoving herself back from him, she glanced down and there was something odd on her inner thigh. It was hard to read through the blood. But when realisation dawned on her she could hardly breathe. He had carved his name into her inner thigh with the knife.

THREE DAYS PASSED in a similar fashion except that his violence grew worse with each passing hour until he seemed to be timing how quickly he could leave her unconscious on the floor. It had become a game to him, revelling in her ability to heal, and when he grew bored, or it became too much for him, he pleasured himself over her.

He was true to his word at least, he never touched her aside from her breasts. She was glad when he said his time was up and he left, waving a cheerful 'I'll be seeing you soon,' over his shoulder.

After the first day, she had stopped trying to fight back, but he was good at angering her enough to try and defend herself. It only ended in him beating her mercilessly and then humiliating her. He was incredibly skilled at what he did, steadily chipping away her confidence and self-worth until she was nothing more than a doll for him to move around as he pleased.

Her submission made him more sadistic and he began to torture her, testing her body's limits. Sometimes he would leave her broken and bleeding, barely clinging to life, and yet, he always seemed extremely careful not to tip her over that edge into the freedom of death.

She dropped her eyes to avoid his scorching gaze. She did not want to talk. All she wished was to hide and be alone.

No, that was not entirely true. She wanted to have Kai and Jaia telling her that she was going to be alright. She needed that comfort from someone who was not another abusive man.

So, she let her mind wander. It was easy for her to track the time as it passed, watching as her finger began to regrow. Her eye had regrown too, but her vision through that eye was incredibly blurry, the barely illuminated room making it burn if she tried to open it.

It was a good three hours before the sound of running footsteps had them both looking up.

Kai burst into the room and then immediately wheeled back out, the scent of blood, degradation and fear hitting him like a wall and blow to the gut all in one. They heard him taking three deep breaths and then one bigger, holding it before he turned and rushed into the room with bulging eyes.

Epharis was sitting with his legs outstretched before him, his head back against the wall though he had not taken his eyes off her in hours. He looked mostly fine, bloodied and dishevelled but—all things considered—relatively okay.

IT WAS her side of the cell that looked like someone had been murdered and it was not far from the truth. For a moment, Kai seemed torn but, eventually, he hurried to Epharis to undo the two simple knots that held him in place as he was the easier fix. The second the Lich was free he was crawling to her, his hands cold and bloodless on her face. She met his gaze with her own neutral one, but the second she was free, she would take care of some things.

Kai yelled in surprise as she threw herself on the Lich, her fingers on his throat, digging in and he struggled to get her off him. She screamed her fury, doing her utmost to rip his lying throat out.

She managed to rip a significant amount of skin before Kai dragged her off him, his arms wrapped around her middle and pulling her back in a panic.

"This is your fault!" she screamed, landing a hard kick to his ribcage before she was dragged out of range.

Fighting like a captured feral, she turned on Kai and sank her teeth into the base of his throat, jerking back to tear away the flesh. Kai screamed in pain, but he refused to let her go, not even when she bit him again.

Epharis moved to help, her arms trapped behind her back and she thrashed against them. Leaving him with no other option, Kai slammed her to the ground on her front, her arms trapped behind her back.

Realising with sudden horror what he had done, his eyes dropped to her middle and all colour vanished from his face.

There was no more swelling, no life, only a large and angry red scar running just above her pubic bones.

"What happened?" he gasped, turning horrified eyes to the blood and gore on the floor and wall in a spray. "Drizdan?" he demanded but neither of them was talking. All Etani did was to glare at Epharis with murderous intent. "Basement?" Kai finally asked and Epharis nodded, without looking away from her.

Kai dragged her from the floor, taking the gold chain and reluctantly using it to bind her. He then removed his long coat and wrapped it tightly around her before he pulled her from the room and up the stairs that led to the rest of the castle.

Up until the wall came between them, she did not stop staring at Epharis. When she finally looked forward, her eyes burning with a blinding rage that she gave into willingly. She was dreading the anguish hiding behind the rage and decided to cling to that fury like a protective shield.

Kai rushed her through the castle halls, heading for the rooms he shared with Jaia. But Jaia wasn't present. Down yet another flight of stairs, Jaia was locked safely away in the room with Versalis sitting on the bed on the other side.

The sight was so reminiscent of the first time she had come there that she paused and shook her head.

"Let me go, Kai, I'm not going to run."

Versalis looked up at the sound of her defeated voice and, taking stock of the sight before him, he slammed against the glass with eyes wide in horror. A moment later, her scent hit him, and he gagged, his eyes sliding shut in disgust.

Kai released her and she crossed the room to Jaia, her eyes on his. He was smiling slyly at her, feral and knowing what had happened to her. That knowing smile promised to finish what the other man had started if she went in there with him.

Instead, she opened the hatch and thrust her arm inside, the vampire too eager to feed his addiction to care. He bit her hard, digging and clawing at her arm as he fed and she shuddered, her eyes shut, focusing on keeping calm and not crying.

When Jaia released her, she dropped onto her side against the glass, her bleeding arm limp in her lap.

"Who gave him the blood?" she asked when the feral growling from Jaia had stopped and his breathing became regular once more.

"Who?" Jaia asked from the other side of the glass, her position making it hard for him to see her. "What's happened? What's that smell?"

Kai wanted to speak but the horror of it all glued his mouth shut and he could only watch helplessly as she buried her face in her hands and started to cry.

Jerking on the door that was still locked, Jaia was furious as he tried to get out and eventually demanded Kai release him. Once out, Jaia stalked from the cage and towards her, stopping a good three feet back as he realised what it was. He all but lunged for her, clutching her trembling body against him.

"What happened?" he snarled at Kai, turning on his brother as his arms went around her.

Turning her face into his chest, she tried to block it all out.

"There was so much blood," Kai said in a barely audible whisper. "So much blood... The Drow. He cut her open. The baby is gone....

then he…" he could not finish, suddenly sitting down on the bench and rested his head in his hands. "Mother, how could anyone do that?" he asked the floor.

Jaia had gone still at her side, his eyes on his brother. "What did he do to her?"

"I think… I think he raped her, Jaia. He cut out the baby and after he had raped her, he beat her and raped her again."

Kai's voice sounded dead and Jaia's grip on her was suddenly too tight, painfully tight.

She wanted to tell them the truth, but to admit she had been abused in any way only had her trembling harder. She could only cling to Jaia, desperate for his comfort and the security the twins could provide her.

Versalis had gone silent, a statue in his cell at the words he had already known were coming.

Pulling her up with him, Jaia led her upstairs, not uttering a word as he took her into the bathroom. Stripping the jacket off her and throwing it to the floor, he turned on the water and waited. When he thrust her under the stream, she jumped at the unexpected fall of water.

They had a water fountain like the ones in Weorene, the water wonderfully hot.

He stalked from the room only for a moment, leaving her staring up at the shower of water but when he returned, her eyes found him again, blank and staring.

He worked briskly and without feeling, ordering her to stand still while he lathered her body before directing her to rinse off. They repeated the process twice more, also scrubbing her hair clean of the blood and fluids she did not want to think about. He studied her naked, bruised, and broken body, ensuring he had cleaned her as much as he could and then he sighed.

"Etani I need you to trust me, okay?"

She could only nod and he dropped to his knees before her in the shower. She remained still as he withdrew something from his soaked pants and inserted it into her. She did not know what it was, some smooth metal device. The thought of him inserting something into her body left her trembling in fear, frozen and unable to think.

What if Jaia wanted to finish what Drizdan had started? Would he abuse her? Could she trust anyone or was she just a stupid, naive girl to think that anyone cared about her?

Frozen in her panic, she stared ahead as Jaia worked. His low voice soothed her, but she did not hear a single word he said. Something clicked and she screamed as small spikes snapped out of the thing and he pulled violently on the device.

She dropped like a stone, blood turning the water crimson, but the vampire was already gone, along with whatever device he had used on her.

Almost hyperventilating on the stall floor, she tried to understand what he had done. It felt like he had shredded her internally, the thought reminding her so much of the agony of Drizdan cutting out her womb. Tears welled in her eyes, and she looked up as Kai burst into the room at her scream.

"Jaia?" he cried, seeing the blood and her on the ground.

"Kai, stay back."

HER PANTING GREW HEAVIER and she found herself entirely unable to control herself as everything began to boil up inside her. All the rage and terror, the loss and the anguish. It flooded her body and she clenched her eyes shut, trying her best to control her emotions.

The two vampires moved into the corner, but she no longer cared. The scream burst out of her chest of its own accord, her body leaning over her empty stomach as water drummed down on her.

Her scream lasted longer than it had any right to, especially when she had not taken in any extra breath.

The mirror exploded along with several windows in the cabinets and something downstairs. She thought it had happened upstairs too, but she could not be sure.

The scream faded into a keening wail and she fell on the floor of the stall, curling into a ball and cried so hard that shudders raked her body.

Arms soon found her, hard and warm and the scent of Jaia filled her nose. He was in the stall with her, soaked to the skin but unwilling to let her go. He cradled her against his chest, his shoes squeaking while he settled himself with her between his legs.

She leant against him as racking sobs ripped her heart and soul into shreds until she was left with nothing. At some point, Kai had joined them, his arms connecting with those already around her and no one thought to turn off the fountain of water that failed to wash away her sorrow.

They stayed there, rocking gently for over an hour, Versalis now free and standing guard outside the door. His ears had bled, but he did not seem to care.

When the water finally went cold, Kai bundled her up in his arms and carried her from the room while Jaia collected things she would need. Setting her down in a room that smelt strongly of Jaia, the twins made quick work of drying her off and wrapping her in a large and oddly fluffy, powder blue dressing gown. Only the garment's sight made her laugh but, almost instantly, the humour turned into sobbing once again as she was pulled onto the bed.

Stripping and changing into dry pants, Jaia climbed into the bed with her, pulling the blankets over them both. She immediately moved to him, her head on his bare chest and his warmth enough to soothe her into an uneasy, exhausting sleep.

SHE WOKE GROGGILY SOMETIME LATER, the spot beside her empty, but she found Versalis sitting across the room, watching her with an angry look on his face. When he noticed she was awake, he stood and moved to her, his hand gentle on her hair and she bumped her forehead against his stomach.

His touch was gentle around her shoulders, his fingers combing through her now dry hair and he murmured in a language she did not recognise.

Finally, he tilted her head back with two fingers and leant down, placing a soft kiss against her forehead.

A zing of energy went through her, but it did little to help her.

"Where are the twins?" she asked, staring down at his feet when he had moved her head back against his stomach.

"They are talking in the sitting room. They wanted to let you rest," he explained in that low, hypnotic voice that barely contained his fury.

Making a soft sound, she wriggled out of bed in that ridiculous blue dressing down, padding across the room and out into the living room.

"He's not talking at all," Kai said, frowning.

"He knows exactly what he is doing, the whole thing stinks of him even if he was not there," Jaia retorted.

At the sound of her scuffing feet, Kai looked up and immediately stood but her eyes went to Jaia, and as soon as he was up too, she was in his arms. She did not say anything, only keeping her body as close to his as possible, soaking up the warmth of him like a leech.

"I'll go see if I can find her something to eat," Versalis said and left the room quickly.

Jaia stroked her hair and looked over her head at his brother, finally leaning down and kissing her temple.

"How are you feeling at the moment?" he asked, lifting her chin to look up into his eyes and frowning at what he saw there.

She could only shake her head and sit down, shamelessly stealing the warm spot he had just vacated.

He turned to see that she had sat directly behind him and narrowed his eyes in a show of challenge, but she just looked back at him, her eyebrows lifting in a silent dare.

Pouting, he skulked away to fetch her a mug of water.

"What were we talking about?"

A little spark of enjoyment started in her at their game, and, accepting the water gratefully, she sipped the cool liquid. She was glad for any excuse to think of anything aside from last week.

She watched the two exchange a glance and she knew what it meant.

"He told us it was Alaric," she stated simply, watching the look of shock on their faces.

Letting out a soft sigh, she told them the story of the walk in the garden, Jaia's face going dark at the implications.

"Is there anything we can do about this?" he asked Kai and his brother frowned, trying to think.

"He's the King."

"I'm going to kill him," Etani said bluntly.

The silence was deafening, so much so that they clearly heard footsteps a floor above them.

"You can't kill him," Kai said in a small voice.

"He wouldn't be my first King," she retorted.

They both looked at her and she arched an eyebrow.

"What? I kill people for fun and eat people to live, sometimes they happen to be the same person. How is this a surprise to either of you?"

17

FEAR AND DISTRACTIONS

"I just assumed you started killing for hire once you got here," Kai said, awestruck.

"I'm over nine hundred years old, Kai, what do you think I did to pass the time? Your world isn't all that interesting, killing people holds back boredom."

The saddest part was that she was telling the absolute truth. Her track record could show that she had killed solely for the purpose of giving herself something to do. No one who knew her ever claimed she was a good person. At least she tried to kill only bad people when she was bored. But when she was hungry, everyone was fair game.

Jaia shook his head to clear it. "Exactly how many people have you killed?"

"Recreationally, professionally, or for food?" she asked, somewhat wary of the turn the conversation had taken.

"All!" Kai barked and she looked between the two.

"A lot."

"How many is a lot, Etani?" Jaia asked, his expression turning wary as well.

"I did not keep track," she lied. She had kept track of them all. Every, single one.

"You're lying," Kai said, and she slumped back in her chair, crossing her arms.

"Why are you picking on me?"

"We'll stop when you tell us," Jaia quipped and she glared at him.

Letting out a low breath, she scowled. "Fine. I've killed one human roughly once a month for the past nine hundred-odd years for food. That's what? Ten and a half thousand? Again, boredom accounts for about half of that, and then there are around fifteen hundred professional killings." Seeing their expressions, she got defensive. "Nine hundred years is a long time to be stalking *your* world, you know. It's not like I could steal food from Ceress and bring it here with me."

"Ceress has food you can eat?" Jaia said suddenly and she suspected he was trying not to focus on her significant undercounting of her actual kill count.

"Of course, pulling humans from this world into ours would be too obvious when it came to feeding so many people. I suspect Epharis came up with a food source like the fruits that grow there. It's not that different really when souls are simply a shred of Faerie given sentience." She looked up from examining her toes to see them both gawking at her. "What?"

"That's not what souls are," Kai said, sounding horrified.

"Of course they are." She was officially confused by their troubled expression. "You hadn't figured that out? And here I was thinking you two were some of the smartest men in both worlds."

The silence stretched on and she was back to wiggling her toes, with the sole purpose of keeping her mind off her memories.

"No! That's not what souls are," Kai cried as she stood up.

He was angry now and she shrank back, sudden panic filling her at the sight of his anger.

"Why are you so upset? What did you think souls were except magic?"

He clenched his fists and she tensed, ready to move and move she did. He had only meant to brush his hair back, but she had already leapt over the back of the couch and flattened herself against the wall as far away from him as possible, her heart racing.

Kai froze at her retreat and defensive posture, connecting the dots. "Oh, Etani, I'm sorry, I did not mean to frighten you."

She could not really hear him, her heart was pounding in her ears and her chest felt tight.

Sinking to sit on her heels, she stared down at the floor as she tried to breathe but it was getting harder by the second and her mind was racing, flicking from thought to thought and then delving viciously into terrors of Kai's face on Drizdan's body as he beat her. She could still recall his sadistic joy as he taunted her and Epharis over what he had done to their child.

Crossing her arms on top of her knees, she buried her face in them and focused on trying to breathe, her lungs dreadfully insufficient to get in enough air, making her gasps incredibly loud in the silent room.

A HAND TOUCHED her shoulder and she jerked away so violently she nearly fell, eyes wild as she found Jaia standing beside her with his hand outstretched.

"Shh, it's okay," he crooned, and she immediately latched onto the sound of his voice in a desperate plea for something—anything—to focus on.

"Talk…" she gasped, and he dropped onto his backside beside her.

She did not listen to what he said so much as the sound of his voice, slow and even with a gentleness one used around frightened animals. It was working on her, the minutes ticking by as he constantly talked.

When the door opened, Kai flung out his hand to Versalis who immediately went still, sensing the tension in the room and finding them in the corner, the loud sound of her breathing as it finally started to calm.

"That's not how you fix this," Versalis said, crossing the room and picking down a trinket from the shelf.

He approached slowly, offering it to her and when she took it, he backed away again.

The thing shimmered in her hands as she spun it, her attention focusing on the way the candlelight shone from its polished surface. She found a tiny seam in the wood and opened it slowly, a waft of spice reaching her nose. Lifting it, she took a deep breath of the spicy scent and her shoulders eased.

"What was that?" Kai asked, looking terrified.

"Haven't you ever seen the men after war? They look exactly like that. You give them something to play with and it usually helps."

She opened and closed the little hinge, admiring the craftsmanship on the wood that it blended everything together perfectly.

Looking up from the little circular box, she found Versalis and then Kai, her smile slightly nervous and apologetic. "I'm sorry Kai, I did not mean to do that."

Jaia wrapped his arms around her and she dropped to her hip, leaning against him even as he pulled her to him.

"I should have realised, I did not mean to get angry," Kai approached her cautiously, but she extended her empty hand to him and he took it, pressing her fingers against his lips.

"You two need to keep calm for a while, no getting anxious or yelling. It will take time," Versalis said, coming back now that it was safe to do so, sitting on the floor in front of her.

Kai sat on her other side and she felt incredibly safe with them on every side and the wall at her back.

She offered Kai the little circular box, but he shook his head. "Keep it, you might need it again."

Smiling, she slipped it into her pocket and reached out, drawing Versalis closer and kissing his cheek, not entirely sure of him, but grateful none the less.

Giving a little pleased sound, he pulled a flask from his pocket and handed it over. She opened the cap and peeked inside, and the smell of the strange elixir Epharis had made hit her nose. She made a happy sound in her throat and lifted it to her lips, drinking about half of it in one go before she leaned against Jaia once more, content in their little group.

"How long do you think it will be before Epharis comes looking?" Kai asked and when she went stiff, he looked panicked.

She did not want to talk about it and so she shook her head. "I don't want to see him right now."

Not until she was strong enough to rip his lying head off his body and then gleefully follow him into death.

"We'll make sure he stays out," Versalis reassured her, and she noticed he had lumped himself in with them, making the four of them one unit.

She rather liked that. "Careful Versalis, you don't want to associate with the crazies. You're the most normal one in our midst."

Jaia snorted, tightening his arms around her.

"I am normal," Kai protested, looking put out but then he thought about it. "Mostly," he corrected.

She laughed with the others, at least, up until the guilt hit her and she suddenly cut off. She could feel their concern, but she could not bring herself to talk about it. Not yet.

A WEEK PASSED with her staying down there with at least one of the three vampires, Kai and Jaia not always able to get out of their duties.

She was fine so long as she was not left alone and they made sure that was the case, even when she bathed.

Versalis was the most competent of the group when it came to handling her. His experience in active warfare made him resort to all sorts of tricks on how she could get herself out of a panicked state or able to keep herself at present. He was even good with her nightmares, calming her down and getting her back to sleep quickly. Kai was the worst, blaming himself for not being able to find her, his fears for his brother overlaying any concerns he had for her and the missing Prince.

She did not blame him, he was loyal and sweet, but not particularly good at looking after a damaged—and sometimes— violent Fae.

She had been having an episode, screaming at Versalis not to touch her after he had tried to help her up from the couch when a knock sounded at the door.

Instantly she fell silent, barely breathing. She and Versalis were alone and while he was a powerful vampire, she did not know the full extent of his powers.

"Open the door," Alaric ordered, and she sprang to her feet, eyes blazing that he would dare.

He would dare!

Stalking towards the door, she had made it halfway there before Versalis caught her around the waist and spun her, his lips hot against her ear.

"Don't make a sound, it could be a trap."

That instilled terror into her, and she immediately headed to Jaia's room, hiding behind the half-closed door.

Versalis opened the door and Alaric shoved his way in, glaring around the room.

"Where is she?" he snarled.

"Where is who, your majesty?"

Convincing herself that he could hear her breathing, she held her breath and listened.

"Princess Etani"

"I haven't seen her in a while," Versalis lied smoothly. She admired his ability to lie like that in the face of Alaric's rage.

"I heard a woman's voice."

"That was me acting," Versalis did not miss a beat and she almost laughed.

"Is that right?" Alaric sounded doubtful.

She did not think Alaric believed him, but she knew he did not wish to start anything with the vampires. A war with them would be catastrophic, considering the possibility of the other war that was looming.

"If you happen to run into her, please tell her I need to see her," Alaric said, his tone angry.

"Certainly, your majesty," Versalis said and bowed the King out.

Only once she was sure he was gone did she come back out,

hugging the startled vampire. Versalis hugged her back and they settled in to read.

EPHARIS ARRIVED the next day and he was also politely informed she was not there, but that time by Jaia who was not quite as diplomatic.

"My wife belongs by my side, Vampire," Epharis snapped when Jaia told him for the third time she was not in there.

"Then I suggest you go find her," Jaia hissed back, refusing to give in.

"Tell her and make sure she understands that I want her back with me."

When he left, she remained in the room, toying with the box and working hard to get her thoughts in order again.

ANOTHER WEEK PASSED and still she hid out, worrying that she was inconveniencing them, but they were adamant that she ought to stay for the rest of eternity if that was what it took. But she felt she was a strain on them.

Versalis seemed to feel the same way, as he was spending more and more time out of the suite.

Still, they were careful to never leave her alone if they could help it.

She found she was starting to get a little desperate for freedom though, mentioning to the twins how much she longed to see the sky. They were a little nervous at first but decided they would all go up around midnight. The three of them could protect her and protect others from her if the need arose.

When midnight rolled around, everyone was feeling giddy with the excitement of going out on a mission, though she was not sure if it was their feeding off her excitement or her feeding off theirs. Regard-less, she was fidgeting in her seat in the last hours and when Jaia returned, holding clothes and a cloak for her to wear then, she had almost raced to the door.

Hurrying into the bedroom, she changed into a simple pair of black pants and a dark grey tunic. The cloak had a large hood and it hid her face well, trailing down to brush the ground and her bare feet.

Stepping out, she approached Jaia and smiled, watching his tense face as he fixed her cloak to better hide her from view. His tension was making her nervous and she caught his hand. All the time they spent together along with their blood connection meant that she did not need to ask the question. He put on a smile and touched her cheek, drawing her in to kiss her forehead gently.

Handing her over to Kai, she gripped his hand in both of hers and Versalis hovered just behind her, almost looming over her, but it was comforting rather than annoying.

Jaia looked at the three of them tensely before he nodded and motioned for them to follow.

Creeping up the stairs, they paused at the top, waiting for Jaia to give the all-clear from the hall before venturing into the main castle.

Etani quickly realised why Jaia was tense. Security around their little underground room had been increased significantly and no less than nine guards were slumped against the wall or lying on the ground. Their breathing told her they were still alive, only unconscious or sleeping.

They passed almost silently down the hall, the vampires always moving like a breath and her training ensured that her bare feet did not make a sound on the marble.

Their pace was slow and careful, Jaia was scouting ahead to ensure their protection until, finally, he was leading them into a small room. There was no door to the outside, but the window was open and big enough for them all to get through easily. The smell of the outside had her itching and her nervousness made Jaia smile. Going first, he jumped through the window and quickly confirmed that the garden was empty before turning to help her out.

Etani stepped up into the window and grinned when he lifted her from the waist and eased her down onto the grass, taking the opportunity to kiss her cheek before letting her go to make way for the others.

As soon as she was free, her head turned upwards and the glittering night sky was magical.

Sitting cross-legged onto the grass, she stared up and simply breathed in the air. She could feel the three vampires moving around her, pacing and alert to their surroundings, ensuring their privacy, but they failed to look up.

A loud thump sounded behind them and Etani froze at that feeling of power looming over her.

All three vampires followed the sound, ready to rip whoever it was apart.

"Epharis," Etani said simply, not interested in witnessing his rage flowing off him in waves.

"Etani," his voice was a low growl, furious at her continued ability to evade him whenever she wanted.

She did not take her eyes off the sky, listening to the tense breathing of the men around her.

"Where have you been?" he demanded when the silence had stretched on too long.

She had been ignoring him, drawing patterns in the stars.

"Recovering," she said simply and frowned when he moved around her, coming to stand in front of her so that his face blocked out the sky.

"MOVE," she said, her tone not angry or tense, but there was a definite threat in the single word.

His eyes narrowed, forcing her to look at him and she hated it. She had come out for the sky, not him.

"I wouldn't do that if I were you," Jaia said calmly even as Epharis had reached for her, the Lich going still.

Her eyes had followed the movement of his hand with clinical detachment as it stopped only a foot from her shoulder.

"Why not?"

She followed his arm up to his face and her calm demeanour met with his glare.

"Well, it's your arm," Jaia quipped and Epharis closed the distance to her.

He did not get the chance to touch her. She got there first.

In one move, she rose to her feet, her right hand landed on his wrist and her left just above his elbow. Lifting her left foot, she planted it against his ribs just below his shoulder and heaved.

She neither knew nor cared where that strength was coming from, only that in a breath she was holding his arm.

The Lich had not made a sound, blinking first at the arm and then his shoulder that was oozing blood.

He seemed relatively calm at the loss, right up until she slid her left hand down to her right at the wrist, swinging the arm back like a bat and stepping into the swing, she almost took his head off, the tense muscle making a satisfying thud and blood spraying.

The Lich flew back several feet, crashing down on his feet, crouched and sliding with teeth bared.

She watched him dispassionately, lifting the arm against her shoulder, ready for the second swing.

The sight was so utterly absurd, yet it was completely terrible at the same time.

In her mind, he had it coming. All he had to do was say her name. All he had to do was let her die with their child and that thought tore at her. It burned inside her, digging itself into her heart and branding her soul.

Approaching him, she felt her friends coming up behind her to see what she was going to do.

She had not told them what Epharis had done, she had not been ready and their confusion at her rage at the Lich was what stopped them from detaining her.

Walking forward, the Lich watched her and when she drew back the arm, he made no effort to stop her.

The arm and her body seemed to blur as she swung, the weapon slamming into his chest and sending him flying once more. She followed, the anger that had formed in the dungeon bubbling up inside her and the knowledge that as soon as she killed him, she would die, was keeping her from losing her mind.

The Lich landed hard, but he was on his feet in the next instant, watching her approach, her face devoid of any emotion.

Jaia moved to stop her, but it was Kai who accomplished that. The exchange between them was silent behind her. Kai had seen that room and her response to the Lich. She needed to do that.

Dropping the arm, she came upon the Lich and between steps, she drove her foot up under his chin.

His body snapped back, landing hard on the ground and he did not bother to get up that time.

Stepping over him, she dropped down onto his chest, her face grim and her hands went around his throat, squeezing.

He looked up at her, not making a single effort to defend himself and she resented that.

Squeezing, she watched as his face began to turn purple, smiling at the joy the sight gave her.

The feeling it gave her was odd, something like her body squeezing even as she tightened her grip, the urge to let go growing stronger but she refused, fighting it with every ounce of strength inside her.

18

CURSES, HUSBANDS, AND A SCORNED KING

Something hit her like a bull, and she was thrown off him. Steel arms closed around her as they rolled to the ground. Etani knew exactly who it was, Jaia's scent was as familiar to her as her own but she still turned on him, indignant that he would dare interfere.

Baring her teeth, she shoved him off her, but he was on his feet in an instant. Pushing herself up, she glared at the sight of him between her and the Lich. When his arms stretched towards her to appease her, she growled and started to plot how to get past him.

She did not care that there was fear in his eyes, and she realised where the urge to stop was coming from. The deal she had made with him meant she could not be there for him if she were dead and the deal was unbreakable.

"You'll die if you kill him," he growled, angry and scared.

"I know."

His eyes widened at the realisation of her intent. She was planning to use the curse against the Lich and free herself from suffering.

"No, no you can't," Kai gasped from across the garden. He had not moved but she could see his panic.

Epharis was staring at her, his face confused and then he closed his eyes when it hit him.

Making her move, she stepped forward and struck out with her foot; the vampire not expecting her to attack and he was sent flying to the ground at some distance.

With her next step, she pushed off at full speed for the Lich. By the time she reached him, his arms extended for her, the removed one having regrown in the brief time they had frozen.

She met him, her fingers finding the hair at the back of his head and his cheek, his head turning up to meet the kiss. One arm curled around her back, the other trapped between them, his fingers touching her chest over her heart.

Pain ripped through her, her delving into him halted as her heart skipped a beat. The vampires were almost on them when the air around them exploded and everyone was thrown back several feet.

Landing hard on the ground, she gasped and clutched at her chest as it tried to remember how to beat again. She wondered if that was how it felt to have a heart attack.

The vampires seemed to be stunned, the Lich was standing and approaching her with something unfathomable looming in his eyes. As the vampires got back on their feet, running for them, the Lich touched the point of his finger against her chest, the long nail piercing her skin and as he drew back, a thin line of red drew back with him, connecting her chest to his finger.

The line snapped and suddenly the pain in her chest was gone, as her heart stopped for a whole two beats before starting again.

The line of red dissipated slowly into mist and his face was grim.

"I cannot allow you to kill yourself. Kill *me* if you wish, but you will not die. Even with my dying breath, I'll do everything in my power to ensure you live. This world cannot exist without you. You are free from my curse," he said slowly, his eyes never straying from her. "I love you, now and forever."

His voice lingered in the air between them and then he was gone, vanishing in a blink.

It took her a second to realise what he had done, and then another for her to realise why, and she screamed her anger and misery. He had removed the curse, twice denying her the death she had craved because the Lich had fallen in love.

The vampires were on her, two holding her down and the third covering her mouth but she did not care. How could he be so cruel?

She remained still under them, even as they searched the grounds for the Lich or anyone else who might be a threat, but they were alone.

"What do we do now?" Kai asked, terrified at how close they had come to disaster.

None of them had any idea the thought would ever cross her mind, none of them knew how deeply the damage had cut, except perhaps Versalis who was leaning down, his hand over her mouth and his forehead against hers. He wiped away her tears and he crooned softly to her.

But she was not listening.

Inside, she was raging, Letari shrinking back as her twin screamed and did her best to tear herself apart. It did not work and that only made her angrier.

Any attempt to break something permanent was met with resistance from the deal, any desire to die on her own was impossible. The deal would not allow her to actively kill herself. Killing Epharis had been the compromise, it was through his actions that her death would then come and now it was gone, he had stolen her ability to circumvent the system.

The Lich knew about the deal, but she did not feel he had cared about that when he freed her. No, he had done it because her death would be agony to him.

She snapped back to herself as they lifted her from the ground, their return to the castle quick and quiet and they made even quicker work of stuffing her into the cell when they got back, ensuring there was no escape for her.

She did not fight them, remaining still and quiet until they left. She knew they would be planning their next step, trying to figure everything out but without the information she had, they would not get any conclusions.

THEY LEFT her for two days and she spent her time thinking. Was there anything she could do? Nothing intentional, it had to be another's fault, but that was difficult. It was hard for any creature to kill willingly, especially when it came to killing a creature like her. She was stronger than many.

Jaia moved and she looked up, realising he had been watching her though she had no idea for how long before he finally made her aware of his presence.

He approached the door and her eyes followed him. His every step was cautious as though moving too fast would trigger an undesirable reaction. He slipped inside the room and headed for her, still treading carefully as though she were a deer who would take flight at any instant.

Finally, he stopped at the foot of the bed and he looked hopeful. She did not speak, simply held out her arm to him and even though he looked distressed at her silence, he accepted her wrist and bit as gently as he was able. He did not linger longer than necessary, biting down on his tongue to smear blood over the bite to heal it faster. Even after he was finished, he did not let go of her hand and instead, he pressed her palm against his cheek.

"Tell me what happened," he said gently, his lips placing a tender kiss against her palm.

She watched him silently for several minutes, just listening to his slow breathing, his fingers tracing small spirals on her arm.

Etani took a slow, fortifying breath. "I don't know how we got there. Last I remember, we were walking in the garden when something hit me in the head. I can't recall really. When I came to, we were in that cell about three to four hours after the garden ambush. I tried to wake up Epharis, but he would not budge. I assume they hit him harder because he took longer to regain consciousness, but I don't know for sure. We tried to get out, but the chain had been knotted and I could only just reach him. Several hours later, Drizdan came in and told us that we were going to play a name called *Choice*."

Her tone was flat, level and calm until she uttered the name of Drizdan and his deranged game. Jaia slid his arm around her shoulders and drew her closer, listening silently.

"He said he would offer Epharis two choices, and whatever Epharis chose, would be lost. My finger or my tongue, Epharis chose my finger—" she paused to stare at the finger in question, noting that the dark tattoo had come back with her finger.

"My eye or my foot. He chose my eye and he cut it out. He said he did not like the green flecks and so he took it—" her voice broke and the eye in question slid shut.

"The last choice was me or the baby. Epharis chose the baby and Drizdan cut out my womb. I wanted it to be me, I wanted to die with my baby." She sobbed at the mention of her precious unborn baby, her body trembling against the vampire.

"After that... he told us he had been granted permission to keep me for a few days. He said I would be his soon and that he didn't mind waiting." Everything in her had gone cold as she recalled the fear and agony. "He tried to do that to me... When they took me to the Under Dark, but there was a horn and he stopped. He promised to finish, but then when he had the chance, he said he would wait," she whispered that last and her eyes finally opened.

"He gets off on abusing women. He would beat me repeatedly, and then when he got too worked up, he would pleasure himself. Over and over again. I don't know... I don't know if he did anything while I was unconscious, he would beat me so badly... I don't know Jaia... Then he left and said his time with me was up but that he would see me again soon. It was a while later that Kai found us and set us free."

Finally finished with her story, she stared into nothing and tears fell freely down her cheeks.

"What did you do in the fountain?" she asked, realising he had not taken a breath in a good three minutes.

"I had to make sure you didn't... Not to him. Not another one," his voice was strained, and she frowned, realising that he had destroyed her internally so that she would not fall pregnant to the Drow and she nodded her understanding. She did not know if the Drow had gone that far, but she was glad for Jaia's actions, just in case.

Finally turning to him, she found him staring at her with eyes that glowed a soft red in his anger.

"I'll kill that Drow," he growled, and she gave a faint hint of a smile. "Not before *I* do."

He pulled her hard against his chest and she stayed there, safe in his arms.

SEVERAL HOURS later he decided to let her out, taking her hand and leading her from the cell and upstairs where she could bathe in the fountain. She knew he would be relaying her story to the others, but she did not care, so long as she did not have to tell it again.

Her thoughts were confirmed when she walked from the bathroom in the fluffy blue robe and found them looking at her with various degrees of horror on their faces.

"What?" she said defensively, glancing behind her and then down at herself, first making sure that there was not something following her and that she was covered.

All seemed well and her body was fully covered. When she turned to them again, they had all carefully schooled their expressions to neutrality. Her cheeks flushed and she looked away from them. It was not hard to imagine what had transpired between them, but she did not want to see their pity or their fury.

She wanted to forget.

Approaching slowly, Versalis was the first to reach for her and she took his hand gladly, settling herself at his side rather than next to Jaia. She knew Jaia cared for her, but Versalis understood her better right then and she needed that.

It was the next evening when a thought came to her. She had been obsessing over the sight of the night sky and that longing to see it again was gnawing on her. But there was something she needed more. The plan she had come up with was insane, but it was the memory of her precious Nayishma that set her actions in motion.

On the plus side, at least for her, she knew her plan would make life difficult for those in power. That, along with her own need to do something good for herself, set her off after everyone in the basement had fallen asleep. Smiling at the sight of Jaia, Kai, and Versalis all crowding Jaia's bed, she crept silently from the room.

Silently, she weaved her way through the palace with her head hidden under a stolen hat from Kai. That, coupled with the long cloak from the night before, somewhat guaranteed her secrecy. At that hour, she looked like just another person travelling out into the city.

Pausing only once for a helpful guard to confirm her destination, she set off in the direction of the doors as though she were leaving.

However, she was not heading out of the city. Leaving the palace, she made a sharp turn and walked quickly through the gardens, glancing back to ensure she was not being followed. She could not hear anyone, but she had to be sure, especially with what she was about to do.

The large building was set in behind the castle, squished between its rear and outer wall, surrounding the castle grounds. It looked enormous, at least two storeys, with flat stone walls and an unadorned, angled roof.

The entrance to the building was a simple set of large wooden gates, a massive beam holding them closed in case anyone inside managed to get free. It was the royal stables, but not like any normal stable.

It was where Alaric was keeping his favourite pet monsters. Those he wanted to use later on. Where he was keeping those Nayishma's father had given him.

The thought of Yish made her stomach ache, but she focused on those creatures she had seen, the need to set them free growing stronger as she approached the building.

Pausing beside the door, she considered the size of the beam and tested its weight. It was heavy, but she felt she could lift it. After all, it was designed to keep people in, not keep *her* out.

Deciding to be smart, she headed to the left and she started wiggling and pulling on the heavy beam, inching it along. Finally, there was a groan and a loud thud, and the end of the plank was yanked free of her hands and the far end hit the ground.

Smiling to herself, she headed for the other end and lifted it just enough to drag the door open, dropping the plank back onto the ground once the opening was wide enough for a large creature to escape.

Heading for the other door, she tugged it open too and took in a deep breath.

Yes, she was in the right place. The smell of all that magic was tickling her nose. She was doing the right thing.

She was doing something her sisters and Yish would be proud of.

19

THE GREAT ESCAPE

Slipping into the stable, she paused as she stared around at the sheer mass of beings hidden in there. Not only the unicorn, dragon and chimera she had seen that day months before, but others, even an enormous tank with a siren who was looking back at her curiously.

Slowly making her way down the narrow row, she stared around in horrified fascination at the mass of figures, all of them that noticed her watched her every move. Pulling off the hat, she set it down on a post and bit her lip, already knowing which creature needed her the most.

It was the unicorn she headed for first, looking so sweet and perfect, not a hair out of place.

"I'll get you out," she whispered to the beast as she approached the pen.

It looked back at her with what could only be described as a sceptical expression and that brought a smile to her face. She grimaced at the gate, noting the iron bolt on the door. Glancing around, she rushed to grab a nearby blanket and was horrified to see that a saddle had been set out. Surely no one intended to try and tame a unicorn, would they?

The idea repulsed her, and she pulled the blanket from the railing and headed back to the unicorn's pen.

Wrapping the end of the blanket around the bolt, she wiggled it free as quietly as she could, the bolt giving a soft thud as it slipped free of the bracket. The unicorn stirred, moving closer as she swung the gate open.

"Not yet, let me get that bridle off," she gasped, holding her hands up as she saw the beast about to bolt for the open doors at the end of the stable.

It was trembling as she moved forward for it, matching her hands as she reached for it and she whimpered as her fingers touched the feather-soft fur on its muzzle.

The unicorn's eyes slid shut as it nuzzled its face into her palms and she revelled in it, a flood of warmth and love filling her that pushed the darkness in her soul down and left her tingling. Moving around quickly, she pulled the catch of the bridle free and gently lifted it away, hushing the beautiful creature softly as she soothed the small rub marks.

"You'll be okay," she whispered, almost falling over when the unicorn turned and nuzzled her with enough force to send her stumbling.

Something gold caught her eye and she noticed that its back hoof was tied as well. Crouching down, she undid the simple knot that held the golden rope in place. Once back to her feet, the unicorn turned to her and she stared up at the incredible radiance of the creature. Without the shackles, it seemed to glow from within, throwing rainbows of light in all directions.

Reaching for it, she held the muzzle gently before she bent down and pressed a tender kiss against the silken nose. "Go, precious. Go and be free of this place."

The unicorn nuzzled her again once and then turned, heading silently for the doors.

Now, she had the undivided attention of many of the other creatures and she squinted as she considered who she should free next.

The fairies and pixies were the easiest and she hurried for them, unscrewing the lids of their jars and allowing them to flutter up, chittering and buzzing around her as she released them all and then moved for the imps. In turn, they bowed to her and vanished into a scattering of leaves and she was glad they had escaped.

"Go, you're not safe here," she hissed at the pixies as they zoomed around her.

They were reluctant to leave, but, right then, she did not have the time to deal with or even talk to them.

THE CHIMERA WAS something of a concern for her, but she still headed for it and looked up into the magnificent face of the eagle. The sharp eyes of the dragon peered down at her, the flickering tongue of the snake tasted the air as it bobbed and weaved, while the majestic lion cocked its head in interest.

"If I free you, will you promise to leave this place without causing harm? Not to the city or anyone here?"

The chimera looked annoyed, but then nodded and Etani sighed in relief, using her blanket to open the gate to its pen and hurrying forward. Releasing the golden chain from its back ankle, she moved around it to remove the chain pinning its wings and then finally around to its beak.

"Forgive me," she whispered as she gave the chain a hard yank and it slipped free.

The eagle opened its beak and stretched its wings as much as the pen would allow. The head of the snake looked at her as she reached to release those chains as well, then finally the head of the lion while the previous two worked to free the dragon. All four looked incredibly relieved to be able to move and stretch after their long confinement.

"Thank you, little Fae," the creature murmured, eyeing her curiously. Its voice was both incredibly deep and almost a screech at the same time. "I will honour my promise. Be safe."

With that, the beast followed the path of the unicorn and she headed for the dragon, not having the first clue on how to get the siren free.

The dragon was so beautiful, his golden scales mixed with bronze, browns, greens, and tan, looking small and scared as she carefully opened the pen gate and slipped inside.

"You're okay, baby," she reassured him.

He had a distinct reptilian look to him, though it was not always the rule with the dragons. They could look like anything. They could range from being akin to cats and dogs to snakes and lizards. Some were even heavily feathered like birds.

The creature before her was all scales and leathery skin. He looked at her with huge, golden-green eyes and growled as she approached.

"Hush, I'm going to set you free," she scolded him.

He blinked at her, lifting his head and looking around the stable to see that she had indeed released others and then he looked back at her, curious and alert.

"I need you to stay still so I can release your wings. Behave."

He gave a huff as though telling him to behave annoyed him, but he remained still as she worked on the multiple chains that bound his beautiful wings. The membrane between each wing was a deep crimson and clearly showed the veins inside, beautiful and perfect until she saw that his right wing had a large section cut out of it

"They grounded you?" she whispered, horrified.

It was too clean and perfect not to have been intentional. It was hard to tell whether it would heal or not. She knew very little about the dragons for that matter. Regardless, she still released his wings and the muzzle from his face, turning for the golden chain around his ankle.

When he was freed, she grabbed her blanket and turned back, almost screaming bloody murder when the dragon was no longer there. A man was standing before her.

He lunged for her, covering her mouth with his overly hot hand and staring down at her with large golden-green eyes. "Don't scream, I'm not going to hurt you."

His skin was a deep golden-brown colour that looked incredibly smooth, a set of black horns starting just above long, tapered ears to point out and down towards his shoulders with a mop of golden blond hair that darkened to almost red at the tips. He wore a black shirt that was ripped, barely clinging to his strong, defined frame, and long pants and no shoes.

"Why are you freeing us?" he demanded, studying her face carefully.

"You were trapped," she explained the moment he removed his hand from her mouth.

He nodded slowly, not sure he believed her but willing to accept her words. He looked to be around twenty. That was obscenely young for a dragon, barely a teenager, and she was concerned as to how he had been captured in the first place. Where was his mother? She should have been protecting him to ensure he was not captured or injured. Their mothers were very protective of their young. Did he happen to wander off, or was his mother killed to capture the baby dragon?

"I will help," he announced, and grabbed her hand, half-dragging her to the next pen.

HE DID NOT HAVE the iron allergy that troubled her and so he had no issue releasing the gates and allowing her to slip inside. The dryad there hugged her tightly before she ran from the stables and vanished into the wind. A Centaur could not use magic to travel and so she looked up at him, his skin so black it was almost blue in the candlelight.

"Winter, Summer or unaligned?" she asked, his dark eyes boring into her as he rubbed his red wrists.

"Winter," he stated simply, and she nodded.

"I will take him and come back," the dragon offered, reaching his hand out and placing it on the Centaur's shoulder. But the Centaur did not take his eyes off her face as she stepped back, and the pair vanished into a pillar of crimson fire.

The dragons were amazing creatures if one really stopped to think about it. Their magic changed to adapt to their current form. If in their dragon form, they could breathe fire and fly, in their human form they could wield fire and transport themselves anywhere they wanted. It was what gave them a better chance against creatures like her, since she could not simply take herself anywhere.

A man with his face covered by a veil turned out to be an incubus and he grinned at her wickedly as she slipped into his rather lavish pen and removed the veil. He was incredibly good-looking, perfect to the extreme, and she found that his lack of shirt was rather distracting.

But he was shooed away the moment he was free, pouting and staring at her hungrily. "What is your name?" he asked quietly, following her from the pen to the tank where the siren had been watching the show.

"Etani," she offered, wondering how she was going to get the beautiful creature out.

"I'll take your siren friend home in exchange for a kiss from you," he teased, his eyes clouded with greed.

Frowning at him, she glanced from the siren to him and back again before she sighed. Unless her dragon friend came back, she was not going to be able to get the siren home.

"Deal."

Grinning he reached for her and she let out a small yelp as he spun her and dropped her into a dip over his arm, his lips coming down on hers hard. Her entire body melted at the taste of his lips, the flood of hormones his kiss pumped into her body and she found herself kissing him back eagerly, draping her arms over his shoulders.

After a solid thirty seconds, he finally lifted her back up again. "I won't forget you, sweet, little, Etani," he crooned, kissing her cheek before he turned to the siren. "Let's go, beautiful."

The siren pointed up and they saw that a wooden platform had been built into the roof of her tank, a set of stairs leading up to it at the back of the tank.

Heading up, she used her blanket to release the trap door and the siren swam up for them.

She was stunning, with skin that shimmered in the candlelight, greens and silvers mixed with pinks and purples. Large black eyes and a mass of emerald green hair. Her skin was covered in stripes from around her face to the tip of her long tail. The siren looked a lot like humans, complete with breasts though she had no nipples. Webbed fingers and that long tail would only be noticed up close, making them exceptionally good hunters. It was not often a man could resist that level of beauty when it was calling to him.

The incubus reached in and took the siren's hand, pulling her out of the water and as he did so, her long tail melted down into a pair of long legs.

That was the main difference between the sirens and mermaids. Sirens could change their tail to legs at will, while mermaids had to forsake the water to gain legs and could rarely return to it after that.

"Thank you," she murmured, looking between the two of them curiously.

"Where do you live?" the incubus asked, wrapping his arm protectively around her tiny waist.

The siren moved closer to his ear and murmured something. Smiling, he nodded before they both waved at Etani and vanished.

Heading for a pen that appeared to be sunken into the floor, she was glad to see she had nearly cleared the stable. Pausing by the gate, she peered inside and blinked as she found a green face looking back at her. His face resembled that of a duck, with a flat, wide, green beak and small black eyes. He had no feathers, his skin resembling that of a frog with black hair and a large indentation on the top of his head that contained water.

"Will you save me too?" he croaked, sitting in a pool of water that reached to his shoulders, filled with lily pads and pretty water flowers.

"So long as you agree not to try and eat me," she told the kappa.

He smiled at her with sharp teeth, nodding his agreement. Lifting the blanket, she carefully wiggled the bolt free and stopped at the edge of his pond. He seemed to be considering her too, but after a moment he stood on amphibian legs and waded to her, lifting one webbed foot to place it on the ledge.

Crouching down, she carefully dealt with the knot while he breathed a deep sigh of relief.

"Thank you, strange woman. I will not forget this."

"Just don't get captured again," she said, offering her hand to him.

He took it and she pulled him from the pond, watching as he padded from the stable with his webbed feet slapping on the ground.

Approaching the second to last pen, she peered inside at what appeared to be an almost normal-looking man. That is unless she could overlook that he had been meticulously bound at multiple points.

He was looking back at her, calm and collected. His arms were stretched out at his sides, his legs bound together to his chair. He had a set of horns that arched up and around in a large '*m*' pattern and long, waist-length black hair. Deep grey skin and an incredibly toned, muscular body.

"Who are you?" she asked warily, immediately suspicious of the sheer amount of chains required to contain him.

He looked to be in his forties, white-eyed and clean-shaven. Perfectly normal on the outside, but she knew better.

"Typhon," he said, and she drew back, her heart beginning to race.

"How were you captured?"

"A trap was set using my wife. I believed her to be in danger, and they seized me. I was sold to this King to be used as a defence."

Nodding slowly, she studied him.

"You are one of mine," he said after a lengthy pause.

"Yours?" she asked sharply, looking up at him.

"A monster," he explained calmly. "All monsters are mine, and you are one."

"What does that mean?"

"Nothing really, only that I will cause you no harm if you release me."

Letting out a slow breath, she decided to chance it. Having Typhon in the control of Alaric would be devastating.

"You're a Fae," he said as she collected the blanket and slid the bolt free. "Fae are not mine."

"I'm a half-breed," she explained as she approached, mindful of him but when he made no threatening move, she set to work releasing him from the chains.

"You smell like a great many things. Vampire, death, Fae, but others as well. You smell like the Fallen, of Bean Sídhe, of a witch," he was sniffing at her and she edged away from him, frowning.

"If you keep doing that, I'll leave you here."

"No, you won't. You don't want that King to hold me," he was smirking at her, seemingly reading her mind.

She managed to get one arm free and froze as he took her wrist, his fingers tracing over her skin before he smiled and let her go, allowing her to finish her work.

"You're young for a hero," he remarked as she knelt before him, working on releasing his legs.

"I'm not a hero, I just don't like seeing my kind enslaved," she muttered, watching as the skin on his legs darkened with each chain removal.

"That sounds like a hero to me," he teased, patting her head when she glared up at him.

Tugging the last chain off his foot harder than was necessary, the man grinned, and the room exploded.

FALLING BACK ON HER REAR, she stared up as serpentine coils began to move around her. He had changed, his legs becoming a long, black and grey tail. Out of his back sprouted white feathered wings.

He looked terrifying, but at the same time, he was radiant and dazzling.

Lowering himself onto his hands before her, his long hair trailed on the ground and he inched closer.

"You have my thanks, little hero Fae," he breathed, jerking forward to kiss her cheek before he seemed to simply vanish, the incredible length of him whipping out the open doors.

At first, the last pen appeared to be empty, but when she turned to look around for more prisoners, something behind her moved and she squeaked as someone seemed to step sideways out of reality.

"Hello," he said conversationally, grinning with razor-sharp teeth.

His skin was deep black, along with his eyes and hair. He was naked, even though he seemed to have no male anatomy. The only part of him that was not black was his unusually large number of very white teeth.

"You're a shadow walker."

"Indeed, and you're a Fae," he said almost playfully.

Shadow walkers were exactly that. Beings who could walk between shadows and manipulate them. If he pinned a person's shadow down, it prevented them from walking. That made him dangerous and useful in many ways.

"How are you contained?" she asked warily.

He pointed towards the back of the room and she looked to see a simple jar wrapped in a golden chain. Inside there was nothing but a small pool of what looked like black liquid.

"Free me and I will cause no harm," he murmured from close behind her. "I swear it."

Looking around at him, she was not sure if his kind could lie, but she was going to risk it because he deserved to be free. Carefully releasing the golden chains, she undid the lid of the jar and turned to him, tipping the jar out onto his hand. His form rippled and he sucked in a breath, growing in mass before settling down again and looking up at her.

"Thank you. I will remember *this* day, the Fae who freed us all," he murmured, reaching out to touch her cheek before he melted down into the ground before her eyes.

Stepping out into the open space, she looked around slowly and jumped as a pillar of fire appeared at her side, the dragon looking rather confused and ruffled.

"Did you know Winter doesn't much fancy unaligned dragons?" he asked, looking down as he flicked icicles from his skin.

"Thank you," she said, turning to him.

"You got them all?"

"Yes, they are all free now. What is your name?"

He smiled at her. "Mune. I shall be leaving now. My mother will be worried."

Etani reached out and took his hand, pressing a gentle kiss against his fingers. "Thank you, Mune."

"You're welcome, Etani, I hope we can meet again in the future," he said, watching her face before he bent down and kissed her cheek.

Grinning, he stepped back and disappeared in a pillar of fire.

Once alone in the stable, she stared around and let out a slow sigh of relief. She felt her soul beginning to heal just a little bit. It was not enough to repair what had been done to her, but it was something to start the mending process. Saving the lives of all those who had been imprisoned certainly started to make her feel a little better about herself.

Picking up the hat, she left the stables.

Alaric would be furious, but she had done the right thing.

A DIFFERENT KIND OF BETRAYAL

The news of the escape reached them the next day when Alaric exploded into a rage. Etani did not share her nightly activities with her new little family, and they did not seem to be aware of her managing to slip away in the night to do the deed.

As much as she had come to love them all, she felt she had to keep that part of herself a secret. Letari seemed to agree with that, even though she had not said a word in some time. While she was grieving, she needed something to cling onto. Being surrounded by the vampire trio made her feel better, but the knowledge that she had done something for those beings, greatly improved her mental state.

So, when they heard of Alaric's breakdown, she very nearly smiled. It was hard to keep a straight face, to the point where she found Versalis watching her, his handsome face showing a hint of a smile.

"What is it?" he asked in a tiny voice, the twins busy accepting a list of the missing creatures and their descriptions from a servant.

"Nothing," she lied, patting his hand gently.

He knew something was up, but after a moment of studying her, he nodded his acceptance.

Kai seemed rather irritated, though he had been looking that way for days, ever since the incident. She knew he and Jaia had been talking, but she did not want to know what it was about. They would tell her if and when they were ready.

The fact that she was so unconcerned seemed to be bothering Versalis all the more, but she did not think they were going to do anything against her. If Versalis thought otherwise, he was not going to tell her and, so she let it go.

"I'm not sure what they're expecting us to do about this," Kai grumbled as he dropped the list of missing creatures on the table. "It was sabotage. Some guard reported a cloaked woman in a hat asking about the stables, but he did not see her face. He did not have any real information."

She saw Versalis moving, his eyes going to the place the twins stored their hats, but neither Kai nor Jaia seemed to share his suspicions.

"I get the feeling this list is being distributed across the city, not just to us," Jaia sighed, slouching back on the couch as his eyes lingered on her.

Studying him for a moment, she dropped her eyes back to the list, noting that there was no name for any of the beings. Alaric wanted to keep the identity of Typhon and the incubus a secret. At least, she hoped the man was back with his wife.

Versalis narrowed his eyes at her. "Hopefully, he isn't expecting us to go looking for them. By now, they will be long gone."

"We can't find them. Some of those are fairly common creatures. It's not our fault he is incapable of keeping his wards safe," she quipped, looking back at Versalis with a slightly quizzical expression. She did not think it would fool him, but she did not want him asking questions either.

"The kappa is common, but the unicorns aren't. No doubt that one went back to Summer," Jaia said as he flicked the paper in his frustration.

"Do all the unicorns live in Summer?" Versalis asked, the conversation piquing his interest.

"No, some live in Winter. I don't think there are any in the Heathen Court and there's none that I ever saw in Ceress," she said slowly, wondering at that. "They don't like being in the human world as they don't handle the lack of magic very well.

Grunting his agreement, Kai flopped back onto the couch, still looking angry though she did not know why.

T HEY WERE GIVEN several days of peace, the twins blowing off their work to stay in the rooms that had been fondly named *'the basement.'* The company was delightful, and she was not about to tell them to go to work if it meant she would get more time with them.

"You can't kill yourself," Kai suddenly burst out one late afternoon.

Apparently, his growing tension had finally reached its peak and everyone jumped at his words. Etani had been butting heads with Versalis and they had finally settled on a game of checkers. He had to teach her how to play, but she quickly learned it and— much to his disgust—had beaten him sixteen times in a row.

Three sets of eyes fell on Kai and he flushed, looking at her angrily.

"Kai, this is neither the time nor place," Versalis said softly, holding a black disk in his fingers.

"When is, Versalis? It's not your life or your brother's depending on a suicidal Princess!"

He had begun to shout, but Etani remained calm, her eyes returning to the board. She had known that would come up sooner or later and she frowned at the disk in Versalis' hand, he had not set it down yet and that meant she could not make her move.

She could feel Kai glaring at her, growing angrier at her silence. "Etani!" he yelled, and she flinched, looking up at him and then to Jaia, who was staring at the table, his mouth set in an unhappy line. "You're so selfish! You would destroy everything around you to get what you want!"

The words stung and she recoiled from him, shrinking back into the couch. She came up empty in the search for the little wooden box, she must have left it in the bathroom.

"Kai, shut up and sit down," Versalis growled, but Kai did not hear him, pointing at his brother.

"What about him, Etani? Will you let him die just because you are sad?"

Her own anger flared, and she met his accusing stare. Versalis stood at the words but she caught his hand, keeping him from attacking the smaller vampire.

"Sad, Kai? Do you call my having my child cut out of me being sad?" The rest of what had been done to her hung in the air, demanding an answer, but they all ignored it.

"I will not allow you to kill my brother. I will keep you alive by whatever means necessary," he growled, and he reached for her.

She was out of the seat before his hand had left his side while Versalis moved between them even as she backed away. Jaia also rose and went to stand behind Kai.

She looked between the two of them. "Do what, Kai?" she demanded, resenting her fear.

"I'll lock you in the cells until this castle crumbles into dust."

Suddenly, she started worrying about both herself and Versalis. The two had been talking and she knew it would end up being them against her and Versalis. Versalis would try and protect her, but would he be stronger than the two young vampires?

She watched the scene playing out before her very eyes even as it was thought up.

Kai tackled Versalis and the two wrestled on the flattened table. Her eyes followed a single black disk rolling across the floor before lifting to see the approaching Jaia. He was so calm, as though the fight behind him had never started and he was just coming in to embrace her. But her body tensed as he approached, preparing to defend herself against a stronger being.

Her body coiled and then rebounded, driving her foot into Jaia's side and throwing him across the room.

"Run," Versalis screamed and she did exactly that.

Kai was only a breath behind her as she sprinted for the door across the room, arms clasping her waist before she could get it fully open.

ONE ARM LEFT her and curled in her hair, forcing her head to the side. Pain ripped through her body as his teeth sank into the soft flesh of her throat and she cried out. His grip tightened around her and though she could not see what was happening behind her, she knew Jaia was doing his best to defend Kai's back from Versalis.

Struggling, she drove her elbow into his ribcage, stamping down hard on his toes but he refused to let her go. She had underestimated how strong Kai was. Her vision began to blur as he fed off her, moving with her as her legs gave out and he lowered her gently to the floor. His grip on her finally began to loosen as she slumped against him, unable to keep her eyes focused on the door or the darkness of the stairwell.

His fangs left her slowly and his grip on her hair eased as his hand moved to cup her nape, easing her onto the floor. As his fingers stroked her cheek, he seemed satisfied when she moved weakly and he left her, off to do whatever it was he needed to do. Someone approached, and she sleepily watched Jaia's determined face as he started moving things around, doing something she could not see.

She could not even lift her hand to touch his hair that tickled her cheek when he leant down, feeling her shallow breaths on his cheek and listening to her slow heart.

He said something and Kai joined him, his eyes alight and glittering as though he were high. She had to suppose that he was, on her blood. They spoke quietly, moving over her and shifting things around, but she could only hear the slow rushing of blood in her ears, her heart fighting to push through what little blood she had left.

Silver flashed over her and she tried to focus on it, but it was gone too fast and then she felt something sliding under the skin of her right inner elbow. The sting of pain was minor, and she found herself staring up at the ceiling, deciding then and there that the colour of their ceiling was much better than the one in her rooms in the royal quarters.

A pressure at her elbow made her look to Kai; he had something in his mouth and was pulling it tight. Had he applied a tourniquet on his arm? She tried to figure out why he would do that but, in the end, she decided it did not matter. What she really wanted was to sleep.

Kai reached over her to help Jaia and her eyes were barely able to open, her breaths slowing to almost nothing and she had a moment of peace realising that she was about to die. Not the death she wanted, but it was ironic given their argument about her killing herself, and they were the ones who ended up killing her instead.

Jaia nodded and looked down at her, his face going pale as he saw her. He turned his attention to something else and then the little prick at her arm moved, jerking and making her arm sting.

On her other side, a trembling pair of hands touched her, and a new sting started in the crook of that elbow too.

She could see death, that old friend of hers, and she smiled for him, glad to be able to reach him and yet he did not look particularly certain, assessing her. Eventually, when his arms dropped, they both looked somewhat annoyed.

Warmth had started at her arms and had begun to spread through her, which was rather odd all things considered. She thought about that for a moment, contemplating the two points where the warmth started, both at her inner elbows, at the veins most often used for needles.

She contemplated that fact for several seconds, unable to make heads or tails of it in her drowsy state.

The warmth was spreading, each side racing the other until, in unison, both sides met at her heart and her world went white.

2 1

CHANGES

Bolting upright, she looked around the room frantically, her breath rapid and her heart racing. A glance around told her she was in Jaia's room, bound to the bed with the obnoxious gold chain. She had been certain Epharis would have destroyed them all, but either he decided not to or the twins had somehow stashed that one away.

She wore a long black nightdress, modest and lovely with little sleeves that covered her shoulders but did not go much further.

She felt weirdly warm as if she had fallen asleep by the fire, and her eyes swept the empty bedroom, which was rather odd when there used to be furniture in the room. But it now contained nothing but a bed and mattress with no sheets or pillows and two metal racks on either side of the bed with a red bag hanging from each, leading to her inner arms by a long red tube. The spots around the points of contact with her arms had gone a weird dark red she had never seen before. It was not like blood poisoning, but brighter.

She was baffled by the change and gave the chain a little tug, trying to pull herself free but she was stuck. The other side had been tightly chained as well, leaving her impossibly trapped and having no idea what was happening.

A short while later, the door opened, and Kai slid into the room with two bags in his hand. Seeing her awake, he turned and called out. "She's up."

Jaia appeared next, swinging the door wide. They stepped inside, approaching her from either side. She watched them warily as they disconnected the almost empty red bags and replaced them with new ones, the tubes turning dark with the flow of new fluid.

"What are you doing?"

The liquid on the tube on Kai's side reached the point at her arm, the same time as the other side and she gasped at the heat that flooded through her body. Leaning forward slightly, she sucked in as much air as she could manage, her head spinning, and she jerked at a gentle touch on her head. Jaia had tried to soothe her by stroking her hair. Looking up at him, she panted softly at the heat radiating out of her, the pounding race of her heart that made her feel queasy.

"We have to make sure you don't kill yourself," Kai explained gently, and she looked to him, frowning.

"How?" she said quickly, not entirely sure what they could do that had not already been done to her.

Kai did not speak, instead, he leant down and peered into her eyes, frowning and looking up at Jaia.

"She looks flushed," he said concerned.

Sighing, Jaia sat beside her. His hand was gentle as he cupped her cheek and drew her slightly closer.

She flinched as Jaia bit deep into her throat and began to drink, her body trembling at the sensation and rush of desire that flooded her. Resenting it, she whimpered as Kai bent down and his teeth sank into her wrist, both taking what little blood she had managed to produce while their blood made her feel too hot.

They did not linger for long and were gentle with her.

"Jaia," she pleaded in a tiny voice when he pushed off the bed.

He turned to look at her and blood was still oozing down her shoulder while Kai still at her wrist, bound and helpless. He scowled at the sight of Kai pulling back with his lips red from her blood.

"I'm sorry, Etani, we can't lose you," he said gently before he left and Kai soon followed, licking his lips clean as he went.

Dropping her head back against the headboard, she sat in silence until, eventually, she dozed off.

When she woke, Jaia was touching her cheek.

By the time the twins had replaced the bags and Kai left, she felt sick. Her head spun as she looked up at Jaia, confused at the gentleness and his touch.

"It'll be done soon, Etani, don't worry," he murmured, and she made a soft sound of protest, facing away from him.

His smile was grim as he drew her face back to him and shook his head.

"Don't do that, I swear it's going to be okay."

Not even for a moment did she believe him, but nodded in agreement nonetheless.

He smiled and kissed her cheek, leaving her alone once more.

She was still awake when they returned and replaced the bags, her pink cheeks an indication that she was getting too warm, but both looked like they did not want any more.

"Bring up Versalis, he needs to eat," Jaia told to his brother.

The vampire King was livid when he was dragged up from the floor below, his face going pale as he was pushed into the room and saw her. She looked back at him, giving him a little wave and smiled weakly, but she felt hot and uncomfortable, her hair sticking to her sweaty skin and her body aching.

"You sick bastards," Versalis snarled as he struggled to get free.

Jaia punched him in the stomach and he dropped on the floor. He was no doubt weak from hunger.

"You're going to feed today, bring her down a little."

Kai shoved Versalis forward, but he turned on them. "Do you know what you're doing to her?" They knew exactly what they were doing. "You can't do this, it's forbidden." He seemed terrified, and he shook his head, observing her confusion.

He did not get a chance to tell her, as they had grabbed him and forced him forward. Kai used his nail to make a small cut on her neck, forcing him closer. That was all it took for his fangs to add to the draw and he fed greedily off her. Her taste was too sweet and his desire growing strong.

When she started to look pale, they forced him back, and his horror-struck gaze met her confused one.

"Versalis," she sighed, her eyes growing heavy and he fought them, but they dragged him away and she fell asleep, warm and content.

By the time she woke again, she felt like the warmth in her had turned to fire and she was already panting hard. Her heart had begun to race at a pace she never thought possible, more akin to a human's steady beat, and it burned. Clenching her eyes shut to try and calm herself, she breathed slowly but the change of pace only made her head spin.

Someone walked in but she ignored them, her body slumped forward and her eyes tight to calm herself. It was not working at all.

"Etani?" A low voice asked, and she jerked at the strange voice.

It was Jaia and she frowned up at him. She could not put her finger on it, but he looked different. Sharper. Shaking her head, she strained against the chains, but it did nothing but make her arms hurt.

"Too hot," she breathed, sweat beading up on her forehead and making her skin glisten.

"I know, baby," he crooned, joining her on the bed and stroking her hair gently. "It's almost over and everything will be alright."

She flicked her gaze around the room, everything looked different there, too. Everything seemed more detailed and refined. She could see the individual fibres of the mattress and her dress or the tiny freckles on her legs that she had never noticed before. She could discern the tiny motes of dust in the air when, normally, she could only see them when the sun shone in the room.

"What are you doing to me?" she whined, trying to understand the differences but her mind was flicking from idea to idea at a pace she had never experienced before. Her teeth were burning and if she were right, her first premolars on her top jaw were oddly, worryingly loose in her mouth

"We're making it so you can't die, sweetheart. Not ever."

She jerked away from him in horror. "You can't turn the Fae," she whispered, hoping it was true, even though no one knew for sure.

"No, not completely at least. Just enough that you get our immortality... and get addicted to our blood." That last part was an afterthought and she whimpered at his words. "I'm afraid it's going to hurt quite a bit since we don't have a lot of time. Usually, the process is much slower."

Shaking her head, she pulled at the chain, but it was not budging at all.

"We only thought about it after your little screaming episode," he said and she looked up at him once more, confused by the subject. "What kind of creature could make a scream like that but the banshee? Neither of us could think of anything and we had heard you scream before, but it was nothing like that. I had a theory and we assume that it was a response to the change Epharis brought in your system," he sounded calm, trying to soothe a scared, hostile creature.

"That left us wondering what else had. The Fae and the Banshee seem similar, but they are vastly different species of the magical realm. Kai did a little digging and it turns out the Fae and the Banshee can procreate even though it is quite uncommon." Taking a deep breath, he smiled softly. "Your dear father was not a true-born Fae. Your grandmother is part banshee and that little talent had been hidden inside you, waiting to be used. So now we must deliberate what else might be hidden inside you. What other secret powers does the Winter Princess possess? There was very little public record on your Grandmother's parentage that we could find though, so now we are left with endless possibilities."

Sounding delighted by the challenge, he looked up when Kai entered and they replaced the bags once more, neither of them feeding off her.

"You won't have the strength to try your scream. From what we read, it takes a certain amount of energy. Until the time is right, we are keeping you below that level," Kai said gently, yet his face was cool towards her, wary and mistrusting.

"This is the last bag, I'm sorry for what you will be going through but this has to happen," Jaia said and he caught her head to keep her from turning away, planting a hard kiss against her temple. "I love you, Etani, we both do, and you're going to be magnificent," he breathed into her ear and the two left her alone.

'Lee?' she thought, searching her mind for that other voice that would give her so much comfort in a moment like this. 'Letari?' There was no response, not even a hint, and she sighed, knowing she was alone.

Sitting against the headboard, she looked between the two bags and marvelled at how closely they matched when it came to draining into her. Curious but unable to get either tube to bend or crease in order to stop one flow or the other, she simply watched the bags slowly empty.

It started when they were both at around the halfway mark, her stomach suddenly heaving and she rocked forward but nothing came out, at least nothing from her stomach.

One of her teeth dropped onto the bed and she felt at the spot with the tip of her tongue, horrified to feel a sharp point there. She found that the same tooth on the other side was ready to fall out as well.

Digging her tongue into the roots, she forced it out and spat it onto the bed with the first.

Looking down at them, they were perfectly white and clean with only a little smear of blood on the second where she had pushed it free of the gums.

Her face began to burn, and she clenched her eyes shut, her tongue still feeling the spot when the sharp point pushed free of the gums. They were not large, only a millimetre or two longer than her little, sharp canines, leaving her with two sharp sets of teeth and the feeling was incredibly odd.

Something strange came to her attention and she cocked her head to the side, listening hard to the sound of footsteps that seemed to be coming from inches above her. Heaving again, she groaned at the pain of her stomach refusing to settle or give up its contents.

Fire began to spread from the inside of her elbows and creep down her arms, leaving her skin burning like acid but visibly unchanged. She was shocked to see tiny, tiny little clear hairs on her arms when she had previously thought there to be none.

Looking down at her feet, she saw the same on her legs and the tops of her feet. At first she was amused at the hairy humans, considering that her body remained clean from birth. But now, she realised she had hair almost invisible to the naked eye. Her hair whispered as she shook her head, a sound she had never noticed before, but it was loud now.

Gritting her teeth to keep from making a sound as the fire reached her shoulder, she began to pant once more, her heartbeat rapidly increasing the closer the fire got to it.

"No," she whispered, the sound of her voice making her jerk.

She had never heard her own voice like that before, a low purr that screamed pleasure and yet sounded cold at the same time, a distant promise of what the listener could have and she was left wondering at Jaia's words on what her lineage might be.

Shaking her head at the thought, she pulled at the chain and grinned when she heard the wood groaning. But freeing herself was not going to save her.

The fire had turned her cheeks a warm pink, sweat glistening on her body and she felt as though she might catch fire.

When someone entered, she could smell the scent of warm male and that immediately made her think of Jaia, the spicy smell of his skin and the taste of his blood that had appeared on her tongue, mixed with a blood she did not know and she could only assume it was Kai's.

Raising her head, her eyes trailed up a rock-hard body to a face she both knew well and had never seen before. With eyes sharpened by the blood, she could see every tiny detail that made him the demonic seducer he was.

Etani wondered if that was how humans saw their kind and the thought made her want to laugh, right up until the fire licked at her heart and it suddenly stopped beating.

Her scream was terrible as the fire spread to every last inch of her body in an instant after the first teasing lick of her heart, the pain of burning alive coupled with the pain of her heart suddenly no longer wanting to beat and a horrific ripping sensation in her brain as thoughts and memories seemed to expand out of what she previously had known to be herself.

Her scream was endless, a plea for death and an end of suffering that did not come.

Her torture lasted for hours, her screams cutting off after the first ten minutes as she fell into unconsciousness. But she was still alert, her soul thrashing like a trapped fish as the fire pecked at it, pulling and twisting it.

Letari had found her immediately, clinging to her as the place that had been her home was ripped apart by flames and her soul was consumed by it and changed, no longer a soft blue but flecked with red, little sparks of fire that gave it a hypnotic beauty and terrible suffering.

She felt a mouth on her throat, flesh tearing and the fire beginning to leave her; could feel hands at her elbows, two more mouths and the drawing out sensation of having venom sucked from a wound.

She felt herself drifting, high on the blood and lost to the void of nothingness that had been herself and yet she realised that the void was *not* nothing. What she had come to perceive as herself had expanded, grown greater than it had been, able to know and understand more.

It was magical and the two swam in it, revelling in its vast size.

Yet, they both knew that things were going to be very different, and people were going to die.

2 2

VARLING

The twins had underestimated her tenfold and their efforts to try and contain her were like wet paper before a breeze.

The gold chain snapped, and the headboard was ripped and thrown into the wall, spilling dirt and confused worms into the room. All three doors that blocked her and the outside were removed with little more effort than it took to blow out a candle, before she was loose on the city.

Physically she had not changed much; her skin appeared smoother, the scars that had littered her body had vanished into perfection, while her feline eyes appeared more cunning than ever before. Her long hair that had been lank mere hours ago now glistened in the dim light of the night.

She moved like a panther prowling the castle grounds, naked and exquisite in the moonlight.

The men before her did not so much as try to defend themselves, the sight of her approach and the purr of her voice enough to bring any man to his knees.

And when they *did* kneel before her, she killed them.

Helmets were thrown, throats were ripped open and she fed on the warmth of them, drinking in their lives and their souls in a way she found addictive.

Morning came, she found herself sitting on the parapet that ran around the castle, her bare feet swinging as she softly sang to herself and smiled when men came to her, leaning against the wall and telling her all the pleasures they would bring to her if only she would let them.

Wearing nothing but blood, she watched the men and her voice called to them, a siren song of womanly need that pulled them in and would have had them begging her for death.

She had been free for only three or four hours, but during that time, she had massacred almost half of the guards on the castle grounds, gorging herself on their blood and revelling in their lust and then their terror.

The sun would be rising soon, and she waited with morbid curiosity at what would happen if she were to meet it. All the while, she sang under her breath, the group below her coming to ten and then eleven defenceless souls.

The scent of him had her smiling, her eyes lowering to the group below her who looked rather confused when her singing stopped and they shuffled away, not understanding why they had come to be there and not looking up to see their death above them.

"If you want to sneak up on someone, you should be downwind," she murmured, watching as one man bumped into the corner of the wall before rounding it and vanishing from sight.

He stopped several feet back from her and she could smell the tension in him as he realised what he was seeing. She had not left the bodies where they fell. She fancied making herself a pile, so she collected them and neatly stacked them together

Nineteen guards were stacked neatly behind her, two men to a level to leave one at the very top, looking somewhat lonely up there. She knew he was looking at it, knew what he saw, and his head shook. She knew because she could hear his clothes rustling against his skin, his hair swishing and then the sound of him swallowing.

"Etani," he breathed her name, and she shivered.

The vampire King had a voice like silk on her skin, whispering a kiss that had her breath catching and she knew then why he was the King. He lured her to him with the promise of pleasure and blood, sex and carnage at levels she could only dream of.

Her eyes found him, and his pupils dilated at the sight of her, her lips tilted up into the faintest hint of a smile. She wondered what he saw in her, but judging by the engorging at his groin, she thought she knew.

"Versalis, did the boys send you to collect me?" she said in a pouting lilt, delighting at the way her voice affected him.

His skin tightened with gooseflesh, his breath freezing only to start up faster.

"Yes," he replied, and she let out a gentle sigh.

She did not want to go back just yet.

She patted the spot beside her. "Come watch the sun with me."

She heard him taking two steps forward before stopping again. "No, we have to go. We don't know what will happen when the sun rises."

He had latched onto concern as a means of distracting himself and she frowned.

"Don't you want to find out… together?" she drew out the last word, her voice lowering slightly and she laughed internally as his eyes widened, his body responding to her in ways she had never seen before.

"Not tonight," he said through gritted teeth, fighting his carnal instincts that she was twinging with every breath.

Finally, she lifted her feet and stood, the movement fast enough to make her blur in the eyes of most, but he caught every microsecond of it, every muscle moving, and every brush of her hair against her exposed skin.

She turned to him, he watched her hips sway as she approached, swallowing hard before his eyes met hers and she lifted her hand to touch his cheek. He was no longer warm to her, they matched closely.

"Spoilsport," she murmured.

Her fingers trailed down his jaw before she turned away from him, heading towards the castle. He directed his hungry eyes on her but then followed a few paces behind, leaving the pile of corpses to whoever would find them later.

The twins had prepared for her arrival and the sight of them made her pause. The sound of a hitching breath behind made her realise that even her laugh whispered of sexual fantasies to the vampire King.

The twins did not fare much better and they kept gawking at her. They had blocked their noses with little clips, their ears stuffed with wool and they stood at the opposite side of the room, ready to confine themselves if need be.

If a vampire King responded so strongly to her, then she wondered how *they* would respond.

"What's wrong, Jaia? Aren't you satisfied with your creation?" she purred, her tongue snaking out to trace over her lips and the double set of canines in a way that had the man trembling.

He shook his head, horrified at his own reaction.

"It will settle," Versalis said, but his resolve seemed to be faltering.

She turned her eyes on him, and he swallowed hard, as he scooted across the room to join the twins.

Kai seemed unable to look away from her or move, his entire body locked in place.

Stepping across the room, she lowered herself onto the couch and crossed her legs, relaxing her posture, while everyone remained watching the others.

She counted two hours passing where they simply stared at each other, the men too scared to move and her revelling in the intoxicating scent of their fear before her skin began to irritate her.

In an instant she was on her feet, the air seeming confused and not knowing where to go as she moved.

The three men jerked, but she ignored them, making her way to the bathroom.

"You two are going to have this entire world on your conscience once she is done with it," Versalis whispered as she turned on the water and stepped under the fountain, smiling.

SHE BATHED THOROUGHLY, marvelling at each drop of water she saw and the way it glittered on her skin, reflecting every speck of light she had not seen before. Only one candle lit the room and it was more than enough for her to see.

Washing the blood from her hair and skin, she listened, but they were talking so quietly she could only hear their hiss. Once done, she dried herself and pulled on a pair of tight black pants and a vest, her bare feet silent on the tile as she swept from the room and paused.

They either had not heard or ignored Epharis standing at the destruction that had once been the doorway. "What the abyss happ—" he choked as his eyes fell on her and his already pale face first turned into a delightful shade of grey, before settling for red.

"Epharis, how delightful," she said softly, trying to recall why she had been angry at him, but the thought eluded her at that moment.

"What did you do?" Epharis said to the twins, but his eyes were still on her, raking her body slowly.

"They did something very bad, husband darling," she whispered, and her voice had the desired effect. His breath hitched and he shivered, taking an involuntary step towards her before he caught himself.

"They turned her into a Varling. A vampire hybrid, usually half-human," Versalis said and flinched when her eyes turned on him.

The word seemed to mean something to Epharis because he looked positively appalled. "Isn't that forbidden?"

Since he was intentionally avoiding her, she took the opportunity to creep closer to him.

"Yes, entirely. It's dangerous and reckless and turns innocent humans into sexual blood toys for a vampire's pleasure and food."

Versalis was also avoiding looking directly at her. Kai, however, was unable to look away, hypnotised.

Epharis *did not* notice her nearing him, until her fingers trailed along his forearm, making him jerk back violently. He was rather shocked to find her and then his eyelids dropped, hunger burning in them.

"Does it matter what they did?" she asked quietly, watching as his throat moved with his swallow.

His muscles quivered with the effort to stay still and even not to breathe around her.

"Varlings are dangerous creatures when they are vampire and human, but vampire and Fae? There is no knowing what she is capable of," Versalis said in a tiny voice.

Reaching for Epharis again, she caught his arm and slid it around her waist, smiling as his muscles seemed so tense they might snap.

Leaning up onto the balls of her feet she grinned at Versalis before whispering in Epharis' ear. "We should go back to your rooms. Safe, dark, *alone.*"

Epharis quivered against her, and she exhaled softly against his ear. That broke him. His arms tensed around her and drew her to him, tight as a vice. Versalis coughed and Epharis shook his head violently, pushing her back but there was no hiding his arousal.

"You two… you deserve to be thrown naked into the day," Epharis hissed, forcing himself to stay away from her.

Disappointed, she watched as he worked to shut parts of himself down so as not to be affected by her. Pouting, she focused her attention on Versalis who swallowed hard. Unlike Epharis, he could not discipline his body.

"I can't even get my husband to love me," she said in a tragic voice and he stepped forward, but he was restrained by Kai and Jaia.

Frustrated at the lot of them, she turned away and pouted, resenting their self-control.

SHE WAS CONFINED to the cell downstairs, at least until it was time for Jaia to feed and she smiled at the sight of Kai who, in order to save his brother, had allowed himself to be captured by the spell of her blood.

"Kai," she crooned through the glass, pressing herself close.

He glared at her and pointed to his ears which were again stuffed with wool.

She pouted and the sight of his body tensing at the tragic sight of her disappointment was delicious.

"Etani," Jaia said, hovering near the hatch and she smiled at his slow, deep breaths of the air that carried her hypnotic, erotic scent.

She crossed to the hatch and lowered herself to her knees, her eyes meeting his through the square opening.

"It would be more fun if you came in, Jaia," she teased and watched his pupils dilate but he shook his head.

That was not nearly as fun when they were prepared, and she stuck her arm through the opening.

The feeling of his hand so gentle on her arm made her skin tingle and the bite, while painful, felt wonderful.

Her blood had replenished enough that he was able to feed, though he took more to compensate for the tainted blood that still lingered in her veins.

He pushed himself back when he was done, and Kai was quick to replace him. She only watched Kai, curious about him. He was an exceptionally intelligent man, young when he had been turned and he seemed both captivated by her and utterly repulsed. It fascinated her, especially when he had taken so little interest in her as a woman before.

"So, Kai, what do you make of your Varling?" she said gently, her eyes lingering on the wool bud in his ear.

He fed slowly, drawing it out but, in the end, he let her go and she withdrew her arm, the hatch closed and the two men sat, looking at the wall and riding the high that was her blood.

"Varling," Kai breathed, watching them.

Licking her lips, she imagined her teeth sinking into Jaia's throat. The thought startled her slightly and she wondered where it had come from.

Neither of them said anything more on the subject and they left her alone once more. They were waiting for the bloodlust and sexual hunger caused by her change to fade.

She had started to get hungry after the third day, her calls ignored until she kicked the glass and the loud crack had Jaia appearing, his eyes tracing the long cracks that had formed.

He breathed a slow sigh and approached the hatch, but she shook her head, her lips curling into a smile.

"Come on Jaia, come in here with me. I'll be gentle."

His reaction was immediate, and he shuddered, closing his eyes to keep his head clear.

They could not let her die. They both knew it and he was left with no other choice if she refused to feed.

Opening the door, he was immediately hit with the scent of her, a low growl escaping his lips.

Smiling, she approached him, and her fingers found his waist, slow and gentle as she pushed up, exposing the hard stomach he had worked for in life.

He caught her hands, pushing them down, and met her eyes.

"You're only getting blood," he whispered, but she could feel what he wanted, his groin was pressed against her hip.

Making a soft sound of disappointment, her hand traced up over his chest to his neck and snaked up and around, drawing him down to her height. He did not protest when her lips found his, the kiss slow and gentle, broken after a moment.

His breathing was ragged when she moved away and her nose brushed his throat, her lips and then the double point of her teeth.

HIS SKIN MELTED under her bite like butter and he moaned at the sensation, his hands dropping to her lower back, clutching the stiff fabric of her vest.

She sucked on the wound and his blood flooded her system, her growl of satisfaction sounding loud in the still room and his hands dropped to her rear, lifting her off her feet.

Her legs went around him, and he staggered to the bed with her in his lap. Latched onto him, she was drinking heavily. She could feel his arousal, the tension that was his restraint as he tried his utmost to keep from doing what his instincts told him to do. Shifting, she knelt over his lap and drew back from the bite, her tongue warm and wet on his neck as she licked away the trickle of blood.

His hands had slipped up under her vest, feeling the skin of her lower back and she sighed, delighting in the sensation. Her nose brushed his, nudging playfully as she leant against him, her hands resting on his shoulders and her grin feral.

"Don't you want me, Jaia?" she whispered, her lips only an inch from his.

He nodded helplessly and she brought her lips down on his, his blood tainting the kiss.

His self-control snapped when her nails bit into his shoulders.

Gripping her roughly, he moved and her back slammed against the wall, his entire body pressing into hers as she enclosed him in her legs.

Their kiss was passion and need yet it did not last long. He broke from her and sank his teeth into her throat, her cry one of pain and pleasure.

Versalis found them there against the wall, Jaia pressed against her with his mouth at her throat, blood smeared over her lips and chin.

Her eyes met his and she frowned as he pulled something from his pocket and opened the door.

Distracted by a second bite, Jaia froze at a scuff and she let go of him even as he turned, protecting her from that new threat that interrupted their pleasure.

Lifting the device, a bolt of light jumped from him to Jaia and the vampire dropped to the ground.

Eyebrows lifting, her hands went up in a show of surrender, Versalis narrowing his eyes at her before he reached down and dragged the unconscious vampire from the cell, locking it securely behind him.

His eyes never left her and hers never left him, hunger dancing in his every step. But he knew better than give in.

Her racing thoughts began to calm after another day of sitting in the cell by herself, her mood calming and she felt her senses dulling only a tiny fraction, but she knew what they meant by keeping her there.

She had been what the humans had feared long ago, the vampire of legend who killed indiscriminately in an orgy of sex and violence. She had to wonder if that legend had not been a Varling set loose on the world.

She did not know, and she made a mental note to ask the twins at some point, but they were avoiding her.

It had been curious that Versalis had not become addicted to her blood as the twins did, but perhaps one round of trying to turn her had set him straight for life. It had taken two vampires to change her.

It was Versalis who visited her when her body had calmed and he still looked shocked at the form of her sitting there, looking bored and swinging her legs to watch them move.

"Etani?" he asked and when she looked up, his breath caught. "I suppose that won't dull," he breathed.

Her brows lifted and she gave a hint of a smile.

"Disappointed?" she asked, and he shook his head. Her smile made him bite his lip and he moved for the door, opening it and inhaling.

The scent of her was softer now that she had used up the blood that had filled her, he breathed a soft sigh of relief, opening the door fully and sweeping his hand out.

Pushing herself to her feet, she found him watching her every move and shaking his head in disbelief.

"I don't think they created a Varling, I think they created a Goddess," he breathed and as she passed, she traced her fingers over his jaw and swept from the room, leaving him engorged and wanting.

ONE, TWO, THREE, ARREST!

The twins were wary of her freedom, but when she did not try to jump them, they relaxed. She got tense when they came near her though, the smell of their blood singing to her the same way she had sung to the men. She had self-control, however, and she resisted.

It had become a game to her, seeing how close she could get only to resist and pull back.

Epharis had visited again, finding her sitting on the couch with her legs crossed, the three men sitting opposite her stared with hypnotic fascination as she raged at Kai who had beaten her again at the game she had learnt to hate since she could not win. Throwing the red and black board, she sent the little disks flying, and all the while she glared at the vampire who consistently outsmarted her. Jaia could do it too, but he let her win sometimes, Kai did not.

Clearing his throat, he jerked slightly as she whipped around faster than he could see, all eyes on him.

"Good evening," Epharis said, eying her with that same desperate want that he had shown the first day.

"Epharis, what brings you down to our lair?" Jaia asked a little desperately.

"I am the messenger to bring you all an invitation to dine with King Alaric this evening," he said in a sarcastic tone.

Four men tensed at her feral, gleeful smile.

"We shouldn't keep the King waiting," she purred.

Protestations were immediate and violent, but she ignored them and wandered into Jaia's bedroom to get changed.

She was going and there was nothing any of them could do to stop her. Well, there was, but she was ignoring that fact.

When she was clad in a long black dress that left her back, shoulders and a fair amount of her chest bare, she walked back out and straight past the lot of them.

It was not until she reached the door that they even stopped arguing enough to realise she was there.

"Etani!" Jaia gasped, but she was gone before they had even gotten out of their seats.

The faces that turned to her turned from shocked to awestruck as she swept through the halls of the castle, the men behind her rushing to keep up with her and trying to get her to stop, but she was not having any of that rubbish. She was not going to stop, it did not matter what they said and when she found the room, the door opened with such force that it slammed against the wall.

Alaric jumped along with the servants and his eyes went huge as they found her.

Her eyes locked onto him as if they were glued there and she stalked forward, the man sitting in his chair dumbfounded.

She reached him and her fingers curled in the front of his shirt. Yanking him down to her level, her nose was a mere inch from his.

"Alaric, dear precious Alaric," she whispered in a lethal voice. "I'm going to rip out your spleen and feed it to you for what you did to me... I'm going to bathe in your blood and bring your precious Kingdom to its knees," her voice was breathy, her grin manic and her eyes on his. He stood frozen, unable to look away from her, with his grip tight on the arms of his chair, bent forward.

"I'm going to make you wish you were never born for letting that man touch me. You will die begging me for mercy, but I won't have any for you. To your last breath you will be screaming in agony, dying like a broken and *worthless* sack of meat."

Three sets of hands found her, and she was dragged back from the King, her grip ripping a hole in his shirt.

She did not fight them, did not so much as put up a mild shrug to try and escape. She was staring at Alaric with her teeth bared, wanting nothing more than to scream for his blood.

But she would wait, they had her now.

Epharis stepped away and left her to the three vampires who had detained her, her hands behind her back in one strong grip, a set of hands on each shoulder and upper arm.

"Well brother, let's have dinner, shall we?" Epharis said dryly, his hands linked behind his back.

Alaric took a good three minutes to come back down from whatever high state of panic she had put him in. He was starting to turn red, fuming by her threats even though he did not so much as glance her way.

With so few of them eating food, the silence was stony, and the King ate with only Epharis for company.

Etani had not taken her eyes off him the whole time and he was pretending not to notice.

Halfway through the meal, the door flung open and a Drow walked in, silver eyes sweeping the room for Alaric, finding him and then realising he had company.

Dark skin turned darker at his flush and his eyes slid sideways, landing on Etani.

She had frozen in place, blinding terror filling her at the sight of the Drow though it was not the one she had come to fear.

Izziah was staring at her with his mouth slightly open, disbelief in his eyes.

Epharis had stood, thinking the same as her but when it turned out to be the wrong Drow, he looked only slightly less like he would enjoy setting the man on fire.

A hand had found her arm and she knew it belonged to Versalis; he was sitting to her left with Jaia to her right, guarding her and guarding others against her.

"What… What happened?" Izziah asked in a whisper.

"Izziah, why don't you come and join us?" Alaric suggested, desperate for an ally.

"I was looking for my brother."

The words struck her like a blow and her attention swung lightning fast to Alaric.

"He's still in the city?" she hissed.

A new hand landed on her, this time on her right as they sensed her tension.

"Of course he is, why wouldn't he be?" Izziah looked confused, his eyes lingering on the hands that held her and then back up to her face, baffled and anxious.

Shoving herself to her feet, she swatted the hands off her and Izziah jerked, stunned by the movement he had barely been able to track.

"Where is he?" she snarled.

Jaia had stood a second after her, his hand finding her upper arm. "Calm down," he whispered but she was beyond words.

The chair crashed into the wall several feet behind her and she swept around the table, heading straight for Izziah but the movement behind him caught her attention.

Epharis had seen it too and his eyes went huge

"Stop her!" he yelled, but it was too late.

She was on the Drow in a breath, the force of their collision throwing them both through the window across from the door to the dining room.

They crashed to the ground and Drizdan kneed her in the ribcage, knocking her off him but, before he could blink, she spun, getting back on her feet. He took in the changes in her and his lips pulled up into a smile.

"Why, Etani, how you've changed," he purred. "I guess I didn't beat you hard enough last time. Oh, well, I'll have to try again."

His smile vanished when she took two steps and drove her foot into his gut, sending him flying.

Versalis had landed several feet away, the twins unable to help until the sun was fully set and she was gleefully spiteful that the sun did nothing to her.

A second, third and then fourth set of boots landed with a thud, but she ignored them, already running after the Drow as he launched himself to his feet, blood dripping from his mouth.

He had turned, ready for her as she ran for him, three sets of feet going after her, but she had a good head start on them and he grinned as he ran to meet her.

They hit hard, her knee going up into his side as his fist landed on her jaw, both staggering back and going again, and then again before the three were on them.

Versalis caught her around the middle, dragging her away while Izziah grabbed Drizdan. Epharis had moved between them, ready to defend her and then changed his mind, punching Drizdan in the face.

She screamed her joy at the sight of the Drow's head whipping back, but Epharis had turned and was helping Versalis to drag her backwards.

"I'll kill you!" she screamed at Drizdan, his eyes hot on her and he licked his lips, that stupid stud glittering in the dying light.

"Come and try, Princess, and we'll go for round two. I miss the sound of your screams!"

Epharis nearly turned back but decided it was better to get her away and finally she was free, turning to see the King standing only two paces away.

Chancing it, she closed those two steps and drove her foot into his chest. He flew back, hitting the wall hard enough to knock the stone loose. Versalis tackled her, but she did not care. She was glad to see Alaric on his back.

Drizdan cackled when she kicked Alaric, his vicious grin on her

with renewed desire. She knew he would try and get to her again, but this time she was ready.

THE KING WAS LIVID, and she glared at him, waiting for him to retaliate, but his eyes fell to her belly and he looked away. He knew she had a right to her fury at him and he was not going to argue it. Limping away, he glanced back at her over his shoulder, grim determination on his face.

She was concerned about that look but there was nothing she could do about it until he made his move.

The Lich and vampire led her away but instead of following them to the basement, she simply refused to go, wanting to head up to her room and collect supplies.

She was getting bored down there and Epharis offered to accompany her.

Reluctantly agreeing, the vampires allowed them to leave and they headed up to her old rooms.

Sweeping inside, she scanned the room and began to collect items, stuffing them into a bag or the Lich's arms when they would not fit in the bag. He simply watched her in silence until she had loaded him up.

"Etani, we should talk," he said gently. She ignored him. "Etani, come on, it's not just you who is suffering. We can help each other if you just let me in."

She went still, her back to him as she gritted her teeth, Kai's calling her selfish echoing in her head.

Keeping her eyes on the floor, she let out a soft breath.

"Fine," she whispered, and heard him putting the things down she had loaded onto him.

Approaching her, he wrapped his arms tightly around her shoulders from behind, hugging her against him. Her hands found his forearms and she clenched her eyes shut, recalling his words when she had tried to kill him.

Her fingers gently brushed his forearm. "A Lich can't love, Epharis."

"A Lich has never been known to love, nor lust, hesitate or care," he whispered in her ear.

She stilled, listening to his breathing and going over his words in her head. His grip tightened around her and then released, and she turned, looking up at him. He seemed momentarily stunned but he quickly shook it off as he studied her face, his hand rising to her cheek.

"Can a Lich love?" she asked finally, her eyes on him.

"This one can," he said simply.

Her sob was quiet, but his arms engulfed her and hers moved around him, clinging to each other in their combined pain and suffering.

Drawing him to the couch, they sat together in silence, their joined misery bringing them closer together than either of them expected and when his lips touched her forehead, she melted into him.

Her chin lifted and his dropped to meet hers, their lips tender and lingering while his fingers became lost in her hair and hers found the front of his robes, holding each other as close as was possible.

For a long time, they remained like that until he finally drew her from the couch and into the bedroom.

Every touch was gentle, brushing the straps of her dress away to allow the fabric to pool at her feet, her hands sliding down his front to release the buttons, pressing the fabric away, until it pooled at the belt around his waist.

He reached behind her, releasing the clasp of her brassiere and dropping it, her hands doing the same with the belt, leaving him naked.

Her underwear was brushed away, tender and slow while their lips moved in passionate, longing brushes.

Drawing her to the bed, he laid her down and settled atop her, her legs willingly parting to give him access and he did not hesitate.

They made love, slow and gentle for the first time, their breaths mingling as they made soft sounds of pleasure. His lips found her ear and he bit gently just to feel her shiver under him and see her smile, her returning nip against his lip earning her a smile in return.

Her fingers explored his back, scraping her nails over old scars to make him shudder atop her and finally when he found his release, he breathed, "I love you."

They lingered there in her room for hours, exploring each other for the first time and trying to figure out how it all worked. Neither of them had been in love before, neither knew what to do and neither was overly comfortable with the concept.

They made love again close to morning and as the sun rose, they stood together in the warmth of the sunlight, naked and watching each other warily.

In another hour, guards burst into the room and they were both arrested for treason.

IRON BOUND her arms in three places; her wrists, elbows, and just below her armpits to keep her arms stretched out down her back. She had been permitted to get dressed, but that was all and Epharis only had enough time to pull on his robes.

Once she had been bound, he was less interested in fighting and more interested in making sure they did not hurt her, their stunned hunger at the sight of her making him worry about her.

The timing had been perfect. In the middle of the day the twins would have a harder time getting to them, leaving only Versalis who had not been informed, as far as she could tell.

A fourth set of shackles ran between her feet, allowing her to walk but not run.

Rough hands held their arms and they were led through the castle and into the throne room where Alaric was sitting, a smug smile on his face and his eyes sweeping between the two of them.

There was no crowd that time, no one to see what happened and no one to defend them.

The entire trial was a sham, made up, and Alaric revelled in their indignation, but he had his plan and he was going to see it through to the end.

They were charged with attempted murder, attacking the King, and trying to overthrow him. In all honesty, she could not fault him on his ability to make those up, though the last one had been fabricated, the first two were entirely true.

She could not help but note that he deliberately ignored what he had done to them, which was to try and have the Prince killed and the foreign Princess mutilated, her child ripped from her womb and then beaten for hours.

But who was counting?

The Drow entered the room at some point; Versalis had crept in and the three watched, two with horror and one with delight.

Their punishment was simple: death. Not the most original plan but a good one.

"You can't do this, Alaric," Epharis had snapped, cutting the man off on some great long spiel that she had stopped listening to a good three minutes beforehand, her eyes finding Versalis and offering him a little wave.

His eyes slid from hers and she frowned in confusion. A moment later, though, she found out why. Hands gripped the shackles between her wrists and jerked her arms up, forcing her to her knees.

Bent forward, the scent of Drizdan made her stomach clench and she was certain she was going to vomit at the thought of him being so close.

Epharis had turned, but Izziah had grabbed his chain and held him back.

The Lich was beside himself at Drizdan being anywhere near her.

"Touch her and I'll rip you to shreds," Epharis snapped and the Drow laughed, something hard and metal tracing along her inner arm and drawing blood.

He had attached a guard to his fingers with long, sharp points that cut her skin easily.

Fear turned her blood to ice and Versalis had started to move forward, but Alaric stopped him, raising a brow at the four of them.

"Perhaps death is too good for you two..." Alaric said, and the hand gripped her arm, pulling her up from her bent position to better see the King though she was unable to stand with his grip on her.

She was seriously considering biting a chunk out of his arm when Alaric made her look around.

"Perhaps we can have Drizdan take the Princess back to Faerie and hand her over to the Winter Court?" he said casually.

The silence was deafening as she imagined that trip. Alone with him, unable to escape or defend herself as she was right then.

Epharis looked like he was going to set the entire castle on fire.

"You, brother, surely you will return to yourself once this witch is gone?"

"That witch is my wife, Alaric," Epharis warned, but he was just as trapped as she was.

"And will you cling to that when she is married off for some alliance and you are alone in fifty years?" Alaric asked, Drizdan's hand tightening on her arm and making her flinch.

"For an eternity," Epharis said, glancing down at her just as she looked up at him.

Drizdan slapped her when her eyes left Alaric and she gasped. Her cheek was burning as she felt her temper flaring. Shoving herself back, she flicked herself around and sank her teeth deep into the front of his thigh, just above his knee.

His blood tasted divine, but she blocked it out, focusing instead on biting down and jerking her head back, the chunk she ripped away enough to fill her mouth and she spat it out.

Screaming profanities, he gripped her hair and drove his good knee into her face, her body hitting the floor as he released her with blood pouring from her nose.

"We shall see, Epharis, eternity is a very long time," Alaric said calmly, watching as Drizdan's boot landed in her stomach and she slid back on the marble. "We shall see just how long you last once she is gone."

SHE WAS NOT EVEN GIVEN a full day, the twins arriving just in time for her to be thrown into a carriage with a grinning Drizdan binding her tightly, making sure to hurt her as badly as possible.

The King ordered him not to bruise her too badly, but he knew how quickly she healed, and it was not going to be long before he was hurting her.

The hole in his pants showed pink flesh, fresh and new.

The twins knew they could not follow, panicked at her loss but before she had been dragged from the hall, she had demanded that enough blood be taken to supply the twins and that she be permitted to return to keep them supplied. She had been woozy as she was loaded into the carriage, a year's worth of blood depleting her almost entirely. But she figured she probably did not want to be awake for the ride to the Under Dark.

It turned out that the Drow brothers had returned to ensure the Princess was delivered to Winter, requesting access to her and Alaric had gleefully agreed, punishing her and patient enough to wait.

She could not guess his endgame, but she suspected she was not going to like it very much.

Within the first half hour, Drizdan had turned on her, slapping and punching her repeatedly for the sheer fun of seeing her pain, her weakness and lack of retaliation making him angry. Instead, he only brutalised her further, leaving her bleeding and almost comatose.

Wiping the blood on his pants, he watched her with a smile on his face.

"You know Princess, they're going to want a husband to keep you busy. Since the Lich isn't a viable option for you, I might put my hand up for the role. The Winter Princess and the Drow Prince, what do you think?" he asked, leaning in to whisper in her ear and he laughed when he heard her breathing stop.

"An eternity with you, what a dream that would be."

He pulled her up off the floor by her hair, his eyes going down over her exposed backside and thighs that glistened with blood from his finger guards.

"Just imagine what our children would look like," he purred, his eyes lighting up in the face of her fear.

She snapped at his nose, but she was not close enough and it only earnt her another slap, his hands rough as he turned her around and shoved her chest down on the seat of the carriage. He did not violate her, but instead, he used the claw-like attachment to tear her skin, leaving her unable to sit for hours, forcing her to watch as he pleasured himself.

THE WINTER COURT

When they arrived at the Under Dark the next day, Drizdan was still tying the laces of his pants as he jumped down the steps to face his mother and her entourage.

Looking past him, her eyes met Etani's and the woman cringed at the state of her. She was bleeding from her lip, her dress torn, bruises were covering her arms and legs, along with a myriad of cuts and scrapes.

"You're an animal," she hissed at her son, disgusted.

"I am what you made me mother," he replied, smiling as she was pulled from the carriage, the gasp going around when she was free of the darkness that hid her.

She had no way of covering herself with her arms behind her back and the front of her dress had been badly tattered, Drizdan's eyes lingering on her chest as he grinned.

"She's valuable, idiot. Damage her and they won't let us keep the gate," the Queen said.

"She'll heal. Take her to my rooms, she'll be safe there," Drizdan said and the guards obeyed without question.

They left her in the room, and she perused it. It was remarkably similar to the one he had in the compound, all greys, silvers, and blacks with just a hint of green.

She did not have long before he arrived, removing two sets of the chains that bound her and cutting the remainder of her dress from her body.

He groped her roughly, growling his delight when she managed to shove herself back from him.

"Going to start fighting it, are we?" he said cruelly as he grabbed her arm and dragged her into the bathroom.

Alternating between getting her cleaned, beating her further, and forcing her to dress while being slapped and pinched, he finally got her into a presentable state and dressed in a soft pair of grey pants and a vest.

Keeping his grip on her constantly, she was pulled from the palace and taken along with everyone else down a small path that led to a large gate. It had been made out of twisted thorns growing up out of the rock and manipulated into a large square doorway, the inside of it showing a Winter forest covered in snow and icicles but they could not smell nor hear the forest from their side.

"You will take her to the palace, you will not touch her again until she is safely in their custody. Then you are free to throw your life away as you wish," the Queen said to her eldest son, he gritted his teeth then shoved her through the archway.

Stumbling through, the archway touched her skin like a feather, brushing over her and she stepped through, turning to see shocked faces, and even Drizdan looked surprised.

Glancing down, she saw odd patterns glowing gently on her skin, vines and swirls that she had never seen before. They were silvery, barely visible but beautiful and giving her an exotic look she rather liked.

It was only an hour to the palace and the snow made it even harder, taking them longer to get there.

"I'm going to miss that body," Drizdan sighed, dragging her along behind him.

"We all are," said the guard to their right and she flushed, hating that they had watched as he had beaten and abused her, ripping her clothes to leave her exposed and threatening to do worse.

Drizdan laughed, yanking her harder to get her to hurry up.

When the palace came into view, they all went still.

It was enormous. Ten times bigger than Ayathian, with tower after tower sticking up in the shape of icicles. The whole thing looked to have been made of ice and was glowing faintly blue.

Drizdan looked at her, hunger in his eyes but they were too close for him to touch her.

"Don't worry, she'll be legally yours in a few weeks. Then, you can have her any time you desire," the guard said, glancing at her.

She frowned at him. She could not understand what he was on about, but she shook her head and dropped her eyes.

THEIR TREK down to the palace was slow, unable to see what was under the snow and ice as they walked, and, crossing a pond, she got a fright as a creature bumped against the underside of the ice.

It had a human shape to the waist and then a long fishtail, blue skin and blue eyes, with darker blue diamond patterns on its chest and back.

It grinned at her, showing pointed teeth and pressed one webbed hand against the ice before it vanished again.

She had never seen a mercreature before, the exotic, lethal beauty of it making her understand how so many humans had fallen prey. That one was a male, and she would have gladly swum to her death to be with him. She could only imagine the radiance of their women.

Finally, they reached the palace and the doors were wide, a small group of women standing in a line, the middle wearing an enormous and elaborate black gown.

The Queen was tall and slender, her creamy pale skin marked with silvery diamonds and her eyes a crystalline blue. Her lips were black to match her hair, which trailed down to disappear into her train on the ground.

Atop her head rested a large crown of frozen roses and tall, thin icicles that only added to her height with a single chain running from one side of the crown to the other, with an unblemished diamond hanging from it to rest between her perfect black brows.

Drizdan and the guards bowed deeply to the woman. Etani, however, could only stare at her, even as the Queen stared back, trying to discern any similarities.

The hair was the same, along with the full lips and long ears, but otherwise, they looked different.

"Granddaughter," she said finally, breaking the silence.

"Grandmother," Etani returned coolly, still refusing to bow.

The woman's lips twisted into a smile and Etani saw she had the same sharp little canines as her own and the woman stepped forward, sweeping down the stairs to embrace her.

When she was unable to return the embrace, the Queen looked behind her to see Etani's arms were bound and raw.

"Take that with you as you go," the Queen snapped at the Drow guards who moved quickly to release her.

Rubbing her arms gently, she very seriously considered making a run for it, but she would only end up in the Under Dark again. Ceress was too far away for her to reach.

"Are you Drizdan?"

They began to converse, but Etani's attention had turned away from them to the neat row of young women. Each one looked similar even though their eyes and hair varied from one to the next. She assumed they were distant relatives. The youngest met her eyes while the rest looked strictly forward.

She was around eleven or twelve and she grinned, revealing little pointed canines, her eyes a bright blue not that different from her own.

Smiling back slightly, she looked back to her grandmother, who had invited the Drow inside.

The Queen set off into the palace and she hesitated, looking longingly back into the trees before she turned back and followed the group inside.

From the outside, it appeared to be nothing but ice. On the inside, though, it was infinitely more than that.

Marble, glass and ice all mixed with hardwood and soft cushions. There were creatures everywhere, of all shapes and sizes though she noted they all had similar colouring, all colder tones of blues, greens, purples and the like, except for the occasional splash of bright red or yellow.

She had to assume they were from Summer and had defected.

People stared at her as she passed, curious and fascinated by that new creature who had the markings that, at least to her own eyes, seemed to be unique to the royal family.

It was somewhat safe to assume there was no escaping her heritage.

The throne room was enormous with a huge ice throne carved into a shape of a large rose lying on its side, the Queen would be seated at its heart where a small cushion lay waiting.

Their appearance had caused a stir in the large gathering of what appeared to be the upper class.

The Queen approached the dais, her massive dress clearing a path more than her actual presence did and once she stepped up, she turned, holding her hand out to Etani.

"Please welcome Princess Etania, the daughter of our much-beloved son Lutheral," the Queen proclaimed and Etani's hand slipped into hers as she stepped up onto the dais beside her grandmother.

The woman smiled, turning her to the crowd and the cheer was enough to make her ears ache. She had never felt so completely and utterly terrified.

WHEN THE CHEERING CEASED, Drizdan stepped forward, his timing impeccable in the general buzz of excitement and joy at her return.

"Your majesty, the great Queen of Winter. I wish to ask Princess Etani's hand in marriage."

The room went suddenly silent at the proclamation and the Queen turned to her. She saw then that the Queen was not all she seemed to be, a cold light coming into her eyes as if she knew everything.

"It would bring Winter great honour to join Winter and the Drow together," she said, and Etani's heart sank.

They had planned the whole thing, right down to Drizdan's proclamation and the Queen agreeing.

That had been the deal all along. Drizdan would recover her, provided he got to keep her.

"You can't, I'm already married," she said, lifting her hand and, to her horror, the dark mark around her finger had vanished.

"No dear child, your marriage was annulled the moment you set foot in Winter. It is forbidden to marry the dead. You will marry Drizdan."

Taking a step back from the Queen, their entire conversation drowned out by the cheering of the crowd, the wild clapping, and she turned; Drizdan's grin was feral.

Pulled from the dais by two enormous trolls who had been dressed to look like guards, she was yanked away under the guise of getting her safely to her new rooms. Drizdan followed with his hands in his pants pockets, basking in the light of his success. They shoved her inside and she immediately turned on him, resenting his grin.

"You and that witch had this whole thing planned, didn't you?" she whispered, hating him.

"Of course we did. Isn't this place wonderful? All the rules are different."

"I will never marry you," she said and that made his smile slip.

"I'm afraid you don't have a choice, Princess. If Winter declares us married, we are married."

"That's rubbish!" she cried, hating everything about that place.

Approaching her, he smiled cruelly.

"Get used to it, Etani. There is no Epharis, no twins, no vampire

King, no one here to save you this time. You will belong to me in a matter of days."

"Why do you pursue me?" she whispered, and his eyes narrowed.

"A strong King must have a strong Queen. One who bows only to him."

"You're not the King," she said slowly, not understanding.

"No, but I *will* be once my mother and sisters are dead. With no one left, I will take the throne with you by my side and Winter at your call."

"I will never bow to you," she breathed, and he smiled at her as his hand flew out to strike her and she gasped, staggering back.

"You will obey your husband. I'm not as sentimental as the Lich. I will not tolerate disobedience from a woman."

Soon after that he left, and she crawled into a huge bed with fur covering it in layers, falling into an uneasy sleep.

SHE HAD BEEN TOLD that the wedding was due to take place in three days and so she used that time to do as much research on her family as possible. It turned out that her grandmother had indeed not been a pureblood Fae, but it was not surprising, considering how many Fae chose to bring in other species to keep the bloodlines free of degradation. The Queen's name turned out to be Tatialia, a name she thought rather odd, at least until she learnt that one of her middle names had been Ysabel and the connection was made.

Her name at birth had been Etania Ysabel Alicia Vellorie Selene Laelia Daewen, something not even her parents knew. It was simply something you knew at birth.

The name number depended on birth, the first always having six or more and the rest having five and occasionally six with those names being taken from family lineage. One name for the eldest child came from each grandmother and one from the mother. Her mother had told her that Alicia had come from her, and now she knew that

Ysabel came from her grandmother. The other names were random and sometimes even words that did not make sense at all or were in another language.

No one was willing to study names for fear of someone else finding out theirs because that would spell doom. If someone had another's name, they could command that person to do anything at all so long as they had it and knew how to pronounce it.

She had not even told Letari or Avadari her full name, it was too risky. They had all exchanged the one name they had adopted from their mother, Belladonna Lyla Deanne Alicia Rivenden. Etani got Alicia, Letari got Deanna and Avadari got Lyla. The order in which the names were taken were random and if the parent gave birth to more children than the number of names they had, names would be recycled. A first or last name was never used.

Should she have children, she would have to have five before one of her names was recycled and unless the parent told the child, there was no way of knowing which name it was that had been taken.

It was all entirely too complicated, and no one was all that keen to test theories.

It was during one of her adventures in the library when she stumbled upon something unexpected. She had found a family tree between a couple of books, not well hidden, but if one were not looking for it, they would not have found it. It was strange, clearly outlining each person starting at herself with Letari, going up to Lutheral, Tatialia, higher to a woman named Tephanie, Ameline. It was so odd, each line marking a clear straight pattern down with others being brought in, but on and on it went, a name and a species. She was very quickly figuring out a pattern. No species duplicated, woman after woman, back and back, generation after generation in a solid straight line. One child, always a girl, always marrying a new species, birthing a girl except for three abnormalities that broke up the smooth, singular line. The first woman had birthed five, Lutheral was born a male, and she had been born a twin.

The line had been marked out as far back as the page reached, starting with a single name, Villaria and she had been a human who had remained unmarried, the five children seeming to sprout from nothing. Four of the children were male, judging by the names and their lines ended within one or two generations; it was the girl who married a vampire, their daughter on to a dragonkin, and down with one man entering the picture only to birth a daughter and then, no more.

The sight made her feel sick, it was too perfect, too clean and she felt suddenly that someone out there had been in control the whole time.

She stuffed the tree into her dress and headed back to her room. It had taken the better part of the time she had allowed, leaving her one day left to try and escape with the tree.

Packing herself a small supply of weapons she had scavenged, mostly kitchen knives and the like, she had tried to sneak out only to find a large number of troll guards keeping her from leaving.

The Queen knew she would try and run. Her rooms had no windows and no access to any other part of the palace.

Retreating to her room, she sat and waited, knowing what was coming.

THE DAY ARRIVED and she stood as the Queen entering with five ladies. They were all elves, all looked snobbish and they were all there to help her dress.

Forced to sit and have her face applied with subtle tones of pigment, she watched the women in silence, many of them looking irritated at having to be there.

The dress she was forced into really was lovely, made of creamy satin in a soft silver that enhanced the visibility of her markings. A large coat was placed over it, lined in grey fur with elaborate snowflakes stitched into it with silver thread and pearls.

Her neck was left bare and, oddly, they took special care to keep her ears uncovered.

They had been horrified by the single rings that had still lingered in her lobes from Nayishma's maids and they removed them quickly, hoping no one had seen.

The robe was to remain off her shoulders, exposing the long line of her neck and shoulders as well as the top of her chest in the strapless gown. She did not know why, but she accepted it.

Her long hair was pulled up into a series of braids and knots, looking beautiful with strings of pearls and silver loops.

With her pale complexion, she looked every part the Winter Princess she was.

The time was fading fast and she was forced to slip into a pair of simple flat slippers that would be removed at the doors to the throne room. A bride was to go barefoot into her wedding.

The Queen dismissed the ladies and the two women stood silent for several long seconds. She was in shock, unsure of what was going to happen if she was going to survive.

"You are a Princess of the Winter Court," the regal woman said, staring down her nose at her granddaughter. "You understand what that means, and what your role is for the Winter Court. You understand that an alliance between the Drow and Winter is beneficial."

Remaining silent, she stared blankly at the wall in the hopes that she could vanish into it. The Queen did not seem to need a response, something she was glad for as she did not think she could formulate one.

"As a Princess, it is your duty to submit to what is best for the Court and your people. This was always a possibility for you. You will marry Drizdan, and you will submit to him as his wife. You will not fight, or I will be forced to do worse than give you to a Drow. I will keep you here, never to return to the human world. Right now, that is still permitted, but if you try and stop this… I will ensure there is nothing left of that world for you to run to."

Looking up, she swallowed as she took in the cold indifference of the woman. Did she really hate her granddaughter so much? What had she ever done to deserve that?

"Marry the man, submit to his pleasure, give him a child if that is his wish, and I will be generous with your freedom. I will not harm those little vampires in the human world. Then, when you are Queen, you may do as you wish. You are the heir to Winter, keep your emotions private and your opinions to yourself. The Court comes first."

Without another word, the woman turned and left the room.

Leading her through the halls, she had begun to tremble at the events before her, fear burning through her soul.

The throne room had been set out with many chairs in rows, the aisle strewn with black petals, and she lifted her eyes to him. Slipping off her shoes, she started her slow march towards her doom. He would have been handsome had she not hated him so much.

His black hair was long and trailed to his shoulder blades. He wore spikey black and gold armour that did nothing to make him look less intimidating and his nearly black eyes were unfathomable as he looked back at her.

His ears had also been left uncovered and she gritted her teeth as she approached him, her hands clasped before her as she had been instructed.

Strong jaw, high cheekbones and sharp eyes. He would be gorgeous to any other woman; to her he was a monster. Lips turned up into the faintest hint of a smile, strong shoulders and a chiselled chest, a slender build but muscular, designed to move fast and dodge easily.

She came to a slow stop before him, her face paler than normal as he took her hand and she shuddered.

His ear piercings had been removed and like her own, the holes had closed entirely. The fact made her terribly nervous.

Black eyes left hers as he turned to face the throne, their hands held up between them for all to see.

The Queen approached, her blue eyes gleamed with joy at the sight of them.

He had not spoken to her, no one was speaking at the rushed royal wedding. She did not think anyone was all that thrilled by the events though, she thought people mostly just looked confused. The girl who had just been returned to them, suddenly belonging to a Drow rather than a Fae or any other species that would be preferable. But no one said a word and she felt crushed by everything that was happening.

"We are gathered here to celebrate the greatest union there is, joining two mighty empires. Prince Drizdan and Princess Etania will bring great joy to our peoples."

Her hand was shaking, and he gripped it tighter, not painful but enough to keep her still.

"Do you, Drizdan of the Drow Court, take this woman as your lawful wife in this world and the next, for eternity and beyond?"

"I do," he said, his voice husky with his triumph.

"Do you, Etania of the Winter Court, take this man as your lawful husband in this world and the next, for eternity and beyond?" the Queen intoned

Her silence was met with whispers and he squeezed her hand sharply.

She gasped in pain. "I do."

"So, may it be," the Queen said simply, and she lifted a small pillow from a table behind her giant dress. Atop it was a large collection of rings and she frowned, realising they were earrings, two sets each.

Scooping up the first set, Drizdan moved to her side and his breath was cool on her cheek as he touched her ear.

Each ring stabbed her ear, causing her to flinch in pain but she did not move. She realised why her chest and shoulders were bare, so blood would drip onto them, which he then licked away.

Switching sides, he did the same to her other ear and then stepped back in front of her, his smile disgustingly smug.

Taking the rings from the pillow, her fingers shook as she split the pile, four on each.

Her eyes lifted to his and then slid away to his ear. It was smaller than hers, short but with a sharper point. Faint hints of marks showed her where the rings would go.

He did not so much as twitch as each sharp stem pierced his ear and then the other, the blood that dripped onto his shoulder quickly wiped away with her tongue and he shuddered at the sensation.

Stepping back before him, they turned back to the crowd and it was done, they were married.

It was such a solemn affair, not what she had ever heard a Fae wedding to be like, and the crowd was grim. But they still cheered for her, even as she saw many craning to see the young couple better.

25

IS TWO REALLY BETTER THAN ONE?

He wasted no time taking her then. The crowd expected the newlywed couple to flee into privacy and he did exactly that, dragging her behind him and into her suite where he practically threw her inside.

"Now was that so hard?" he said as he removed the armour, dropping it onto the floor to leave him in only his shirt and trousers.

He approached her, roughly tugging the robe from her shoulders and throwing it to the floor.

"No," she breathed, fear radiating through her while he moved around her, tugging at the laces of her gown and forcefully yanking it down to leave her in nothing but her undergarments.

Turning to stand before her, his eyes trailed over her bare breasts and down, the scar on her belly vanishing with her transformation.

He did not seem to like that much, finally looking up at her.

"Undress me," he ordered.

After only a brief hesitation, she lifted her hands and caught the hem of his shirt, lifting it over his head and dropping it to the ground beside them.

His muscles were tense, every cord on high alert, expecting her to try something.

She did not.

Instead, she dropped her hands and pulled the ties of his trousers free, pushing them down with as little contact with his bare skin as possible.

Smiling, he stepped out of them, delighting in her discomfort. "Remove those."

She went still, it was one thing to have him strip her, it was another to strip for him but when his hand lifted to hit her, she hooked her thumbs in the band and slid them down over her hips, stepping out of them and leaving her naked.

Wrapping her arms around herself, she chewed on her inner lip. She knew she was trapped, that she was never going to be able to escape him. She also knew that to fight him would lead to disaster. They were married now. That meant she had to submit, but the thought of surrendering to him had her stomach clenching in fear.

He pressed her backwards, knowing full well she would retreat until the back of her legs hit the bed.

"Are you going to be difficult?" he asked, and she shook her head.

Nodding, he pressed her back and he waited for her to scoot back from the edge of the bed, following her a moment later.

He knelt between her knees, one hand scooping under each and parting her legs for him. He immediately settled between them and breathed a soft sigh at the feeling of her against him.

"If you try anything…" he trailed off, but she could only shake her head again, panic filling her and he smirked, glad to have her submissive that one time.

Gripping her right thigh, he dug his nails in as he shifted her and pressed forward.

Her eyes slid shut as he claimed his new bride, gentler than he had ever touched her but it felt more domineering that way. He did not hit her or try to hold her down, he simply knew she belonged to him and he could have her however he wanted.

The sounds he made had her entire body going cold, staring up at the ceiling with the sight of his broad shoulder above her, his muscles bunching and relaxing as he moved against her. His hair tickled her shoulder, but she did not dare move or risk him hurting her.

It was not as unpleasant as she thought it would be, but her unaroused state still made it uncomfortable. He did not seem to notice or care if she was eager. He only wanted her body and he had gotten it.

His hips ground against hers and he moved smoothly, his breath coming in pants as his pleasure mounted and finally, after what felt like an eternity, he found his release inside her and got off her.

Leaving her to head to the bathroom, she rolled onto her side and remained there, cold and broken as her husband cleaned himself up.

SHE HAD no concept of the passage of time. Winter only had one season, the perpetual dim of Winter. It made her confused and irritable when she did not know how long they had been trapped. She and Drizdan had come to an uneasy truce. If she did not fight him, he would not hurt her or be unnecessarily rough. He was also not permitted to stay in her rooms if she had fulfilled her duties as a wife. That had caused an argument and he learnt first-hand just how much she had changed.

He had stalked into her room, furious that she had asked that he not be granted access to her and had been kicked back through the wall. It had been a bad night for her. When he realised he could not contain her he had enlisted the troll guards and they had mutely held her between them by the arms while he took what he wanted from her body.

After that, a truce had formed. He would not get the guards to hold her down, but she would allow him into her bed once per day.

It was not perfect, but they made it work.

Time had escaped her entirely and after a quiet enquiry, she was horrified to learn that she had been in Faerie for just over eight months. Her body clock had told her perhaps two, but not eight.

She had been working silently in that time to first study her family, and then collect some items. She wanted weapons, but she required something special.

She had finally found what she needed, stolen from a guard who had been distracted chatting up some pretty little elf. No one said trolls were intelligent.

The news had forced her to decide, either go to Tatialia or go to her husband, she needed to go back.

When she knocked on the door to his rooms, he had first been shocked and then smugly pleased that she had come. He was not much thrilled when he learnt of her reason, but he revelled in the fact that she had come to him asking for permission to do something.

"I have to go back," she said simply, the door behind her barely shut.

"No, you don't. You belong here with me," he had retorted automatically.

"I have an agreement with Jaia and Kai that is in danger of collapsing. It was part of my agreement to come here quietly," she narrowed her eyes at him and he frowned, recalling the discussion.

She could not leave them and her own need for their blood in return had driven her to distraction whenever she thought about it. She knew it was not the addiction they had hoped to get out of her, but even the thought of the twins drove her wild with hunger.

He reluctantly agreed, provided he was to accompany her, and that he was to be allowed into her room an extra time in a twenty-four-hour period.

He had been frustrated that he had not managed to impregnate her, and she had not told him that every time he did, she had found ways to destroy it, usually by inserting a long, thin knife into her womb through her abdomen. She did not know how many times she had done it, but it was too many.

She did not want him to go with her, but those were the terms and she agreed, before submitting to his pleasure.

Once he was done with her, he had smiled and left her to dress on her own.

Before they left, she returned to her room to collect the family tree she had stolen and she paused to see three new entries, Drizdan and a double line leading down from their union. The two names had her staring in horror. Kailee and Lorelle.

The new additions had baffled her, and she studied herself, finding no two lights inside her as she had done before. Were they a mistake? She did not know but she did not have time to worry about it just then.

She shook her head and bundled up the papers, stuffing them into a bag and then shoving the entire bag down the front of her corset.

They had not been permitted to leave in casual attire. She had been forced into an enormous black gown, a diamond hanging between her brows on the long silver chain. Her hair decorated very similarly to her wedding day and she sighed at the lack of manoeuvrability the stupid thing had. But she had agreed simply to avoid having to fight anyone on the subject.

The gown was made from velvet with a silvery thread around the sleeves and hem; pretty, but it was heavy.

Drizdan was wearing his armour and he looked fantastic, judging by the wistful stares that many of the women wore. She thought they could have him, though she resentfully noted that yes, he was incredibly attractive, and his arrogant smile made her shiver.

He took her hand in his and a young, dark-haired woman had stepped forward to open a gate for them. Etani had wanted to make it herself, but it turned out that they had gatekeepers that were capable of opening gates to anywhere in the human world.

The thought had confused her; she was fascinated with the young woman.

She had drawn a rough arch in the air and then vines had cracked up through the ice, forming a large archway that opened with a pleasing rippling effect.

She had to wonder at the girl, and why none of the others did it themselves but that would have to wait.

They stepped through and into a hallway just off the hall in Ayathian.

Marvelling at the talent of the gatekeeper, she turned to Drizdan. "One day?" she asked, and he nodded, his eyes hard on her.

"Back here," he agreed; they both had things they needed to do.

He kissed her cheek and left. Sighing, she dragged the ridiculous train behind her. She had managed to get down the stairs to the twins' rooms and smiled at the low sound of murmurs.

When the door swung open, only one seemed to notice her. Versalis looked up and went still, the twins and Epharis were still talking quietly, looking angry. She was pondering how she was going to fit the bulky dress through the doorway, unsure of her ability to get it through without help.

"You really shouldn't pout so much, or you'll turn grey," she said as a way of greeting, and three heads snapped up, taking her in.

They were on her in an instant, dragging her into the room with ecstatic voices. Their hugs were tight, the jibes against her attire half-hearted. There was no denying she looked magnificent in that dress, even if it was massive.

"I only have a day," she said once they had all calmed down.

Her eyes settled on Epharis, the only one who had not hugged her. She went to him, her hands gentle as she drew him down into a prolonged kiss. When his arms went around her, she sighed at the warmth of him against her. They did not linger for long, though, because Versalis was the first to notice her ears.

"Who did they force you to marry?" he demanded and Epharis let go of her as though she had hit him.

She remained silent, too busy missing Epharis' touch.

"Etani!" Kai shouted.

Jerking her eyes from Epharis, she looked around at the three vampires and frowned at their concerned looks. "What?"

"Your ears," Versalis pressed.

Flushing, she averted her eyes. "The Winter Queen Tatialia in her great wisdom has decided to join the Drow to the Winter Court through my and Drizdan's marriage."

Her voice was flat, devoid of emotion, but the ensuing silence was absolute as the vampires first took in the news and then drew their conclusions of what her marriage to the Drow would look like.

No one moved, and Etani's face was set in a mask.

"No," Kai whispered, horrified.

"How can they do that?" Jaia exploded, grabbing her arms, and pulling her forward.

But he had nowhere to take her, and no way to protect her.

"Winter is absolute," Versalis said with a calculating gleam in his eyes.

"What of our marriage?" Epharis seethed, and they all drew back from the Lich's fury.

His arms licked with green fire and they all knew to get back from him while they had the chance, pulling her behind them.

"I don't know. I have to think about that. It's possible that Etani would be married to you here, and him in Faerie. Or her marriage to Drizdan may be nulled because she was already married. You will need to tell me more about your laws, Epharis."

Versalis was calm, far too calm for her liking, and she shivered.

"Why is he so obsessed?" Kai demanded, looking unreasonably angry compared to the others.

"I asked him that. He says he wants a strong Queen when he wipes out his family to take over the Drow Throne."

For a moment there was silence and then Versalis barked out a laugh that made them jump.

"Well, if nothing else, the man has dreams."

AFTER THEY MANAGED to calm Epharis, his arms found her, holding her tight to him like a vice. No one was willing to discuss what was being done to her or the implications on their lives.

Finally, when everyone was calm enough to think, Etani wriggled the bag out from where it had been crushed between her and Epharis, and handed it over to Kai.

"I found this, *easily* I might add. It's my family lineage and the whole thing was just too perfect, too easy. It's convenient."

Her eyes met Jaia's and they knew it had been planted for her to find, but the question was why.

"A name, a species, a single female child."

Epharis was looking over her shoulder at the parchment and frowned.

"It was a girl?" he whispered, and she immediately shut the idea out of her mind.

Since she did not want to think about that, she focused on Kai. His eyes were trailing from the top to the bottom and then freezing.

"Epharis is on here," he said, frowning.

She blinked and, forcing Epharis to let go of her, she circled to see what Kai saw.

"In Winter it wrote Drizdan," she breathed, glancing first at Epharis and then at her left hand. The dark band had returned.

"Who are Kailee and Lorelle?" Kai asked slowly, his eyes sliding down and to the right, two names were linked up between her and no one.

She remained silent, looking down at the two names. She had thought they would disappear with the loss of Drizdan, but no, they were still there.

"Etani, who are they?" Kai asked again, all eyes turning to her.

She shook her head and when Epharis snatched the paper, he stared down at the names and then up at her.

His eyes burned as they dropped from her face to her stomach. She was pregnant with Drizdan's offspring.

Epharis had started towards her once it clicked in his brain what the names meant, she had immediately started to back away from him.

"I've been taking care of it, every time. It's not possible," she gasped, shrinking back from the furious Lich.

Kai looked green at the realisation that she had been forced to terminate them more than once on her own. Jaia's eyes closed as he processed the information, but Versalis stood, prepared to stop Epharis if the need arose.

"Etani," Jaia said, devastated. "We can't let her go back to that monster. She can't do this forever. We have to do something."

"The law is clear," Versalis whispered, disgusted. "He has a right to her body, just as Epharis has."

Jaia looked appalled while Kai seemed close to vomiting. There was nothing they could do to protect her from either of her husbands.

Her back found the wall, her eyes on Epharis as he approached.

"I know exactly what to do," he said, his voice that calm that told her he had moved past fury and gone to that special level of anger where people died and things burned.

Versalis only lasted a second, dropped by the Lich when the vampire made to stop him and she was left alone, the twins knowing full well they were just as helpless.

"Don't hurt me," she pleaded, her eyes wide and terrified as he pressed closer, stopping only an inch from her.

"You are mine. Your body is mine," he hissed, pressing his forearm to her throat.

Gasping, she gripped his wrist and tried to pry him off her, tried to squirm but she was tired, weak, and scared.

His hand found her stomach and she whimpered at the realisation that she could not protect herself, could not protect her children. She could not do anything. Her eyes slid shut as a green fire lit up in his fingers as her skin sizzled. Her dress was burnt away and then, she was falling.

Kai looked down to the list. "Gone," he said gently, horrified by what he had witnessed.

Curling herself into a ball, she remained silent in her grief as the smell of burnt skin and clothing filled the room.

"How could you?" Versalis breathed, pulling her into his arms.

Looking up at him, an idea started to bloom in her, even as Epharis stalked across the room to check the parchment for himself.

"It had to be done," he said, but now that his anger had faded, he looked distressed.

Jaia was watching her in Versalis' arms, and saw as she leant up to whisper in his ear.

"Help me."

Versalis did not look down, but, setting his jaw, he gave an almost imperceptible nod the same time her eyes met Jaia's, and he did the same. She buried her face in Versalis' chest, his arms tight to protect her.

Kai had noticed a change between the three and when Epharis stalked from the room to calm down, they moved.

They all knew he was not going to let her leave without him, even though he would be hunted down by Alaric. Jaia pulled her to her feet, tossing his jacket over her ruined dress while Versalis swiftly swept from the room.

"We're taking Etani," Jaia said and Kai nodded, not questioning a thing.

Setting up a drip in her arm, she pumped the little ball carefully and withdrew as much blood as they had time for, combined with what had been stored. If he were careful, he would have six months.

Kai would remain behind to keep Alaric and Epharis happy.

As soon as Versalis returned, she lifted her finger to her mouth and bit the tip.

The vampires had never witnessed it before, but they needed to get out now, they were running out of time.

Drawing the line in the air, she pressed the veil forward and smiled at the hint of forest. She had wanted Ceress and that was what she got.

The two vampires went first while she paused, staring anxiously at Kai.

"I love you, Kai, I'll keep him safe," she promised, and he nodded, looking scared.

Sweeping through the door, she pulled it shut behind her and left Kai to deal with the backlash.

Stepping into Ceress, she glanced at the two vampires who had gone still, panting at the change in their world. Standing between them, she wrapped her arms around herself, providing them the time they needed to adjust.

"Don't get used to it. We won't be staying long."

They turned to her and, almost immediately, both sets of eyes affixed to the enormous spiral city behind her.

"Welcome to Ceress, the Fourth Court of Faerie, and home of the Celestrials."

Versalis' mouth was hanging open, but Jaia was looking at her now, his eyes huge.

"You opened a gateway to Faerie? You can open a gateway between the worlds?" he almost choked, shaking his head at her nod. "What are you?" he whispered, but she ignored him to check on Versalis, who looked shell-shocked.

Etani patted his cheek and he blinked rapidly at her, taking a long time to finally be able to focus.

"Come on, the longer we stay, the harder it will be to leave."

After she was sure they were both following her, she pulled them on and they skirted the border, finally walking free of the trees when she was pulled up short.

The forests of Ceress stopped rather suddenly, the same as the forests of Winter and Summer. It was unnerving to see, as the ground did not change gradually, one step there was grass and fallen leaves, the next there was snow in a perfect line.

The two men had frozen at the impossible sight, though Jaia had stopped at the sunlight that was no longer being held back by the thick canopy of leaves.

Turning to the two men, she tilted her head and considered them and their options.

"There is a place we can go, it's private and empty, or at least it was last time I was there."

Etani wanted to keep them moving, nervous about the possibility of their being found out.

The hunt never came into Ceress, but with them standing so close to the border, they might risk coming over for them.

26

FLEEING THE TORTURE

Giving them another tug, they followed reluctantly, eyes sweeping over everything as they tried to take it all in while they had the chance.

She led them back into the woods just enough to hide them from prying eyes of the Courts, they headed in the direction of Summer for about an hour, moving as quickly as they dared without using excess energy. She knew the two were straining to keep from tapping into a store of energy they had never known existed and the longer they stayed, the harder it would be for them to resist.

When they reached the location she thought was correct, she pulled them to a stop and ignored their fidgeting as she paced back and forth, trying to find the right spot. It looked slightly different now than it had when she was there years ago. When she was fairly certain she had the right spot, she bit the tip of her finger and drew a line. The blood hung in the air and she pressed the door open to reveal darkness. Smiling, she turned to the two, but they were hesitating.

"Move or I'll move you," she said, her tone as pleasant as she could make it, but the threat was clear.

Versalis swallowed hard, but Jaia took him by the arm and shoved him through. Following after him, she threw one last look at Winter and went still, her eyes on those of a man with pale skin, two dark blue triangles pointing down from his eyes. His hair was midnight black and his eyes were a deep, shockingly vivid blue.

He opened his mouth to speak, but she had already slipped through the door to greet two incredibly angry vampires.

Jaia mostly just looked irritable, Versalis was in full-rage mode and by the time she stepped through, he had ripped a large tree out of the ground and thrown it. Even she was struck by his strength and he turned to her, muscles hard and teeth bared.

"You!" he barked as he started for her. "How could your kind keep this from us? How can they deny us?"

She backed away as he approached, knowing full well he had just tasted the strength his kind should have but had been denied by hers.

"Think about what you are feeling, then think about what one hundred vampires with your current strength can do. Think about the destruction," she was trying to calm him down, but all she could do was let him rage himself out and calm on his own.

When he swiped for her, she danced back, and his miss seemed to agitate him all the more. Deciding that he had turned his rage on her for the time being, she decided to keep his attention from a safe distance. Darting past him as she knew she should not do, she took two steps and then launched herself at an enormous tree, climbing up easily with her nails digging into the soft bark.

As was instinctual for him, he took chase and prowled the base of the tree, looking up at her.

He might be an exceptionally powerful vampire, but the tree she was perched in was too big for even him to rip out and she thought it was too difficult for him to scale. He seemed to think so too, as he stayed on the ground glaring up at her.

"Come down here and let's talk," he said as she dropped her rear onto the branch, settling in for a long stay.

"I'm not so sure you're interested in talking at the moment, Versalis," she replied calmly, looking down at him as he rested his hand on the tree and gave it an experimental shove. The tree did not even shudder. Cursing, the vampire King sat down on the ground and the three settled into a long staring session.

Jaia was jittery and moved at an alarming pace where she could barely follow his movements, but he seemed to be calm enough.

"How're you holding up, Jaia?"

His eyes found her before she could blink, and he smiled in a way that made her distinctly nervous.

"Just fine Etani, thank you for asking." He was too calm. The man was a genius at strategy, and she could see his brain working but she was not entirely sure what it was working on.

She was right to suspect him, as he had wandered off after around ten minutes of their stalemate. Searching for him below, she did not see him coming from above.

Boots thudded beside her and she very nearly fell out of the tree in her surprise.

She scrambled back from him, he smiled as he followed, his hands in his pants pockets.

"So, Etani," his hands were suddenly on the tree on either side of her head, appearing out of nowhere.

"Let's talk," his arms seemed to materialise all around her and suddenly she was airborne.

She fell through the air and landed lightly in a different pair of arms. Looking up into the face of Versalis, she swallowed, and his lips pulled up into a savage grin.

JAIA APPEARED with a thud and she looked between them, afraid and doing her best not to show it.

Teeth grazed her neck in the next instant, she had not seen anyone move but suddenly they had both vanished and they bit, Jaia at her throat and Versalis at her shoulder.

She refused to scream or make a sound at all, instead she clenched her jaw and trembled between them.

By the time they had withdrawn, she felt woozy and when she

finally fell to the ground, she clutched the grass for support to keep the world from spinning.

They had begun to talk but it was too fast for her to understand and so she tuned them out and tried to figure out what to do. She had no idea how to handle the situation, having never dealt with a vampire or a vampire King high on Faerie and her blood, but she could only assume it was going to be some time before they came down.

After their conversation, it had come as a surprise to her that they had decided to use her dress to bind her rather effectively and she was thrown over Versalis' shoulder, his expression smug.

It was uncomfortable and humiliating, but she could only assume they wanted to keep her alive or else they would have drained her. She had to wonder at what would happen if they had done that, given what the twins had gone through to turn her.

Given she was their willing companion, she did not comprehend their thinking process, but she was determined to placate them until they were able to get themselves under control again.

At least, they were heading in the right direction. The building was visible in the distance and the two vampires looked to each other before heading that way, relatively calm all things considered.

The building was small and had a very abandoned look to it as if it had been left unoccupied for years. A single storey affair, relatively low with a single room. It seemed so incredibly random that it immediately piqued their interest. It was even more interesting to the two when they stepped inside, and the interior was enormous. It was sectioned off using long strips of colourful fabrics and little folding screens that divided it up into five sections. One for sleeping, another for bathing, a kitchen, an area for her experiments and attempts to make a host, with a little sitting room being the centre.

The outside looked as though the place were going to fall apart; the inside, however, looked as though they had left mere hours ago.

Dropping her onto the couch in the centre of the room, they snooped around the place before turning back to her some ten minutes later.

"What is this place?" Jaia asked.

"My sisters and I hid out here in the early days of our coming to this world. This is fairly similar to what the average apartment looks like in Ceress," As she spoke, she squirmed to get more comfortable and to twist her arms, allowing her to get her nails against the strips of her dress that bound her.

She began to cut at it and when it came free, she held it to keep them from sagging around her.

Versalis prowled the room to ensure that everything was as it seemed before moving to her and looking her over, his eyes hungry on her face.

"I can see every detail," he whispered, and she jerked back as he was suddenly a mere breath from her face.

"Versalis, you need to think—" She cut off as he licked up her cheek with that long tongue and he laughed at her shock.

Moving away from her again, he picked up a small bottle and sniffed the contents.

Behind her, Jaia seemed to materialise and she shivered as she felt his breath on her skin before she felt the air moving at his approach.

"You might as well take them off, we heard you cutting them," he whispered a mere inch from her ear and tugged the fabric from her fingers.

Letting it fall free, she turned her head just enough to see her friend and he smiled in delight at her discomfort.

She knew it would wear off, but until then they were hostile, violent, hungry and dangerous.

Several hours later she found herself on the bed between them, Jaia's leg over her hip as he breathed heavily, sprawled out against her back in an exhausted sleep.

Versalis stayed awake with her, his eyes searching her face and taking in every tiny detail as though he had to memorise them.

"You are young," he finally observed, and his eyes focused on her lips when they pulled up into the hint of a smile.

"I only look it," she responded, her eyes lowering as she shifted and

Jaia grunted at her movements, jostling him. The man was like an overgrown puppy when he slept.

Versalis looked at her in confusion and she lifted a brow, realising he may not know.

"I could die, before. I don't know if I can die now. When I died, I would be reborn into the form I had when I died the first time," she yawned, opening her eyes to see Versalis looking at her mouth with a slight frown. "I died when I was in my twenties. Pushed off Ceress when I accidentally almost killed a boy," she gave a sleepy smile at the memory, wondering what had ever happened to that boy. "He did not like it and so he pushed me off the city wall. It was a long fall and then I was in this place with all these misty creatures. I followed a ribbon and came back to my body. We did not know about the age reverse until a few years later when Ava had come to realise that Letari looked older than me even though I was the firstborn."

Nuzzling herself closer to Jaia, who growled softly in his sleep, she allowed her eyes to drift shut.

"You are a strange creature, Etani," Versalis whispered and she smiled, drifting off to sleep.

SHE WAS awoken the next day by a sharp movement beside her, Jaia scrambling away and she sat up, her eyes burning at the sudden light as she looked around. They had formed a dog pile at some point in the night and she was under one of Jaia's legs and Versalis' entire upper body, which had slid off her waist and he had bolted upright, alert for the threat.

Instead, they both turned to Jaia who had flattened himself against the wall in the tiny pool of remaining shade. He looked utterly terrified and it took her a good fifteen seconds to figure out why. The sun had been on him, but he had not been burnt.

Blinking stupidly, she looked from him to the window and back again before she reached out and took his hand, drawing it slowly into the sunlight.

Nothing happened except that his hand reflected the sunlight in a bright white glow. She tugged him along, he inched closer to put his whole arm in the sun. Still nothing.

He pulled his arm free and stepped fully into the sunlight, staring up with wide eyes, his lips parted as he looked at something he had not been able to see properly in centuries.

She could not understand what had changed but suspected it might have been the trip to Faerie and it would fade away with time, but when she turned, she found Versalis looking at her throat, a crease forming between his eyebrows.

"It's you. Everything always comes back to you," he whispered, and she shook her head, not understanding. "You're always the link. The special twist no one ever expects. Your blood allows him to walk in the sun."

The words did not make any sense to her and she shook her head again.

"It was Faerie, it has to be," she said, refusing to accept that she could have any effect on the vampires in such a way. "If that were possible it would have been discovered by now. The vampires lived in Faerie and fed off the Fae in the past."

"But you're not just a member of the Fae. You're a mixture of many creatures in this world combined," he said, and she frowned at him, refusing to believe him.

Jaia had vanished, crossing the room and flinging the door wide.

Scrambling after him, they stood in the sun and watched Jaia bathe in the warmth and light.

"Maybe it's you... Being close to a King? You can walk in the sun," she said, watching her friend almost glow with his paleness.

"No Etani, it's not me. You're the one changing all the rules," he breathed in her ear.

Refusing to accept that, she stepped out and approached Jaia, his eyes finding her, and he took her into his arms, hugging her tightly.

She had to wonder though if Kai would be that happy and if he would be willing to test the theory or not.

They had spent the rest of the day in the sun, relishing the warmth of it and their freedom, however short that freedom might end up being. None of them had any delusions about their being free forever; eventually, someone would find them, it was just a matter of time.

The plan was then set to start Etani's training, something she was anxious to get to as quickly as possible but they had decided to wait for the next day, both to give Jaia time in the sun and to give them all time to scope out the area for possible spies.

When none were forthcoming, the three settled in and training began the next morning.

Training with the vampires was exceptionally hard, especially when they were still so powerful, but she was determined to get through it and her prior experience meant that she was a fast learner.

They pushed her body to the absolute limits until she was screaming in pain, forcing her to bend and contort her limbs to make her more flexible, forcing her to punch and kick harder and faster, teaching her how to move and lunge.

Jaia was not only an incredible fighter, but also an expert at how things were supposed to be. He critiqued her until she got it perfect, scolded her when she got it wrong and then praised her when she got it right. He was an expert swordsman and she was learning that, too.

Her change made her lethally fast, her appearance a distraction and her body a weapon, her mind sharp and her attention focused even when Jaia tried to attack her from behind one day; she heard him as Versalis had lunged with his sword and Jaia had kicked for her back. She had crouched and thrown herself backwards in a perfect arc, landing on her feet with her sword at Jaia's throat and he grinned, incredibly pleased with her.

They kept so busy none of them noticed the passage of time, fighting daily and talking of an evening, feeding off each other when they needed it and Etani hunting when the blood of her companions could not satiate her.

They never noticed all six months that had passed until they were finally, eventually found.

They had been training, Versalis and Etani in the clearing moving with lightning speed to try and land a blow on one another when something had clicked and she had caught Versalis by the wrist and thrown him over her shoulder, catching the arrow to her upper chest instead of his taking it to the heart.

She gasped at the quivering fletching and looked up to see a guard looking horrified.

"Jaia!" she screamed, knowing they would be after him too and it was all the warning he would need.

They had come for them during the day, knowing that he would be easy to kill with his sensitivity to the sun. Her scream hopefully would allow him to be spared, it had however given the guards time to come down on the pair of them.

Versalis had landed hard, not expecting the move and while he was down, a black metal net had been thrown over him.

He screamed as the net burnt his flesh where it touched and she moved to rip it off him, arms coming down around her.

Her training immediately kicked in and when a grinning man came before her, reaching for the arrow in her chest. Planting one foot on his chest, she used him as a springboard, throwing herself and the guard behind her to the ground. Landing with the grace of a cat, she ripped the arrow free and twisted, using it to stab through the eyehole of a helmet.

The man dropped and she picked up his spear, grinning wildly at the hesitation of the guards.

She did not recognise their armour, but they seemed to be mythical beings of some description or other.

They decided to come at her as a set, she spun the spear and drove it into the ground. Catching hold of it, she used it to lift herself off the ground and drove both feet into the chest of the guard in the middle, springing off him in a smooth arc to land left foot first, pulling the spear out of the ground with her and turning, launching the spear across the clearing into another guard.

She had begun to laugh, relishing the actual fight as she turned back to the two still standing. One was stupid enough not to be wearing a helmet and his tanned, reddish face was pale with fear.

Grinning at him, she started forward, leaning forward into a handspring that had her airborne and hitting his chest backside first. Wrapping her legs around his neck, his backwards fall pulled her upright.

Two small knives had been strapped to her thighs and she drove them both into the sides of his neck, his landing on his back brought her to her knees and she rolled forward in a tumble to flick herself back onto her feet.

SPINNING, she threw the tiny blade into the mouth of one of the last remaining guards before turning on the last two. Neither looked overly interested in trying to come for her.

With the small knife still in her hand, she watched the two, her breathing coming in heavy pants with the exertion of the fight and with her eyes still on them, she paced slowly sideways towards Versalis, who was whimpering quietly. Crouching, she gripped the edge of the net when he cried out and she spun, driving the knife forward and up.

With a clang, the tiny blade broke and the knife spun off into the grass and she looked up. An enormous man was standing before her, smiling as his hand drew back and he punched her hard in the face.

Her body hit the ground and she rolled, avoiding a brutal kick that would have broken her ribs had he struck her. He followed her and so she rolled again, tucking her knee and flinging herself onto her feet, her arms up in front of her body, ready to defend or deflect.

She did not get time to move when a soft whistle sounded behind her and she jerked, moving like a startled cat and spinning to find a small puff of feathers in the back of her thigh.

She reached behind her, plucked the offending little dart out, squinting at it but she could not see what was on it. Her world tilted and she swayed as whatever it was on the dart hit her brain.

Throwing the dart onto the ground, she sucked in a slow breath to calm herself. The more she panicked, the faster the toxin would work.

"Now Princess, glad to see some things work on even you," the man said gently but his voice seemed to echo in her ears and she struggled to understand what it was he had said.

Doing her best to focus on him and not the two copies of him that appeared and vanished at will.

"What?" she asked, her voice slurring and she knew she was in trouble.

The man before her appeared to be a giant of some sort, hairy and wild looking. Clad from head to foot in armour that seemed to be tailor-made for him.

"Who are you?" she asked, trying for a civilised conversation but as there were now three of him and they were beginning to glitter, she was having trouble figuring out who to speak to.

"Lord Pharley," the man said, and she squinted, trying to remember if she knew that name.

She did not.

27

SOMETIMES A MAN JUST WANTS TO HAVE FUN

"Pharley? Are you Alaric's?" she asked.

At least he was polite enough not to be trying to detain her yet, possibly because she was solely barely standing by her willpower or because her ability to fight the toxin fascinated him. She did not know what the reason, but she was glad he was not punching her.

"Indeed, our esteemed King asked all of us to keep an eye out for you. How lucky am I that you came into my lands," he sounded genuinely pleased to have run into her.

"Glad to have been of service Milord," she quipped. Her right leg gave out and she was rather suddenly on her knees, not sure how or when she got there.

She knew her body would be trying to burn off the toxin but it would take time, the toxin itself though might make for an interesting defence later if she could just figure out what it was made of.

"It's taking longer than I expected," he said as he approached, reaching down to cup her chin and lifted her face to his.

Her entire world seemed to swing backwards and around in a somersault and she paled, thinking the lord was not going to like it very much if she threw up on his pretty armour.

"Surprisingly long," someone else said and she was surprised to see a new man dressed just as well in classy silver coloured armour.

She looked up at the new man and frowned, sure she had seen him before.

"Hello again Princess, how're you holding up?" the man asked.

"It's not very polite to dart a lady," she replied, the hand under her chin now the only thing keeping her up.

"It's also not very polite to kill ten of my men."

"We were only defending ourselves," she said, and he gave a slight nod.

"This is true, but you are trespassing."

He had her there and she smiled vaguely.

"Touché good fellow. Where do I know you from?"

He grinned to show long pointed teeth and it clicked. He was her supplier of the poisonous substances she needed to make many of her chemical weapons.

"Harla?" she asked finally, and he smiled. "And here I thought we were friends."

"Oh, we are Princess, but the King comes first, and I'll admit to a professional fascination with your biology."

"I don't blame you," she said wryly, knowing that she probably would have done the same thing if their roles were reversed.

"Would you be terribly offended if I took some blood?" Harla asked.

"Do I have a choice?" He shook his head and she took a deep breath, speaking on the exhale. "Feel free then."

He was delighted, Pharley was polite enough to keep her upright with a light hand on her shoulders while Harla set up a little kit of supplies.

She looked over the man's armoured back to the net and it took her a long moment to realise it was empty. She did not know when Versalis had escaped, but she was glad for it.

Harla drew a full syringe of blood from her arm with an air of a man who knew exactly what he was doing. He bent her arm up when he was done and stored the blood back in the pack.

"We can keep her drugged, I have enough to get back to Ayathian," Harla said, bending down to study the size of her pupils.

"You have a freckle on your nose," she observed, he was so close that she could see all three of them.

"Do I? I'll have to check that out," he said. She knew he was humouring her in her drugged state, but she had become obsessed with that freckle and followed it up as he stood.

"Why are there two lords here?" she asked and the two exchanged a look and it dawned on her a second before they told her.

"We're married."

She nodded slightly, the tiny gesture making her pitch forward onto the grass. The grass felt delightful against her face.

"WHAT DO we do about the vampires?" Harla asked from above her. She was quite content to stay right there, watching an ant crawling up a thin blade of grass while he seemed shocked to see the giant alien watching him.

"Hello, little ant. You're a tiny little thing," she remarked, but it did not respond.

"They are to come back too if we can get them but she's the priority. Is she talking to an ant?"

She had begun to talk to it at some point, telling it all about a flower she could see out of the corner of her eye. The ant did not seem overly interested in what she had to say.

"Talking to bugs is better than her ripping us apart, I'd say," Harla said and they shuffled around her.

One of them swore.

"Where's the damned vampire?" Pharley asked and the low growl from behind them told them exactly where the vampire was.

She knew from personal experience that it was difficult to kill a man in full armour when one did not have a weapon. But when they went down, one usually had a good twenty seconds before the armoured man was able to get his lungs working and stand up again.

Versalis seemed to have the same thought as she, for when the two men were down, he did not try and kill them, and instead he dragged her off the ground and interrupted her continued conversation with the ant, who was still refusing to speak to her. She did not know what she had done to offend it, but she thought it was rather rude not to talk back. The ant never got the chance to learn how to speak, as Pharley rolled onto it in his attempts to get up.

Making their way quickly to the house, they found Jaia had been waiting, three dead guards and his cheeks flushed.

She cheered at the sight of him and he looked confused, Versalis only shook his head and handed her over. Smiling wide, she kissed his cheek and settled into his lap.

"Jaia, they killed my friend," she complained, frowning at the grip on her chin and she looked up at him, his expression wary and stern. Studying her face and, her eyes in particular, he sighed and let her go.

"Which friend is that darling?" he said gently, his arms going around her.

"The ant!" she almost yelled, throwing up her arms in exasperation. How could he not know about her friend?

"Is that right? Why did they do that?" His tone was very calm, and she found his calmness to be just as frustrating.

"Because they're bastards!" she cried, and he pushed her hands back down into her lap where they belonged.

Versalis snorted a laugh and was back at her side, a large bag in his hands.

"We need to move out of the area, then wait for her to come down before we can think of a plan," Versalis said, giving her head a little pat and she wrinkled up her nose, irritated.

"I'm not a child," she grumbled.

"No, just high off your gourd," he said gently. "I'll carry her, you take the supplies."

She was exchanged for the bag and she was happy in his arms, his grip tight and smelling strongly of a male vampire.

"North?" Jaia asked from somewhere behind her.

"Yes, we should get out of this area before what happened to them is found out. What do we do with the house?"

Two sets of eyes turned to her and she frowned.

"Burn," they said together.

She watched as the house was quickly torched and she was still watching it as they ran from the area, her mind still for a moment as she realised a part of her life was destroyed. She felt Lee stirring, attention focused for a short time on what she was seeing.

'Everything is vanishing,' she whispered to that other voice, aching at the thought.

Lee did not respond, only turning away in silence with the sense of a deep, heart-wrenching pain filling their shared mind.

BY THE TIME they reached wherever they had been heading, her head had begun to ache, and she was in a sour mood, her high gone and left with the lingering effects of the toxin.

When she was set down, she watched the two vampires setting up a basic camp. She did not think her legs would support her yet, so she sat still and watched them grumpily.

"Feeling any better?" Jaia asked an hour or so later when a fire had been started and a small tent erected. They had scouted the area and deemed it safe for them to stay and there was even a stream nearby for bathing.

She had just decided that she was going to crawl to the stream when Jaia approached.

"Better after I've had a bath," she said, and he tilted his head then smiled.

Holding her arms out to him, he helped her to her feet and she was relieved that they at least held her up, but when she tried to walk, they gave out and Jaia caught her before she hit the ground.

Clutching him tightly, she grumbled in his ear and he laughed, scooping her legs out from under her and heading for the stream.

Without preamble, he had her stripped and, in the water, where she moaned softly at the coolness on her skin. With his back to her, he waited as she used a handful of sand to scrub her skin clean, water plants to wash her hair and the cold seemed to stimulate her legs somewhat.

"We have to get back to Kai," she said, watching the little fish swimming around but never getting close to her.

"Yeah, I know," he sounded tired and she watched him for a few moments.

"What's wrong?" she asked, looking down at the fish once more.

"I'm not sure. Everything about this feels wrong. Why would Alaric have people looking for us?" Turning, he began to pace, and she watched him.

"I don't know, maybe Winter is holding him responsible?" That answer did not seem to fit but what else was there?

"Maybe, but that seems convenient doesn't it?" he asked, turning to look at her.

She frowned, running her fingers over the surface of the water and watching the ripples.

"Maybe it's an excuse to get you or Versalis back?" she asked

"I'm not important enough, but Versalis maybe," she met his eyes and frowned in thought.

"Maybe it's all for show, an attempt to make it look like he is trying to find us, and their finding us was pure chance. I did not think that area would even be populated."

"The entire world is owned, Etani, there is no free land left," Jaia said and she squinted at him.

"That's not true," she said, not entirely sure.

He gave her a slight smile and jerked his head back towards the camp.

Pushing herself up slowly, she extended her hands to him and she managed the three paces to the edge of the stream and stepped out. Her grip tightened on him as she did so, almost falling on top of him.

"What was in that dart?" he asked.

"A neurotoxin of some sort, but I can't figure out what one or what it was mixed with," she was frustrated by that, wanting to know badly.

With his hands on her waist, he picked her up and set her back down by her clothes and she dressed under his watchful eye in case she toppled over.

"We need to discuss getting back to Kai, regardless of the lords trying to find us or not," she said, and he nodded.

Sweeping her into his arms, he carried her back to camp and the waiting Versalis.

Sitting down around the fire, she stretched out her legs and worked on getting her toes to work on command, but they were being stubborn.

"We have to get to Kai," she said as she watched, clenching her toes and then releasing them again and moved up to get ankles.

"They will be prepared for us. It could be a trap," Versalis said slowly and she nodded, her ankles rotating and her eyes sliding her attention up to her calves to get them to clench and release a few times.

"Yes, but he will be running out of blood and I can't let him go without," Kai was not part of the deal she had with Jaia, but she still cared for him and was not about to let him starve.

Looking up at Jaia, she found him watching her with an intent she did not understand.

"What?" she asked defensively

"They are going to be waiting for you. They know you can pass through," his voice was tight, and she gave a slight shrug.

"Would you rather we did nothing and Kai suffer?" she asked, knowing full well that he would prefer his brother to be with them but they had to leave someone behind to keep Alaric happy.

"No, but what if you are captured?" he asked, his hands in tight fists on his thighs.

"Nothing is going to happen to me, Jaia. I will go in and ensure he is taken care of, otherwise, I'll bring him back with us," she stated with a confidence she did not feel.

"And what of Epharis?" Versalis said and she glanced to him, wondering whose side he was on just then.

"What about him?" she asked, her eyes returning to her legs as she moved up to her thighs. It seemed her legs were mostly back into working order.

"Are you going to fight him if he tries to stop you?"

"I was banished to Winter, what he wants is irrelevant at the moment. My main concern is not being dragged back to Winter."

"And Drizdan?" Versalis said firmly.

Her muscles tensed and she refused to look up, her mind going to her husband and his expectations of her. She was struggling to keep up her conviction as it was, they were not helping.

Shaking her head, she pushed herself to her feet.

"Etani, I'm sorry," Versalis said, but she was already on her way to the growing darkness.

She knew he intended nothing by it, but she did not want to have to think of the Drow who owned her life in Winter. She wanted to be alone, or with Epharis, but after what he had done in the basement, she was not quite as sure of him either.

They left her alone as she pulled herself up as high as she could into a large tree, leaning her back against the trunk and watching the sky darken.

They did not seem to understand the depth of her emotional and mental scarring, and she was not about to tell them about it.

If it came to it, she would return to Ayathian on her own to get to Kai. She did not need their help nor their approval to do what she needed to do.

They remained as they were for several hours, simply waiting for someone to do or say something when, finally, Jaia decided he had put up with enough and he approached the tree.

Starting up, he was below her in only a minute. Swinging himself up, he plopped down on the branch facing her, his eyes narrowed and hands resting on the branch between his legs, leaning forward to get into her personal space.

"We are going to get this plan in order before we try and take on the castle," he said, his bare feet swinging in the air.

"And how long is that going to take, Jaia? You have to have realised that I can just leave you two here."

He nodded once, lips pursed.

"Yes, I thought of that already. But if you had intended to do that, you already would have left and been back by now. You're worried but you won't admit it. You know perfectly well that it is going to be a huge risk. You are fully aware that you are important to Alaric for some reason and you know he wants to get his hands on you."

She frowned slightly as she watched him, trying to figure him out.

"This is Kai we are talking about. He's worth the risk, Jaia."

Leaning back, he moved his hands to behind him and rested back against them.

"He is, but so are you."

She snorted and frowned.

"I am important only because Alaric decided I am important. That is all. Kai is important because he is your brother. We *need* to get to him, and we need to do it now before word gets back of our still being on this continent. For all we know, he could be waiting to see if it's even worth having a defence."

"You really think he's going to be happily sitting by and waiting for news that maybe we're here and maybe we're on the other side of the world?" His tone was condescending, and she looked away from him, frustrated. "Etani, we can't risk you getting killed or injured," he said.

"Why, Jaia?"

Jaia stopped and blinked, looking slightly confused and she watched him, curious at the expressions that passed over his face. He was trying to figure it out too.

She was only important because they made her important, without that she would not be.

"Jaia, I'm not important unless you make it so. I'm just another creature in this world."

Jaia scratched at his jaw and then shook his head.

"You're important to my sanity," he finally came up with and she laughed.

"It's entirely possible that we could fabricate something, you know that."

"You can't fabricate Fae blood," he said flatly, and she cocked her head to the side.

"What do you mean?" she asked, curious.

"It's impossible. It's been tried before, many times in fact, but it's impossible. You can fabricate something similar to human, something similar to vampire and all the rest, but you can't fabricate Fae."

She had not known that, and it shut her up immediately, though she was now pouting.

"Well, you have no one to blame but yourselves for being in this situation. If you had only minded your own business right from the beginning," she did not mean it and he gave a low growl, yet his eyes were laughing.

Lifting her brows in challenge, she pursed her lips and gave her best haughty stare.

"Come at me vampire, I'll put you in the ground."

"Challenge accepted Princess," he said silkily and when she grinned, he leapt off the tree.

Following him, the fight began and while she overpowered him, his superior strategies had him winning and she was left to slink off in defeat.

Versalis had been waiting for them, knowing Jaia would get her down from the tree better than he could and she stepped up behind him, her chin on the top of his head and her arms draped down over his shoulders, linking just before his sternum.

"Why did not you save me from abject humiliation, Versalis?" she whined.

He laughed and his fingers curled around her wrists, holding her gently while turning his head to kiss her inner elbow.

"Even against two, my love, we would not win."

"I think he cheats," she said, seeing the man in question approaching out of the corner of her eye.

"Never," he said and dropped down beside them, smiling at her when she made a face at him.

"So, let's talk about Kai," Versalis said gently.

The plan they set out was simple; they would all pile through the portal, grab Kai and pull him into Faerie where he would get a hit of energy from Faerie as well as her blood. They would fill up as many bags as they could and then get him back, hopefully before anyone realised he was gone.

Best-case scenario, everything would go to plan; worst, they would be caught.

But Etani had a different theory about what the actual worst would be.

Jaia was not immortal. Versalis was exceptionally difficult to kill, but Jaia was not and when she raised that fear, Versalis looked at Jaia and the two frowned. She wanted Jaia to stay behind in Faerie, but it would mean leaving the door open and that was a risk. Something could come through, or something could get to Faerie.

CHEWING ON HER LIP, the two vampires outvoted her and she let out a slow breath, knowing she had to go along with it, but she would be very aware of his presence and the risk he was in.

Her fears for him were a surprise to her; she did not know why she felt so worried, but she did, and it gnawed at her.

Knowing the best time to go would be during the day when Kai was likely to be in the safety of his room, they waited the night out in preparation.

They had no weapons to polish now, nothing to clean and so they waited anxiously, packing up their supplies when they were ready and dumping water on the fire.

Finally ready, she looked to the two and frowned, wanting to go alone but knowing she would be held down and the plan abandoned if she tried and Versalis seemed to be thinking along the same lines as her.

Letting out a breath, she bit the tip of her finger and drew a slow line in the air. Pressing on it, the two stepped through and she followed along behind, finding themselves in snow.

Shivering at the sudden change, the vampires turned to her and jerked, surprised by the markings that had formed over her body.

Giving a slight shrug, she looked around to gauge where they were, finally looking up at the sky and finding the border between Winter and Ceress.

Motioning them that way, they trudged through the snow in a straight line for the closest border they could get to.

They reached it three gruelling hours later and they stepped from knee-deep snow to soft, springy grass and warmth.

Stopping to shake snow and water out of her boots, she squinted while trying to figure out where they were. She had made it a point to never go that close to Winter when she mapped out the locations that she frequented and so she was a little lost for where to go.

Deciding her best option was to scale a tree and locate the city, she stripped out of everything but her pants and vest and started climbing, leaving the rest behind with the buzzing vampires.

She had been wary of them, but they seemed to be controlling themselves relatively well, only giving her a passing sly glance in contemplation of her blood. But so far no one had tried to bite her, and she was glad for it.

Pulling herself up as high as the tree allowed without bending, she searched the horizon and found Ceress to be a relatively small cone on the horizon.

Frowning, she had to wonder just how big Ceress was and turned, looking the other way to see nothing but forests. If Ceress was just one-quarter of Faerie, the world must be bigger than originally thought.

It was well known that Faerie was smaller than the human world, but no one knew exactly how much smaller because no one knew how big the human world was.

Setting their course, she began her descent and looked down to see Jaia watching her, his arms crossed and looking fidgety.

"Are you alright?" she asked warily, not wanting to have to fight him off. While he looked anxious and as though his skin was too small for him, he nodded and took her hand to help her drop the last several feet to the ground.

"How far do we have to go?" he asked.

"I think we will be walking for most of the day, but if we stick close to the border, I think we can run most of the way. You two should be fairly full of energy." She saw him squirming and smiled slightly.

"Running will help burn some of it off."

Versalis approached slowly, carrying her boots and what few supplies they had. Accepting the boots, she pulled them on, tapping her toes on the grass to settle her feet.

"Run?" he asked.

She nodded and bounced on the balls of her feet, grinning.

"Try to keep up. I'm not slowing down for slackers."

Versalis' eyes narrowed and Jaia clenched his jaw in a grim smile. It would be interesting to see if she were faster than them or not.

Taking off, the two vampires streaked after her and she was pleased to see they could keep up with her. They ran like the wind, a blur of movement and muscles singing with the exertion.

It still took several hours to get to where they needed to be and she began to slow, the two breezing past before turning back.

Versalis had a wild grin on his face, his eyes alight with the freedom. Jaia looked as though he was going to cry at having to stop and she patted his cheek gently.

"Is this what you always feel when you run?" he panted, coming to her side.

"Generally, yes, it's a wonderful feeling, isn't it?"

Both vampires nodded and stretched while Etani worked on finding the exact location.

Settling herself in the spot, she noted that there was a scuff in the grass and shook her head, wondering what creature had been in the area.

Biting her finger, she opened the door and the three stepped inside into the darkness and cool of the dungeon.

The scent hit her like a slap to the face and she moved without thinking as twangs filled the room.

Turning, she drove her foot into Jaia's side and threw him across the room, just as arrows found her and Versalis, slamming them back against the wall and driving into the stone.

Jaia was just bounding back to his feet when someone hit him, a long silver knife against his throat.

He lifted his hands in surrender and looked to her and Versalis.

Versalis had been hit with at least five, all around his torso region and one in his neck.

Her movements had caught three in her side and another four in her chest and she wondered dryly why so many had been aimed at her. Her last thoughts were that someone must really hate her before the world went black.

HOME, SWEET HOME

As it turned out, she could not die even from so many arrows to the chest, something she was rather curious about.

Looking to her side, she found a limp Versalis with a large knife sticking out of his forehead and she had to wonder what had happened for him to deserve that.

Pushing herself to her feet, she found herself to be unrestrained, but one of those obnoxious gold chains had been tied around her ankle. She turned and found that they had all been bound in a similar manner. At first, she had not registered that there were four of them in the cell.

Moving to Versalis, she placed one hand against his head and gripped the handle, pulling it free of him and she wondered at the stupidity of their captors, leaving her a knife. It would take time for him to recover, but it may take hours for the healing process to expel the knife on its own, so she thought it best to remove it. Turning to Jaia, she blinked as she realised that Jaia had been propped up against a bound and gagged Kai.

"Kai?" she asked, baffled by why he was there.

His eyes snapped open and she flinched at the feral state of him, his hunger burning into her soul. He growled as she approached and she knelt, looking first to Jaia who seemed mostly fine. He was still breathing, and she gave him a gentle pat on the cheek.

He jerked and sat up, her attention going to Kai, and she gave him a warning look as she reached behind him, releasing the gag. The second it was gone, he lunged, and she jerked back even as his teeth sank painfully into her shoulder.

Drinking fast, he growled as Jaia made to pull her away, but she remained still, allowing the vampire what he needed, and he released her on his own. Moving away from him, she pressed on the wound to ease the bleeding and sat down against the wall hard, her brain feeling a tiny bit fuzzy.

Jaia seemed to be affected by the smell. "Where are we?"

"My second home, the dungeons in Ayathian," she said dryly, checking to see if the blood had stopped before applying some more pressure.

Versalis stirred and groaned, his eyes opening only to snap shut again at what must be excruciating pain. It was unlikely the knife to the brain did not give him a migraine.

"Why are we here?" Jaia asked.

"I'll be sure to ask as soon as we find out," she replied, brushing back strands of Versalis' hair and wiping the blood from his face. "I'm sure they'll be turning up sooner or later."

Kai had started to get back to himself. "You had to know it was a trap."

"We suspected it, but we thought we needed to take the risk. You would be almost out of blood," Jaia said, shifting to sit up straight.

"I have been on starvation rations since I got here. They arrested me the day you all left."

Jaia and Etani exchanged a look, feeling terrible for his suffering.

"Don't worry about it, I had hoped you would come up with a great exciting escape plan to rescue me when you found out, not get stuck in here with me."

"We had no idea Kai," Jaia said, sounding wretched.

"I'm so sorry, Kai, we would have come straight back if we even suspected you would be taken. There was no reason for it."

Kai nodded and smiled at her.

"I know, it was entirely unexpected. But I think Alaric has finally had enough of you running off that he decided he needed bait to get you all back," he seemed quite chipper to have them there and she had to wonder when he had last had company.

"I'm surprised they dumped us all in this cell together, unbound like this," Etani said, looking between the three men and wondering at the reasoning.

"It is odd, but maybe they are short on room? I've heard Alaric had been in a sour mood and arresting people left and right," Kai said.

"How did you hear that?" Jaia asked, curious.

"Epharis has been sneaking me in blood under the guise of experimenting on me. He feeds me information."

Jaia and she exchanged a look of wondering before they both shrugged it off, unable to understand the reasoning the Lich had for anything. She could only assume it was because he thought she would probably kill him if she ever found out that he could have helped Kai and refused.

IT WAS ABOUT three days later when their captors had finally come to meet them in their little box. At the time she had been asleep against Jaia's shoulder, having fed the three vampires enough to leave her woozy and exhausted.

A boot hit her leg and she jerked awake, blinking as she looked up at the King.

"Alaric," she said simply, the sound of her voice waking Jaia at her side.

She had never realised how much vampires slept and if her guess was right it was for the same reason *she* did. Sleep preserved their energy and meant less need for feeding especially when one did not have anything to do.

"Princess," he said gleefully

"How've you been? Well I trust." She really was not in the mood to deal with the maniacal man and he seemed to find her irritation amusing.

"Very, how about you? I hear you've been having fun camping up north."

Word must have gotten back to him about their fight with Pharley and his husband.

"How's Pharley and Harla?" she quipped, recalling the two tall men and their delight at finding the three of them in the woods.

"Both well, Harla sends his regards. I think he has taken an interest in you, he keeps asking if he can meet with you," Alaric said, his tone suggesting intimidation, but she was not buying it.

"Is that right? I did not think he was interested in women."

"I get the feeling it's not your body he is looking for, at least not in a sexual manner."

Ah, another Epharis who wanted to take her apart to see how she worked.

"Well, please politely tell him that I have other obligations at the moment and his desire to experimented on me will have to wait."

Alaric grinned and she frowned, knowing he was about to tell her something awful.

"I've already agreed on your behalf."

"Of course you did…" she said dryly, more annoyed than anything.

"Of course. I'm sure you two will have plenty to talk about," Alaric was still grinning, taunting her.

"When is our date?" she asked and she shifted, realising her foot had fallen asleep.

"I will have him called from his home in the city. He wanted to wait for you to wake up."

"How nice of him. Run along then," she quipped.

He did not like that and Jaia growled as she was struck but she shook her head to keep him from being hurt as well.

She licked her lower lip free of blood and looked up at him, glaring.

"Why do you keep trying to catch me, Alaric? What do you want?"

He frowned at her questions and shook his head.

"Be prepared for Harla," he snapped, and she watched him go.

"What is wrong with this world?" she demanded, baffled by the men around her and wanting to give them all a good smack.

"You're like a drug," Versalis said in a hazy tone; he was still suffering from the knife to his brain. "One taste and you can't get enough."

She looked from him to the twins and they nodded their agreement.

"Rubbish," she snapped, refusing to believe that.

Versalis shrugged and flopped down against her, his head in her lap.

She sighed and stroked his hair gently, Versalis dozing and the twins waiting to come and collect Harla.

About an hour later, the sound of boots echoed, and her tension peaked. Looking to Jaia and Kai, she stuck out her wrist to each of them. "In case I'm gone for a long time."

They both obediently fed and when they were done, she forced her wrist down on Versalis as well, who grunted but accepted.

Harla and Alaric were talking quietly outside, discussing something, and then the door rattled.

Biting his tongue and wiping the blood on the bites, the holes sealed just in time for Harla to come into the room, his sharp teeth in a wide grin of excitement.

He did not try and manhandle her, instead, he offered his long-fingered hand and she took it, standing slowly. Swapping the chain out from her ankle to her hands, he seemed to almost vibrate in his excitement.

He was taller than her, but not as tall at Pharley, perhaps six eight or so. The men in that place had to all be mutants, she was sure of it.

Versalis sat up, all three vampires alert and anxious.

"Harm her and I'll come for you personally," Versalis said as Harla slipped one arm around her waist, pulling her towards the door and tugging the chain free of the ring that held her in place.

"Don't strain yourself, vampire, or your head might end up sprouting a knife," Harla said and when she looked back, smirking, the three realised that the knife had disappeared.

She had stuffed it into the back of her pants, armed and dangerous.

Pulled from the room, she looked between the two men.

"Care to observe, Alaric?" Harla asked as he guided her down towards the stairs.

"You may be better off doing it here, Harla, she has a remarkable ability to slide out under doors," Alaric said dryly, looking down at her.

"Is that right?" Harla asked, tightening his grip on the chain.

"It's not my fault you are remarkably dense, Alaric," she said and when he swung at her, she darted back from him, grinning.

"I'd be glad to observe," Alaric said spitefully and considered where to go, then he grinned and opened the door directly across from the cell the vampires were in.

"You're a bastard," she growled, watching as a young human male was dragged from the cell and thrown at a guard.

"Get in," he snapped and when she did not move, he shoved her inside, Harla following in behind her.

"Guard, have the boy bring my supplies down here if it is better to keep the Princess contained," Harla said, following in and considering the cell.

It did not take long for a large number of supplies to be delivered to the cell, including things she had never seen of before, two chairs, and a hook.

With her chain in Alaric's hands, she watched as Harla stood on the chair and carefully screwed the end of the hook into the support beams of the cell ceiling, tugging at it sharply to ensure it was in and then accepting the chain from Alaric.

"I found your blood to be fascinating, Princess. It's unique and not entirely matched to the species of Fae."

She thought he could not be more correct, but she went along with it. She was not about to start telling him about Ceress.

Feeding the end of the chain through the hook, he pulled it firmly and when he was satisfied with the height of her arms beside her head, he looped it through three more times and then tied it off.

"This chain is ingenious, I wouldn't mind getting to spend some time with your brother one day," Harla said as he stepped down from the chair and gave the chain a hard tug. It did not budge.

With her standing, her wrists were a few inches up above her head, she would not be able to sit or even kneel.

Curling her fingers around the chain to ease the strain on her wrists, she studied the collection of supplies.

"You are feeding the vampires, are you not?" Harla asked but she did not reply. "I would be curious to know how your blood affects them if you are drugged," he said, laying out an assortment of needles and syringes.

EYEING THEM, Alaric grunted and stood to move the table back.

"I'm going to kill you one day Alaric," she said moodily, thinking she might still be able to get to the table, but acting like she could not.

She had no way of defending herself as his fist sank into her stomach and she gasped, wheezing as she hung from the ceiling, her legs not wanting to hold her up.

"You've been a right pain this whole time. If you weren't a Princess, I'd..." he trailed off and she glared at him.

"Your stupid prophecy wouldn't matter, and I'd have killed you already," she growled.

He hit her again and she whimpered loudly.

"However, the prophecy does matter and I will be the greatest King this world has ever seen, even if I have to kill my brother and force you into my bed," he said in a lethally quiet tone.

"You can take tips from Drizdan, you two think remarkably alike when it comes to *forcing* women into your beds," she did not know why she was goading him, but the anger on his face gave her a perverse joy.

"Yes, and he can teach me the best way to make you scream while I fill you with my dynasty."

The words made her stomach twist and she fell silent, the fanatic zeal in his eyes finally getting her to shut up. She knew he was not joking when it came to what he would and would not do for his precious prophecy and keeping her bound to his bed would barely warrant consideration from him.

Harla had been ignoring their conversation as he worked and she resented the lot of them, wishing she had never come to that damned city of monsters and sexual sadists.

"No more smart comments, Etani?" Alaric taunted and she looked to him, affecting a glare.

"Go jump off a cliff, Alaric."

Refusing to give him the satisfaction of hearing her scream as he drove his first for the third time into her stomach, she used his close-ness and the chain to hoist herself up and drive her knee into his ribcage.

He grunted and stumbled back, watching as she clung to the chain and he realised he had made a mistake letting her legs go free.

She glared at him, prepared for him to come closer again.

"Harla, got a sedative?" Alaric asked and her eyes snapped to the slender man.

He made a soft noise of agreement and picked out a bottle and a syringe.

She moved as Alaric did and he swiped at her, but she had prepared and as he tried to grab her, she drove her foot into his gut, using the chain and her foot in his gut to hoist herself up just enough to spin and slam the top of her foot into the side of his face.

He went flying and she spun back to the ground, her eyes on Harla as he watched the two of them, the syringe ready. He seemed to be mostly disinterested in their quarrel, only concerned that he completed his task.

"Might I suggest you take her from one side and I the other?" the man asked as Alaric got up.

"She's not usually this good," Alaric growled, and she grinned at him.

"We had a lot of time to kill."

Harla began to move around behind her and she watched him, trying to keep them both in view but he moved out of range and she growled softly in warning. Alaric was grinning at her, his shoulders hunched and looking remarkably like a street brawler. She knew she was going to be in for a world of hurt when they got that needle in her, so she wanted to get in as many hits as she could.

"Come on Alaric, stop being such a coward," she goaded

Her arms were tense as she turned her head just enough to see them both but was unable to do so. Not if she did not move her head. Alaric rushed her and she stepped forward once, driving her foot up between his legs. His hand dropped to deflect most of the blow, but he still staggered back, and something pricked her back.

Swearing, she jerked away but a slender, bony arm slipped around her middle and the needle pressed deep into her flesh. Alaric had straightened, grinning maniacally as Harla drew away and returned to the table with the empty syringe.

"Stay back for a minute or two until it takes effect," Harla said but Alaric ignored him, wanting to punish her for her cheap groin shot.

Again, he came for her and again she moved. She was faster than him, but he was bigger.

Kicking off the ground, her foot hit the underside of his chin and his head snapped back. By the time he hit the ground her cheeks had begun to flush.

Taking advantage of his slow rise, she waited until he had gotten onto his knees and with one flick, her foot was above his head and then she drove the heel down onto the top of his head. He went forward, catching himself on his hands and she rebounded from her foot returning to the ground to drive her knee up into his downturned face.

He landed hard and she knew she was done, her cheeks a rich pink colour as the sedative began to take hold of her body and she felt herself drooping.

Panting, she glared down at the King and his furious glare that faded into a malicious smirk at the sight of her face.

She was getting tired and she tried to fight it, forcing her eyes open as wide as she could as she watched him get up. She felt warm, warm enough to want to lie down and take a nap but that was a bad idea right then.

He loomed over her and she gave him a weak, sleepy smile.

"Fuck you…" she breathed as his fist came towards her face and her head snapped back, her body going limp.

"Don't worry, I will later." She vaguely heard, but the words had little meaning.

She felt every blow to her body and while it hurt terribly, her brain seemed to be stuck inside a washing basin and someone was spinning it like a top to leave her spinning and sloshing all over the place.

Regardless, she refused to scream, knowing it was what he wanted, and she was too stubborn to give him the satisfaction.

He was enjoying her helplessness and she knew he had been keen to get revenge on her in private. Harla seemed perfectly fine with it and she had to admit, she had humiliated Alaric several times. Had their roles been reversed, she probably would have beaten him into a bloody pulp as well.

She did not really notice when the hitting stopped and the cutting began, Harla going to work on her for his research. She was beginning to come to, hanging limply from the chain and when a bony hand cupped her face, she was able to open her eyes just enough to see his narrow face and sharp teeth.

29

BOYS AND THEIR MAGICAL TOYS

"Welcome back, Princess," he said happily, his hands smelling strongly of alcohol and blood. "How are you feeling?"

"Like you drugged me," she said, her voice sounding slurred and tired.

"That's because I did. It did not last as long as I thought. I had hoped you would be out for several more hours, but it's been only two."

He glanced at the book on the table and she was reminded strongly of Epharis.

"Are you related to those two?" she asked, making a vague gesture to Alaric, who was sitting in the corner looking satisfied with the work.

"No," Harla said simply and lifted her chin higher to better see her eyes.

Shifting her feet, she found the floor and stood, deciding that yes, the sedative was leaving her system.

"Do you know her species?" Harla asked of Alaric, who was staring her down.

"Winter Fae of some description. There is a rumour she has other abilities and that walking through realities thing is exceptionally uncommon even amongst the Fae."

"No it's not," she retorted, jerking her head out of the bony grip and glad for the chain, her body swaying back and she would have fallen if she had not been held up by the chains. "Most of them can do it, they just choose not to. Your world isn't exactly desirable and the creatures who populate it are even less so."

That was a little mean, but she was smarting over the sheer number of times he had hit her while she was out.

Alaric snorted, amused now that he had worked out his anger.

Getting her balance back under control, she contemplated giving Harla a good boot to the shin but decided she should keep her feet to herself for the time being.

"What did you do to me?" she asked when she finally looked down. Her clothing had been removed except for her undergarments and blood had dried on her skin accompanied by a significant number of new pink scars.

"Testing your ability to heal," Harla said dispassionately.

"Is it up to your standards?" she looked to Alaric when she started seeing what she thought were patches of dark blood, were just large bruises. He smirked as she glared at him.

"Beyond my expectations, really. You aren't a full Fae, are you?" he said, picking up the book and adding several notes.

"That obvious?" She was not about to tell him anything worthwhile.

"It is if you know what you're looking for," he said, looking first from her to the book and back again.

"You're from one of the hidden Courts, right?"

She went still, staring at him with her mouth slightly open.

"What?" she asked, unsure if she had heard him right.

"One of the hidden Courts, not Winter or Summer."

She was floored by that, even Alaric sat up with interest.

"I don't know what you're talking about," she breathed, but he could tell she was lying, and he smiled.

"Yes, you do, you can pretend all you like, but the fact that you can lie at all tells me a lot about you," he said, adding more notes.

Her eyes went to Alaric and she found he was staring hard at her, angry.

"Does Epharis know about this?" he demanded of her and she shook her head.

He seemed placated by her lie and her eyes went back to Harla as he approached fast. She jerked but had nowhere to go really.

"Which one is it, Etani?" he sounded frantic, desperate for the information.

"There are only two," she said, trying to sound convincing but even that he would suspect something like that had thrown her entirely for a loop.

"Several years ago, a Fae Lord was captured and tortured," he began, the tip of one long, bony finger tracing the shape of her ear and she tilted her head away from him.

"They wanted Faerie's biggest secret. The best secret. Do you know what he said? That there are four Courts. No one believed him, thinking it was just a trick and he died swearing to the truth of the four Courts," he breathed, his face a mere inch from hers and she could almost taste the sweat from his excitement.

"The report was filed away and forgotten, but I have been trying to get into Faerie for years and I found that little report. It got me thinking about Winter and Summer. Why were there two Courts when there are four seasons? Why Winter and Summer and not Spring and Autumn? Why wouldn't there be four? It was a logical conclusion, one for each season, one Court for each quarter of the year. Winter and Summer are significant in terms of extremes, but nothing lives and grows without spring, and nothing wilts without autumn. Which one is it, Etani? Which one are you from?"

She had pushed herself as far back from him as was possible given her situation and he had followed after her, breath brushing her face and she was utterly terrified of that man and what he knew.

"Winter, only Winter," she whispered, and his face showed first disappointment and then anger.

"Do not for a second think I will not torture the information out of you, Fae," he said in a flat tone and she swallowed, now wishing she only had Alaric to deal with.

"There are only two," she said, her mind racing at how to get out of her situation. That man was dangerous, far more so than any others she had met thus far.

"We shall see," he breathed and moved away from her. The book snapped shut and she jumped, looking to Alaric who was himself looking a little uncomfortable.

"Alaric, you have to let me go," she said, looking from the King to the Harla and back again. "Please, just let me go. I won't retaliate, I'll do what you say, just let me go."

He looked at her, seeing the genuine fear in her and then looked to Harla, frowning.

"Harla, I think we are done for today," Alaric said, but Harla was not listening.

Standing, the giant King approached, and she watched Harla filling a syringe, her head tilting to try and read the label.

"Alaric!" she gasped as she saw what it was, but Harla had already jabbed the needle into the side of the King's neck, flooding the King's system with a strong dose of muscle relaxant and sedative.

The King staggered, his rapidly pounding heart sending the toxin shooting through him and he plopped down on the chair, drunk on the drugs.

Harla turned to her and smiled as he prepared a second syringe, approaching her and jabbing it into her abdomen. She jerked back, her muscles suddenly not wanting to work anymore.

She found herself hanging loose from the chain, her hands still working but her legs were unresponsive.

"Good, now we can have some privacy," Harla said as he pulled the chair up and sat down in it in front of her.

He had a small knife in his hand, and she gritted her teeth.

The bite of metal on her skin had her trying to move again, but her legs refused to function, and she whimpered softly.

"Which Court, Princess?" he asked in a calm voice.

Looking past him to Alaric, she found the man awake but mostly unable to move, calm and watching.

"Winter," she said immediately, clenching her jaw tightly to keep from making a sound as the knife drew blood, pressing into her side just above her hip.

"Which Court?" he asked again, and she shook her head.

She gave a muffled cry as the knife slid smoothly and cleanly into her flesh, her lips clamped shut to keep from screaming.

Disappointed, he returned to the table to retrieve the syringe. "Which Court?" he repeated, giving the syringe a little tap to check for bubbles but it was a clean draw.

"Winter," she replied and flinched as he slid the needle into her left thigh and pressed down.

It started slowly, a burning that started relatively mild and then began to heat up until she was sure her leg was on fire.

Gasping, she kept her teeth clenched and tried her absolute best to stay silent, but a whimper escaped her.

"Which Court?" he was not going to change his question and she shook her head.

The second jab had her crying out in pain, both legs on fire and she could see that the areas around the injection site had turned black. He had injected her with a corrosive element that was eating away at her body.

"You only have to tell me which one and we stop," he said calmly, studying her for the next place to inject.

"Winter, you bastard!" she cried and finally screamed as he injected the next dose deep into her stomach.

It spread through her, given a larger area to destroy and she could do nothing to stop it.

"Last chance," he said as he lifted the syringe with only a little of the compound left in it, hovering over her heart.

Did he know she was immortal? She did not know but she wanted it to end.

She refused to speak, and he hesitated, not willing to kill her. Instead, he smiled and moved away, leaving her hanging limp and whimpering as the corrosive ate away at the repairs her body made.

He had left the room and she could not see what he was doing, unable to turn herself and so it was a shock when he dragged in Jaia.

Her heart froze at the horrified expression on his face as he looked at her, his eyes trailing down her tear-streaked face, her bloodied body to the dark black holes in her flesh.

Jaia was shaking though she thought it was more from fury than fear.

"There's a good man, just stand there," Harla said and tied Jaia's chain to her own, just above her hands to leave them standing close together, facing each other.

"Etani," he whispered, and she shook her head, resting her forehead against his.

"Tell me or I kill the vampire," Harla said and she looked up to see a large wooden stake in his hand.

Her eyes went wide as she saw it, terror filling her and even Alaric seemed to be struggling.

"Get away from him!" she snarled, but Harla only smiled.

Looking up at Jaia, he had frozen in fear with his eyes on her.

Placing the stake against Jaia's back, Harla aimed up and drew back the stake.

Panic flooded her at the mental image of losing Jaia, her entire world ending with him. The stake flew forward

"Autumn! Ceress! I'm a Celestrial, stop!" she screamed, frantic as the stake stopped, an inch of it buried in Jaia's back.

He looked utterly terrified at being so close to death and his body jerked at the removal of the stake.

She began to cry helplessly, and he moved closer, allowing her to rest her head against his cheek at the fear and relief of his surviving.

Harla had vanished to make notes, the stake discarded.

There was a choking sound coming from Alaric, but she ignored him and pressed herself against Jaia, relief flooding her and countering the fear to make her feel dizzy and unable to keep the tears back.

His cheek rested against the top of her head, his eyes on Alaric in a hateful death glare.

Returning, Harla seemed pleased at the results and pulled her back from Jaia, turning her to face him and Alaric.

She thought she was starting to get control of her legs back, but she could not tell if it was that or simply muscle spasms as the muscles had to regrow.

"Autumn is Ceress? What is Spring?" he demanded.

"It's where the leftovers go. The freaks who don't belong anywhere else. It was the Drow home before they were banished," she was exhausted, drained from the fear and near loss of someone she cherished so dearly. "It was dubbed the Heathen Court by the rest of us."

He began writing again and she looked at Alaric, who had been staring at her with a murderous look on his face.

"You Fae and your secrets," Harla breathed, delighted at getting confirmation after all that time.

"I don't suppose you would permit me to keep her for a few weeks or a year? To study of course," Harla said to Alaric, who looked angry enough to breathe fire.

Harla shrugged and turned back to her, gleeful as he picked out a new syringe.

"Now tell me, Etani, how do you get into Faerie?"

"Only the Fae can get in unless you are taken in by a member of the Fae," she realised his glee and she shook her head, lying for all she was worth. "It has to be a genuine desire to take the extras. A genuine need or it will just spit you out somewhere in this world."

He looked disappointed and then looked to Jaia and back to her.

"You took him there did not you?"

"We needed to escape, that is a genuine need."

Harla nodded and inched closer to her, his eyes eager.

"What happens to the vampires when they go to Faerie?" he breathed, so close his nose touched hers though the angle made it impossible for her to be able to force a kiss before he moved away on reflex.

"We get incredibly strong and fast," Jaia said, his breath warm on the back of her neck.

Harla looked from her to him and smiled happily at the new information.

"Do you feel any different?" he asked, scribbling down his notes at a feverish pace.

"I get ravenously hungry and feel like a god," he said.

She gave her toes a little wiggle and Alaric looked down at them, his lips turning up into a grim smile as their eyes met.

They both wanted revenge against Harla now.

"Do you feed off her?" Harla asked and Jaia sucked in a breath, nodding once at the personal question.

"What does she taste like?" Harla whispered and she felt Jaia tense behind her.

"Like the sun and ecstasy," he said. "Honey and sex."

Her cheeks flamed, but she was focusing on her legs and willing her body to heal them faster, trying to direct the healing but she had never been able to do that.

"Interesting," Harla whispered, leaning in to breathe in the scent of her throat.

She flinched back at him, but he had grabbed her, examining the scarred skin.

"How long have you two been together, or do you share her with your brother?" the insinuation had her blushing brighter and Jaia growled a warning.

Harla laughed at their embarrassment and moved before her, his eyes dragging down her form.

"Where else do you bite her?" he knew he had gotten to them and was going to try and torment them even further.

He tugged at the band of her undergarments to check her hips and she shoved herself backwards into Jaia's chest.

"Stay still, I'm not going to defile you. I don't fancy women," he snapped and she clenched her eyes shut as he tugged her undergarments down to her knees and knelt, examining her hips, pelvic region and her rear, grunting when he found her free of bites and checking her inner thighs just to be sure.

She hated him, though when her eyes opened, she found Alaric looking away and was glad for that at least.

Harla moved to her chest next, finding nothing but a number on her shoulders and then up to her wrists.

"I see two different sizes, possibly three. Yes, these two have a wider space between the fangs and that one has larger fangs," his face was at her shoulder, examining the barely visible scars.

Stepping back, he slid her undergarments back up into place and looked between them, then at the door.

"All three of them? Etani, I'm surprised at you," he said, laughing at her embarrassment.

"Necessity," Jaia said through clenched teeth, almost shattering with his restrained fury.

"In what way?" he paused and then he recalled the information. "Her blood is addictive, is it not? I didn't know for a fact," he added the note to his book and examined her carefully, licking over his sharp teeth.

She had never stopped to think about his teeth, only finding it weird but never bothering to ask. It was not the weirdest thing in that world but now she was very much wondering what he was. There were a lot of creatures with teeth like that, but so many could change their shape.

"What are you?" she breathed as he inched closer, his grin growing wide.

"They say he tried to tear down the world to escape captivity, the world was crushing him. But if he ever gets free, he will bring the world crashing down," he seemed to delight in her realisation. "But that's just a story. I don't want to destroy this world, only Faerie."

He moved forward and sank his sharp teeth into her shoulder, carefully picking a spot that had not been scarred already.

He did not linger, but she still screamed as his saliva burned and she found herself getting woozy.

Harla moved back from her and licked his lips, frowning as he considered the taste of her blood and watched them as Jaia bit the tip of his tongue and dragged it over the bite marks. The bleeding stopped, but the bite did not heal over.

Whimpering at the burning that refused to stop, she tried to calm herself and focus.

"Why does every creature here have to be some great mythical creature?" she demanded, her body burning.

"Who is he?" Jaia asked, looking down at her inflamed skin.

"Nidhogg, the world ender. He's supposed to be the one who consumes the world," she said through gritted teeth.

Jaia looked up at the slender, tall man who was looking thoughtful.

"That's supposed to bring about the end of the world?" His tone was doubtful.

"He's supposed to be an enormous dragon, not a man."

Harla looked at them, contemplating the two of them curiously.

"This form makes moving around easier," he said simply and Jaia nodded but she was frowning at him, wondering.

"You're cursed aren't you…" she said, laughing through the pain when his face went sour.

"Someone cursed Nidhogg, that's rich. Who was it? Old Jenny Greenface?" she taunted, knowing she was getting the name wrong, but that witch and she had never gotten along.

"Hecate," he said angrily, and his eyes narrowed as she began to laugh, though every peal hurt.

"Be quiet…" he growled.

"How did you manage to anger Hecate so much that she bothered to pay even the slightest bit of attention to you?" she asked, genuinely curious. "Did you eat some of her girls?"

He looked away and she laughed again.

Hecate was one of the more powerful creatures in Faerie, a step above even the Queens of Faerie. She was one of the oldest and was obscenely powerful. Called a goddess by the humans, but she was the woman to give certain humans the ability to tap into Faerie from birth. They had been called witches and Hecate was fiercely, insanely protective of her girls. It was assumed that Hecate looked after and created Faerie, but she doubted it. Hecate only cared about the Fae as much as supervising them to create the humans. Hecate only cared about the witches.

"How many did you kill?" she asked.

"A coven."

"You don't mess with the witches, everyone knows that," she said, shaking her head at his stupidity.

"At the time, I didn't know they were witches." He sounded like a petulant child and she laughed again.

"Is she ever going to turn you back or did you get the full parting shot before she booted your arse into the human world?"

30

CAN'T KEEP HIS HANDS TO HIMSELF

His expression had her pealing laughter again, unable to help herself. It was just too funny to her, that great world-destroying dragon cursed by Hecate and then shoved forcefully into human guise before being dumped on the human world like an unwanted puppy.

She had never met Hecate before, but she had heard about the woman coming to the human world from time to time, scoping things out and making sure her girls were safe.

But she was sure to stay far away from the witches. They tended to smell different to humans and you did not want to be a predator near a witch if Hecate was nearby. She was rumoured to have a nasty habit of simply exploding people like dropped eggs.

He was glaring at her then and she grinned back at him, delighting in his suffering.

"Oh, come on, Nid, you have to laugh at these things. Maybe she'll take pity and give you back your pretty form."

He flinched at her nickname for him, glowering as he jabbed a syringe into her stomach, and she began to scream as the corrosive agent ate through her.

So, she had deserved that, she knew it. But it had just been too good a story for her not to rub his nose in it. It was one of the first things she learned when she met another mythical when coming to the human world for the first time. It had been told to her with the very first mythical creature she had met, a cat incidentally.

A little ball of black fur with a large white spot on his chest. She had taken to the beast instantly, offering him meat she had stolen after she had seen him and getting excited when he had settled in her lap.

It was the first creature she had ever seen in the human world that was not a human and she loved him blindly. He had purred and kneaded her legs, letting her pet him and then when she sighed and went to place him on the ground, he told her off sternly for stopping.

She had dropped him and scrambled back, shocked at the talking beast.

He had laughed at her and sat down, calm as you please and told her not to trust creatures, nothing was ever what it seemed in that world.

He had gone by the name Catsit, though none of the humans had ever bothered to ask him his name. He had asked her for what she called herself and she had told him, as well as telling him she was new to the human world.

He had then told her what to expect and to avoid the witches and a few other choice species that no one wanted to mess with.

She had thanked him for his help, and he had asked for a bowl of milk in payment, which she gladly stole for him and he lapped it up before prowling away.

She had only ever seen him once since then, returning to that same village several decades later and he was still sitting there, calm as could be.

She had joined him for a time, offering him milk and a mouse to eat, they had talked and then she had left. One day, she would have to go see if he were still there, assuming she survived Ayathian.

Harla was yelling something, but she could not hear what it was in her blind pain. It seemed the saliva and the corrosive had interacted badly, and she had fallen unconscious. She did not imagine Harla had liked that very much.

When she came to, she squinted and saw that Jaia's lip was bleeding, Harla's knuckles were bleeding and he was hunched over his ribs.

It seemed Jaia had booted him hard enough to break them and Harla had punched Jaia in the mouth in retaliation.

"Can we go home now?" she mumbled.

"We are home, sweetheart," Jaia said gently, looking down at her limp form.

"Can we find a new home?"

"As soon as we get out of here," he said, looking up as Harla appeared above her.

"At least you're not dead..." he said dryly.

"You know, I don't think I can die anymore," she said conversationally. "Before it was easy, you die and go for a nice stroll, then a swim and *whoosh*, you're back. But now? Being immortal isn't any fun when you can't actually die any more. Living is hard..."

She did not know why she was talking, it had simply spilled out and Jaia looked down at her, confused.

"Are you okay?"

"That bastard bit and drugged me, then that other bastard in the corner beat me," she turned her head to Alaric. "Because he's a *child!*"

Then she turned her head back to Jaia, though it was dangling limply on her neck.

"And then, after all that, the first bastard is going to try and get into Faerie. I just know he is. And you know what? He can go to Faerie and then Tatialia can eat him, and everything will be fine."

"Why would Tatialia eat him?" Jaia asked dryly, seeming to realise something.

"Because she's *mean*," she dragged out the last word. "And she probably eats bastards for breakfast. She's that type of mean. How I could possibly be related to her I don't know, I'm not that mean."

She was spilling way too much information, she knew it, but she had suddenly gotten the urge to talk and was running with it.

"How are you related to Tatialia, the Queen of Winter?" Harla asked.

"She's my grandwitch," she said, smiling at the play on words and thinking it was quite clever.

"Grand what?" he asked, looking at Jaia.

"Etani is the granddaughter of Winter's Queen. She's a Princess of Winter," he said, frowning down at her.

"I thought she was a Princess of Ayathian."

"Ayathian doesn't have any. She's a foreign diplomatic prisoner," Jaia snipped.

"Yeah, a diplomatic prisoner of that bastard," she gave a little wave in Alaric's direction.

"What's wrong with her?" Jaia asked.

"I think she is having a drug reaction. Etani how do you get into Faerie?" Harla asked, realising his advantage.

"That's easy, you just open the-" Jaia had driven his knee up into her back and she yelped in pain.

"Jaia, what is your problem?!" she demanded, distracted from the topic.

"Stop talking," he said, and she scowled up at him, irritated and sore.

"Open what, Etani?" Harla asked and she looked at him blankly, not understanding the question.

"Open what, what?" she asked, confused.

"How do you get into Faerie?" he asked

"Well, there's a gateway in the Under Dark, you could go there."

"You said you just had to open something. How can *you* get into Faerie if you need to?" he demanded.

She opened her mouth and Jaia kneed her again.

"Jaia, stop it!" she cried, distracted again.

"Do that again and I'll kill you," Harla growled.

"How did you even get to be a lord? You're a jerk," she said of Harla, not giving him time to respond before she looked at Alaric. "You need to pick your people better, they all suck."

Alaric snorted a laugh in agreement and Harla turned on him.

"Should I sedate you further, Your Majesty?" Harla hissed.

"You should, Alaric isn't very nice," she looked up at the chain above her, her hands turned red from the strain of her weight on them. "Can your hands fall off from blood loss?" she asked Jaia and he looked up at her hands.

"I don't think so," he said but did not sound very certain.

Settling her feet on the ground, she pulled herself up, only to sway dangerously and find herself face to face with Jaia, grinning at his startled face.

"Hi handsome, fancy meeting you here. Do you come here often?" she purred, teasing him.

"Too often," he said, wary of her tone.

She inched closer to him, biting down gently on her lower lip and smiling when his eyes flicked down to her lips and then back up to her eyes.

"You know… I like you a lot," she breathed, and his eyes went wide. "More than just liking, for a long time."

He looked like he would very much like to run away just then but he had extended the full length of his arms to draw away from her and still she was close to him.

"I think I may be in love with you…" she whispered. He opened his mouth to speak but then he looked behind her and something jabbed into her back.

She frowned, moving on instinct and turned, cupping her fist in her palm and driving her elbow back and up into the face of Harla.

He fell flat on his back and she smiled, stepping lightly up to him and placing her foot hard down on his throat. She could feel the buzz wearing off, anger coming to her.

"You know, Nid, I'm getting sick of you injecting me," her buzz was turning into a foul mood at an alarming pace and she was in the mood to rip that man's head off his scrawny shoulders.

She pressed down hard on his neck and he choked, trying to push her off him but she kept pushing down, anger burning inside her at everything all these men had done to her.

"I'm going to take your head, and I'll hand it to Hecate on a silver platter. She'll be thrilled," she snarled, unable to do much more than choke him to death with her foot.

Jaia was still in shock, Alaric was still barely able to move and Harla was being choked out by a half-naked bound Fae.

That was the sight Epharis walked in on as he came looking for his brother.

He looked at her, then to Jaia, then Alaric and then finally down at Harla, who had turned red.

"Epharis," she said pleasantly, but he could tell by her tone that someone was going to die.

"Etani, what is going on?" he asked warily.

"This here? Think back to our first date, but instead of a psychotic Lich, it's a psychotic demi-god with a size complex and a bone to pick with Faerie. Then we have King Voyeurism and a shell-shocked vampire. That's what we have here. How's your day been?"

He watched her, looking up to the chain and then down to Harla again, who was by that point turning blue.

"It'll be a real hassle if you kill him, and his husband will cause a scene, Alaric will have to deal with that and there'll be another trial," he sounded like it was all simply too hard for him and she frowned, glaring at the man who was her husband.

"Why don't you come here and take him then?" she said in a lethal tone, but judging by his expression, he was not going to do anything stupid. "How about you come over here and release me so I can speed along the process?"

"If I let you go, do you promise not to kill him?" Epharis asked calmly, knowing the best way to deal with his angry wife was to try and stay calm.

"No, I'm going to wring his neck and then hand his mutilated corpse back to Pharley."

Epharis let out a soft sigh and looked down at Harla, who by now looked as though his living long enough to be strangled properly was not going to be an issue.

He moved forward and she growled at the approach, but it was either stand still and Epharis would stop her or defend herself against Epharis and stop killing Harla. Neither outcome appealed to her.

Stopping before her, he reached down and curled his hand around the back of her knee and pulled up sharply, his eyes locked on hers and refusing to back down from the challenging stare.

Harla rolled away and Epharis let go of her leg, allowing her to lower it to the floor.

Staring into each other's eyes, they tried to force the other to look away. Neither was willing to be the one who looked away first. Alaric coughed and they both looked to him in unison.

"This is what happens if you let your anger get the best of you brother," Epharis said, finally reaching up to release her wrists and then moving to Jaia, who had not budged.

IGNORING HARLA, she moved to Alaric and he jerked as she reached for him.

"Oh, calm down, I'm checking your pulse," she said moodily, pressing her fingers against the skin under his jaw.

Nodding, she crossed to the table and picked up bottles, checking the labels for the one she needed.

Picking up a clean syringe, she drew out a portion and then stabbed it as deeply into his arm as it would go, making him flinch.

"If you ever threaten to rape me again, I will ensure you die a slow and painful death, and then I will find you in death and kill you again," she murmured in his ear, pushing down on the plunger and then jerking the needle out.

He was glaring up at her as she moved away, throwing the empty syringe at Harla, who had the thing bounce off his forehead.

Grabbing her clothes, she stalked from the room to free Kai and Versalis.

The instant Versalis was free, he was on her and checking to make sure she was okay, the black patches looking terrible, but they were healing, the bite on her shoulder still inflamed and even slightly infected.

"We could hear…" Kai said, looking pale.

"Don't think about it," she said, turning away from his agonised look to get dressed.

"How can you be so calm?" he whispered, and she looked at him, buttoning up her vest.

"It's not the first time I've been tortured, Kai. You get used to it," that was not true, one never got used to being tortured, but she did not want him to worry about her and he looked horrified.

Walking back into the cell with the rest of the men, she glanced at Jaia, frowning as she tried to recall what had happened to him.

She left Kai to deal with him, needing to check on Alaric again.

His pulse was fast but steady and he was getting control of his limbs back.

She filled a mug with water and lifted it to his lips, and he drank gladly. She knew that sedatives tended to dry out one's mouth terribly.

Satisfied with her work, she turned to find Epharis glowering at her from a mere foot away, looming.

"If you yell at me, I'm going to neuter you," she threatened, seeing he was about to blow up.

"Six months you've been gone, Etani." He was using the 'I'm going to kill you later' tone

"And before that, I was in Faerie," she retorted, hearing the slap, and seeing Jaia jerk, looking at Kai and then the two left the room, Kai almost dragging his brother.

She watched them go, concerned but unable to remember what had happened.

"Do you want to stay down here?" Epharis warned and she turned on him.

"Is that a threat?" she snapped, his jaw clenching making her believe it was one. "Do not threaten me Epharis. I am not yours to control."

"You are my wife," he exclaimed, grabbing her arm.

"You married the Lich?" Harla demanded and she turned on him. He was still on the floor, trying to breathe through a crushed throat.

"Shut up, Nid!"

Epharis wrapped his arm around her middle, predicting her move, and she managed to clip Harla's jaw, but did not kick him in the face as she had intended.

Epharis heaved her up under his arm and stalked from the room, ignoring her struggles and profanity.

Taking her up to his room, he threw her in and locked the door behind him. She turned on him, glaring at him even as he started for her, fury in his eyes.

"If you ever talk to me like that again…" he hissed and she backed away, seeing the fire beginning to dance in his eyes.

"You can't threaten me," she snapped back, but he was not going to tolerate her mouth.

He slapped her across the face, and she staggered, finding the back of a chair to keep herself from falling.

MOVING AFTER HER, he gripped her by the hair and forced her forward over the table, sweeping the books off in his haste.

Keeping a tight grip on her hair, he reached down and released the ties of her pants and jerked them down, followed by her underwear and he leant down over her.

"You are *my* wife, I will do whatever I want with you," he snarled, kicking her legs apart and hitching up the front of his robes.

He bit down hard on her ear as he forced himself inside her, his low groan sounding loud in her ear and he gripped her shoulder with his free hand, nails digging into the bite wound as he thrust hard, grinding her hips into the edge of the table.

He had been without her for so long, angry at her and the world, furious that she had not found him when she had arrived and then their argument and his rage had escalated. Now all he wanted to do was have her and make her hurt.

Keeping his hand in her hair to keep her from standing up, he took what he wanted from his wife and released her when he was done, panting hard and finally relieved although only momentarily.

Sliding to her knees on the floor, she tugged her pants and undergarments up, ignoring his growl of warning that he was not done with her yet.

She did not speak to him as she stalked from the room and into the bathroom, throwing her clothes in a heap and running the bath.

He followed her after a few minutes, angry that she had walked away yet captivated by the blood and damage to her body with new bruises blooming at her hip bones.

Stripping off his robes, he joined her in the bath without a word, still angry but wanting to help her.

He helped her to wash her hair when her shoulder made it difficult and when she turned around, he kissed her hard and forced her up against the wall of the bath.

She grunted in pain but did not fight him as he took her again, knowing he would have her willing or not and it was easier not to fight him.

Having expended himself twice, he seemed to have calmed down, looking at her shoulder and frowning at the discolouration.

"That's infected," he observed, moving to pull at the skin around the bite, feeling the heat radiating off it.

"I thought that too," she sighed, flinching when she tried to lift her arm. "I've never had an infection before."

Epharis grunted softly and climbed out of the bath to collect supplies, returning to drizzle a stinging, thick liquid onto it.

"Keep it out of the water but stay in the bath, the steam will help," he said, drawing her closer to him and into his lap.

His arms were tight around her, protective as she leant against him. She felt his need for her again, but he resisted the urge, for the time being, leaving her to heal.

"Where have you been?" he asked, watching the infection oozing from the bites.

"In the North, Pharley's territory. That's how they found us. Dumb luck."

He nodded and ignoring her protests, he pulled the skin to help expel the infection.

"Stop, Epharis that hurts," she complained, and he hushed her, watching in fascination as a small barb came loose and he picked it out of the mess of blood, medicine, and pus.

"He bit you, didn't he?"

"Yes," she said, trying to see what he saw. He let it roll onto his palm and she frowned at it.

"You know what this means," he said, and she put on her best 'pity me' look.

But he was not about to give it to her. He climbed out of the bath and drained it, having her lie on her back with her shoulder over-hanging the edge of the bath.

He sat on her hips to keep her from struggling and he grabbed her shoulder, squeezing it.

She screamed, blood and pus pouring free along with small frag-ments of the barbs.

SECRETS IN THE BASEMENT

For over an hour he worked until, finally, the wounds began to heal over to leave her with a shiny pink scar that covered most of her shoulder.

"There you go," he breathed, looking down at her.

She glared at him and his brow lifted in challenge. She was hurting and angry, resenting them all and so she drove her knee into his back, throwing him forward and rolling as he flipped to his feet and came at her, aiming a kick for her side.

She threw herself to her feet, but he was on her in an instant, pinning her against the wall.

"Now wife, I think you're in no state to be fighting me," he growled in her ear as he grabbed her hip and jerked her into his groin.

"Epharis stop," she pleaded but he ignored her, grunting as he took her again and then again until he was finally spent completely, several hours later in bed.

Rolling off her, he sighed and pulled her into his arms, ignoring her protests.

He had satisfied himself upon her and punished her for running off, now he was calm.

She sighed and rested against his chest, frustrated but helpless. He was her husband, she knew she had to submit to her duty as a wife, but it was hard when she wanted to be left alone to lick her wounds or be with her friends. Her last thoughts as she fell asleep were of Jaia and his desire to kill Harla for hurting her.

An odd sound woke her in the night, curled up against Epharis' side, or at least she thought she had been. Something was touching her head, eight gentle points of contact that were drilling into her mind.

"Epharis?" she asked groggily, trying to turn her head but he kept her still.

"You will not kill him until I'm ready," he whispered, his voice echoing inside her mind to make her brain ache. "You will no longer hate him, will not try and kill him. You will remember what he did, but you will not rage. Not until I am ready to move, my precious wife. We will have our revenge for what he did, but not yet."

Squirming under the force of the pain in her mind, she groaned but there was no escaping him, no escaping the words that were drilling their way into her brain.

Looking to the side, she whimpered as what she thought had been Epharis at her side turned out to be the corpse of a human man, his skin grey and eyes wide. His mouth was hanging open in an anguished scream. Looking up, she found Epharis leaning over her, his eyes glowing a toxic green.

"You will not kill Alaric. You will treat him as though he did not give the order. And now, sleep."

She did sleep then, the memory of the corpse, his words and the fear fading into nothing more than a vague dream in the back of her mind.

She slipped out of bed hours later, a headache leaving her grumpy as she made her way into the sitting room and noticed the plans that had replaced many of the books on several tables. Crossing to one of them, she frowned as she looked down at the maps and realised they were troop movements. The King and his brother were preparing for the war that she had forgotten all about.

Her stomach knotted when she thought of Nayishma and she shook her head at the stupidity of men.

"You play a significant role in the war," a voice said, and she glanced up to see Epharis watching her, wearing nothing but a pair of black pants.

Her eyes trailed down from his long silver hair to his toned, yet slender chest and then down to his bare feet.

"How so?" she asked, her eyes flicking back up to his face as he brushed his hair back. At that moment, he looked almost human and she shivered at the sight.

"You will be on the front lines with Alaric, I'll be back with the twins," he slouched into the room, looking tired but content, especially when his eyes traced over her nudity as she bent over the table, her hair not doing anything to cover her.

"I'm not sure if I would be that good on the front line and Alaric certainly shouldn't be."

Epharis snorted and came to her side, his hand trailing up her back to make her shiver again.

"You haven't seen Alaric when he is in his titan form and you are an exceptional fighter. You just don't have training in swords."

He met her frown and doubt with confidence.

"You can learn while you're here."

"You know I will have to go back to Faerie."

"Alaric… Isn't going to tell them he got you back," he said warily, and she straightened.

"That is an exceptionally bad idea. If they think you're hiding me, they will come."

"Have you ever heard of what happens when Faerie goes to war?" she asked, certain he had not.

He shook his head and she frowned.

"Ayathian will be wiped off the map. A future warning for anyone who thinks they are clever enough to go up against them again. No one will survive"

He frowned at her and she shook her head, knowing he would not believe her.

"Well, I only hope Alaric knows what he's doing."

"We all do," he sighed and pulled her down to detail the map and all the movements in it.

Later that day she had slipped away in search of the twins, knocking gently on the door to their rooms and finding Versalis.

He greeted her warmly, pulling her into a tight hug and guiding her inside, the twins reading.

"Etani, glad to see you're back," Kai said brightly, getting up and hugging her.

JAIA HESITATED, watching her warily, and his reaction made her nervous.

"What's wrong?" she asked, anxiety in her voice. "Are you still unwell from yesterday? Are you injured?" she approached Jaia, ready to yank up the back of his shirt to check his back when Kai stopped her.

"He's fine, Etani, he's just a little shocked."

"By what?" she demanded, angry and scared for him.

"With what you said in the dungeon," Kai said slowly.

She looked from him to a sullen Versalis and then, to Jaia. "What did I say?" she asked, defensively.

"Don't you remember?" Jaia asked and she shook her head.

"What do you remember?" Kai asked, glancing at his twin.

"I said a lot down there, what point are you talking about?" she asked.

"After Harla bit you and before Epharis showed up," Jaia said.

She frowned, thinking about it.

"Harla bit me, I was laughing because of what he did and how he ended up as a humanoid, and then I was thinking about Catsit and then Epharis was there and I was trying to squash Harla's throat."

"What's a Catsit?" Kai asked.

"Catsit is the first mythical I came across in the human world. He is a little talking black cat with a white circle on his chest. He told me a lot about his world and to avoid the witches."

She looked between them and shook her head slightly.

"I was drugged was I not?" she sounded irritable again.

"Yes dear, you were drugged," Kai said gently.

"What did I say?" she demanded, looking between the three.

Jaia was watching her, his face both relived and terribly sad.

"Jaia?" she asked, wanting to go to him but afraid of his rejecting her.

"It's not important now. You're safe, everything is going to be fine," he breathed, his tone sounding devastated.

She looked at Kai, who had been watching her intently, almost accusatory.

"What did I say, Jaia?" she demanded, starting to get scared.

"Don't worry, it isn't important now," Jaia said gently and took her hand, leading her down onto the couch.

She did not like it one bit and she knew they had been talking about her. But she sat down, and her eyes levelled on Versalis. He looked back at her, and then he looked suddenly nervous as the intensity of her stare. He knew she was going to grill him for information later.

SETTLING down at Jaia's side, she inched closer but her attempt to get close made him stiffen and she moved away again, hurt by the rejection.

"Did you know about the war preparations?" she asked Kai, moving further away from Jaia under the guise of picking up one of the books until a good foot separated them and she hugged the book to her chest, not even reading the title.

"War?" Kai asked, looking up.

Versalis had watched her retreat, a small crease between his brows at the sight of her slumped shoulders.

"Epharis has all these maps and war plans. They are gearing up against Weorene."

The three men looked at her, startled.

"Already?" Jaia asked and she shrugged.

"We've been gone some time," she replied and began to explain the plans Epharis had told her. After a while she got up to get some water, and Versalis made room for her beside him and she sat down at his side, his arm going around her protectively.

Jaia had already gotten lost in the strategic side of it, Kai was frowning in thought and she finally fell silent, resting her head on Versalis' shoulder, his hand gripped tightly in both of hers.

She did not know why Jaia had suddenly rejected her, but it hurt.

"How long?" Jaia demanded, turning to see her with Versalis and flinching slightly.

"Weorene is already preparing, perhaps a month or two at most. Alaric wants me on the front line and you two in the back with Epharis. I assume you will be with Alaric and me on the front, Versalis."

The vampire nodded his agreement.

"Why you on the front lines?" Jaia demanded, suddenly angry. Pushing himself up from the seat, he began to pace.

"I'm immortal and a skilled killer," she said, not understanding his anger.

"So, he's sending you out to be his killing machine while we sit back and watch?"

"He needs the brains to be behind the scenes," she said finally.

"You're more intelligent than I am," Jaia said, frowning at her.

"You're a master at strategy, Kai is a genius. I can kill things. It makes sense."

He stalked forward, angry that she was agreeing with the plan to put her in the line of fire.

"Jaia, I'm immortal," she said, and he threw up his arms, stalking away again.

Looking to Versalis, she shook her head at her confusion.

"Alaric has it right, she would be best on the front lines, trying to get through to King Varsas."

She blinked and then realised that yes, Varsas would be there and she was likely going to be able to get to him. Jaia had frozen too, frowning at Versalis and then at her.

"She's a trained assassin. If anyone is going to get to that man, it's her," Versalis said.

"Aelen could," she said, taken aback by the ferocity of Jaia's stare.

"Aelen is mortal and an elf. You are immortal and a Fae. You're going to be the one to get to that King and put a stop to the war."

She did not bother fighting and instead, she let them fall into discussions about war.

Finally, she rose and Versalis looked up, standing suddenly, and following her to the door and out onto the stairs to the rest of the castle.

"Versalis what happened?" she pleaded but he shook his head.

"I'm sorry sweetheart, it's not my place," he said gently and smiled, brushing her cheek. "You look tired."

"I am tired," she breathed, allowing him to pull her into his lap once he had sat down on the stairs.

She leant into his chest and buried her face in his neck, his arms painfully tight around her but it felt amazing to be held so close.

She traced a gentle kiss against his throat, and he gave a low growl, tilting his head in invitation.

She bit down hard, her hand sliding up to curl around the back of his neck as she clutched him to her. Her tongue traced over the bite to taste his blood and he shuddered, his fingers digging into her back as she fed.

It was rare that she would feed on him, his blood potent and leaving her tingling, but it also caused a reaction between them that was hard to describe to themselves.

It triggered a primal need in them. A desperation that neither of them was willing to give in to and so they courted disaster, never intending to, but always ending at the very brink of destruction.

His breathing was heavy as she drew on him, her tongue teasing as she traced the four cuts in his skin.

He shuddered and shifted her so she straddled him, his hands finding the small of her back and pressing her down on him.

She rocked teasingly, feeling his arousal under her and she bit him again, adding four new holes.

With movement like lightning, he had her up against the wall of the stairwell, her arms and legs around him as he pressed into her, desperately wanting her and yet both knowing it could not happen.

His fingers were hot as they slid up the back of her vest, dragging his nails down her back to leave deep gouges in her skin and she arched her back, the move grinding her against his erection.

At the opportunity, the pain forcing her to release the bite, his lips came down hard on hers and his tongue explored her mouth, tasting her and his blood on her lips before his fingers found her hair and yanked, exposing her throat.

He bit down with intentional force, causing her to groan aloud in pain. The sound electrified him, and he pressed against her, rolling his hips against her to make her moan quietly.

She traced her nails down under the back of his shirt, the lethality of those steely nails enough to arouse him to a whole new height, a threat of danger.

She ached for him, her entire body screaming for him to take her there violently against the wall and his body responded in kind.

A noise above them had them both freezing in place, panting hard and clutched so closely together they could be one being.

He let her slide to the ground, licking away the last traces of blood and smiling sheepishly, knowing they both needed to be more careful. Their becoming sexually involved was not what that world needed, not what would lead to its survival.

Their ever coming together would lead to the end of that world and they both knew it. His lust triggered her need for blood and that would lead to thousands dying. Her lust triggered his bloodlust and more would die, hundreds of thousands would be killed within a matter of months, all because they had given in to their need.

She gripped his hair and forced him to her, kissing him hard and passionately before finally drawing away and heading upstairs, leaving him panting and erect, his burning eyes lingering on her as she fled.

SHE NEVER INTENDED for things to turn out that way, but she had given in to her desire for blood and affection and had stepped too close to the edge with the vampire King.

Running her fingers through her hair, she flushed as men turned to look at her, their sensing her carnal needs drawing far too much attention to her.

She found herself heading back in the direction of her rooms near Alaric's and she tilted her head at the open door, stepping inside to find Drizdan and Izziah standing there, arguing.

"What are you doing in my room?" she demanded, both men looking at her and then breathing in sharply.

Narrowing her eyes at them, Izziah seemed to flush while Drizdan's focused sharpened on her and he smiled. It was not a nice smile, but rather one suggesting terrible thoughts.

"I've come to collect my wife," Drizdan said, approaching her.

"I'm not sure if you're aware of this, but…" she lifted her hand and his eyes focused on the shadow marking around her left hand.

His cheeks flushed with anger.

"What does that mean?" he snarled, and she turned away from his anger, crossing the room to collect her belongings.

"I'm only married to you in Winter. I'm not in Winter right now, I am married to Epharis here," she sounded angry about both. "Isn't magic fun?"

He gripped her bag and threw it, slamming her back against the wall with his teeth bared.

"I went through a lot to get my hands on you… I am not giving you back to the Lich," his face was inches from hers, his fingers leaving bruises on her arms.

"Then you should have made a better deal with Tatialia. If you can't handle the Fae, get out of Faerie," she snapped, pushing him off her.

He slapped her and her cheek burned, blood pouring at the cut his metal glove left on her cheek.

"Drizdan!" Izziah said, outraged at his brother's actions.

"Get out," Drizdan said to his brother. "If you don't want to see how I handle my wife, you should leave now."

Izziah watched as he gripped her hair and drove his fist into her stomach, doubling her over before he fled, closing the door behind him.

"I don't think you understand the gravity of the situation," he said as he began dragging her in the direction of the bedroom. She gritted her teeth and dug in her heels, refusing to let him touch her.

"You belong to me," he snarled, hitting her a third time and forcing her through the door. She could feel her hair tearing, parting from her scalp but still, she resisted.

Growling, she shifted her feet and drove her fist up into his kidney.

He let go of her immediately and she darted back. He looked livid.

"Get on the bed or I will make you," he said slowly but she shook her head, her posture defensive.

She did not expect him to draw a sword, the sight of it making her pause and then prepare herself for pain.

He came at her, scoring on her upper arm while she scored a hard kick to his ribcage and sent him flying. Turning for the door, she gripped the handle and then yelped, looking down to see that the handle had dark grey metal on it.

Looking down at the ground, she saw the drips and realised it was a very new addition, leaving her unable to open the door easily. He had trapped her in there.

She turned as he got up, burning with anger, and he grinned.

"You smell good, Etani. Been getting frisky with the vampire?"

He was leering, but she knew he was furious at the mere thought of her either getting worked up over a vampire, or that a vampire would dare touch her.

"Jealous? I'm not getting worked up over you?" she taunted, knowing better but she hated him, and it made her feel better.

He glared at her and she knew that if he got his hands on her, she was going to suffer dearly for her smart mouth.

He came at her and they broke apart quickly, a deep cut in her stomach and she thought she might have broken one of his ribs. His sword had greater range, but if he were not careful, she could get a hit in on him.

"Last chance, bitch," he snarled. She shook her head and he came for her again. He did not try and cut her, did not try and slash at her. The back of his hand found her cheek and then his sword drove straight through her middle.

She cried out, his grin a feral mask of triumph as she dropped to her knees and he slid the sword free of her.

"Exactly where you belong," he said, looking down at her.

Wrapping one arm around her, he pulled her to the bed and threw her onto it, her fingers going to the wound to try and stem the bleeding but he knocked her hands away and used the cut in her vest to rip it open, leaving her exposed.

She did not care about his greedy stare down on her chest, she was too busy pressing against the wound to try and stem the bleeding.

"If you try and struggle, I will stab you again," he warned, motioning to the sword at her side as he straightened and untied her pants, roughly pulling them down along with her undergarments.

Leaning down, he kissed her inner thigh before biting her painfully.

Blood welled and he lapped it before he started up her body, leaving his mark on her flesh for Epharis.

TORTURE OF A NEW KIND

Whimpering, she looked up at him as he removed the plating around his thighs and then undid his pants, shoving them down just enough to release himself.

"You are my wife, you will submit!" he yelled in her face, furious that she was still being difficult.

"Only… in Winter," she wheezed, not wanting to surrender.

"No Etani, I will never stop being your husband. Here or in Winter, you belong to me."

Dread filled her as she looked up into his cold, dark eyes.

She did not know if she still belonged to him, she did not know if it was in Winter alone, or if he owned her no matter where they were. Could she fight him?

The resounding 'no' rang in her head and she bit her lip, hating him for everything he had ever done to her.

She was too weak to fight him, and she knew the law. She knew he had a right to her, but that did not make it any easier when he was violent.

He read her cracking resolve and smirked in the face of her doubt.

"Submit to me and I will be gentle," he coaxed, hesitating as he leant over her. "All you have to do is submit and it will be easier."

Doubt ran through her and, finally, she could only nod once. If she obeyed, he would be gone faster, right?

Biting her lip, she found a spot on the ceiling and focused on it. She needed to focus on something else, something that would keep her away from what her husband was doing to her.

He at least kept to his word, he was not excessively rough with her as she assumed he would be, but he did make sure that his sounds of pleasure were loud in her ear.

At that moment, her mind wandered to the twins, and especially Jaia. She did not know why it was him she thought of then, but his hard, stern face lingered in her thoughts. She wished she were in the basement with them, she wished she were anywhere else but in bed with her Winter husband.

Grunting in pain, she came back to herself and looked up into the sweaty, bloodied face of the Drow. He had bitten her breast. She could feel the blood rolling down her ribs to stain the mattress under her.

He looked confused, almost high before he looked down at her in return. "What did you do?" he asked in a dazed voice.

"What?" she asked, not sure what he was talking about.

Drizdan paused and then leant down again, biting hard into her left breast before shuddering atop her.

"Sweet mother," he groaned, his entire body clenching as though in pain.

However, when he began to move at a feverish pace, she knew it was not pain he was feeling.

She did not know how long he kept her, only that he was growing excited by something with the more he hurt her. She knew he was a sadist, but she could not explain his response to the pain that drove him wild.

By the time he was done with her, the stab to her abdomen was healed but she was left littered in cuts and bruises. A rib had been cracked, leaving her unable to breathe properly. Her lip bled and she tasted blood where her inner cheek had been cut against her teeth.

He had focused mostly around the sensitive parts of her body, her breasts, ribs, inner thighs, and backside. Long cuts and punctures marred her body while his name was scrawled over her right breast in large letters.

Sitting at her side, he was panting heavily as though he had run a marathon, staring at the blood-soaked bed in wonder.

"What are you?" he gasped, brushing back sweaty hair from his face. "This isn't normal. You aren't normal."

Looking up at him through a haze of confusion, she did not know what to say and so she remained silent.

After a moment of looking down into her eyes, he grunted and pushed himself off the bed. Turning back to her, he scooped her limp form up and took her into the bathroom to get cleaned up.

"Can't have my wife looking and smelling like a whore when we go back to Winter," he growled as he began to scrub her down.

It was incredibly painful, her wounds stinging all over again, but he ignored her feeble attempts to escape him, keeping one arm around her middle to ensure he could finish the job.

With both of them clean, he set her down on her feet but did not immediately let go of her, a faint hint of concern showing in his face as she swayed.

"You are weak," he said in disgust, as though his abusing her was her fault. "We'll get you something to eat before we head back."

Nodding once, she remained silent and watched him.

He was a handsome man if she looked past the fear and hatred. If she ignored those for a moment, his physical appeal was enough to set her heart to fluttering, but he was a monster. He was abusive, violent, and cruel.

He was also her husband and she did not think there was anything she could do to stop that… unless she killed him.

THE THOUGHT LINGERED in her mind as he moved around the bathroom, roughly pulling a black robe over her shoulders, and using a towel to scrub her hair dry. He was muttering to himself about not wanting a lazy wife, but he still did the work while she simply struggled to stay standing.

"Can't wait to see what Epharis makes of that," he grinned, touching the no longer bleeding spot on her chest that showed red on her pale skin. 'DRIZDAN' sprawled over her skin. It looked angry and inflamed, but it was healing quickly enough.

The thought of what Epharis would do made her distinctly nervous, glancing towards the bedroom. She would need to hide the evidence. She wanted to kill Drizdan, not leave it up to her husband.

The thought eased some of her distress, and she began to plan, looking back at Drizdan. She was going to kill him, but how?

He deserved it, even if he was only following orders, their kind did not kill children. It did not matter that the child he murdered had not been born yet. Even a child still in the womb needed to be protected. But she wanted to do it herself. She *needed* to do it herself.

The plan settled into her mind and she took in a deep, slow breath as her suffering began to ease in the light of a plan.

She would be the one to end his life, she simply needed a way to do it. Right then, she was too weak. She was tired, angry, and hurting.

She needed to hide what he had done to her body, she needed to reset herself. She needed to be stronger.

Drizdan seemed entirely unaware of his wife's plans, drying himself off and dressing before guiding her back out into the sitting room and setting her down on the couch.

"We will be heading back to the Under Dark in two days," he was saying, setting a case out on the table and beginning to throw her possessions into it. "This time we won't be coming back. You will stay there and have your blood sent to your damned vampires. You will stay in Winter with me."

She tuned out his angry ramblings, looking around the room she had come to know as hers.

Even with her living there so long, there was little to show for it.

She did not tend to collect trinkets, she did not stockpile shoes or pillows as some ladies did.

However, she *did* have a small collection of items she had been collecting without knowing why.

A SMALL SHARD of glass that shone a pretty green in the sunlight, a smooth golden coloured rock, and a tiny silver bell. She did not try and understand her need to keep those items. They had meant absolutely nothing to her, but the need to keep them was still there.

Drizdan's hand tapped sharply on her face, jarring her out of her thoughts and back into reality.

Looking up at him, she tried to recall what he had been saying but she had been so caught up in her thoughts of the tiny collection of items that she had been completely ignoring him.

"Did you hear what I said?" he demanded, looking angry.

Shaking her head, she flinched back as his hand collided with her cheek, sending her already confused mind reeling all the more.

"You will listen when I'm speaking to you, Etani," he snapped, glaring down at her.

"Yes Drizdan," she mumbled, as a new wave of anger burnt inside her.

"Get dressed, we will be returning to the compound until it's time to leave."

Nodding, she pushed herself to her feet and headed slowly for the bedroom. Pausing at the scene, she stared in horror at the sight of her ruined bed.

There was a large amount of blood on it, her sheets had been ripped and the bloodied sword was still on it. Along with that, there was a small collection of knives and a gauntlet with sharp, talon-like fingers.

Deciding not to think about it, she headed for the dresser and held onto the wall to keep from toppling over. It did not work and the thud of her shoulder hitting the wall drew in Drizdan.

"I'll get you something to eat," he said, disgust evident in his tone.

Nodding silently, she pushed herself upright once more and dragged on her underwear.

Setting the robe to the side, she looked up at the quiet click of the door to her suite. Her mind was sluggish, but it was coming up with a plan.

She needed to be stronger to handle him, and what was the quickest way for her to get stronger?

A grim smile pulled at her lips. She needed to die.

Giving up on trying to get dressed, she pulled on her robe and tied it off. Her movements were slow as she shuffled across the room and picked out a leather thong, using it to tie back her hair.

Satisfied, she looked once more around the room and lifted her finger. Biting into the tip, she filled her mind with the thought of escape and drew the line in the air, stepping through into freedom.

SHE HAD HEARD LONG AGO of a place that was overrun with odd humans, many of them having darker skin than the ones she had seen in the places she had visited. She had been curious about them, wanting to know more but had never gone. For her, the deciding factor had nothing to do with the people there, but the place itself.

The vampires had enough blood to keep them going for around a month. That gave her time.

Slipping easily through reality, she stepped out into a place she had never seen before.

Looking around, she frowned at the scenery. It was exceptionally dark, and the mist was thick.

She assumed she was in heathen territory and her skin crawled, brushed by the mist.

She had never been able to see into Spring because of mist and she had never wanted to try and get in.

The trees were enormous, twisted and like claws with no foliage at all. They looked dead but she could hear them whispering.

A movement caught her eye and she turned to see a dark, richly brown coloured figure moving in the trees.

Frowning, she tilted her head and moved in the direction of the figure, wondering what it could be.

It giggled and she went still, squinting. It was a young dryad, small and skinny.

It saw that she had stopped and so it had stopped, moving just enough to catch her attention and try to draw her in and that alone was very odd. Dryads were all females, that meant they only tried to lure men but here she was being lured by one of them.

Clicking her tongue gently, the little creature flitted forward, fascinated by the sound. She clicked her tongue again and the dryad crept closer.

She was shocked to see that the little creature was male, naked with big brown eyes and odd, triangular markings on his skin.

She was still trying to figure him out when she realised he was not a dryad. Looking up, she saw an enormous black spider looming over her. The sight of the giant thing had her wanting very badly to run away, but that was not a good idea.

He was a lure alright, a young spider in human shape that was drawing her into the web for consumption.

"No," she said simply, and the spider froze, seeming confused. "You will be wasting your energy, I'm immortal."

The young male creature approached her, touching the blood on her robe that she had not noticed had soaked through, and tapping it against his tongue. He looked disappointed.

"Better luck next time," she said, giving the boy's hair a ruffle before she moved away.

Predators understood predators to a certain extent, and she was glad for that. She was also glad to be away from the spider.

Making her way through the creepy black forest, she decided to head back to the human world, not wanting to come across any other monsters from that place, nor a member of the Court.

She pictured the location in her mind and bit her finger, drawing the line in the air and stepped out onto the most beautiful sight she had ever seen.

She had no idea how she had come across the location, she had never been there before, but she was not going to complain at her success.

She was standing atop a cliff, a stream rushing past her into a sharp fall. The roar of the falls was tremendous, but that was nothing to what she saw.

The forest was so enormous she could not wrap her mind around it. It stretched on for an eternity and beyond. She had to think this was the entire world and everyone was inside it, but she had never seen that cliff before. She looked down and smiled, the height making her dizzy.

She was certain it was enough to do the job.

She spent the day there, just watching and listening to the world live and she shook her head at the magnificence of it. There were no thoughts she could come up with that could describe that place.

She watched the sunset and it was breathtaking enough to steal her heart.

She was in love.

Once the sun had set, she got up and moved back away from the cliff face, turning back to it, and taking a running leap off the side of the mountain.

She fell for an eternity, ten seconds and then twenty and thirty, falling and falling and finally she hit the stone, and everything was no more.

WAR GAMES AND PRETTY CATS

er eyes opened and she looked around, realising she was in the spirit world and she had to laugh at the impossibility of it all. While it was incredibly hard for her to die, she could still do it if she put her mind to it. Letari was holding her shoulder gently, her eyes sad but Etani was simply relishing, wanting to enjoy the free fall and the sudden stop.

She had not felt any pain, just a blinding joy at flight, the feeling of air whipping past her, the beauty of the world.

Standing, she looked down at the ribbon that pulled tight towards life and she sighed, looking to her twin.

"Kill them all," Letari said though she had no way to say it.

She stared at her twin and then she nodded, her eyes turning and she started for the entrance back to life.

She burst out of the pool under Ceress and sighed as she looked around, hating that place. But even as the guard ran, she dragged herself out of the water and her mind was on Ayathian as she drew the line and stepped through… into the middle of the throne hall.

She pulled up short and spun, entirely shocked at the turn of events and eternally glad it was the middle of the night and the place was empty, except for a young maid who had dropped her tray.

Lifting her finger to her lips, she made a shushing gesture and the girl nodded, collecting her things and running.

How she ended up there she had no idea whatsoever. She should have ended up near that town she always went to. But there she was, naked in Ayathian's throne room.

Guards gaped at her as she passed, but none of them said a word, simply staring at the exotic creature as she stalked for the basement.

She kicked the door in and found all three already on high alert as she swept into the room and turned in a circle, looking.

The smell of her hit them first and they inhaled sharply. She lifted her hand with her index finger extended upwards to ask for silence, as she knew Versalis was about to speak though she had not heard or seen him moving.

Finding what she was looking for, she picked up her panic bag and undid it, dumping the contents out on the table and pulling on her best pair of dragon-leather pants, a long black cotton top and her backup supply of weapons and chemicals.

She turned to the three as she bundled up her hair and started braiding it, her eyes going from Kai, who looked as though he had been crying, to Jaia who looked wary and finally, to Versalis who was trying to suck in as much air as he could.

"Are you alright?" she asked Kai as she reached the bottom of her hair and used a small leather thong to tie it off.

He nodded and while she doubted it, she nodded too.

Lifting two long daggers from the pile, she tucked them under her arm and slid on her gauntlets, the daggers fitting snugly against the underside of her arms.

"You two?" she asked Jaia and Versalis. She was still stinging at the rejection from Jaia, but she had tucked that away as well. Versalis looked ready to start shouting.

"You were dead!" he finally roared, and she looked at him.

It was not only her smell that alerted them to her. She looked different, no longer scarred and broken, no more cuts and bruises, everything was new, and she was ready.

"So?" she asked, adding two knives against the small of her back in custom sheaths.

"For three days! How did you die?" he demanded, and she lifted a brow at the length of time. Unusual, but it did not matter at that stage.

"There is an exceptionally large mountain on the other side of your world. It is a very lovely place and a big fall. I believe they say it's the sudden stop that kills you though. Enough damage and it does it."

Kai had gotten up off his seat and had fallen against her, his body shaking with sobs and she wrapped her arms tightly around him.

"Kai, talk to me. What's the matter?" she asked quietly, looking up at the other two in confusion.

"He went to find you. He walked in on Drizdan throwing a world-class fit about your running off somewhere. He saw…" Versalis trailed off as her eyes slid shut.

"It was like… like the dungeon all over again…" Kai whimpered, his arms tightening around her until it began to hurt but she refused to let him go.

"It's okay Kai, I'm okay now," she whispered, her cheek resting against the top of his head.

She was watching Versalis, who had relaxed somewhat, and he rushed over to hug them both tightly.

Jaia hung back, watching her with the two men and looking confused. She watched him in return as she held the wildly sobbing Kai.

She did not know what had happened in that room, but she was not about to let him go. She would do whatever it took to help him, and she knew he would have done the same for her.

Epharis burst into the room shortly after, his eyes wild as he found her.

"You!" he barked, and she arched a brow at him.

He realised the scene a second later and stopped, taking them all in and Jaia off to the side.

"Is this because of Drizdan?" Epharis asked warily and she nodded once, having no idea how he knew but not denying it. "Your Winter husband has been banished."

She jerked her head up at the words and stared at him, overjoyed, and yet horrified at the news.

"Banished?" she demanded. How was she going to kill him if he was not in Ayathian?

"Yes, banished. The guards were called at a raving Drow in the Princess's suite. They had him arrested thinking he had killed you when they found your bedroom. I saw the… bed," he had gone pale, his eyes boring into hers. "I heard rumour of a black-haired goddess walking naked through the halls with an intent to kill and assumed."

"Flattering," she said, as Kai squeezed her painfully.

"Etani, we need to speak."

"Not now. Later," she replied and turned to Versalis who was breathing in the scent of her hair. She swatted at him to get him to stop and he slunk away, looking pouty.

She knew he could not help it, she knew she would smell amazing to him but that did not mean she wanted them sniffing her like that.

"Hear that Kai? He's gone now," she crooned as she led him to the couch and he curled up at her side, his head in her lap while she stroked his hair.

Epharis was looking down at the vampire, baffled, and she tilted her head to Versalis, the two moving away to talk and she began to sing gently to cover up the whispers.

Her voice did not seem to affect Kai like it did with a human. It made him rather sleepy and, true enough, a few minutes later, he was asleep.

She sighed gently, stroking his hair back from his face and closing her eyes, her attempt to get dressed and armed forgotten for the time being.

"Why did you do it?" Jaia asked quietly and she looked at him, her expression neutral.

"I was so tired. I just wanted a break. But then I also wanted to get stronger, a reset," she said simply and Jaia looked angry. "But Letari said something to me that made me realise that there is a better option."

She smiled as she brushed over Kai's forehead.

"What did she say?" Epharis asked and she looked up at him.

"Kill them all."

No one said a word, all of them realising that she had come back for that exact reason.

She had been pushed and pushed, finally, she had snapped, and she was not going to take any more abuse.

Epharis swallowed and looked to the two vampires as her eyes dropped back down to Kai who looked troubled even in sleep.

The men exchanged worried looks as she began to sing again.

News about the war had spread throughout the city and people were getting nervous. It was getting harder for her to hunt with so many humans opting to leave the area rather than getting drafted into the war, and the lack of food was making her moody.

The elixir that Epharis made her worked, but it was not the same as a fresh human. She noted that he had suddenly turned nice to her. It amused her, though it was not overly surprising.

She had made a deal with herself that she would spend her day training under the Kai's obsessively watchful eye. At night, she would take at least three hours to open one of those little packets and try to deal with the trauma she had endured.

It was hard, but she felt as though it might be working. Especially when she had Kai with her, cradling her while she sobbed and screamed, often crying with her.

She was a quick study and within a few days she had learnt how to use a long black bladed sword she had been given. It was simple and elegant, only needing one hand, and she could carry two. Within the first week of her return she had taken on Epharis and it had been close; two days later she kissed him on the cheek after she had beaten him. Three days after that, she had taken on Jaia and that was an entirely different story. The man knew exactly what to do and how to attack her at her weakest points, landing blow after blow on her with his wooden sword and she had gotten frustrated and tackled him.

At that point, the fight was called off and she had been banished from the field for cheating.

She came back the next day to train and by the end of the month, they had faced off again and she had scored several times, but still lost to him.

The news about the war was getting dire and the lords had been called to provide soldiers who flooded to the city to help. She was annoyed to learn that so few of them were human.

She watched them from the balcony of Epharis' rooms as he had been trying to convince her to keep up her studies, but she had been more interested in watching the people, and he had been more interested in watching her back as her dress revealed a hint of her thighs every time the wind blew.

She had drawn a fair bit of attention from the soldiers, who were quite eager for someone to talk to and so she had worked it, leaning on her elbows and grinning at them, the cut of her dress giving them an exceptional view of her full cleavage.

They seemed to rather enjoy looking at her cleavage and it annoyed Epharis, so she liked it even more.

Standing on the balcony, she was watching a tall feline male in bone armour with spots all over his furry body as he sang to her in a voice that could have made angels weep.

She had never seen a beast like him; he told her he was from the forest and she wanted to go down there, but she had been stopped. That was a few days earlier and she had decided to sneak out while Epharis was looking for something.

Dressed in her usual leather pants and vest, she watched the feline male as he sang to her, his long tail swaying and she decided to simply go down there and talk to him.

Due to the risk of men in the city, she was always required to carry her swords, along with all of her usual weapons, and he saw as she hopped calmly off the balcony and dropped.

The fall was not huge, and she landed easily, her knees bending, and the men around her moved back.

She was taller than most expected, and up close she was rather intimidating in her weaponry and leather.

The feline had stopped singing, his golden eyes on her as she approached him, and he smiled.

"Come down here," she said to him and many of the men seemed to lean in, hearing her low voice for the first time and all that it promised.

He leapt from the wall and landed with perfect form beside her, on all fours. She had an affinity for cats, and he seemed to like her just as much as she liked him. He prowled around her once before standing up on his hind legs.

His armour was made entirely out of bone, a large spine running down both of his legs, a loincloth giving him modesty and a belt around his waist. His left arm was covered in a leather guard with a large number of needles and darts, the right having a large skull of some creature she had not seen before. His chest was bare, muscled, and huge.

He carried an axe and a strange bone talon-like thing that she found interesting. It looked as though it went on his paw, three large spikes coming out of it and feeding down to protect the back of his arm and wrist. It made for a large set of claws.

Fascinated, she tilted her head to the side and took her turn examining him.

"Who are you?" she asked him calmly, his ear flicking in her direction.

"Jagum of the forest clan," he said, his chin up high in pride.

"Jagum of the forest clan," she said slowly, and he turned to her, his eyes burning as she spoke.

It was odd to see a feline on his back legs like that, his muzzle and large teeth giving him a strange accent that worked well, even more so with singing. She tilted her head and realised that he had pierced his skin with the bone sections, they were attached to his skin instead of leather.

"Etani!" Epharis bellowed down at her and she looked up. Many of the men dropped into low bows.

"Go back to bed, Epharis," she called, and many looks were thrown her way at the casual use of the Prince's name.

Epharis looked ready to spit fire and he stalked away from the balcony, no doubt heading down there.

The cat was over seven foot on his hind legs, and he looked down at her, pinkish-brown nose twitching.

"You're a predator too," he said, and she smiled, his breath catching.

"I'm called a soul eater here."

"Your name is Etani?"

"It is," she was enjoying their game of cat and mouse.

"I recognise it," he said slowly, trying to think.

"Yes, it was just shouted at us."

The cat snorted his amusement and they turned to see the Lich stalking towards them, looking livid.

"I am curious to see you in action. I have never seen one of your kind before," she said, ignoring the path the soldiers were making for the Prince.

"I would gladly fight any of these men for you."

She grinned at him and he looked wary at her double set of canines.

"No Jagum, you're going to fight me," she breathed.

He looked shocked and she turned on Epharis, giving her new friend time to think.

"Yes, husband?"

Her use of the title had him slowing down warily and Jagum choked as he realised who she was.

"Get inside the castle, now."

"My friend Jagum and I are going to practice," she said and saw Epharis' eyes slide from her to the cat.

"You're going to fight a werecat?" he demanded, and she turned slightly to see Jagum.

"Yes," she said simply, looking back at Epharis

"Fine, go fight the beast," he said angrily.

She smiled and turned her back on her angry husband and back to the cat, who was looking nervous.

"Is that wise, Prince Epharis? I don't want to harm your wife."

His eyes found hers and he flinched back from her expression. Her smile had vanished, and she was glaring at him with murderous intent in her eyes.

"Yeah, that was a bad thing to say…" Epharis said dryly as he looked down at her.

She had started to walk away, and the crowd followed, the cat following after several seconds and then they found the ring.

He reached behind him to draw the axe and slid his paw into the claw contraption. Standing across the field from her, he looked enormous next to her slender frame.

She drew her swords and took a moment to snap a ribbon into place around each wrist, keeping the swords from leaving her hands, and adding a trick she had not told anyone about yet.

SHE SMILED at the cat and he bared his teeth, letting out a feral roaring scream before he came charging.

She moved like the wind, allowing him to get close before she turned and stepped to the left, her body bending backwards in a graceful arch to avoid the slash with the claw, as she turned she spun both swords and blood spilled.

Standing back to back, she looked down at her swords and the blood, the cat having two long cuts along his ribs.

"You are a beautiful creature, Jagum, and your voice could make a Goddess weep, but you underestimate people," she said gently as he touched his ribs, neither of them moving for an instant.

"I won't make that mistake again," he purred, realising the challenge he faced. "Who are you really?"

"My name is Princess Etania Daewen of the Winter Court of Faerie and royal assassin to Prince Epharis."

"Makes sense…" he breathed, and they moved, he swung the axe and she bent forward at the waist, allowing it to swing over her back and miss by a foot.

Turning her sword backwards against her arm, she shoved it back, but the cat had moved to avoid it, spinning with reflexes that spoke of his species.

She went on the attack, her movements blurring as she struck again and again, the cat unable to do anything but defend against her with her sheer determination and speed.

Finally, he roared and swung as she leapt back, landing on her knuckles and then her feet.

She had scored any number of times on him, leaving him bleeding but he looked exhilarated and the crowd had grown around them.

"You're a tricky little beast," he said happily, his tail whipping behind him.

It seemed as though he had been holding back and he came at her with a speed she had not expected, the blows coming thick and fast and she had time to defend against them but little more and finally he struck. His claws raked viciously across the side of her face, one barely missing her eye and the other two leaving the bone exposed.

She staggered back, blood blinding her and she knew Epharis would be coming for her.

The cat had gone rigid, realising he had scarred the face of the Princess, but she had a wild grin on her face, and she dropped her sword, a black ribbon sliding free of her sleeve. Jerking up on the sword, she used the ribbon to spin the sword in a circle.

She was blind in her eye, but she did not care. The cat looked utterly terrified as she spun the sword and then let it fly.

Deflecting it only barely, she yanked it back to herself and then the game began.

Throwing her swords at him and retrieving them, alternating between vicious kicks and frenzied sword attacks.

She finally caught him, and he went down, both swords coming up and then down to stop directly over his heart, double points just brushing his fur.

She was panting hard, blood dripping from her jaw and ear and she smiled. Stepping over him and bending down, she placed a kiss on the tip of his nose.

Straightening, the giant cat got up and the crowd cheered.

Turning to see Epharis smiling, her eyes found Alaric and he was looking smug at her success.

She allowed Jagum to kiss her hand and she used her sleeve to wipe away the blood, the cat looking shocked to see it had healed almost entirely but she still had no vision. It would return soon enough, and she headed for Epharis, who pulled her from the ring and back towards the castle.

Glancing over her shoulder, she found Alaric still watching her, the cat getting slapped on the back and cheered by his fellows.

She had fought a werecat and won; it was a good day for her.

THE WINTER LORD

Training continued and she had taken to training with the soldiers, shaking them up and getting them to see a smaller, more delicate adversary as a real challenge.

She had not been out to humiliate anyone, only to practice and train. They had been glad for the new challenge at first, at least until she started kicking their arses, and leaving them sore and resentful.

She had to remind them that she was over nine hundred years old and had been fighting for survival the whole time, but it did not seem to do much for bruised egos.

Being female meant they did not think of her as a threat and that was going to get them all killed. As a result, she was eagerly beating a healthy fear of women into them, refusing to let any of them die as a result of a strong female fighter.

"Faerie is made up of a majority of women. If you underestimate them you will die!" she screamed to the crowd that had come to see her latest fight.

"Yes, it is," A voice said and she turned, her eyes falling on the strange male she had seen in Winter and she realised he was also the male that had appeared at the ridge after they had returned from the Under Dark.

"Who are you?" she asked warily, and she approached him, circling him once.

He was tall, willowy slender with a pale fawn-coloured skin and those dark blue triangles leading down from his eyes in a sharp point.

He had long fingers, long ears and a small frown set into a devastatingly attractive face.

The smell of magic wafted off him and she noted with a flicker of fear that he was a member of the Fae.

"Uzo," he said simply as she moved back before him, her eyes searching his face.

"Uzo?" she asked, only two feet from him and able to see every detail.

He was wearing a black, long-sleeved shirt that was open to just under his sternum, the collar lifted to draw more attention to the area. Black pants and smart, expensive-looking black shoes.

His hair was unkempt and spikey, reaching just below his ears in a mess that looked annoyingly attractive, as though he ran his hands through it so many times it simply grew that way.

"Uzo Ernin, High Lord of Winter."

She took a step back from him and frowned, her eyes trailing down and then back up his form.

"We're not related," he said after a pause, the crowd had gone silent and tense, unsure if there would be a fight or if they should be protecting her as the Princess.

"Why are you here, Uzo of Winter?" she asked warily, her hand resting on the grips of her swords.

"I've been looking for you. I knew your father."

She narrowed her eyes at him, her body tensing.

"Why have you been looking for me?" she asked, not understanding.

"Your father and I were comrades, he asked me to find you just before he died and ensure you were safe."

She was getting angry now, that man coming into her life with some idiotic well-meaning attempt to obey her dead father. "That was a very long time ago, Uzo."

"You're not exactly easy to find. You're good at hiding," he seemed irritated by that.

She shook her head and drew her sword, pointing it at him. "I don't need your help, Uzo of Winter. I never needed your help."

He looked angry and hurt for a moment, but then he smiled.

"We shall see, little Princess," he said and called for a sword.

He was given one and she was nervous to see him moving seamlessly into an attack posture.

"Now, Etania, I'll try to go gentle on you," he said, and then attacked.

He moved like lightning and she could barely hold him off, his attacks calculated and smooth, seeming to blur even to her eyes and she slid her second sword free of the sheath, working to push him back but he was physically stronger than her and his age made him fast.

He pushed her back until the crowd was forced to move or get involved.

GETTING IN CLOSE TO HER, she found him to be grinning, but it was a nasty grin and she had needed both swords to block a powerful overhand blow.

He drove her to her knees, and they left deep gouges in the packed dirt.

Looking up at him, she gave a low growl and pulled at both swords. They screamed as his sword was thrust up and she rolled, spinning herself up to her feet and backing away from him.

The crowd had gone entirely silent, watching the fight between the Fae.

He came at her again and she was forced to defend herself and she had the sudden, terrible realisation that he was not really trying.

His hand flung out and he struck her across the face to send her flying.

She rolled, landing on her back and she blinked up at the sky, her hands empty. He approached at an easy pace, calmly cutting the ribbons and as she pushed herself up onto her elbows, he levelled the point of his sword against her throat.

Her hair had come free of its braid, partly covering her face and sticking to her skin.

He did not even look ruffled as he met her eyes.

"You're still a child, Etania," he said softly, pressing her back down with the sword.

She lifted her hands in surrender, his blank face making her think he might try and kill her regardless.

"You have no choice in my being here, girl. Your father and I have our deal and you are going to have to endure."

At no point did he raise his voice, speaking in a low tone as he studied her, trapped under the point of his sword.

"I surrender," she breathed, swallowing at the blade pressing lightly against her throat.

"There is no surrender in war, Etania. You fight or you die."

Jagum moved forward, angry that she was still pinned down.

He swiped at the Fae, Uzo seeming to melt and appear back several feet, the sword at the ready.

"We are not on the field yet," the enormous cat growled, holding his hand out for her. She took it and he pulled her to her feet. "We allow our partner to surrender and we fight again at a later time."

"You are teaching your soldiers to be weak," Uzo said, throwing the sword to the one who had given it.

Jagum was looking down at her, the pad of his thumb brushing away a small drop of blood at her throat.

"We are training. We are getting stronger, not weeding out the weak," Jagum said as he turned on the Fae.

"That is enough for today," she said, glancing towards the castle, and she frowned at the sight of Alaric.

He had been watching every one of her fights and now his attention was on Uzo. She knew what the King would be up to and she did not think she liked the idea of Uzo being collected by the man.

Jagum bowed and she swept from the field. Collecting her swords on her way out back to the castle, the crowd parted for her, looking shocked and almost afraid of the Fae.

She had shown them what Faerie could offer, Uzo had shown them that the strongest in Faerie would bring to a war, and it was terrifying.

RETURNING TO THE CASTLE, she swept into Epharis' rooms and he looked up from his book, smiling slightly at the sight of her.

"How was training?" he asked, watching as she began to pace.

"There is a Fae in Ayathian. How long has he been here?" she said angrily but turning to her husband, she saw his confusion.

"A Fae in Ayathian? Surely, we would have known by now if there was another of your kind in the city," he said, and she could see his tension. "What is he here for?" His tone had turned dark, assuming it had something to do with her.

"He's said he's a comrade of my father's and is here to fulfil some deal to keep me safe."

Epharis looked irritable, looking her over and seeing the smear of blood.

"He fought you?"

"Some abject lesson to tell me I'm not strong or fast enough for war," she spat.

He grunted and stood, coming to her and catching her by the shoulders. He looked down at her and frowned.

"We aren't fighting Faerie, there will be no Fae in this war."

She nodded and closed her eyes as he pressed his lips to her forehead and drew her down to join him in his studies.

Sometime later Versalis turned up and he smiled at the sight of her, her head in Epharis' lap with a book in her hands.

He was stroking her hair gently, his elbow on the backrest of the couch with his book.

Peeking around the corner of her book at the knock, she waved him in and he moved inside, shivering at the pressure that told him to stay out, but her invitation had been enough.

"The twins are back," he said gently, and she sat up.

Jaia and Kai had been sent on a trip out into the country to play spy. Their abilities to be in the sun had come in exceptionally handy for the King and he was readily abusing it left and right, but she had become concerned about his interest in the ability. She was not about to become a blood mule for an army of day-walking vampires.

Epharis looked up at the loss of her presence and glowered at the vampire, neither liking each other.

"Any news?" Epharis asked and Versalis nodded tersely.

"It's only a matter of weeks now, Your Highness. Weorene has invaded."

She and Epharis exchanged a look and the two followed Versalis out into the hallway and down into the throne room where the twins were looking tired and irritable.

Kai turned at the sound of their approach and Alaric's moment of distraction, heading to her immediately.

She slipped her hand in his and he squeezed hers tightly. Jaia had not moved from his report and she felt a warm breath on her neck.

Glancing at Kai, she turned her back to Alaric, her long hair providing privacy for Kai as he greedily bit into her throat.

She felt eyes on her, but she ignored them as she traced her fingers through the soft black strands, his arms tight around her middle in a way that crushed her against him.

It had not been all that long since they had been gone, but the stress was affecting them all and she flinched as he bit her again and again, more chewing on her neck than anything. But he drank eagerly and bit the tip of his tongue to lick over the wounds, sealing them almost instantly.

He looked slightly guilty as he drew away, but she smiled, feeling pleasantly sleepy.

She used her thumb to wipe a smear of blood from his cheek and he kissed her palm, turning back to Alaric with cheeks flushed.

Versalis swept to her side and slipped his arm up under her ribs to help support her as she turned, watching Jaia's rigid back. He was ignoring her, she knew it.

"Right now, we are seeing minimal casualties. Their military is not overly interested in destroying smaller towns and villages."

Alaric frowned but she realised what that meant immediately.

"They mean to conquer. The less destruction means less resentment against the new ruler," she said, and Alaric looked to her.

"It makes sense," he said finally, returning his attention to Jaia.

"They are taking prisoners, anyone who fights them, but keeping them alive in rolling cages. They're getting full and so they started making more while on the move. I don't think they expected so much resistance."

Alaric nodded, staring at nothing as he thought and finally Jaia turned, glancing back at the group that had formed around him.

"How many?" Epharis asked and Alaric frowned.

"Around thirty thousand."

The room was silent for a long time and finally, Versalis gave a low whistle. It was an exceptional number of beings, obscenely large.

"How many do we have?" she asked.

"Around fifteen," Alaric said, and she exchanged a glance with Versalis.

"Fifteen at best," Kai said, sounding worried.

Things were not looking good.

"You will all need to be fitted for new weaponry and armour. Have it prepared," Alaric said as he stood and sighed.

"Alaric, you know this is bad. Is there no way to get a diplomatic resolution?" Epharis asked while Alaric shook his head.

"We've tried that already, Varsas is set on his goal."

"What is his goal?" Kai asked, confused.

"Expanding Weorene, obliterating Ayathian."

Letting out a slow breath, she turned to Epharis and he was watching her. They were both worried, her for him and him for his family and their legacy.

After a time, the group dispersed and Jaia swept past them, stalking from the room.

Hurt, she dropped her eyes and turned to follow him out, pausing at the sound of her name.

Alaric motioned her towards him, and she obliged, not having a reason to refuse him.

"That man you fought. Who is he?" the King asked, and she let out a slow breath.

"Uzo, he calls himself," she said, wondering what it was this man had in store for her father's friend.

"I would like you to introduce us," the King said, and she squinted up at him, wondering but still unable to find a reason to refuse.

"Yes, Your Majesty, I'll ask that he come up to the castle," she said after a brief pause.

He looked pleased and she was dismissed.

She swept from the room and figured she might as well go find the Fae while she knew where to find him.

Stepping out onto the ramparts, she searched the area around the castle, trying to locate the Fae in question.

It did not take her long to find him, he was battling six men and she rolled her eyes at the show of force.

As she watched, he took them down at a rapid pace and she frowned, knowing just how easy he had taken it on her. The thought angered her severely, but she forced herself to let it go and start down the stairs in his direction.

Men moved out of the way, bowing and murmuring to her but they did it out of respect for her rank more than her ability as a fighter. She did not like that they saw her as a Princess and not a soldier but there was little she could do to change that right then.

BY THE TIME she reached the field, he had put them all on the ground and was waiting for a new fighter, but she cleared her throat and he turned.

"Come for another beating, Princess?" he teased, and she clenched her jaw.

"King Alaric has asked to meet with you," she said sourly, and his head tilted to the side.

She motioned for him to follow and he looked irritated at having to stop, but he knew how royalty worked. One did not refuse without good reason, and wanting to train was not a good reason.

She led him back towards the castle while he hurried to catch up to her.

"I was only teasing, Etania, do not feel that I am here to harass you. I am here to help and protect you."

"I don't need your protection Uzo," she said, and he caught her arm, forcing her to stop.

Turning to him, she frowned as he looked down at her.

"Your little Kings are not the only ones who are wanting war, don't get complacent."

"Who else is wanting war?" she demanded, and he frowned, shaking his head. "Uzo?" she stepped in front of him, refusing to let him pass and so he leant down, his lips brushing her ear.

"Winter wants their Princess back, Etania," he breathed, and she shivered, a slow fear building up in her.

She had known that would happen, and still, they had not believed her.

She looked up at him as he moved away, and he gave her a sly smile.

"Don't worry, I'll keep you safe," he said cheerfully, and she glared.

Sweeping past her, he burst into the throne room with a booming, "Alaric!" And she was forced to follow after him, frustrated at the games of Fae.

The two men spoke joyously while she glared at them, her arms crossed.

Alaric seemed to enjoy her irritation and so he worked hard to get his claws into Uzo, but Uzo did not seem even vaguely interested in sticking around to play pet Fae for the King, he was quick to make it clear that he was there for the Princess, and that was it.

Alaric was not impressed and yet he smiled and eventually the two parted, Uzo smiling at her as he left.

"Satisfied? Fae aren't that easy to capture," she said to Alaric and he gave a slight nod.

"While you are here, we must discuss our tactics for this war," he looked tired and she decided to give him at least a small break, approaching and dropping onto the top step of the dais.

He seemed surprised, but did not complain as she sat with her left foot on the top step, the right on the ground two steps below. "You have some great secret form, isn't that right?" she asked, watching the guards as they rotated shifts.

"It's not much of a secret," he said dryly as he slumped in his throne, looking moody.

"Oh, don't be so grumpy, Alaric. Wars are fun," she quipped, turning to look at him.

"How many have you been in?" he asked, looking put upon.

"A few," she said evasively and smirked when he looked like he did not believe her.

"So how big are we talking, Titan King?" she asked, resting her arm against her knee.

"Around fifty feet," he said, and she looked at him, shocked.

"What are the rest of us supposed to do, sit around and watch while you stomp on everything?" she had not expected that height, not at all.

"I may be tall, but I am relatively slow," he said.

"Alright, so you need fast movements around you while you stomp on things," she said finally, squinting at him. "How.... How do you wear armour when in that form?"

He looked down at her and met her curious gaze before he grunted and looked away.

"My armour is enchanted, much like everything else in this castle. It grows with me."

"Fascinating," she breathed, and his attention returned to her, brows lifting at her show of interest. "Will you let me see it before the battle?" she asked and a pout formed over her lips as he shook his head, smirking.

"No, it's too risky."

She shifted, scooting on her butt to face him with her legs crossed and he watched her with amusement. She was like a child getting a new toy and he seemed to like her attention.

"I have to ask, is it possible to kill you in titan form?" she asked, and he narrowed his eyes at her, she shrugged. "I need to know if you have weak points that need to be protected."

"With enough hacking, you could kill me just like any other man. I am only bigger, not invincible."

She tried to imagine how many times she would have to hack at a neck in order to sever the artery and she shook her head.

"That's fantastic," she said, amazed at this new creature.

He looked pleased and finally stood, offering her his hand. She took it and stood gracefully, his hand was wonderfully warm and large around her delicate one.

He kept hold of her for only a moment before he bowed and then left her there, stomping from the room.

Watching him go, she bit down on her lower lip and considered what the war was going to look like. It was going to be huge and it was going to be terrible. She could only hope that she could help keep those that she cared about alive.

OVER THE COURSE of the remaining weeks they had before Weorene turned up on their doorstep, she had been stockpiling supplies under the watchful eye of her irritable husband.

He was so moody because she refused to let him touch her and while he understood, he resented her not wanting to be intimate with him.

He wanted his wife and she was terrified of letting him touch her, though she did not want to admit her fear and so they had fallen into a tense truce.

She made up for it by keeping him distracted and entertained with her attempts to make new evil concoctions and even having a go at making the philosophers stone, which ended in the room filling with acrid black smoke and their fleeing to the balcony.

He found it hilarious and she sulked. She suspected he had intentionally let her mess it up, given she was going off his notes and still it failed early on, not giving her a chance to move into the long-term steps of the instructions.

Once the air had cleared, she went back inside to clean up the mess and then stuck to the more basic supplies she knew how to prepare.

Versalis joined them a few times, but the twins had stayed away for the most part and she missed them both terribly. Still, the vampire King refused to tell her anything about why they were upset with her and she was left feeling lonely and depressed.

In order to keep her busy, Versalis had begun to learn more of the difficult concoctions and they both worked hard under the instruction of Epharis, who seemed to enjoy teaching them what he knew.

It was possible to see the looming darkness that was the army marching towards Ayathian and they were now down to a matter of days.

People were scared and she could understand why. That army was like a black river moving along the mountains and valleys, coming to drown them all and she found she was just as scared as the rest of them, but also, she was excited.

Epharis had grown steadily touchier with her and she worried about his thoughts, his hands stroking her arms and he breathed in the scent of her hair, kissing her any chance he got.

When another concoction blew up in their faces, she gave up for the day and stalked from the room and into the bathroom to bathe.

Epharis followed, a large hole burnt in the front of his robes and they left a coughing Versalis to go to her room and bathe there.

"What is wrong with you?" she demanded, as he had been responsible for the explosion that time.

Pulling off her simple dress, she threw the ruined thing into a corner and ran the bath.

"I know, I'm distracted," he said moodily, looking at her when she grabbed his arm.

He looked down at her and frowned, worry in his eyes.

"Talk to me, what is going on in your head?" she insisted, worried about him.

"I am preparing for what is to come, Etani. Not everyone is going to survive this war," he breathed, and she blinked, fear washing through her.

"Epharis, neither you or I, or even Alaric, is going to die. We are going to make it through this."

He stared down at her, searching her face for a lie but she was certain.

"I will not allow you to die, Epharis. I will go into the underworld and I drag you back, kicking and screaming. You are not allowed to leave me here with Alaric."

He laughed and wrapped his arms tightly around her, hugging her in a crushing embrace that she leant into.

His fear had chipped away at her resolve, but she could hide her fear from him, and she tilted her chin back to meet his lips in a hard kiss.

His hands traced down her back and she shivered, his kiss deepening. It was his touch against the underside of her breast that had her jerking back from him, leaving a good three feet between them with her arms wrapped tightly around herself and that packet groaned inside her mind, demanding to be let out.

"Epharis… I can't," she whimpered, hating herself for not being able to comfort him the way he needed.

He moved to her and slid his arms around her tightly but there was no hiding his disappointment.

They bathed together, ensuring to get all the residue off their skin and then dressing.

She left the bathroom quickly and cleaned away the mess.

As Epharis walked from the bathroom, a huge booming horn sounded and she jumped, spinning to the window.

Versalis burst through the door and was at the balcony, staring out.

"They've stopped," he said, squinting into the distance at the movements of the army.

"Do you suppose they are calling for a meeting?" she swept to his side, staring out and Epharis joined them a few seconds after.

"Most likely."

A servant burst into the room and spun in a frantic circle trying to find them. He looked utterly terrified.

"King Alaric is demanding all of you attend to his council," he panted and then sprinted from the room.

"Where?" Epharis boomed, and the fading voice called back as the man fled to find the others.

"Throne room."

TRAITORS AND COWARDS

The three left the suite and swept towards the throne room, pausing to see the fortifications that had been made to the giant doors that had allowed access to the castle.

Turning into the throne room, she found Alaric in full armour, his helmet adorned with horns.

"Varsas has called for peace talks. I will require you all to be there. We will be leaving in an hour. You will all be prepared," he growled, and she looked around the room, seeing all the important faces.

The twins stood off to the side, their faces grim. Izziah was alone, looking nervous and tired. Aelen looked bored, Versalis, Epharis and she stood close together with varying looks of nervousness and seriousness. Catherine had dressed in strong leather armour, her short brown hair tied back in a ponytail. Uzo was even standing nearby, his eyes on her with a little crease between his brows.

She turned away from him and focused on the King.

"I will require you all to gear up and return here as soon as possible," he said and when they nodded, the groups dispersed.

Saying goodbye to Versalis, she left Epharis and returned to her rooms beside Alaric's and pulled out a leather case from under her bed.

She set it on top of the bed and opened the clasps. Stripping down to nothing, she pulled out a pair of tiny undergarments that had been ordered specifically off the specifications of Nayishma's ladies.

Pulling them on, she wondered at the dainty size of them but found they did not tend to bunch.

Next was a pair of skin-tight black dragon leather pants and a pair of thigh-high leather boots with a small heel, lacing up from ankle to above her knee and folding down the leftover.

On the inside of each boot, she slid three throwing knives. Pulling on a long sleeve, tight cotton top, she tucked it into her pants and, finally, the corset was pulled on, cinched tight around her.

Just under the back of the corset, she tucked her pouch of poisons and elixirs, a string binding it around her waist. Two knives crossed against her lower back and a belt hung around her hips, laden down with her swords and a small pouch for a garrotte, a length of rope and several long needles.

Her armguards were made of hardened leather that held two more knives up under them, and along the top was a series of needles in a neat row.

She pulled the hood out of the dwindling case and tucked it into the top of her shirt, a mask pulled up over her face and the hood pulled high to make it hard to grab her hair, braided and shoved down the back of her shirt.

Lastly, a strap went around both upper thighs with six of the tiny little blades she had crafted, and she smiled at the sight of them, their blades padded with black dyed cotton.

Once ready, she moved towards the mirror and turned, searching for bunching or fabric that sat incorrectly.

Satisfied, she headed for the door and opened it to Epharis. His eyes raked down her and he smiled slowly.

Her eyes swept him as well, lingering on the elaborate gold and black guard that protected his sword arm from collarbone to the base of his fingers.

His robes were long and black, undecorated, with a belt around his hips for Anduril. His arms were covered by heavy gloves.

His long silver hair was loose, but it was unlikely that anyone would get close enough to grab it.

A finger guard protected the middle finger of his secondary hand and she was surprised to see he was holding a humanoid skull, the eyes glowing an evil green.

She did not ask, instead, she tugged down the mask that covered the lower half of her face and kissed him hard, tugging at the front of his robes so they would fall open just enough to show his muscular chest.

Neither of them spoke as they left her room, her fingers pulling up the mask once more.

The vampires approached from the opposite direction and Versalis gave her a feral grin as he saw her in her full battle attire.

He was wearing black from neck to toes, his armour light and simple with spikey angles. The guards over his hands extended past his fingers to make lethal-looking claws.

The twins wore no armour, having opted for black robe-like suit constructions. Kai's was made of a stiff fabric that curled up to around his ears in a sweep, the front buttoned tight and unadorned. Gloves covered his hands and his boots reached his thighs.

He moved with a feline grace that she could appreciate.

Jaia opted for slightly more style, the hems of his robe striped with silver along with a striking detail around his sleeves.

He wore a white shirt underneath, adding class to the outfit. A symbol she had never seen before was stitched into the back of it and he wore a metal glove over his left hand, protecting his hand though she did not know why. Each of them wore a black belt with two swords, but she felt they looked unprotected.

Sweeping into the hall, they found the rest of the team already waiting, grim and unsmiling.

Izziah had opted for plate armour of dark blue, gold and silver that looked exceptionally light on him, his elbows and fingers ending in sharp points. His silver hair shifted in the breeze of the open window and he looked lethal.

The King had been given more armour, large plates that doubled up the protection of his shins and there were gold-coloured spikes in neat rows. His thighs were reinforced, as well as his shoulders and chest. His enormous sword rested against the throne and she noted that there was a wolf engraved into the reinforcements on his shoulders.

"Very good," he said in a deep voice and he rattled when he stood. Picking up the sword, he slid it into a sheath that ran across his back and he led the way out of the castle.

It was going to be about an hour walk and so they had opted for horses.

The horse Alaric got was a monstrous beast with a black glossy coat and mean brown eyes. Its back was level with her head, and she wondered how it could possibly be that big.

It looked like it would happily bite her arm off and so she moved away, glaring at the beast.

Left as the only one without a horse, she watched as they mounted and she took a deep breath, stretching her arms. She was ready.

A snort behind her made her look around and the horse was so very dead she was surprised it could move. Rotting flesh and eyes that glowed a toxic green had her looking past the disturbing head to Epharis, looking down at her.

He offered her his hand, but she shook her head and his smile was smug at the knowledge of her strength and speed.

She noted the skull was hanging from his belt in a little net bag and she wondered again, but she would ask later.

The group set out, along with a regiment of guards in fine silver and blue armour, their horses huge and angry looking.

She let them go first and then went after them, her muscles aching at the lack of use.

She moved like the wind, easily passing the horses, and keeping pace with the King. He lifted two fingers and pointed forward. Grinning, she took off and circled, her lips parted to suck in air in search of any odour that would suggest outrunners.

She found the ambush within a few minutes and they did not know what hit them.

Three men, the first one falling to his death from the tree he had been perched in. The second had his neck snapped and the third was met with a feral grin and a hard kiss. He fell, his lips turning a deep black as he hit the ground and the group slowed to see what had happened.

The last man was a dead giveaway of what had happened and so they moved on, knowing she was nearby.

She watched as Versalis searched the trees for her, his eyes snapping to any hint of a sound but by then, she was already three trees away. Leaping and bounding or using branches to swing herself forward.

It was utter joy for her, the ability to move and run at full speed and she was buzzing from the soul she had ripped from the assassin.

As the group burst free of the trees, she flew alongside them, her hands finding the last branch and launching herself out into open air, unable to help but recall the moment she flew from the cliff.

The King glanced up, his eyes wild as he saw her, and he bellowed his war cry.

Landing on her feet, she rolled and flung herself back onto her feet, not missing a beat as she kept up with the group and she saw the twins exchanging a look, but she ignored them.

She had never shown them just how fast and easily she could move, nor had she allowed herself to push her limits. But now she did, and it was utter bliss.

THE ENCAMPMENT WAS AHEAD, and they began to slow, not wanting to start the war before they had to.

Coming to a stop when the rest did, her breathing came in short pants and she silenced herself, eyes narrowing on the regiment that had come to meet them.

Varsas had not changed at all. He was still small, round, and angry looking with a large red beard and bushy red hair that made her miss the wonderful Yish all the more.

He looked red in the face at that moment as well as he stomped forward, his regiment following along behind him.

The small group of monsters moved into a neat row behind Alaric as he paced forward, their eyes alert and behind them in a double row of soldiers, the regiment was ready for the fight.

Varsas considered the collection of oddities and smiled grimly as he realised he was out of his depth.

His eyes lingered on her and she smiled slightly at him, making him flinch.

"Alaric, quite a collection of oddities you have here," Varsas said. A low growl started from somewhere to her right, but she could not tell who it was.

Alaric did not respond to the jibe, instead, he smiled and gave a small motion, the three rows behind him coming to a stop though he continued ahead several feet more before coming to a stop himself, forcing Varsas to approach to meet him or have to yell.

"Varsas, please kindly tell me why you have invaded my Kingdom?" Alaric said, his voice booming.

"Your witch priestess murdered my daughter," Varsas snarled, and his eyes found her again. "The wrong woman," he added snidely.

"High Priestess Amalee acted on her own. She is dead and long gone."

"You are lying, you will do anything to protect your fanatic women."

Her eyes narrowed and she felt Catherine tensing on her left, angry at the insult.

"Amalee was punished for her actions. There is no need for this war," Alaric said slowly and Varsas laughed.

"Who punished her?" he demanded. All eyes on their side turned to her and she tensed.

Varsas looked at her and gritted his teeth. He had known that already, but he was pushing to find a lie, wanting an excuse to try and get control of Ayathian.

She realised then that Varsas had no intention of stopping and she glanced to her right to see Epharis' face was hard as he seemed to come to the same conclusion. Varsas wanted power, not revenge.

Something shoved her and she moved without thinking, darting forward as a twang sounded and she heard her name being yelled.

Launching herself up, she planted her foot against Alaric's shin guard, thrusting upwards and in a somersault over his head. Her sword seemed to materialise in her hand as it flashed, and wood splintered.

Landing back on her feet between Alaric and Varsas, her body turned mostly backwards toward Alaric. She levelled the point of the sword at Varsas and a second later, an arrow landed in the grass, cut cleanly in half by her sword. Utter silence reigned as everyone registered what had happened and Varsas backed away, his attempt failed.

The arrow had been aimed right for Alaric's head. They had tried to assassinate him during peace talks.

She wanted terribly to go after the invading King, but she stayed in front of Alaric, protecting him.

Varsas bared his teeth at her as he melted back into the line of his guard, who were all looking a little less certain.

"This cannot be tolerated, Varsas. You have brought this down on yourself," Alaric turned, his cloak whirling around him, and he stalked away. She lingered only long enough for Alaric to retreat five steps before she backed away, fury burning through her at the cowardly attempt to win. She could not abide cowards.

With her sword returned to its sheath, she turned only when she was sure the army had set their goal on retreat and she found them watching her, Alaric's eyes unreadable.

"This means war," Alaric said to the group and the tension shot upwards, but they had already expected it. "At dawn," he said, and they headed back towards Ayathian.

SHE STUCK CLOSE by the group as they retreated, angry at the weakness of Varsas and she let it burn in her until they returned to the city.

When the King announced he would hold a rally for the men, she decided not to attend and instead found herself scaling the tower she had hidden in what felt like a lifetime ago.

Sitting down on the roof, she watched the army in the distance.

She heard someone approaching her from below but did not turn, knowing it would be someone important to her.

Versalis sat down at her side and sighed gently, grabbing her arm from around her leg and gripping her hand tightly.

"What if everything goes wrong tomorrow and we die?" she asked, finally voicing her fears.

Versalis looked at her and frowned, thinking.

"Etani my love, you would never permit any of us to die. You would never allow that to happen."

She looked at him, frowning slightly.

"Am I so selfish?" she asked, hurting at the implication.

"No darling, not selfish. Protective. You will do whatever it takes to keep those around you safe and happy."

He kissed her hand and she watched him, searching for any hint that he was lying to protect her feelings.

"I'm scared, Versalis," she whispered.

"We all are, baby," he said gently and drew her into his arms.

"Come down and join everyone for drinks, it'll be fun," he purred, and she looked up at him with surprise.

"Drinks? You drink?" It seemed odd, but she still allowed him to coax her down from the roof of the tower and down into the basement.

The twins, Epharis, Aelen, Catherine and Uzo were all there and it smelt as though they had already started.

"Etania!" Uzo cried and gave her a hard hug. Versalis grinned and shook his head, moving away as a heavy mug was shoved into her hand.

She sniffed it warily, but Uzo touched two fingers against the bottom of the mug and tilted it up.

She drank quickly, his determined grin remaining in place as he forced her to drink the whole thing or wear it.

Kai approached nervously as he watched and she felt her cheeks beginning to flush, the alcohol hitting her like a slap.

Uzo laughed and swept away, enjoying her response.

"Kai," she said as she took his hands, the room spinning.

"He did that to us too, it hits hard but wears off quickly. It's some concoction he came up with," Kai said, catching her when her legs gave out.

She clutched onto him, her lips pulled up into a smile.

"Kai," she repeated, her voice slurring slightly. "I don't want to go into another war, they're messy," she spoke in a conspiratorial tone, but louder than she intended, and Jaia swept over.

She tensed at his approach and shifted to keep Kai between them, not wanting to deal again with his rejection.

"Everything is going to be fine," he said coolly, and she nodded, struggling to keep her legs under her.

"Yes, yes," she breathed, her eyes on the wall instead of him. His hand was warm on her cheek and when she pulled back, his clenched his jaw, looking away.

"You two need to cut this out. We could die tomorrow," Kai snapped, and he unceremoniously dumped her into Jaia's arms and stalked off.

She blinked, looking from Kai to Jaia and back again.

Jaia looked like he was going to explode, his neck strained to keep his face away from her.

"Jaia?" she asked, confused at his dislike of her. "What did I do to make you hate me so much?"

He gasped, looking down into her face.

"I don't hate you," he breathed, sounding horrified.

"Then why do you not want to be near me anymore?"

"I..." he broke off as an enormous boom shook the castle and everyone in the room froze, looking up at the dust falling around them from the ceiling.

"What was that?" Uzo asked nervously.

"I have no idea," Epharis said and the boom came again.

Jaia's arms tightened around her as she felt him tensing.

"We need to get upstairs. These rooms might not stand."

The room cleared in record time, Jaia lingering with her. As the third boom hit, he looked up and then down at her before he gritted his teeth and suddenly kissed her hard. She froze, stunned back into reality by the kiss. He had never kissed her like that, with so much longing and desperation, fear and need.

She met his feeling with her own, her fingers curling around his hair as she drew him down and she lifted herself to the balls of her feet.

The kiss was passionate and hungry, his arms gripped her back and, finally, they parted.

He was breathing hard, his eyes burning with something she could not understand.

"If we don't survive this, never forget that I love you," he breathed and she pulled him down into another kiss of fear and need, unable to bring herself to speak those words that stung her. They lingered only a moment before they left the room, unsure if it would stand up to whatever was happening above.

Parting ways at the top of the stairs, she watched as he went after his brother and she approached the window. It had shattered and when she looked out, she found an enormous boulder had sprouted on the side of the castle just above and to her right.

Stepping out of the window, she looked up and her lips parted as she paced forward, seeing the enormous spidery contraption in the distance.

It drew back and then launched the ball. Slowly lifting her eyes to the skies, a boulder bigger than a house came crashing down with a boom that made the world shake.

3 6

THE END

She had never seen boulders fly like that, never seen the thing that they used to launch them and judging by the horrified looks of the scrambling guards, they had not seen it before either.

It seemed impossible that objects so huge could move that easily through the air, and yet, there they were.

Turning, she jumped back in through the window, heading for the throne room where Epharis and Alaric were arguing. Catherine and several others were trying to figure out what was happening while Uzo was looking like he had just won a prize.

He found her as she entered and he immediately went to her, grinning happily. "Etania, isn't this fascinating?"

She shook her head, doing her best to ignore the oddity that was Uzo. "What are they?"

"Some invention of the humans, no doubt. They come up with some *magical* tools of death," he sounded far too thrilled and she narrowed her eyes before turning to Alaric, who was heading towards them.

"Have you seen it?" Alaric bellowed and she nodded.

"They look like big wooden scorpions, with a tail that flings up and launches boulders. I've never seen anything like it before."

Alaric looked furious and she thought for a moment.

"Alaric, they can't have brought all that many with them. Those boulders are enormous and would be hard to move. Surely we can wait it out."

He scowled at her but then nodded, agreeing with her logic.

They settled in to wait, agitated and irritable until finally, hours later, it was decided that the attack had stopped, and they piled out of the castle.

The morning would soon be upon them, and she stuck close to Uzo and Epharis as they went to see the destruction. About fifteen boulders had been launched at them, only four hitting the castle and several more destroying large sections of the city, but there was not that much damage, all things considered.

Etani stood at the parapet and frowned. "We need to take the war to them."

Alaric looked at her, frowning in confusion as she studied the city.

"This is too easy for them. All they have to do is start a fire and the whole city goes up in flames. We need to keep them out of the city."

She stared into the streets, seeing the flames moving easily.

"What are you talking about?" Alaric snapped and she looked at him.

"Your city is a tinder box, Alaric. Much is stone but most of it is wood. You need to get out there and fight them before they get to the city."

Alaric stared at her for a moment, then looked at the city and, finally, he nodded. "Bring me Kai," he ordered a guard who ran to collect the vampire.

Stepping onto the wall, she paced along slowly, staring ahead and trying to see what was happening. She could not see any more boulders being loaded and that was a good thing.

Kai appeared with Jaia and she ignored them as she surveyed the opponents, trying to understand what they were thinking. She felt eyes on her back and still she ignored them. She needed to get higher.

She moved to the castle wall and begun to climb, stopped a good twenty feet up, staring out.

"There is a valley between them and us. We could go there," she called down to the group of men who were all watching her.

She must look odd, balancing in one hand and her long braid waving in the wind, clinging to the sheer face of the castle. Looking down at them, she found Jaia and his eyes were burning, but she did not try to decipher his look.

Alaric nodded and they turned to plan for the new location.

IT WAS GETTING close to dawn when they made it to the chosen spot. The scorpion weapons were gone, but they could see the opposing military gearing up.

Looking at the military formations behind them, she bit hard on her lower lip, doubting herself for her suggestions. She did not know what to do, did not know if she could do anything at all to help them, and Alaric had vanished.

Nervous, she examined both armies, knowing they were outmatched.

"We are going to suffer heavy casualties," she breathed as she studied the mass of life that was the opposing army from their position on a small rise.

They had the high ground, but that was all.

"Not necessarily, I still have mine," Epharis said and she looked to him, frowning.

He smiled and moved to the top of the crest, pulling the strange skull from its place at his hip.

The glow was bright in the darkness and so it was easy to see him from both sides as he lifted the skull to his face. Speaking in a deep rumble, she felt a coldness seep through her and she exhaled slowly, suddenly wanting to go to him, needing to be at his side as he called to whatever part of her that had been changed with his attempt to turn her into a creature like him.

That part of her was chomping at the bit, screaming for her to join him and sit at his feet, to worship him as the god he was.

She must have moved, as Uzo wrapped his arm around her chest, holding her back even as Epharis' voice echoed inside her ears and she craved his attention.

She pushed against the restraining arm and then there was a second.

The light changed around her, the world seemed to turn a shade of green and Epharis lifted the skull.

He screamed words that resounded in her and she gasped, reaching for him but unable to escape the arms that held her so tightly.

Something moved around them, the ground lifting and bulging in a way that made people scream, terrified of what was happening.

Arms began to burst out of the ground, rotting corpses and skeletons rising from their earthly graves to heed his call. She wanted to rise too, and her nails left deep gouges in an arm that kept her still, restraining her from doing what she wanted.

Epharis' battle scream made her heart pound and she sucked in a breath, wanting to scream with him but then a hand was on her mouth and the army of corpses screamed for her. The sound was unearthly, haunting, and she knew none of them would ever be the same after seeing the soldiers of long-forgotten wars rising to fight again.

Epharis turned, his eyes bright with green fire, finding her and her captors.

She knew he wanted her, too, the Lich Princess to his Prince, but he resisted when she could not; she was straining for him, biting the hand that covered her mouth and raking flesh but still, they held her, crushing her.

The call faded and she was released, collapsing onto her hands and knees with jagged, panting breaths that seemed to expel that need like mist.

She had no idea what had just happened to her, but it both exhilarated and terrified her in equal measures. She had underestimated his strength as the undead army began to move into formation under his glowing stare.

He was their master and they obeyed willingly.

Each one of them glowed with that eerie green glow, making them stand out amongst the normal mythical creatures.

THINGS SETTLED down into an uneasy silence as the dawn started to peek up over the horizon and still Alaric had not shown up, making them all nervous but she knew he would never miss out on the war.

Turning, she found the twins staring at her and she bit her lip before she approached the two and hugged them both hard. Kai's eyebrows lifted slightly at Jaia's hands lingering on her and the closeness and intimacy of their embrace.

She flushed and something dawned on him, then he grinned, seemingly pleased.

Their movements had sparked others to do the same, farewelling their comrades and hugging friends just in case that was the last time they would be seeing each other.

Epharis hugged her back tightly, squeezing her and kissing the top of her head but she knew he needed to remain focused and in control.

Versalis tried to crush the wind out of her, lifting her off the ground in a bear hug even as she tried to throttle him in her returned hug. He laughed and kissed her cheek, better at hiding the fear than they were.

Uzo squeezed her tightly as well, but his eyes were intense. "Nothing will happen to you," he promised.

"If you cared for my father at all, you will protect those twins and not me. That is all I ask of you."

He drew back, those incredible blue eyes turning to the twins, and then he nodded.

"You have a deal, Etania, daughter of my closest friend. I will protect those you love most, and your father and I will be square."

She took his hand and they both gasped at the zing of energy that shot through them as the deal was struck.

She released him and was almost tackled by Catherine, the strong woman hugging her tightly and grinning maniacally.

"Crazy werewolf," she laughed, the woman's endless joy at war enough to break her tension.

"Insane Fae," she said and turned to lunge after Epharis, who was not expecting the attack.

Aelen took her hand and squeezed it firmly.

"It has been an honour knowing you, Princess," he said in his deep voice and she nodded, smiling.

"And at you too, Aelen."

He smiled grimly and she finally turned to Izziah, who was lingering back.

"I'm so sorry for everything that has happened, Etani," he said softly.

"You know what your brother is now. Do not allow him to harm anyone again," she replied, and he nodded, their embrace tense but genuine.

They fell into silence, standing in a close group as they waited for the dawn to come and the battle to begin.

Looking down, she saw the men below moving into formations and the men behind them had moved as well and she turned to see they had left an enormous gap right down the middle. She did not understand that gap at all but then she shook her head, knowing they were trained.

Something tugged at her hand and she turned to find Uzo by her side, holding out a bow and single arrow.

"Just trust me," he breathed when she looked confused.

She was a decent shot, but she was the only archer with him, and they both only had a single arrow each.

"Ready Princess?" he asked and she gave him a wary look as she notched the arrow and in unison, their arrows rose high.

They waited, her fingers tingling, and she exhaled.

A soft murmur escaped his lips and a sudden glow shot from her fingers up her arms to cover her skin in the same pattern she had while in Winter.

Glancing sideways at Uzo, she was fascinated to see that he too had markings, an exotic fiery pattern that glowed over his skin.

Mist flowed from their bodies as the sudden coldness of them reacted with the warm morning and she began to smile as she felt Faerie reaching for her, touching her soul.

As the first rays of morning blinded them all, two arrows were released.

ABOUT THE AUTHOR

Born in Mackay, North Queensland in Australia, N. Malone's writing journey started at the age of nine. It wasn't until the age of twenty-nine that the career began.

The story of Etani had been building for nearly ten years, daydreams and forums until the character became a reality when book one had begun. Now, with nine books in the works, the story can continue.

"If you like writing, then write."

nmalone.net

AFTERWORD

If you enjoyed Trapped Princess, you can continue the adventure in book three "Always a Fae", available on pre-order:
   https://books2read.com/u/4j2qov

Your opinions are valuable, please take a few moments to leave a rating.

www.ingramcontent.com/pod-product-compliance
Lightning Source LLC
Chambersburg PA
CBHW020543120726
47903CB00001B/109